A Plea for Revenge

"By Enath, I summon you."

A woman's voice shattered his dreams.

"By Elun, I summon you."

The too-familiar flames roared up, filling his consciousness.

"By Anchytel, I summon you."

The flames died to a small fire on a slab of stone. Walter of Jacin, Leader of the Wild Hunt, felt the cool night air on his face, felt the presence of the men he led beside him. "By Enath, Elun, Anchytel, we have come. Who are you and for what do you summon us?"

"I am Richenza of the House of Indes and I have summoned you to avenge my brother and destroy the House of Thaiter as it has destroyed the House of Indes."

Walter's heart sank. Avenge. Destroy. The words were too familiar.

THE WILD HUNT:
VENGEANCE MOON

JOCELIN FOXE

AVON · EOS

*For Ruth Sparks Cottrell,
who believed in this book.*

This is a work of fiction. Names, characters, places, and incidents either
are the product of the author's imagination or are used fictitiously. Any
resemblance to actual events, locales, organizations, or persons, living or
dead, is entirely coincidental and beyond the intent of either the author or
the publisher.

AVON BOOKS, INC.
1350 Avenue of the Americas
New York, New York 10019

Copyright © 1998 by Linda Reames Fox and Joyce Cottrell
Published by arrangement with the authors
Visit our website at **http://www.AvonBooks.com/Eos**
Library of Congress Catalog Card Number: 98-92623
ISBN: 0-380-79911-1

First Avon Eos Printing: September 1998

AVON EOS TRADEMARK REG. U.S. PAT. OFF. AND IN OTHER COUNTRIES,
MARCA REGISTRADA, HECHO EN U.S.A.

Printed in the U.S.A.

WCD 10 9 8 7 6 5 4 3 2 1

Character List

THE HUNTSMEN

Walter—a knight once in the service of the Grand Duke of Hersin, cursed 247 years after the fall of Reasalyn.

Hamon—once ruler of the Principality of Saroth, cursed in 268.

Eleylin ("Ellis")—last heir of the Rensel Empire, a sailor from Onsalm who prefers to live in the present, cursed in 302.

Thomas—lawyer and politician, former member of the Council of Amaroc, cursed in 315.

Michel—merchant's son from Iskandroc who preferred selling cities to selling mercery, cursed in 349.

Payne—a courtier from Yesacroth, descended from Amloth, and cursed in 420.

Reynard—a street entertainer and thief from Rayln, cursed in 511.

Ulick—a warrior of the eastern Sueve, cursed in 596.

Justin—an apothecary and alchemist of Manreth, cursed in 650.

Alesander—a Prince of Tarsia, cursed in 800.

Bertz—a farmer and headman of his nonate of the monotheistic Stros, cursed in 880.

Garrett—a member of the gentry of the Tributary Lordships, cursed in 908.

Brian—a young nobleman of mysterious antecedents, cursed in 1205.

THE HOUSE OF INDES AND THOSE IN HER SERVICE

Lady Richenza Indes—the one who summoned the Wild Hunt.

Annet Rostow—waiting woman to Lady Richenza and the one who knew the old stories.

THE HOUSE OF THAITER AND THEIR RETAINERS

King Rozer III—King of Tarsia.

Queen Betrissa—his third wife.

Prince Ewets—his eldest son, a poor prince and worse poet.

Prince Leot—his second son, the dangerous one.

Princess Meriel—his only daughter.

Prince Wendis—his youngest son, a drunken wastrel.
Lord Claverdon—King Rozer's steward and most loyal supporter.
Jevon—a liveried man.

OTHER CHARACTERS

Firmin Tredgett—a merchant of Tarsia, a man of many parts.
Karina Tredgett—Firmin's wife.
King Ludvic of Arin—a looming offstage threat.
King Daimiron of Canjitrin—yet another offstage threat.
Milizia, Dowager Queen of Canjitrin—a motivator of kings.
Kendrick Loton, Lord Abethell—Canjitard Ambassador to Tarsia.
Master Philemon—keeper of the Tarsit City Records.
Symond Tierse—a Priest of Haldan, the High Priest's confidential advisor.
Jolon Revnal—a young man who regrets cheating at cards.

THE MENTIONED DEAD, ANCIENT AND RECENT

Tarses the Conqueror—destroyer of the Rensel Empire, ancestor of the Royal Houses of Tarsia.
Amloth—son of Tarses, first leader of the Wild Hunt.
Berin and Diertas—Amloth's brothers, who were cursed with him.
Cassimara—Walter of Jacin's wife, last heir to the Rensel House of Morcaston.
Herlind—Hamon's sister, lover, nemesis, and victim.
Anderad—a famous King of Tarsia commemorated in stone.
Brian I, King of Canjitrin—bynamed the Liberator or the Rebel, depending on one's politics.
Mascelin II, King of Tarsia—Alesander's father.
Prince Harmund Vitaut—Alesander's eldest brother.
King Anselm of Tarsia—Alesander's younger brother.
Queen Cassandra—wife of King Anselm.
Prince Colias Vitaut—Alesander's youngest brother.
Queen Lescina ("Lessa") Vitaut—Alesander's twin sister and wife of Thaiter I.
King Thaiter I—brother of Mascelin II, putative founder of the House of Thaiter.

Anelhar Indes, Grand Duke of Amaldrin—ancestor of Richenza, important in securing the succession of the House of Thaiter.

Nele Indes, Grand Duke of Maldrin—Lady Richenza's brother, the cause of much tumult.

Rychart Indes, Grand Duke of Maldrin—father of Nele and Richenza.

Queen Lovisa of Arin—first wife of King Rozer.

Queen Kamilka—second wife of King Rozer, mother of all four of his children.

Geoffry Hassart—Brian's brother.

King Aleyne IV of Canjit.

The Deities

THE HIGH GODS OF THE RENSEL

Enath—Goddess of Fire. The patroness of warriors, artisans, and all those who use the fire of the mind. Symbolized by the half-moon.

Elun—Goddess of Water. The patroness of women, children, and those deserving pity. Symbolized by the full moon.

Anchytel—Goddess of Earth. The patroness of those who delve for the fruits of the earth and of deeds done in darkness. Symbolized by the new moon.

Orien—God of the Air. Overshadowed by his sisters.

OTHERS

Theyad Haldan (Tiat Altan in Eastern Sueve dialect)—the Sky and War God of the Sueve.

Taros—an ancient fertility god who has outlasted the comings and goings of conquerors.

Bis—a minor Sartherian daemon.

Reikos—the neglected and nearly forgotten patron god of the sailors of Onsalm.

Maloc—a Rensel/Selinian daemon of voracious appetite who periodically devours and regurgitates various celestial bodies.

Prologue

A thousand years and more the Rensel ruled their empire of the five lands under the patronage of their tutelary Goddesses: Enath, Elun, and Anchytel. To the rulers looking out from their capital of Reasalyn all was peace and splendor; to the people they ruled, especially those on the northern borders, their rule was harsh. Plague and drought made it harsher, until many of their subjects saw the Rensel as naught but tax collectors and muttered of rebellion.

The Empire might have recovered had the drought not pushed the westernmost of the nomadic Sueve tribes into the Rensel borderlands. The Sueve, led by Ortas, searched for better grazing and found themselves welcomed by the disaffected Rensel subjects. Ortas married a woman of the borderland who hated the Rensel. Their son Tarses was raised in that hatred, and, when he became the leader of the Sueve, he gathered all the western Sueve tribes and all the peoples of the border in war upon the Rensel.

Tarses and his allies conquered all the Rensel lands of the Magnary Valley and finally besieged Reasalyn itself. But the siege dragged on, the allies faltered, and rumors of Rensel relief armies made the Sueve fighters restless. Tarses swore he would take the city or die in the attempt, but not all of the twenty members of his council were equally steadfast. Some wanted to retreat; some looked for compromise. On the Rensel side some nobles, fearing the rescuing armies were fantasies or conquerors as dangerous as Tarses in their own way, also sought compromise. Two of their number, Malivan and Caros, were appointed to parley with the Sueve. Tarses would not listen, but his eldest son Amloth was more reasonable. Amloth and the Rensel nobles agreed that he would put aside his Sueve wife and marry the heiress of the Rensel Empire and in due time rule the Empire under Rensel law. It was necessary to obtain the consent of the heiress, who was being educated in the Temple of the Three Goddesses in the Citadel of Reasalyn.

Malivan and Caros showed Amloth, his youngest brother Berin, and two other Sueve warriors an ancient tunnel into the temple. Before they could locate the heiress, Amloth's ambitious half brother Diertas followed them with a troop of Sueve. Half-angry, half-relieved, Amloth used the warriors to capture and control the temple precincts and allowed Diertas to join him, Berin, and the two Rensel as they entered the sanctuary to confront the heiress.

They interrupted the midnight rites, and Amloth made his proposal to the fifteen-year-old girl. Marry him and he would see that the Sueve would leave Reasalyn and all its remaining lands in peace. The heiress said she would rather die than marry a filthy barbarian.

Amloth had risked too much to take no for an answer and raped the girl while Diertas made the High Priestess watch. The High Priestess cursed the sons of Tarses and the two Rensel traitors in the names of her Three Goddesses: Elun, Enath, Anchytel.

Their hearts seemed to stop at her words, but Amloth refused to be defeated. He ordered more warriors into the citadel, and Tarses conquered Reasalyn that day. But Amloth and his brothers disappeared at daybreak. Enraged that his sons were lost, Tarses razed the city and slaughtered its inhabitants. Then Tarses and his armies retreated north and set up camp where the river Marre joined the Magnary.

Any deity worthy of the name can destroy those who defile her holy places. The Three Goddesses chose not to destroy the five men who had desecrated their sanctuary; instead the Goddesses decided to use the men to restore their worship and the Empire the defilers had destroyed. The Goddesses called these men the Wild Hunt and bound them to perform any task set them by one who summoned them in the Goddesses' name at the full moon. If they failed before the next full moon, Amloth, who led them, and all the Huntsmen except the three last cursed, would face that postponed destruction. The remaining three would carry on the Hunt. Only if someone cared enough about a Huntsman to fight to hold him back from the Goddesses' call on the night of the last full moon of each summoning would that man be free of the curse.

The Goddess also decreed that in the future, any man cursed by their three names would also be doomed to join the Wild Hunt, if his sins were great enough.

For three centuries Amloth fulfilled the letter, if not the intent, of every summons. In that time nine more men were cursed, and one escaped. Meanwhile, the Sueve consolidated their rule in the Magnary Valley and fought their way up the Kelsary Valley, through the Rensel province of Irkeldra, exterminating the Rensel nobility that they captured.

Some Rensel fled to the southern provinces of Arinca and Madaria; others retreated to the mountains to carry on their resistance. These mountains took their name from them: the Selin Mountains, and the Rensel survivors were, in turn, called Selinians. In their mountain fastnesses their already peculiar social customs became odder still.

The only kingdom north of the mountains unconquered by the expanding kingdom named for Tarses was Onsalm on the western sea. Three hundred and two years after the fall of Reasalyn the Wild Hunt was summoned to Onsalm, where through mischance and treachery the Hunt failed. Eleven Huntsmen burned, but Amloth was freed and a new Huntsman was cursed. The Hunt, with Walter of Jacin its new leader, continued into a world the Goddesses could not have foreseen.

Onsalm fell to Tarsia, as did Iskandroc, and with that fortress's fall Tarsia soon reached the southern sea. But by that time Tarsia had become more Rensel than Sueve. Its conquerors had been absorbed by the indigenous population. For three hundred years the Kings of Tarsia ruled a greater realm than the Rensel Emperors had in their day. But the Tarsean Kingdom, too, fragmented.

The Hunt was summoned a score of times, but the summonings became less frequent, though they loomed large in Tarsean legend. Other gods replaced the Goddesses in most men's prayers. For three hundred years there was nothing; then, on one full moon a summons came that would shake the kingdom Tarses had founded.

Full Moon

"By Enath, I summon you."

A woman's voice shattered his dreams.

"By Elun, I summon you."

The too-familiar flames roared up, filling his consciousness.

"By Anchytel, I summon you."

The flames died to a small fire on a slab of stone. Walter of Jacin, Leader of the Wild Hunt, felt the cool night air on his face, felt the presence of the men he led beside him. He paced his horse one slow step forward, and asked, as he must, "By Enath, Elun, Anchytel, we have come. Who are you and for what do you summon us?"

The woman who had tended the fire spun round to face the half circle of mounted men that now surrounded her, her hand groping toward a dagger that glinted near the flames. She looked from face to face before her eyes settled on his. Her hand fell to her side. Startling as their sudden manifestation must have been, it was not the Wild Hunt that she feared. Yet she was afraid; Walter could read fear in the tension of her body, and in her eyes, dark in her moon-paled face.

Fear did not mar her voice as she answered him. "I am Richenza of the House of Indes, and I have summoned you to avenge my brother and

5

destroy the House of Thaiter as it has destroyed the House of Indes.''

Walter's heart sank. Avenge. Destroy. The words were too familiar. The mourning black of her clothes was too familiar. As was the name of Indes. Indes had been one of the twenty companions of Tarses the conqueror, who helped him destroy the Rensel Empire. Even in Walter's time, ten generations later, the House of Indes had been one of the greatest lineages of Tarsia. Whenever this was that could not have changed. This woman, this girl—she could not be much more than twenty—must be a noble-woman. The task she set them would shatter lives beyond hers and the House of Thaiter.

Thaiter. That name he didn't recognize.

This was Reasalyn, the Rensel's ruined capital. They were in the Temple of the Goddesses in whose names the Hunt had been summoned. Here Amloth, Tarses's son, had been cursed with his brothers and followers, the first to form the Wild Hunt. On that altar slab where this night's fire burned Amloth had. . . .

A branch snapped, rescuing him from his thoughts. The girl gasped and swung round. Wordlessly with the power the Goddesses granted him, he dispatched his men—half to search, half to guard.

The silence stretched unbroken as they listened for the sounds of pursuit. She stood looking up at him, studying him. Looking for what? Centuries of age? He had known Amloth. He had seen the fall of Onsalm when Amloth failed. Despite the passage of time he knew he looked only the forty years he had been when he was cursed, his brown hair no more greyed, his face no more lined. On the outside he was the same man he had been the day his wife and son had died.

Like a blow to the gut Walter remembered who had looked up at him with that same questioning gaze. He could not deal with that memory and dismounted.

In the distance one of his men shouted. Stones clattered, falling on stone. Hooves thudded on sod. Someone screamed—a scream cut short. Richenza of Indes flinched.

''My lady.'' He was right: she did not deny the title. ''That was no man of yours?''

"I came alone." She stared in the direction of the scream. "I was afraid I would be followed, so I hid behind the altar till the moon rose. I saw no one, but I could sense someone near."

Hamon—it would be Hamon—rode back into the clearing. He leaned down from the saddle. "I take it that you didn't want him alive."

Richenza shook her head.

"No," Walter answered.

"Good." Hamon straightened. "Otherwise, it would have been a trifle late. He broke his neck falling off what must be the only wall still standing in Reasalyn. Now what?"

"Was there anything to identify him?"

"Nondescript man in nondescript clothes—not livery. No papers. Tarsean coins—a fair number—in his purse, and these," Hamon dropped two bits of metal onto Walter's palm and waited expectantly.

"Hide the body and see if you can find his mount." Walter held the bits of metal out to the Lady Richenza, who frowned over them but did not touch them as they lay in his palm.

"That's Leot's badge." She pointed to a small metal plate shaped like a leopard's mask with holes at its edges. Walter remembered such badges sewn on livery to identify noble retainers in the southern kingdom of Yesacroth, but not in Tarsia. Some things had obviously changed.

"The other is just a foreign coin, Ascovian, I think. Perhaps it was his good-luck charm." She shivered as though touched by the man's lack of luck. Her face was lit half by the full moon's cold light, half by the fire's warmth. Half-live, half-dead, caught between two worlds as he was. He buried the thought and looked away.

Behind the altar the great bas-relief of the Goddesses still stood, stirred to false life by the fire. Enath still stood on the left, fire at her feet, scroll in hand, Anchytel on the right with sheaf and serpent. In the center Elun still held the full moon in her hands, but below only a dark void showed where her waters had once flowed under the altar and down the center of the ceremonial way through the city, symbolically nourishing all the Rensel lands. The carved faces seemed to smile at him, smile not warmly but with the mockery of knowledge, of secrets unshared.

He turned his back on them. They had chosen this girl's task for him, for all the Wild Hunt, to perform or face eternal destruction, and they never told him why. Why this task, not another? There were other summoners; those who went unanswered, whose calls only touched the corners of his consciousness. Looking out over the ruins of Reasalyn he could guess the Goddesses' purpose this time.

A once-thriving city lay in desolation. The moonlight picked out few fragments of paving not swallowed under grass, few fragments of wall not broken by the roots of encroaching vegetation. It must be late autumn—the trees were bare and the grass brown. Dead, dead like Reasalyn. No one lived there, no one had since Tarses razed the city, enraged that his sons were cursed. The Goddesses would send them on any task that spread discord in the state Tarses had founded.

"Who is Leot?" he asked the girl.

She started as if she had expected him to know. "Leot? Leot is the king's son. Leot of the House of Thaiter."

Thaiter. The last time they had been in Tarsia the ruling house had been Vitaut. His Huntsman Alesander was a Vitaut. The questions came flooding at him. But he forced them back. Knowledge must be shared, known by all his men. Ignorance was dangerous.

He wished that they were gone from this dead city and fought the urge to call his men from their search. Half his men kept guard—six men. And six to search. He had a new Huntsman, Brian—he found only the name in his mind—and he had not let himself realize it till now. Careless, he chided himself. He could not afford to be careless.

Finally, his searchers returned, reporting the body hid, no sign of any human presence but the dead man's and the girl's and signs of two horses.

"My mare bolted before I could tie her," said Lady Richenza. *No doubt the dead man's did, too*, thought Walter. Animals were too wise to be here when the moon was full.

Now they could go. Hurriedly he had the nearest Huntsman take her up before him, and, calling in the men who had stood guard, he led the way down the hill and through the ruined city.

Behind them the fire had sunk to embers on the altar, embers that would stay alive until the Hunt returned in success or failure at the next full moon. Beside the dormant fire a forgotten dagger lay.

They rode through forest till they came to a rutted road that paralleled the Magnary as they pushed on north. To Walter's eyes the land looked prosperous, peaceful in the full moon's light. The villages still stood where they had since Rensel times, but he could see new, isolated farms. Only in peaceful times could men live thus, apart from their neighbors.

The Lady Richenza directed them off the high road, up a lane to an open gate. They halted, and Walter sent three of his men to scout the area and the boy Reynard to search the courtyard and outbuildings. A thief had his uses.

The courtyard seemed empty. Walter recognized the characteristic plan of a Rensel villa in the siting of the buildings; old stone had been reused in their walls. The lord's house, though, was not in the Rensel style. He noted the expanse of glazed windows reflecting the moonlight, the height of the pitched roof, the carved doorframe. Yet it was not new; the stones were not fresh-cut and raw, and vines clung to the far wall.

How much time had passed since their last summoning?

Reynard reported. There were five horses in the stable, three men asleep in the hayloft, no one in any of the outbuildings, and one upstairs window showed a light.

Walter looked at Richenza, who nodded. "If my horse returned, there would be five. I brought a groom and two men-at-arms, and my lady-in-waiting Annet is probably sitting up worrying about me."

Reassured, Walter called in his scouts, who had nothing suspicious to report, and led them into the courtyard. Richenza slid down from Hamon's horse and knocked on the door. Walter frowned. He should not have exposed her unnecessarily to Hamon. If she knew of the Wild Hunt, she must know what Hamon of Saroth was. His nearness must have made her uncomfortable.

The door flew open to her knock. A bony middle-aged woman stood on the threshold. "My lady, where have you been? I've been beside myself since your horse—"

"Annet," Richenza cut her short, "did anyone come after I left?"

"No one. I—"

"It's all right," Richenza told Walter. The thirteen men dismounted from their moon-silver horses.

"My lady," Annet quavered, looking at the faces lit by her lamp. "What have you done?"

"Don't fuss, Annet. Light a fire in the parlor. We have guests."

Walter turned to Richenza, who was staring at him, her eyes wide. She had dark eyes, blue with a violet cast, and they conjured up the face he tried so hard to forget. *Her* hair had been silver fair but . . .

He pushed the memory away. "Where is this parlor?" After twenty summonings he was no longer surprised that he knew without asking that that was a new name for a room. "We should move inside before we attract attention."

She led them through the screen passage and the great hall to a large room beyond. Windows filled the outer walls. This would be a sunny room in the daytime and an indefensible one. The western windows framed the sinking moon.

The Lady Richenza stood at the fireplace, gazing up as though she drew strength from the armorial display. Walter's gaze followed hers. In his own time Indes had had a battle standard of the same red and gold, but armory had been a southern innovation newly adopted the last time he had been in Tarsia. How would a pompous herald such as he had known in Yesacroth describe the design? It was a red field, pierced by three sharp golden points bespattered with red drops like blood. That would be gules, three piles conjoined in base or goutty de sang. An apt design for Indes or any other of Tarses the Conqueror's Companions.

Richenza of the House of Indes—Walter looked at her and smiled at the ironies of time. Would Indes the Sueve tribal leader have claimed this delicate, fine-boned girl as kin? Her pale skin, her build, her blue eyes would have marked her as Rensel to Indes. Eyes with a violet cast like hers had been sung by the Rensel bards as like the sky at sunset and dawning. All Indes would have recognized as his was her glossy black hair. And a name, he reminded himself, and the privileges that went with it.

Companion of the Conqueror—how many houses of the original twenty could prove the strict male descent from one of Tarses's council that was necessary to that rank? If Indes were destroyed, how many remained?

She turned and sat in the high-backed chair. Her long hands were folded sedately in her lap, but her back was rigid. The thirteen men of the Hunt settled about the room, waiting to learn the details of the task she had set them.

First Walter asked the question that he most—and least—wanted the answer to.

"My lady, what year is it?"

"The thirty-eighth year of the reign of King Rozer III."

Useless information; the name Rozer meant nothing to him.

"Since the fall of Reasalyn?" he corrected patiently.

Her eyes widened; she must have realized why he asked. "More than twelve hundred years."

Worse than he had feared; three hundred years, nearly, since their last summoning—by far the longest gap since the start of the Hunt. His men registered the time in their own ways, but he could sense their shock and unease.

He put his own feelings aside. Time passed; his only concern should be its impact on the task at hand.

To distract his men and his mind he turned to Richenza. "Exactly what is it that you wish done?"

She looked at her hands clenched in her lap. She consciously relaxed them, then met Walter's gaze. "There are two things I wish of you. First, my brother Nele was executed for high treason without trial or hearing. Indes has the right to choose a champion to fight in trial by combat to disprove the charge. However, all the nobles so fear the king's displeasure that I will find no one to take Indes's part."

Walter nodded; the combat should be no difficulty. Several of the Huntsmen could take care of a simple judicial combat.

"And . . . " he prompted.

"I wish the House of Thaiter to be destroyed as Thaiter has destroyed the House of Indes." This was the crux of the matter.

His men seemed to take this information with indifference, real or feigned.

"What, precisely, were the circumstances of your brother's death?" From the corner of his eye he could see that Alesander was watching the lady intently.

"Murder," she corrected. "My brother Nele became Grand Duke of Maldrin when our father died two years ago. My father was barely laid to rest when Prince Leot befriended Nele. I knew that Leot was up to some trickery, because Leot and his brothers hated my father. There was no reason why Leot should change his mind."

"Why did Prince Leot hate your father?"

"My father was governor to the two older princes, Ewets and Leot, for several years after their mother, Queen Kamilka, died. He always said an untrained man, like an untrained horse, is of no use to anyone, but the princes' other governors had let them run wild. By the time Father was appointed they were nearly of age, and it was too late. Then Rozer's new wife Betrissa tried to seduce Father, and when she failed she had him removed from office. Father retired to Maldrin, but things happened to suggest that Ewets, Leot, and the queen were conspiring against him."

"Your brother knew nothing of this?"

"He knew, but he chose to believe that Leot wasn't responsible—only Ewets and Betrissa. Ewets was openly hostile, and Wendis, the youngest prince, is a useless wastrel, so Nele came to believe that Leot was the only member of the Royal House worthy to rule. Leot convinced him that King Rozer was simpleminded and that the kingdom was in danger."

Lady Richenza's eyes dropped, and Walter wondered if she was ashamed to say what happened next. But she looked up and continued. "So when Leot decided to assassinate his father, Nele followed like a child, all puffed up by his own proposed role in history. But somehow Rozer learned of the plot. When he was confronted by his father, Leot confessed, and said he had been led astray by

Nele, and Rozer, the fool, wept and forgave him.''

Her eyes blazed with anger. ''Nele was left to fall into the trap. They let him and his men get into the king's apartments, then they ambushed them. His men were killed. Nele fought through and escaped into the corridor. I'm told he sought refuge in the Princess Meriel's apartments. She called the guard, and they captured him. They took him out to the courtyard and beheaded him immediately so that he could not betray Leot's part. Leot had his body delivered home to me that dawn in an arrow chest.

''If my brother was a traitor, then the blood is corrupt, our name degraded, and our possessions forfeit. But they slipped; they forgot that Indes is beyond any law but the Laws of Ortas. My brother was not condemned by his peers, and without that judgment they cannot touch our goods. If I do not appeal Leot to prove his accusations, I am left in limbo. I cannot even legally mourn Nele's death because they have named him traitor. If I appeal and Leot wins, he proves his charges and I lose everything. If my champion wins, then Nele was innocent, whatever the evidence against him. But win or lose, the House of Indes ends with me. I cannot pass on its special status even if I had ten sons.''

''Why have them all killed?'' Thomas asked. ''Why not just Leot and the king?''

''Rozer tells Ewets everything. He must have been part of the plot. Ewets is the heir; he would be glad to see the House of one of the Companions ended. And Leot had promised Meriel to Nele, and she encouraged him. In the end, though, she wouldn't hide him or plead for his life. Wendis must have known, too, for he left town so conveniently. The House of Thaiter is corrupt beyond salvaging.''

''How many people comprise the House of Thaiter?'' Walter asked.

''Only Rozer, his three sons, his daughter Meriel, and Queen Betrissa, who is also of the House, the last of the only surviving cadet branch. Thaiter is famous for its history of sudden death among younger sons.''

''Fratricide runs in the family,'' Alesander said suddenly.

The Lady Richenza looked at the prince sharply, angrily, but he met her gaze with laughter in his blue eyes. Alesan-

der had only ridden with the Hunt for two summonings—
he still felt a compulsion to learn all he could of events in
his homeland, events Walter had not had occasion to keep
abreast of.

"Are you of Thaiter?" she asked.

"Haldan, no! Vitaut. The Thaiter from whom the current
ruling house is descended was my father's brother—my
only surviving uncle."

"Why did your father let him survive?" Hamon asked.

"He was absentminded and walked into walls. Besides,
Father was fond of him. I was astounded to learn that he
had rebelled against my younger brother and seized the
throne. Not that it matters now, but I am sorry my relatives
have caused the lady so much grief."

"So you didn't kill all your brothers," Hamon said.

"No, and I was always very kind to my sister."

"But I *was* very kind to my sister." Hamon sounded
more wounded than offended. "The poison killed her
quickly."

"Not quickly enough, apparently." Michel leaned over
the back of Hamon's chair.

Hamon looked up at him. "She never knew when to shut
up either." Then he smiled at Lady Richenza. "Actually,
our old nurse cursed me. Nurse always did like her better."

Walter sent Hamon a silent warning. The lady looked
wary. Walter had seen summoners lose their nerve when
the task began in earnest.

He turned to her. "Has a date been set for the combat?"

"No, it will be set when I present my champion in audience in three days. However, Leot has already agreed to
fight whomever I choose."

"Excellent." Walter looked about the room. His men
had absorbed the nature of their task, but now they were
impatient. Walter began to give orders.

"Michel, go help in the kitchen. Reynard, tend the
horses. Bertz, more wood for the fire. Garrett, see if some
wine can be brought while we wait for the food."

Richenza looked taut to the point of breaking. Time to
turn her mind to something more mundane than the Hunt.

"My lady, we need to go unnoticed in Tarsit. How must
we dress?"

She looked at him and relaxed as her thoughts moved to that everyday subject. "First of all, your hair is too long. The fashion is for hair no longer than his." She gestured toward the new one, Brian, whose black hair curled only as far as the nape of his neck. "Now as for your clothes . . ."

Dawn, gloomy and rain-soaked, lit the room and touched the faces of the Huntsmen. Walter looked down the table as the lady talked. As he had evaluated the strength of his troops before battle, Walter considered his men now.

Hamon, the most notorious of the notorious ruling princes of Saroth, lounged in his chair watching the others work. Walter need not question his willingness to perform a task. Be it rape, murder, or any other filth that needed doing, Hamon would do it and enjoy the doing. His languid air was as characteristic of Saroth as his swarthy skin, black hair, and black eyes. Though he had played other parts, he was best cast as a southerner.

Eleylin, the longest cursed besides Walter and Hamon, would do whatever he was asked, but his coloring showed his origin as surely as Hamon's. Rensel coloring, silvery fair hair and pale blue eyes. Few but Selinian mercenaries had such coloring in Tarsia. His assured decisiveness could be mistaken for a mercenary's brash arrogance.

If there still are Selinian mercenaries. Three hundred years. Elun, don't make the task impossible.

When he looked at Thomas, Walter softened. Thomas he could trust to understand. No need to fear that Thomas would shirk a painful task or change an order to suit his own opinions. With his brown hair and eyes, he might be from anywhere.

Michel came in from the kitchen carrying a platter heaped with food. Square-built, yet pretty with his golden hair and green eyes, he appeared the soul of innocence, but behind that youthful face was a vicious and self-centered mind. Michel would do anything if convinced it was in his own interest.

Payne was helping Bertz carry firewood. He had his ancestor Amloth's dark red hair, but his eyes were green. Uncommon coloring, but as likely here as anywhere. Like

Hamon, Payne would do the tasks set him with no qualms, if not with Hamon's relish.

Reynard, his fox-colored hair straight from the soaking rain, entered and came over to say, "Master, your horse is the bay now." Walter nodded. Thief, cutpurse, and general vagabond, he managed an air of innocence. At fifteen he was the youngest Huntsman, but he often proved more useful than his elders.

Ulick was studying the leaded glass of the window. With his glossy black hair, lynx-colored eyes, ivory skin, and broad face, he was another whose origins could not be concealed. He was one of the nomadic Sueve—the Sueve who had stayed on their grassy plain. At least Tarsia's border with the Sueve lands made his presence here more easy to explain than it had been farther south.

Justin had been given his wine already—Garrett had known who would want it first. Justin had heard that it must be killing. An alchemist could be kept far too busy with this task. He must find someone to watch Justin.

Alesander was listening intently to the Lady Richenza. The prince was valuable in any task that called for a man of station. With hair of gold and blue eyes, he possessed all the skills of a courtier, and on the field he was a fine example of young knighthood. His inbred rashness must be carefully curbed. Here in his homeland he would be an invaluable aid.

Bertz stared out the window. His looks were acceptable, his coppery hair and grey eyes possible anywhere this far north. But his accent was indelibly Stros. The Stros were a sect from the north, insular and of an unlikely monotheism. Furthermore, the man disapproved, seemingly, of everything. Including drunkenness. He could watch Justin, which would, Walter hoped, relieve anyone of watching Bertz.

Garrett had watched Bertz last time—the wrong job for someone from the Tributary Lordships, who were at constant war with the Stros. The young man's baiting of the Stros had caused trouble despite Bertz's indifference. Garrett was a little unpolished for Tarsia, but that could be explained. His light brown hair and pale green eyes were common enough, though his remarkable height—half a head taller than any other Huntsman—made him difficult to disguise or forget.

Finally, Walter looked at Brian, who sat on the stool farthest from the light. All he knew was a name and what he could see. He was young, in his early twenties, Walter estimated. His hair was black and curly; his eyes were blue, and he carried himself well. Nothing else was obvious. He must talk with the boy and soon.

Next to Walter, Lady Richenza faltered and put a hand to her head. She had not slept that night nor, if she had sat up with her brother's body as was the custom, the night before.

The servingwoman hovered, scolding softly. Richenza murmured a protest to the older woman and continued talking.

Walter stopped her. "No, you need sleep. I will hear more later." Annet helped Richenza to her feet and out of the room. Walter watched the women leave, feeling Thomas's eyes on him. Thomas would have uncomfortable questions later.

Garrett filled his goblet and Walter fingered the short stem thoughtfully. Garrett had only ridden with the Hunt once, so he might not have noticed that Walter did not touch wine, only ale or beer or water. He remembered his last cup of wine. It was almost the last pleasant moment he could remember—and that a thousand years before. He contemplated the goblet without lifting it. Did Justin find forgetfulness in the wine? Walter doubted it; he had seen no surcease of pain in the man's drunken eyes.

He pushed away from the table. This was no time to seek oblivion. There hadn't been in a thousand years, or twenty-two moons, however you figured it. This was a distasteful task, but it should not prove difficult.

"Alesander." The Prince of Tarsia started as if he, too, had been lost in thought. "How much does what the Lady Richenza described differ from Tarsia in your time?"

"The conduct of the Royal House seems all too familiar." Alesander smiled wryly, then sobered. "What I see of the estate and household arrangements seems little changed as well."

"Could you pass as a gentleman of the lady's household?"

"Certainly."

"Good. You joust sufficiently well to handle the judicial combat. You will be Indes's champion. Also, if the Royal House is determined to finish the House of Indes, the Lady Richenza is in danger. She will have to be guarded."

Alesander nodded.

Annet returned, disapproval radiating from her every move.

"Did the Lady Richenza get safely to bed?"

"She did."

"Is there some room where I could be alone?"

"There is the room where His Grace worked."

"Show me."

The room she took him to was small and isolated, furnished with no more than a table, a chair, a few books on a shelf, and a window.

As the woman turned to leave he stopped her. Grudgingly she turned back.

"Annet, you know who we are, and why your mistress called us."

"Yes."

"She has set us a task and we must perform it. The others will have questions. Answer them as best you can. A mistake could harm your mistress. Do you understand?"

The woman nodded.

"You may go." Walter turned to the window. He wanted this time alone, away from the old arguments and vituperative baiting of the others, away from Thomas's watchful eyes. He was weary and this was as close to sleep as he would come until the moon was full again and even that would probably be a sleep beset by nightmares.

How long will I dream next time? A thousand years? Forever?

He ought to think of the work at hand. He knew enough to make a start.

It would be hard this time. This time there was the Lady Richenza. If only she weren't just the right age, and if only her eyes were not that exact shade of blue-purple . . . She had even used the same angry, imperious tone that Cassi-

mara had used when things were not arranged to her liking.
Damn! He had too many people to worry about as it was.

Walter looked out the window, across the fields, alone
with his thoughts—thoughts that would not be disciplined
and strayed back to painful subjects. He was almost relieved when Thomas knocked lightly at the door.

"You've found a nice hole to hide in." Thomas stopped
abruptly as if he knew that he had come too close to truth.
"What are the others doing?"

Thomas shrugged. "It is beginning to be noisy out there.
I think the three hundred years bothers them. It certainly
bothers me."

"I know."

"Is that what's troubling you?"

Walter sighed. "No more than usual."

"The task itself doesn't seem that difficult. At least it's
a small family we're to hunt down. What, then, is the problem?"

"It's the girl. We need to be careful. It mustn't look like
a single plot against the Royal House, or they'll blame
her."

"She isn't a fool. She must realize that, and I remember
nothing in her command stating she must survive to have
the task fulfilled."

"Must you remember everything to the letter?"

"The Ladies certainly do, so one of us has to. Besides,
legal thinking is hard to outgrow."

"If I plan carefully, her death is not necessary. To plan
I need quiet."

"Nonsense. When you plan you sound like a Sueve war
leader taking a city. There's more to it." Thomas studied
Walter. "It *is* the girl, though. You are rarely so thoughtful
when gathering information. I've known you to question
someone solidly for two days before you were satisfied.
The Lady Richenza is asked a few polite questions and then
allowed to take a nice nap. Why?"

"She'd already been up for two nights." Walter began
to tick reasons off on his fingers. "Even I can't question
an unconscious girl."

"This isn't a debate."

Walter gave up. "She reminds me of Cassimara."

"Your wife?"

Walter nodded. "Her eyes, her age, even her voice—"

"I see." Thomas stared at the matting. "Will it cause problems?"

"I don't know. I don't think so. It just makes everything ... painful." The pair were silent until Walter's thought drove him to speak. "I need something to do. Go tell the new man, Brian, that I want to see him."

2

First Day—Morning

Brian sat in the parlor and watched the men around him with a firm sense of unreality. Surely this would turn out to be some sort of pageant joke. The biggest, filthiest jest of his brother Geoffry's career.

No, Geoff was dead. Brian had stood over him and known that a head twisted like that meant a broken neck. Geoffry had made his last joke.

So, unbelievable as it might be, he was here with them. Some he could put names to. The dark, slightly built man from the south must be Hamon, Prince of Saroth, who had murdered his own sister. The pretty youth with the golden curls must be Michel Galmot, who had sold the fortress of Iskandroc to the Sueve. The man with the straight silver-gold hair and the air of impatient authority had to be Eleylin, the last heir to the Rensel Empire, who had beheaded his mother for causing the destruction of Onsalm. Brian's knowledge of history did not yield names for any of the others except for the man who had left the room, Sir Walter of Jacin. Brian had looked into that man's bleak eyes and known this was no joke. They were the Wild Hunt, and he was one of them.

He figured the time again. His father had sent

a delegation headed by Geoffry to Rozer's thirtieth-year jubilee. His seventeenth birthday, the only one he remembered enjoying, had fallen while Geoffry was on that visit. If this was the thirty-*eighth* year of Rozer's reign, it was two full years since Geoffry's death. But he could remember only two nights—the one following the funeral and the one now ending. The shocks were ragged cones in the fields, the trees bare. Not quite winter; Blood Moon, he decided. The time for the killing of cattle. His last memory was of early autumn, when just enough leaves had fallen to hide a trip wire if a rider hadn't learned to be wary of traps.

Brian shook his head. He wasn't ready, two years or not, to dwell on that. He remembered the funeral—his mother, dressed in black pointing at him and reciting that curse *by Enath, Elun, Anchytel.* Only the names of three ancient Goddesses, but the words had made his heart pause, just as it had when he'd heard that strange snap that had been Geoffrey's neck breaking.

The three names had seemed to echo endlessly in his head. He had told himself it was just one of her scenes, another incident for the courtiers to gossip about. But her own household, the ones who had accompanied her from Yesacroth years ago, had been silent, expectant.

That last night he had been unable to read or to sleep. He had sat on his bed and watched the moonlight—a full moon, like tonight—creep across the floor, reaching like flames to engulf him. Something had happened when it reached him, something he had no words for. Then there had been a voice and a beacon toward which he must ride.

No, that wasn't right. There had been something in between.

He had been in the presence of a woman dressed in a white pleated gown with wide sleeves, her arms bare beneath them, and her long silver-gold hair unbound. Her face had been young, her eyes old, and Brian knew that he had known her name, but he could not remember it. She had spoken to him, but he could only recall the sound of water flowing, her words just out of reach. Then had come another woman's voice—Lady Richenza's—calling him, using those names again—*Enath, Elun, Anchytel.*

Someone put a hand on his shoulder and Brian spun round. The brown-eyed man with the Madarian accent stood over him. "Walter wants to see you." Brian felt a fool for jumping.

The man led him across the dais of the great hall.

"Walter tells me that your name is Brian."

How does Walter know that?

The man opened the door to the room next to the parlor. Walter of Jacin sat behind the carved wooden table.

Walter looked at Brian, summing him up with ancient grey eyes. Brian debated saying something to end that awful scrutiny.

In the end Walter broke the silence. "Your name is Brian . . . ?"

"Hassart." That was the House name, rarely used now.

"You are from the west. Where exactly?"

"Near Canjit." That was true; his own holdings were well out of the city.

More silence. Brian spoke first. Even a stupid question was better than the judgmental silence. "Is it always like that? I was in my room alone, and then I was at the temple."

"Is that all?"

"There was a woman." He didn't say more; he couldn't.

"The waits can differ. Sometimes it seems no time has passed, sometimes there are dreams, sometimes nightmares, sometimes you are taught things. It is better not to dwell on it." The last, surprisingly, was almost kind. Walter went on more brusquely. "Do you know how much time you have lost?"

"A bit over two years, I think."

Walter sighed and looked up.

"What did you do?"

Startled, Brian blurted, "I didn't do anything."

"Everyone has done something."

Brian made no reply. Walter looked past him out the window. When Walter spoke again it was in a quiet voice, as if he spoke to himself.

"Amloth, son of Tarses the Conqueror, was cursed first of us all for his defilement of the temple where we were summoned tonight. The high priestess cursed him by Enath,

Elun, Anchytel just as I was, and"—the measuring eyes regarded Brian—"just as you were. You will lose years—centuries—between summonings. You will ride to the beacon fire and find yourself perhaps hundreds of miles from your last memory.

"We will be given a task to do; if we fail to perform it by the next full moon, the wall of flame will rise and devour all but three of us. You are the first man to be cursed in more than three centuries and I can promise that you will be one of the survivors. But you will live with the memory of failure."

Walter paused to let his words sink in before he continued. "So you have done nothing. Who hated you enough to send you to ride with us?"

"My mother." Brian expected a comment, but the old man merely nodded. "My brother, Geoffry, was killed in an accident when we were riding. My mother thought I caused it." Did Walter believe him? He was pitting all his experience at looking guileless against Walter's centuries of spotting lies. But no real lie was involved, merely a few omitted facts. "I didn't get along with Geoff and Mother . . ."

Walter just looked at him, and Brian fought the urge to fidget. Finally Walter asked, "Do you understand what the Lady Richenza commanded us to do?"

"She wants us to exterminate the House of Thaiter." That seemed an excellent idea. From what he knew of the reports brought back by his father's envoys, the Royal House of Tarsia was a viper's nest.

"If we fail at this task, you, Garrett, and Bertz would remain. The rest of us . . ." Walter snapped his fingers, ". . . as if we had never been. Not only our bodies, but our souls, would be consumed in Enath's flame." He let that sink in. "Do they still tell of the fall of Onsalm?"

Brian nodded.

"I saw the fall of that city nine centuries ago. We were betrayed, and we failed that day. We stood in the moonlight and the small fire that had summoned us did not die; it flared and spread from man to man until it had devoured eleven of us." He leaned forward. "If you make a mistake, or cause anyone to make a mistake, you will have all our fates on your head. Remember. Now, is there anything else you need to tell me?''

The Huntsman's eyes made Brian want to retreat. In a last defense he responded with the only other fact he could recall about the Hunt and the fall of Onsalm, ''Amloth escaped.''

''So I am told. Trapped by a burning rafter that crippled him. Payne could tell you more. He claims descent from Amloth.

''It takes great hate to condemn someone to this—it takes great love to free you from it. They say that if you find someone who loves you, needs you, enough to hold you back from my summoning till the sun overwhelms the moon on the last night we are free, you are released from the curse.

''I am told that Amloth was held by Eleylin's sister, and another escaped before him. The first was before my time, and all I know of Amloth is that he was not with us after Onsalm, but neither were eleven other men. Once one of his women tried to hold Hamon. He thinks he killed her struggling away.''

Brian stared at the floor, inexplicable obstinacy welling up in him.

''Go now,'' Walter said. ''Don't drink with Justin. You won't pass out, you will get a hangover, and you won't forget anything. Send Thomas, the man who brought you here, to me.''

As he left, Brian wondered how Walter had known he had considered drinking himself into insensibility.

Walter did not look up when Thomas entered. Neither man spoke until Walter leaned back in his chair.

''Well,'' Thomas said, ''what did you learn about Brian?''

''That he is an excellent liar.''

''When has lying been a liability with us?''

''When *I* am lied to.''

''Oh. What does he lie about?''

''Nearly everything. He says his name is Brian Hassart, which is true. However, his clothes are expensive, his bearing excellent, and his manners perfect. All I know about

his birth is that his brother's name was Geoffry, and he
doesn't like his mother. Unless things have changed far
more than I think they have, that boy is wellborn.''

"Merchants may have improved their manners."

"He is no merchant."

"He looks innocent enough."

"So does Michel. He says he has done 'nothing', that he
was blamed for his brother's accidental death. No one is
cursed for 'nothing'."

"Unless the Goddesses finds his talents or the notoriety
of his cursing useful."

Walter frowned at Thomas's cynicism. "I won't, I can't,
believe that." He returned to the subject of Brian. "That
is partly lie and partly truth, but I cannot tell where his lie
leaves off and his truth begins." Walter rested his chin on
his fist. "Consequently, I don't know anything about him
except that he has excellent manners, lies well, and didn't
fall off his horse between here and the temple. Oh, yes, he
knows his history and is from 'near Canjit.' Not, mind you,
the village of Something-or-other, or the estate of Lord
Thus-and-so. But simply, 'near Canjit.' ''

"M-m. Well, on that information you should find something for him to do. Put him with Hamon to test his stomach?''

"No, that might make him worse. Who is from reason-
ably near Canjitrin and might not frighten the boy?" Walter
thought for a moment. "You talk to him."

"Amaroc is nowhere near Canjitrin."

"But he's probably never heard of you."

"A sad lack of notoriety in my case."

"Fortunately."

Walter looked up. "He was only cursed two years ago."

"Brian? That might be a problem."

"Especially if he decides he can go home. Remember
Ulick?''

"Vividly. I thought we'd have to tie him up for the
whole month the first two times."

Walter nodded gloomily, "If I—we—fail this time, do
you realize who leads the Hunt? Bertz. A farmer—a Stros
farmer—leading the Hunt? He only barely believes he's
here. What would he do? Make converts? Not perform tasks

he disagreed with? I don't even know if the man can lead."

"You might try to find out, but you're not the one who has to worry about it, are you?"

Walter sighed and nodded. "I plan to have Bertz watch Justin."

"Practical. Then no one has to watch Bertz. On the other hand, recalling Bertz's reaction to drunkenness in general, I feel sorry for Justin."

"Justin feels entirely too sorry for Justin."

"You can understand that."

"I understand it, but his drinking endangers us all." Walter changed the subject, "The Lady Richenza needs a guardian, that much I do know. Do you know what the guardianship laws are in Tarsia?"

Richenza awoke with a headache, a bad taste in her mouth, and sunlight slanting in her window. She sat up, and all the memories of the night before came flooding back.

Oh, Haldan, what have I done? She settled back on the pillows; but before she could relax, the door flew open, and Annet hurried in, carrying a tray.

"You're awake. I told that man I wouldn't wake you even if he wanted to see you right away, but he insisted and said he'd send someone else." Even this counterfeit victory over "that man"—who Richenza assumed was Sir Walter—did not improve Annet's mood. As Richenza allowed herself to be served breakfast and helped to dress, it became obvious that Annet had had no sleep, but had been questioned most of the morning.

". . . And such things as some of them asked, too, my lady, about manners and how to address people. One of them, before he left, even wanted to know where he might talk to sailors. Sailors! In Tarsia!"

"Which one?" Richenza was amused despite Annet's distress.

"The blond one, who I think was Prince Eleylin."

Annet faced Richenza squarely and grimly. Her grey-green eyes were serious, as if she meant what she was about to say.

"Are you trying to kill yourself, too? Summoning them—" She nodded sharply in the direction of the closed door. "The king and that pack of ill-bred pups he calls sons would give their right arms to finish you off and have done with Indes completely."

Richenza looked at herself in the small hand mirror, inspecting the hair Annet had braided. "Being dead is infinitely preferable to what Leot has planned for me. You heard the message he sent with Nele's body. As for the king, he'll give more than his right arm before this month is up." She put down the mirror impatiently. "Besides, who else would fight the judicial combat? You?"

"Well, it doesn't have to be the walking dead men you've called up. And what will you do about Feracher? You are betrothed to him, after all."

"Robert will want to see which way the wind blows. If the match proves less advantageous than he expected, he'll cry off. I hardly think he'll rush to my side, even if he weren't a month's journey away. Leot took that into account when he planned this." She looked in the mirror one last time and found that her reflection looked far more confident than she felt. "Now, where can I find Sir Walter?"

"In your father's study." Annet pursed her lips considering her next words. "My lady, at least promise me you won't go back to the city so soon? We could stay here."

"And how long do you think I'll be able to hide here, or anywhere, once Leot's discovered I'm not at Maldrin?" Then, repenting of her sharpness—Annet had raised Nele, too—Richenza sighed. "I will be as careful as I can, but there isn't anything else I can do, unless you want to see me in Leot's clutches?"

Annet's lips thinned, and she nodded shortly.

"You're right. I suppose you had no choice."

Richenza fled the room and closed the door, wishing she were half as confident as she had pretended for Annet.

Walter rose from her father's place and greeted her with the same solemn courtesy he had shown the night before.

"My lady, we have much work, and we need information. So, today we must ask questions and you, my lady, must answer them as best you can. Any mistake or gap in our knowledge could hurt you as well as us. Do you understand?"

She nodded.

"Very well," he said. "This will not be a pleasant afternoon, but it should be the worst you will have to bear from your summoning."

The sun was nearly set when Walter of Jacin looked at each of his Huntsmen in turn, as if to be sure that there was not even a single question more to ask. No one spoke, and Walter nodded. The Huntsmen rose and, like schoolboys dismissed from their lesson, crowded out of the room, discussing what they had learned.

Richenza watched them go, as exhausted as if she had ridden all day without stopping. She felt that she had told them every fact she had learned in her life. She turned to Walter, who rose as she did.

"Thank you, my lady," he said smoothly. "I shall see that you are not troubled again by our planning."

Her tired mind took a second to realize what he meant.

"But I wish to be troubled by it. I am not a child to be forbidden the councils of my elders."

"My lady, it may not be safe for you to know too much."

"I am the last of Indes; I have conspired against the throne; am I safe in any case? Even if I had not summoned you, I would have been in danger of my life and more. I am not the fool my brother was. I know what can come of my actions."

"As you wish, my lady." Walter's eyes were grave and thoughtful. "I have decided that Prince Alesander will be your champion. Since he will be part of your household for the next moon, you should understand who he is."

"I know his name, and therefore, his birth."

"That is not what I meant, my lady." He paused as if weighing his words. "Prince Alesander was cursed because he killed his brother."

Did he expect her to be shocked? "Fratricide runs in the family," Alesander had said last night, and she had understood. The Royal Houses of Tarsia were all the same.

"That should make it easier for him to kill Leot, shouldn't it?" she replied calmly.

3

First Day—Evening

Walter closed the chamber door behind him, shutting out the sounds of dining which still came from the great hall. The fireplace was the only source of light in the darkening room, and he turned a chair around to face that light and warmth.

Well, after a full day of questions and answers what did he know? That Tarsia was ruled by a feeble king, whose family consisted of three variously vicious sons, a proud and heartless daughter, and an adulterous wife. Things haven't changed much in three hundred years, he thought satirically. As Alesander had said the night before, the conduct of the Tarsean Royal House seemed all too familiar.

Things had not changed as much as he had feared. Apparently the political turmoil had led to stagnation. Tarsia seemed to be no more advanced now than Yesacroth had been three hundred years ago. This summoning had not, after all, dropped them into the alien world that he had feared when he first heard the year. Reasalyn had been more advanced twelve hundred years ago than anything the Sueve had yet managed to build. He wondered if something had been lost with the Rensel; some touch of genius gone forever. "Walter, you think too much!" Amloth had told him often, and Walter turned his mind back to the task at hand.

The royal sons fought like dogs over the bones of the kingdom. Would their destruction lead to some restoration of Rensel order? The Goddesses must have a purpose to these summonings, though he never could perceive the pattern. But he was only a mortal man in spite of any powers he controlled. Trust, then, that there was some point to the tasks, some justice served. The Lady Richenza did not deserve what had befallen her. Some of his men didn't deserve what would befall them if they failed.

Does anyone deserve that, he wondered, shuddering as if the flames at Onsalm reached for him again. However just or unjust the cause, they must not fail. Oh, how he wished that these killings might be justice disguised. This House of Thaiter, like all the Houses descendant from Tarses, killed their own kind. Like the hunting dogs of Avrian, in the traveler's tale, which, if you threw a stone among them, would forget the outer danger and turn and destroy each other. Perhaps all he had to do was throw that stone.

He summoned Hamon, who did not come alone. Walter had expected Thomas's arrival, but he was less pleased to see Richenza settle herself opposite him. He remembered her statement that since the responsibility of the summoning was hers, she did not wish to be in ignorance of its details.

Thomas had brought a branched candlestick from the hall and busied himself in lighting the candles, so that the fire was now only the largest pool of light amidst the gloom.

Walter turned his chair about to face Hamon, who stood at ease, the firelight full on him.

"I have decided on your part in this task," Walter began.

"You want me to kill the queen."

"No." Walter's face was hidden in the shadows. "I think the king will do that for us. I want you to seduce her."

Hamon smiled contemptuously. "Any special way?"

"I leave that to your experience in these matters."

Hamon turned sharply away from the revealing firelight. "It's an interesting problem. To seduce Queen Betrissa I have to be close to her. I can't be a nobleman from Arin

or anyplace else in the south because no such man would
be traveling in Tarsia for pleasure with the countries close
to war. My looks make me an unlikely Canjitard.''

He turned to Richenza. ''You say she's vain. Does she
choose her dress goods herself?''

Richenza nodded.

''I could be a southern merchant. The borders haven't
been closed to trade. I'll head south and set up a trail north
from Iskandroc in case they investigate. When do you want
me to be in Tarsit?''

Richenza spoke up. ''Merchants of luxury goods often
present themselves at the king's audience with gifts to ad-
vertise their wares. The next audience will be in three days'
time.''

Walter nodded. ''You would be wise to present yourself
there.''

Hamon turned to go.

''Wait,'' Walter said. ''I want you to take Reynard as
your apprentice. Stay while I speak to him.''

Hamon leaned against the table as Reynard half bowed
to Walter.

''Reynard, you're Hamon's apprentice, as he will explain
to you. Hamon will seduce the queen. Before that I want
you to be in position to betray them to the king. Rozer has
a soft spot for entertainers, so it should not be difficult to
ingratiate yourself into his household when Hamon flees.
Keep your ears open for information that might be of use
to us and report to me at the Lady Richenza's town house—
secretly, of course.''

Reynard bowed and took a step backward. He looked at
Hamon, ''Apprentice what?''

''Cloth merchant.''

''And I thought it was going to be something interesting.
Seducer, maybe.''

''Isn't teaching you fencing enough?''

''I'd also like to learn the gentler weapons,'' Reynard
protested, as Hamon shepherded him from the room.

Walter frowned after them. That ought to dispose of
Queen Betrissa and place a competent spy in the palace.
He summoned Michel.

''I want you to befriend the princes—Wendis especially.

Teach them what little they don't know of dissipation. Fan any flames of distrust among them.''

"Noble company. Who am I, to mingle in it?''

"A young noble, finishing his education with a tour of foreign lands—from Canjitrin, I think.''

"My, I must be rich, then.'' Michel slyly jingled the coins in his purse. "Richer than this would indicate. How much more do I get?''

Walter tossed him the purse from his own belt and said as Michel hefted it skeptically, "You can add your inevitable gambling winnings to that.''

Michel started to protest, stopped; thought, and asked, "Do I get a servant? I ought to have at least one. The new man, Brian, would be useful; he knows so much about Canjitrin.''

"I have another use for him.'' He ignored Michel's pout. "I have a use for all my men. If you must have a servant, hire one. I shouldn't have to tell you to choose one who can keep his mouth shut. Report to me or to Thomas. The princes frequent an inn called the Three Queens on Golden Street in Tarsit; that should be your first approach. I trust you can take it from there.''

Michel left, and Walter called in Eleylin.

"Well?''

"Ewets is interested in Rensel antiques.''

"And?'' Eleylin prompted.

"I want you to sell him some. Something with an aura of magic and power. Perhaps we can find a way to make his brothers jealous and uneasy. I leave the what to you.''

Eleylin snorted. "Rensel artifacts never helped the Rensel.''

"No doubt.'' Walter summoned Ulick and Garrett. "The three of you are mercenaries who have been serving at one of the frontier fortresses near Rayln. But the pickings are poor and the winter cold in the north. So, lured by rumors of war with Arin, you are moving south in search of softer employment. You have stopped in Tarsit to squander your pay. You have been serving together but you don't know much about each other and you're not really friends. Eleylin is going to sell Prince Ewets a Rensel antique. One of you will inform the other princes of the fact. Work the

details out among yourselves and don't let anything inca-
pacitating happen to Eleylin. I will get in touch with you
through Thomas. Any questions?"

"Yes," Ulick asked. "How is Ellis to acquire this Rensel antique?"

"I leave that to you, but I suggest going to Reasalyn and
unearthing something. Local superstitions keep people
away from the ruins, so it shouldn't be too difficult to find
something to use as bait."

Ulick nodded. There were no more questions, and the
three left.

After a long, still pause he summoned Payne.

"Payne, I need you to establish yourself in a position to
arrange an accident to Princess Meriel. I don't know when.
You had best be an impoverished noble from Canjitrin
seeking work far from home so as not to disgrace your
family. Take Brian with you—he can give you the information you need about Canjitrin. Your most difficult task
may be to keep an eye on him."

"Why?"

"He's a liar. About himself, if not about other things."

Payne perched on the edge of the table. "Thanks for
warning me. Anything else I should know?"

"He talks freely of everything but himself, and, as you
found out today, he was only cursed two years ago."

Walter called in Brian, whose glance shifted from him
to Richenza to Payne and back to Walter.

"Brian, you are to go with Payne as his assistant. Do as
he tells you and help him all you can. Remember the price
of failure." Brian looked at Payne uncertainly.

Walter turned to Payne. "Establish yourselves as soon
as possible. Report to me at the Lady Richenza's town
house."

Brian followed Payne from the room. Walter sighed and
summoned Bertz. The Stros came and stood composed and
unawed before him, waiting for Walter to speak.

"Bertz, I want you to watch over Justin, get him his
materials, help him as you can, don't let him take anything
stronger than liquor, give him no chance to attempt suicide
or anything that would incapacitate him. Whatever you pri-
vately think, let him drink except when I tell you not to."

Walter called in Justin, who, almost miraculously, was sober.

"You have undoubtedly guessed that we shall likely need your skills as a maker of poisons. We need something that will look like an old man's natural death. One with an antidote in case of accident."

"You don't want much, do you?"

Walter ignored his outburst. "Bertz is your assistant—"

"Nursemaid, you mean."

"Consult with him and draw me up a list of materials and equipment. Especially those which would lead to conjecture if purchased in Tarsit. Finish it tonight.

"The two of you will be the servingmen of my household; comport yourselves accordingly."

Bertz escorted Justin out. Walter called Alesander. He turned to Richenza. "Alesander will be your champion and your bodyguard. Nominally he is a young noble, a neighbor's son seeing the world in my service. I am your distant cousin—I think I remember there was an obscure branch of your family resident in the upper Kelsary Valley."

Richenza nodded.

"It would probably be best if I appear to be your guardian. I won't interfere with your administration of your property, but Thomas says your position would be legally stronger if you had a male kinsman in the offing. Otherwise, we are in your service." He rose, "Whenever you wish to return to Tarsit, we will be ready to accompany you."

She looked from Walter to Alesander to Thomas, standing obscurely in the shadows by the window where he had watched all evening. "We can leave first thing in the morning."

"Does it always come out long?" Reynard complained, as Bertz pushed his head forward to trim the hair in back. Brian watched with sympathy as the Stros made no attempt to be gentle. Michel's fussiness had apparently put him out of temper.

"It's been long every time I've been called." Payne watched the proceedings with a jaundiced eye; his turn was next. "I guess that's more practical than its being the length it was the summons before. You can always cut long hair, but it's difficult to lengthen short hair in the space of thirty days.''

"I suppose." Reynard didn't sound convinced.

"It could be beards," Payne pointed out.

"A beard isn't one of his problems yet," Hamon observed.

"It's getting to be more of a problem every moon." Reynard rose, brushing hair off his shoulders. "I'm getting taller, too."

"Don't make it too short," Payne told Bertz, taking the boy's place. "Or do all Canjitards crop their heads?"

Brian considered. "It varies. M—the queen's courtiers brought in the longer styles from Yesacroth."

Eleylin—or Ellis as Brian had invariably heard him called, except by Walter—wandered over with a still-unshorn Garrett in tow. The Rensel was scowling as if he wanted to kick something, and Garrett's shoulders were shaking with suppressed laughter.

"That's something I'll avoid," Ellis sounded disgusted anyway.

"The barbering? Let me guess," Payne said. "You're to be a Selinian mercenary."

"Don't talk," Bertz said.

"But first we get to do some digging," Ellis began, then shot an irritated look at Garrett, who convulsed with laughter. "We are to go to Reasalyn and find some Rensel artifacts to sell to Ewets. Then—"

Garrett straightened. "I still say we should just find a chamber pot and paint bawdy pictures on it."

Ellis ignored him. "We get to manufacture a magical something or other."

"Why?" Payne asked. "Walter usually avoids that sort of thing."

"I don't think Walter knows; I certainly don't."

"Same here. We've only very general orders. Go and get work in the palace."

"You'll spend the nights indoors, anyway. Want to trade?"

"Red hair makes an unlikely Selinian," Payne replied. "Besides, it's already half-cut."

By the time Payne's hair was finished to his satisfaction

Garrett had managed to compose himself to take his place. Ulick swept the many-colored clippings into the fire. They burned quickly, like old, dry hair from dead men, and Brian shivered.

Garrett called to the Sueve, "Ulick, you want to go dig?"

Ulick looked up, unruffled, and said in his soft voice, "I have heard of the workmanship of the Rensel. I should like to judge it for myself."

In the silence that followed Payne touched Brian's arm. "Let's go."

The rain that had been pouring all day had not let up with nightfall. They passed Michel standing at the window, staring out disgruntledly. Outside, Hamon and Reynard disappeared into the darkness.

Before they stepped out the door Payne stopped Brian. "You can't go dressed like that."

Brian glanced down. His cote of black cloth was too fine for a long ride, but he couldn't see much to be done about it at this hour. Besides, Payne was dressed like a southern peasant, as unlikely a fashion as his own to find on someone traveling in Tarsia.

Brian opened his mouth to say something, then closed it again. Payne was wearing a dark green cote with tight sleeves, which was ridiculous, since Brian had noticed the full white sleeves of Payne's shirt while Walter had been speaking to him. Payne hadn't been out of his sight since then—not for a minute.

Payne sighed at Brian's confusion. "You haven't been shown anything, have you?"

Brian, feeling as if he were five years old and being breeched, shook his head.

"Listen," Payne said. "We aren't sent to do these tasks without resources. Walter can grant certain abilities to us as we need them. The one we are always given is the power to alter our clothes."

"Showing him how to lace his breeches?" Michel had overheard them. Brian felt himself flush.

"Aren't you supposed to be on the way to Manreth?"

"In this rain?"

"It's raining for all of us. If Hamon and Ellis can survive

the weather, I'm sure a merchant's son can."

Michel's charm vanished, and Brian saw pure malignance on the young man's face. Then he shot a glance over his shoulder. Across the great hall Walter was watching them. Michel nodded sharply and nervously to Walter and went out into the rain.

To Brian's relief, Walter sent him no wordless message. The Huntsman's voiceless call had been unnerving enough as an order to stop a man or merely to come to Walter. Brian didn't want to know what such a reprimand would be like.

"Michel is a toad. Ignore him." Payne shrugged. "Now, as I was saying, when you need to change your dress, visualize what you want to wear clearly in your mind. Remember we've been traveling for several weeks, so you shouldn't have new clothes."

Brian obediently pictured a favorite hunting tunic and prudently added a heavy cloak in deference to the season. He felt strange for a moment, as if something shifted on his body. When he looked his black had changed to grey, and he felt a cloak's weight on his shoulders.

"I did that?"

"Someone did; I don't venture to say who, but you were certainly responsible. You're lucky; this is easy. If you were to be at court, you'd spend half your time trying to remember the fashionable number of buttons and hoping you weren't copying something you saw someone wear the day before. That happened to me once in Yesacroth. I had a hard time explaining it. Sometimes it's better just to pay a tailor."

"Where are we going?" Brian asked, as they emerged into the rain.

"We need to set a trail from Canjitrin. Is the northern route from there through Morthrell to Tarsit still the most commonly used?"

Brian nodded, pushing a lock of cold, wet hair out of his face.

"Then we'll stop conspicuously at an inn on the main road. That way, if anyone checks to see if we really came into the city the way that we said we did, they'll be able to trace us part of the way."

"Who are we going to—I mean what are we to do besides find work in the palace?"

"I'm not sure about the details, but I gather that we're to 'arrange an accident' to the Princess-what's-her-name?"

"Meriel." Geoffry had mentioned her; a betrothal had been discussed.

He cast about the stable for the horse he had ridden earlier, wondering how to tell one identical mount from another. His horse, like all the other horses ridden by the Hunt, had been silver and faintly luminescent in the moonlight. No silver, or grey, horses were in sight. In the stall farthest from the door a roan whickered and moved restlessly. Somehow he knew that was his mount, but he couldn't have said why.

He shrugged. His clothes had just changed on his back; why should he be bothered by a mere horse of a different color?

Payne halted before they rode out the gates. "We'll be taking back roads, avoiding even small villages. We don't want anyone to see us until we're much farther north. Walter doesn't like to take even small chances."

Brian understood now the hours of interrogation of anyone who might have information to help Sir Walter's plans. And, on reflection, he also understood how carefully he had been manipulated into telling more about himself than he had planned. Thomas had seemed so harmless when they talked during the early hours of the morning. By nightfall, however, Brian had regretted every syllable as his words and inferences from them had been revealed to Sir Walter.

He didn't think he'd given away anything important. He had revealed nothing that any young man at court in Canjit wouldn't have known. No one could have guessed who his father was, or the details of Geoffry's death. Sir Walter must use everything that came his way. Even small things, like learning that King Rozer's eldest son, Ewets, had once bid against Brian for a Rensel intaglio, had been grist for the mill.

Better, much better, that Brian keep his own counsel to protect his living father, and his dead brother.

Well, if secrecy was to be his plan for now, he had a long ride in which to contrive a story.

4

Second Day

Alesander Vitaut had been talkative for the first part of their journey, but he grew more intent on the countryside as they traveled. Richenza was not offended by his inattention; she had her own thoughts.

She had turned over Sir Walter's plans in her mind and realized that they were not what she had expected. Of course all she had had to base her expectations on were Annet's tales, romances of the minstrels and the history she had studied. The reality was not nearly as moralistically simplistic as the one nor as high-minded as the other.

She recalled Sir Walter's voice giving orders—unfeelingly efficient. The only thing high-minded about these plans was the result.

Richenza closed her eyes and remembered the scene in her own great hall three mornings before, when the small party in royal livery had deposited the arrow chest and opened it to display the gruesome contents. Leot had not come himself, but he had sent a message with the smirking courier who had supervised the party.

"His Highness hopes you will be suitably grateful." Grateful that Leot had sent her Nele's body, that it wouldn't be burnt, that his head wouldn't be displayed on the castle wall. Shock had left her speechless, immobile, until Annet had had Indes's few remaining men at arms eject the courtier. She knew what form he expected that gratitude to take, and her departure for Sulby had been as much to escape Leot's immediate reach as to bury Nele before the king changed his mind.

Now she journeyed back to challenge Leot before the whole world. Even with the Wild Hunt doing her bidding this was a gamble, but a gamble she must make to ease her conscience. Nele would not have been a target if he had not been her brother.

She had disliked Leot from the moment he'd come into her father's custody. Nele had overlooked the prince's petty cruelties and spiteful arrogance, but Richenza had not. She sympathized with the victims and understood why her Father had disciplined Leot.

Too young to realize what a dangerous enemy Leot could grow into, Richenza had made no pretense of liking him. She had beaten him at any game they played, and, worse, she had learned the secret of defeating him. All she needed to do was to frustrate him on another count and he would forget the original contest in his anger. He was like a boar ignoring the spears for the beaters.

So she understood her part in this, whether Sir Walter did or not. Her task was to infuriate Leot with the judicial combat, so that he would not see the Hunt behind him closing in for the kill.

Leot, Prince of Tarsia, stood beside his brother Ewets as they watched their father's litter disappear through the Temple gate on its way back to the palace.

"It seems to me"—Ewets waited as his horse was brought—"that you, not Father, should be making thank offerings to Haldan."

"We all should. It was a dangerous conspiracy. If I hadn't tricked them into trusting me, we'd be dead in our beds."

"Lucky for you."

"Indes felt some sort of twisted loyalty. He thought he should warn me. Of course I told Father immediately."

Ewets hauled himself into the saddle of the hackney his

groom held. "Claverdon told Father a day before you did."
He kicked his mount. "Did you know that, brother?"

Leot scowled after him, waved away his waiting troop
of liverymen, and reentered the inner temple courtyard.
"You can stop lurking in the shadows." he barked at the
plainly clad man who waited under the loggia. "They're
gone."

Firmin Tredgett looked up from the paper he held. "The
shadows seemed appropriate. I have news."

"Where in Anchytel's pits have you been? I needed you,
and you were nowhere to be found. Now the danger's past,
you show up."

Tredgett cut the tirade short. "What danger?"

"What danger? Do you expect me to believe you don't
know? Father found out. Belintor got drunk and spilled
everything he knew to his uncle Claverdon, who rushed off
to tell the king."

"He didn't know that much. "I told you not to let anyone—"

"Nele Indes told him. Everything."

"Indes is a fool."

"Was a fool."

"What happened?"

"Father confronted me. Had me hauled in to question. I
told him Indes had deceived me, that he had tricked me
with a story about having troops ready for a preemptive
strike against Arin, and that when I discovered that he was
really conspiring to kill the king—"

"The king? Ewets was the target."

"Forget that. I said that I pretended to go along so I
could ferret out the full extent of the conspiracy. Father
believed me, but I had to prove my loyalty."

"How?"

"Easy. I told Indes that the time was ripe for action, then
warned Father." Leot laughed. "You should have seen Indes's face when the guards appeared. Within the hour Indes
was dead, and Father couldn't be more grateful."

"Is he grateful enough to listen to your warning that
King Ludvik of Arin will invade in the spring?"

"No, he still listens to my milksop brother, who thinks
Arin is our friend."

"Arin was only our friend while he was at war with Madaria. Now that they have signed a ten-year truce, he's looking for a new victim to keep his armies well exercised."

"Damn it. I know that, you know that, but Ewets won't believe it, and Father doesn't want to."

"It will be harder now to dispose of Ewets, and with Indes out of the way any troops raised from his lands will have doubtful loyalties." Tredgett sighed, then went on, "At least his lands escheated; the kingdom will have the revenue."

"No."

"Why not?"

"Indes wasn't tried."

"But—"

"I couldn't let him talk. Haldan! Father might have believed him. He had that damned honest air."

Tredgett shook his head.

"Look, I did what I could. If you'd been here, maybe you'd have had all the right answers, but you were off Haldan-knows-where on your own money-grubbing business when I needed you."

"Your Highness, you did an excellent job. You thought and acted superbly. I couldn't have done better. And, although I was out of the city, I was on your business, not my own."

Leot snorted.

"I was in Manreth, meeting with a councilor of the King of Canjitrin. The rumors are true. There is a secret treaty between Arin, Yesacroth, and Canjitrin. Canjitrin's negotiations here are a ruse."

"You have proof?"

"He will send a copy when he can do so safely and we will have proof that the king and Ewets will have to believe. I also spoke with a retired captain of the Arinese army at Credom, and he let slip some of Arin's troop dispositions. There were other reports from spies I sent into Arin. Do you want a written report, or do you want to discuss them now?"

"I might as well hear it now, but let's at least go back

to the palace. I need wine to wash down your dead dry facts. Meet me there.''

Tredgett watched him mount and ride away surrounded by his blue-clad guard of liverymen. *I should have praised him more.*

He set off on foot for the palace, wondering when the conspiracy had been widened to include the murder of King Rozer. The possibility had been discussed and, as far as he knew, abandoned because it could cause dissension if there was war. Apparently, Leot, spurred by his ambition to be king, had resurrected the plan and not told him. Tredgett shook his head. Leot was indispensable; his prowess on the tourneyfield made him the most popular member of the Royal Family with the troops, and the troops must be kept loyal at any cost.

5

Third Day

Although the chamberlain was wavering, Alesander knew the argument would continue. The girl would win; she not only had the right she claimed, she had the determination to claim it. In the meantime, he ached to know what was going on in the audience chamber. Snatches of sound drifted temptingly through the arcaded screens that separated it from the anteroom and made him ever more impatient to see his opponent.

A burst of applause came from the hall. He glanced at Richenza and decided she needed no help. Yielding to temptation, he pulled the hood of his traveling cloak up and slipped into the hall. He found an inconspicuous place along the wall near the door and settled down to watch.

He glanced at the crowd of commoners—better dressed than they used to be—and at the few members of the nobility who had deigned to attend court. Did that mean court pickings were too paltry to attract them, or was there a better way to ingratiate oneself these days? The Royal Family was seated on the dais on a Master of Protocol's delight of appropriate thrones, armless chairs, and stools. At this distance the king looked regal enough—silver hair, a long spotless white beard—though Rozer's stare was too fixed as he watched the court poet read from one of those silly scrolls court poets always affected. From Rozer's expression the standard of court panegyrics in Tarsia had not improved in four hundred years.

On the king's right his sons sat in order of age. The first two had their heads together, talking. The son seated nearest the king would be the heir, Prince Ewets. According to Richenza, he was twenty-five years old. He looked older. His hair was so pale and so colorless it seemed to be already greying. He also ran to fat. He lounged in his chair and his clothes, while of fine material, were sloppily worn and soiled. Alesander unconsciously straightened his own shoulders, wondering if Ewets had ever been lectured on the duty of a prince to act regal in public.

The next son in line must be Leot, the chief villain of the girl's story. He also lounged in his chair, but he lounged with a studied grace. Well-cut hose showed off muscular legs and glittering metallic brocade stretched across his broad shoulders. He would be in his early twenties and apparently kept himself in fighting trim. Richenza had said that he was as good as the professional jousters and used his prowess to win popularity with the people. If her deductions were right about the events behind her brother's death, Leot had a tricky, clever mind: a formidable opponent. If he had had to put his money on one of these royal contenders, Alesander would have had to bet on Leot.

For the third prince—Wendis, wasn't it?—was obviously asleep. Falling asleep seated on a faldstool is undoubtedly a talent; especially if you do it inconspicuously and don't fall off. Alesander doubted, however, that that skill would be of much use in a contest for a throne. Leot surreptitiously kicked his brother. Wendis awake was little improvement. He had gold curls, a baby face, and currently wore a dazed, unintelligent expression. Except for that expression he reminded Alesander unpleasantly of Michel.

Something jarred his arm; a liveried usher motioned him to an alcove farther down the hall. Richenza was already there; her traveling cloak shed.

"We're to be presented *last*."

That was an insult; as a descendant of one of the Conqueror's Companions she had the right to immediate audience. Alesander noticed with approval that she had herself well under control. Her high color was the only sign of her anger.

He positioned himself where he could watch the dais end. The poet was rewinding his scroll. The king presented him with a purse. From this distance Rozer looked less regal. He had a round, unlined pink face above a plump, short-legged body. He looked like the Child-King of the Beggar's Feast; as though he wore a false beard and strained his feet to reach the floor. Ewets looked bleary-eyed and sated with the food he let stain his clothes. The boy Wendis squirmed sulkily on his stool. Even Leot was less impressive. His massive shoulders, squat neck, and square head topped with pale, reddish, close-cropped curls gave him a bull-like appearance—all muscle and no intelligence.

"What do you think of the Royal Family?" Richenza whispered, interrupting his thoughts.

"I was wondering if I wished to claim kinship. My twin sister, poor girl, married Thaiter I. I can see very little of her there."

Richenza looked from Alesander to the dais and back again judiciously. "Well, they're fair as you are."

"Lescina was as dark as you. No, darker, for she had brown eyes." Alesander was surprised into laughter he had to suppress. "With all you've said against them do you want them to be not only kindred, but true kind?"

"Oh, no," she said, confused. "It's just that you seemed to want, or find, or . . . oh, never mind."

"Forgive me, my lady, I know you did not. But it is odd to see others in what to me is still my place, my father's place. I have learned everything I could about what happened in Tarsia, and I thought I was resigned to it. But to actually see . . . it's very strange."

The small group of petitioners who had succeeded the poet rose from their knees and backed from the hall. The woman with them was noisily weeping; the king apparently had not granted their plea.

The next group granted audience was Haroc, merchant of Lin'merith. Alesander recognized Hamon, accompanied by his apprentice Reynard and three gaudily dressed porters bearing great carved chests. The merchant and his apprentice were even more garishly dressed in the bright-colored loose clothing of the south. Hamon flourished a deep bow to the king and a deeper bow to the queen and the princess. He punctuated his speech with sweeping gestures. Reynard opened the first chest. In moments the area before the throne was carpeted with silks and rich brocades.

The queen leaned forward pointing to a rich stuff of Saroth. Hamon brought it closer, running it through his hands so that the golden threads of its weft glittered like motes of fire. The queen said something and smiled at him. Hamon smiled back.

The Princess Meriel's glance intersected Hamon's, and she flushed. Her body retreated to its stiff posture and her eyes to their contemplation of the cornice frieze from which they had been tempted. Except for her flushed cheeks she might have been an ivory icon, unmoved and untouched, above daily life.

As he watched Hamon, Alesander felt his own muscles tensing with distaste. How could any nobleman, let alone a once-reigning prince, stoop so low? Hamon acted like he enjoyed it; pimping his own body in that thin gold-trimmed silken robe, his every gesture calculated to appeal. The queen followed every move he made with her eyes.

The king's attention was on another show. Reynard, once the chests were unpacked, had with seeming negligence begun to juggle two balls, then three balls, then five. The king was entranced.

Hamon gestured to the bearers, who started to repack. He clapped his hands sharply. Reynard jumped, sending the balls into a higher orbit; then caught them one at a time, except the last, which rolled to the king's feet. Reynard bowed awkwardly and retrieved it. The king patted him on the shoulder and spoke to Hamon. Hamon gestured in protest, then shrugged.

Nicely done, Alesander thought. *The Royal Family is now well aware of the available talent.*

The mercantile party left. The herald announced, "The Lady Richenza of the House of Indes." The announcement caught the king in the act of rising, and he sank back petulantly.

Richenza straightened her back and, head high, swept forward to confront the House of Thaiter. Alesander followed her. They made a solemn contrast to the previous petitioners. She wore the close-fitting, sweepingly sleeved and trained court dress of Tarsia, but made of funereal black velvet. Her only ornaments were the jet buttons that fastened her gown and the jet pins that held up her braided and coiled black hair. Alesander's clothing was subdued in respect to her mourning. Cote and hose both were midnight blue, made of velvet and fine cloth. Silver buttons set with sapphires fastened the cote's front and sleeves. It was a rich habit, chosen by design to make him seem slighter and softer than he was.

Richenza, as was her right, neither knelt nor bowed. Neither did Alesander.

She pitched her voice to carry, "I, Richenza, head of the House of Indes, appeal Leot of Thaiter of the murder of my brother Nele."

There was a buzz of amazed comment from the spectators. Before it ended Leot had bounced up from his chair.

"That is a lie."

"Then prove it in fair combat."

"You have no right to challenge me. Your brother was a traitor, and his treachery degrades your house."

"He had no trial by his equals; without their judgment Indes cannot be degraded."

"I don't fight women or children. Let your guardian take up your cause, if he approves of such foolishness, and if you can find anyone foolhardy enough to champion such an unworthy cause. Your brother was a traitor, and if His Majesty chooses to hide that shame and shield you from the consequences of his actions by not bringing him to public trial," Leot warmed to his theme, "you should be grateful. Yet you, with no more sense than a sullen child, flaunt that treachery before the court. This is a matter for older and wiser heads. When you have a guardian . . ."

"I already have a guardian, and he approves."

"You'll never find a champion."

"Allow me to present my champion, Alesander Scelin."

Every eye turned toward Alesander, who performed a correct, perfunctory bow to the king. The king, who was wilting like a battered shuttlecock as he followed the argument, blinked.

"Does he understand the seriousness of the challenge? The contest will be to the death."

Does he expect to frighten me with words?

"Yes, I know," Alesander said, meeting Leot's pale eyes. All the Royal Family had those tan eyes except Wendis and the queen. Predatory eyes like a hawk's searching where to rip flesh.

"One moment." Ewets's soft voice cut the lengthening silence. "Who is your guardian? There are no males left of the House of Indes."

"Not of the main line," Lady Richenza conceded. "My guardian is Walter Martling, my cousin. I sent for him when I learned of my brother's death. You will remember that my great-great-great grandfather Ricver divided his holdings in the outlands among his six sons by his second wife—a sister of Otgar of Nentham. One of those sons . . ." She was launched on the best genealogical double talk that Alesander had ever heard. He wondered how much was improvised and how much Walter and she had worked out ahead of time. Even the herald whose profession it was to keep family complexities straight was soon dazed and struggling to keep up.

Alesander realized that Queen Betrissa was studying him, a smile in her green cat's eyes. She leaned forward, breasts straining against the taut green brocade of her bodice and her hand languidly pushed back her diaphanous veil from where it failed to obscure a white shoulder. Movements designed to show the best of an aging body. Hamon shouldn't have to try very hard.

"Now his, Odhard's, second son was the father of my maternal grandmother, so Walter Martling is both my fifth and sixth cousin." Richenza paused as if to consider the matter. "He is, of course, my heir."

Leot, who had sunk into his chair while she spoke as if he hoped to be unnoticed when she finished, jerked his head up at that announcement.

She looked down at him. "Do you, Leot of Thaiter, accept my challenge?"

He glanced hurriedly to his father, who was still mentally

entrapped in a maze of long-dead ancestors, and found no help there. He rose. "If you are a fool and challenge me, I accept."

"When and where shall the fight take place?"

Leot must have known that he appeared reluctant. "Where and when you wish. But for my part, as soon as possible."

"The seriousness of the charges against the Grand Duke of Maldrin and the honor of the House of Indes demand the most public of occasions. I name the time as midday on the Feast of Haldan and the place as the Great Square of Tarsit."

Well chosen. The most public of places at the most public of times, and but two days before the full moon.

"I accept the time and the place."

"So be it." She turned her back and walked from the hall. Alesander followed her.

She smiled at him with her eyes as he handed her into the saddle, then mounted his own horse, afraid every second that if he caught her eye again he would laugh aloud in triumph. She had played Leot like a fish, winning every point they desired, and had made the prince look a coward in the process. She had never lost her composure or needed his help. She had been more regal than any member of the Royal Family, as true as sword steel. What a queen she would make!

They turned north along the river, where he could remember only open fields. Now tall houses solidly filled the four miles between the palace and the old temple of Taros, the Harvest God. The houses on the river side of the road seemed larger and more splendid than the houses on the right, but almost every house proclaimed with carved arms or floating banner that it was a noble's dwelling. Some of the arms Alesander recognized.

Down the broad street came a procession of empty carts, their screeching wheels offending the calm, aristocratic air. The carts were followed by a closed carriage which emerged from the courtyard gate of a great house on the riverside. Richenza spurred her mount and entered the same courtyard. Alesander followed her through a gateway adorned with the arms of Indes. A troop of mounted men in bright blue palace livery with the badge of a leopard's face on their sleeves waited as a tall thickset man in black made a stiff bow to Walter and Thomas, who stood in the carved doorway that led into the lord's part of the house. The black-haired man swung around and mounted and, as he led the troop from the courtyard, his eyes swept across Richenza and Alesander. Cold, dark, dispassionate eyes; Richenza paled under their gaze, although she kept her head high.

By the time they dismounted only Thomas stood in the doorway. His eyes were alight with suppressed laughter.

"What happened?" Alesander asked. "Whose men were those?"

"Leot's," said Richenza. "Led by his chief flunky, Firmin Tredgett. What did they want?"

"Custody of the goods and person of an 'unfortunate, unprotected, orphaned noblewoman'—his words, not mine," Thomas added. "We arrived to find them inventorying the furnishings. They had carts to carry off the best pieces."

"Leot works fast. No wonder he looked so appalled when I said I had a guardian and heir. They even had a closed carriage to muffle any outcry I might make at being kidnaped. That man Tredgett is a toad."

"He's very smooth. You should have heard and seen Walter and him: Tredgett obviously taken aback but determined to carry out his orders, Walter playing the simple, straightforward, country nobleman too much the bulldog to yield a single point. Remember how he did the same at Rayln when we recovered the Talisman of Facry?" He went on before Alesander could remind him it was before his time. "They argued politely, and Walter forced him to concede step after step. I threw in the appropriate legal tidbit now and then until by the time you came Tredgett was in full retreat. Trio for three male voices with stage action from left to right offstage. I wish I could set it to music." Thomas smiled at the prospect and shook himself back to the present. "You didn't tell us about Master Tredgett."

"That slimy, sneaking, lowborn clerk! He's only a snake in the grass who slithers around doing Leot's dirty work."

"Snakes have fangs and some are poisonous. I think Walter has questions. Besides, he'll need your report on the king's audience. He wants to use the chamber that the servants call the summer parlor if you have no objections, Lady Richenza. He should be there now."

Walter did have questions, first about every detail of the audience, then, "About this man Tredgett. What do you know of him?"

She seemed surprised. "He's a moneylender who does Leot's dirty work. Protecting his investment, no doubt."

"Leot owes him money. Do the other princes?"

"I suppose so; nearly everybody does. We don't." Thomas could hear the pride in her voice. "I never let Nele become enmeshed in debt. Probably Leot meant to use our property to pay off Tredgett and buy more allies besides. That's why Tredgett was here." She seemed relieved to account for the man's presence that afternoon.

"I see." Walter leaned back in his chair studying her. "I know I said that I would not interfere, but I have been considering the needs of your household and the size of this house. It is too understaffed for comfort or defense. There are dangers both in hiring and in not hiring new people. We need to discuss it. However, that must wait. We don't have time before dinner. You will want to change. I have been remiss not thinking of your comfort—you had a long journey and no rest since we set out this morning."

After she left there was a momentary silence, and Thomas rolled his pen in his fingers as he watched the others.

Finally Alesander asked, "You think this man Tredgett is a danger?"

"I don't think we can risk underestimating him even if he is only Leot's tool."

"It never pays to undervalue the power of money," said Thomas.

"Is that a proverb?" jibed Alesander. "From what I saw of Leot, I doubt that he knows the use of tools. They might turn in his hand and cut him."

Walter looked at him. "Do any of the princes know the proper use of tools? Your appraisal would suggest an unhandy crew."

"Perhaps the tool uses them?" Thomas suggested.

"Tredgett is known to be Leot's man," mused Alesander. "But all the princes owe him money. That would suggest that it is Leot who is the chosen tool and Tredgett the maker."

"Maker of what?" Thomas asked.

"Kings," Alesander replied.

"If that is his intention, we need to know," said Walter. "I think that you, Thomas, are in the best position to investigate. We need to know all about Master Firmin Tredgett as soon as possible."

"Shall I borrow money or just offer information for a price? Have I your permission to betray you?"

Even Walter smiled at that whimsy, but Alesander sobered and said, "She's afraid of him, I think, more afraid than she is of Leot."

"All the more reason to know." Walter rose.

Thomas felt an uneasy prickle of danger. So the Lady Richenza had already become "she" to Alesander. Had Walter taken that complication into account?

It was nearly nightfall on their second day of riding. Brian wanted to stretch his legs and eat, and not answer any more questions. Payne seemed determined to learn the whole world in a day. Their conversation had ranged from riding to politics and all the possible stops in between.

Payne might have been any one of the young courtiers Brian had been raised with. He knew horses and riding, and more of warfare than a Canjitard might, but he was not an unfamiliar quantity.

What Payne didn't know was the last three hundred years of history. When the Wild Hunt had last been summoned Canjitrin had still been a small city-state, not yet even encompassing Onsalm.

So most of their conversation had been about history. It hadn't been too difficult explaining how Canjitrin stood between Yesacroth and Tarsia. Payne had clearly spent most of his life at one court or another. The difficulty had been in not letting Payne know how much Brian knew, and how he knew it. He hoped that he was passing for the son of some court official.

Ahead, a posting house proclaimed itself with a brightly colored sign involving a rose and a hare. Payne pulled his horse up and surveyed it.

"Looks reasonable. Ready to call a halt?"

"Hours ago."

Since their fortunes were supposed to be slim, Brian had expected to sleep in the common room or to share a bed with two or three others in a dormitory. Instead, to Brian's surprise, Payne bespoke one of the inn's two private rooms. Brian didn't ask why, though it seemed an unlikely extravagance, unless it was to make them more memorable. In the common room Brian sat and leaned against the wall. He wanted to collapse, but his stomach was complaining, and he tried to remember when they had eaten last.

The room was crowded, and the people around him sounded like Canjitard merchants. All he could do was close his eyes and wait for Payne to stop chaffing with the pretty little tapster and bring the ale and food. Payne did eventually, but his appearance was brief. Taking his own food and ale, Payne followed the tapster up the stairs. Good, Payne could pump *her* for information for a while.

Brian ate in silence, but a comment loud enough to rise above the general babble nearly made him choke.

"The whole problem is that the king is letting that woman from Yesacroth run the country."

The woman from Yesacroth could only be the queen—running the country? What was happening at home?

Brian considered going out and getting his horse and riding home to Canjit as quickly as he could. Anything to help his father. Common sense intervened. Brian remembered Michel's expression as Walter had reprimanded him—running would do no good.

Someone hushed the speaker at the next table, and even as Brian listened, the conversation turned to grain prices in Morthrell.

He fled the common room, afraid he would give himself away if he overheard more. In the room Payne had hired, he stretched out on the bed, but he could not sleep. He had had no sleep since he had been summoned—three nights, not counting tonight. But all he could do was stare at the ceiling or the inside of his eyelids, and think and think and think. . . .

Was his father ill or distracted? What had happened since he had disappeared? His father must be beside himself. Was there any way to send word? And what word to send?

Am safe. See you in three hundred years. Don't worry about me.

No answers were forthcoming, and Brian stared at the ceiling for a long, frustrating hour before he heard Payne come in. The red-haired man closed the door and leaned against it with a sigh.

"Well, I think she'll remember me, anyway."

Brian grunted an acknowledgment and rolled over.

"You're not going to sleep," Payne said.

Brian pushed himself into a sitting position.

"What do you mean?" Three nights and no sleep; he'd barely noticed. Brian knew the answer before it was given.

"Just that. You're not going to sleep—not until the next full moon. And then you won't wake up unless we're called again." Payne sat on the edge of the bed. "Sleep isn't something we're granted. I don't know whether it's part of the punishment, or whether it's to give us more time to work. All I know is that there's no rest for us until the moon has passed."

"Walter said something about my not passing out if I drank too much."

"Oh, you can drink yourself into a stupor, where you can't think straight—Justin tries to spend most of his time that way—but you won't lose consciousness. You can certainly be knocked out, but not for long. If you can't share quarters with another Huntsman or room alone, find a woman. It gives you the reputation of a reprobate, but it's safer than arousing suspicion when your roommate notices that you don't sleep. Any complications stemming from your bed-hopping will be cured at the end of the month."

"Bastards or the pox?"

Payne laughed. "The pox. Gods, I think Ulick and Hamon have left bastards from Saroth to Rayln. The pox, like everything from minor wounds to decapitation to plague, is cured at the next full moon. You may be nearly dead at the end of the month, but the next time we're summoned you'll be perfectly healthy. Michel, at least, has found it a fine cure for everything, except his morals.''

''What else don't I know?'' He sounded plaintive, and Payne chuckled.

''You'll learn. We were all novices once—even Walter.''

''I find that hard to believe.''

Payne nodded. ''Empty your purse.'' He gestured to the space between them on the bed. Payne glanced over the small pile of coins and idly inspected a silver selk.

''I'd find it hard to believe that Walter was anything less than omniscient.'' Payne idly tossed the coin into the air and caught it. ''But Amloth the Conqueror's son was my great-great-grandfather, and we have stories in my family— a few of them true.''

''Walter told me you were descended from Amloth.''

''Walter seems to have told you a great deal.''

''But nothing practical.'' Brian wondered what Walter and Payne had spoken of before he had been called into the room two nights ago.

''Naturally not,'' Payne said. ''Empty your purse.''

Brian reached for the purse before he remembered the coins on the bed. ''I just—'' There was weight to his purse again. He poured out its contents. On the rough blanket lay two piles of coins, identical down to the profile of King Aleyne IV and the fountains of Hassart on the reverse.

''Anchytel's purse,'' Payne explained. ''I wasn't sure you'd been granted it. Michel gave himself away once when he was playing the son of an unsuccessful merchant by spending more money in a week than his 'father' should have made in a year. Walter's been very careful whom he lets have a bottomless wallet ever since. You won't run short of money, unless Walter gets word that you're spending gold coins like coppers, and then he'll cut it off.''

''It seems that Walter didn't tell me enough.''

''Don't condemn the man too much. Given enough time and ill luck, you could be in his place.''

Brian thought about that—it wasn't a comfortable idea, but there hadn't been a comfortable anything in the last two days.

Keeping his tone as light as he could, Brian asked, ''So

what brings Amloth's great-great-grandson into the Wild Hunt?''

Payne's hand clenched on the coin, and Brian held his breath.

Payne's fist slowly unclenched. "Stupidity, chiefly.

"When I was eighteen I went to court. An uncle got me an appointment as valet to the Grand Duke of Yesacroth. I was sure I'd be one of the duke's intimates in months. It was my birthright. Four years later I was still a valet while nobodies were promoted. I decided I would do something so daring the Duke would have to notice me.

"There was war on two fronts—on the east against Tarsit, which had conquered Arin, and in the north against the Selinians. The war in the east was formalized static sieges; I saw little chance there. The situation to the north was more promising. The Selinians were still a power, not pushed back into the uplands as you say they are now. It was still conceivable that a Rensel state could be restored, and many in Yesacroth would have welcomed that. The center of disaffection was the Shrine of Enath. It was a nest of spies.

"I raised a troop of volunteers and we raided the shrine. We found enough arms for six companies and the detailed plans of three of the duke's fortresses.

"I'd been raised on tales of Amloth, so I was careful to spare the priestesses' lives, and we didn't desecrate the sanctuary, although I was sure more arms were stored there. But that wasn't enough—the High Priestess herself cursed me.

"The duke promoted me immediately, but after the full moon it didn't matter." Payne looked up at Brian, bitter laughter in his eyes. "So, here I am, twelve hundred years after my illustrious ancestor was cursed, carrying on the family tradition."

He tossed Brian the silver coin, and Brian, to his own surprise, caught it.

"Not bad." Payne changed the subject briskly. "Is fencing with sword and dagger in the Yescovian style common in Canjitrin, or will I be conspicuously southern?"

*   *   *

Even as he listened to Walter and Richenza state, restate, and compromise their views on the dangers of an under-staffed house versus one which might harbor a man whose loyalty was owed to another paymaster, uneasiness lurked in the back of Thomas's mind. He said nothing to Walter. Walter had more urgent concerns. Let Walter worry about how to defend this enormous pile of a house which put such a brave show of strength to the street and exposed such windowed openness to its gardens and the river. That was a problem on which Walter was an expert. A concrete problem to keep at bay the ill-defined questions that wriggled snakelike in the dark of the mind.

I need a like task, thought Thomas, and sought his own familiar solace, the rigors of the law. Walter had asked what was the law of guardianship in Tarsia. That was his excuse for indulgence.

He found no books on the subject in the library, but it was impossible that a family which had accumulated the enormous number of five hundred some books would not own a single volume on the law. Further search revealed the books in the muniment room, nestled among the chests and cupboards. crammed with a thousand years of charters, deeds, and documents. He gloated over a moon's worth of self-indulgence. Best to start on Walter's question. He pulled down *Esquin on Inheritance* and retired to the steward's chair by the fireplace.

Even though he concentrated on the delights of clauses and cases, his uneasiness disturbed his conscious thought, just as the hum of voices overhead disturbed the quiet of the night.

The crash of glass from above, when it came, seemed almost foreordained—a catharsis for the tension. He put down the book and ran up the back stair to the stillroom where Justin and Bertz were working. Walter was already there and Annet's nightcapped head poked 'round the door.

"It's only broken glass." Bertz blocked the door into the still-room. "We were moving a chest to make a convenient base for the distilling condenser, and one of the small retorts slipped off and shattered. We have other retorts, and we can clean up ourselves."

Annet's head disappeared, and Walter, after a characteristic pause to weigh the situation, turned and left.

Bertz still stood in the doorway, and Justin wasn't in sight.

"Are you sure you couldn't use some help?" Thomas wondered why they were so unwelcome. "It sounded like more than just a retort from below."

"Don't bother. Nothing was broken that matters."

Now Thomas could hear movement in the stillroom— the tinkle of glass fragments. Justin began to curse softly.

Thomas shifted, ready to force his way in.

"I wouldn't try it."

"I will unless I get some answers. What have you been doing? I've heard your voices all evening."

Bertz stepped into the larger room and closed the door behind him. "I broke his pitcher of wine. 'Accidentally' of course. I've kept him so busy talking, teaching me how to help him, that he has had little chance to drink. But his craving seems to grow with the darkness and the stillness of the night, so I took more direct measures. Is that explanation enough?"

"Walter said to let him drink."

"Why, if I can keep him from it? Because Walter can't stand to live with him sober?"

"That's not it at all. If he's not allowed to drink, he'll try worse. He's tried before. Since he can't kill his body, he'll do his best to kill his mind. Do you want that on your tender conscience?"

"I won't let him drug himself, either. Will you let me go back to him before he thinks of cutting his wrists on those convenient shards, or do you insist on interfering?"

"You've a high opinion of your talents of persuasion if you think you can stop Justin from drinking."

Bertz smiled, "No, just my talent for asking stupid questions that require long-winded answers. Are you going to tell Walter?"

"No, not for now. But if—"

"There will be no problems." Bertz opened the stillroom door. "Thank you; your help, while welcome, is not needed."

Thomas returned to the steward's office, but it was a long time before he could concentrate on the book he cradled in his hands. It would be best if tomorrow he could use his restlessness to ferret out the truth about Firmin Tredgett.

6

Fourth Day

But when the morning came it brought successive waves of people clamoring for the attention of the Lady Richenza and her newfound kin and his household. It started simply enough; servants who had fled returned shamefaced and apologetic, begging her forgiveness and their reinstatement in their former places. And from the lowest scullion to Hildebert Munsley, her steward, she smiled, commiserated, and forgave. For wasn't there less chance that her own people might be spies than those new hired? The men-at-arms who had died with Nele could not be replaced, and their loss remained a hole in her household, unpluggable until she could quietly call men up from the estates to replace them.

When the first wave had receded it was followed by a second, more exalted one. The wives and daughters of the nobility came to make polite inquiries about her health while their eyes asked more impertinent questions and passed judgment on her demeanor and her household.

Later, when it was seen that the king's wrath did not strike those who called on her, their menfolk came, drank her wine, judged her newclaimed kin, and relaxed into polite talk of treason and its profits. This wave started with

61

mere lords and reached its zenith with the Grand Duke of Morsett.

"If only I had known, it would have been different. My men—"

And Lady Richenza, knowing just how little help Nele could have expected, drowning in this crest to the day's waves of hypocritical solicitude, did what she never thought to do and fainted.

That shattered the pattern of politeness and enabled Walter at last to clear the room.

Thomas and Alesander helped Walter herd their unwanted guests from the long gallery and down the stairs. They watched from the second-story windows as the great courtyard slowly cleared, and Walter's voice floated up the stairs exchanging dismissive courtesies with the last of their callers.

Thomas turned from the window. "Did you learn anything from that?"

"More gossip than I cared to hear." Alesander leaned out the casement. "But little useful knowledge. I learned where the young men practice jousting and what they think of Leot's skill. I even made arrangements to practice myself and show what I can do, though less than my best would be wise."

"Did you learn anything more about Tredgett?" Walter rejoined them.

"No. When I mentioned his name they closed up tighter than a miser's purse. Did you learn anything?"

"They shied off the subject whenever I tried to bring it up, too. Which would suggest they are afraid of him and suspect that his spies were present even here."

"Now, someone did talk to *me* about Tredgett," said Thomas.

Walter and Alesander turned to stare at him.

"Are you more surprised that someone talked about Tredgett or that one of that noble company deigned to talk to a commoner?" Thomas asked mournfully.

"You weren't the cynosure of conversation," said Alesander.

"Still, someone did talk to me. I grant you her eyesight is failing, so, no doubt, she didn't realize to whom she spoke, but according to Margata, Dowager Lady Salpersey, Firmin Tredgett is an upstart merchant meddling with the affairs of his betters. He started out with very little money or backing and built a mercantile empire not only in Tarsia, but in all the five lands, and even has contacts and power overseas on the trade routes to Avrian and in the ports of Ascovia. In the last ten years he has been loaning money to the nobles of Tarsia, buying their goodwill, if not their souls. She thinks it's shameful to have a lowborn man wield such influence. She says it just shows what the world is coming to: merchants are in positions of influence, nobles no longer interest themselves in war and heroic deeds, children don't obey their parents, and the gardeners have spoiled the strawberries by growing them for color and size rather than flavor.'' He followed the other two into the gallery. ''Tell me, Walter, have you noticed any difference in the strawberries in nine hundred years?''

Late that night, long after the waning moon had risen, Thomas sat in the echoing quiet of the steward's office and rested his eyes from the crabbed hand in which *Esquin* was written. He had retired early, deeming his presence unnecessary when both Walter and Alesander spent their best efforts in amusing the Lady Richenza. Since then small stirrings in the night had revealed the separate comings of Payne and Reynard to report to Walter, but Thomas, considering that little could have happened, had stayed apart, intent upon his task. If it were important, Walter would call him.

A gust of cold night air fanned the dying flames in the grate beside him. Thomas looked up to see Alesander standing in the open doorway from the kitchen passage.

Alesander shrugged off his cloak and laid it across a convenient stool as he went to warm his hands at the fire.

''It's colder tonight with the sky clear.''

So Alesander had been out the night before.

''I hadn't noticed.''

''Close by your fire like this you wouldn't.''

''You missed the excitement last night.''

''The crash in the night. Walter mentioned it. I was out studying the city. I shan't have the anonymity to do that much longer." Alesander sat on a bench by the fire and rested his chin on his hand. "It's beginning to be like Yesacroth."

"Is that bad? I see nothing wrong with civilized living."

"Civilized or decadent? It's not the material objects I distrust, it's the atmosphere of overripeness and corruption."

"Corruption, in my experience, flourishes as well in hovels as in palaces." Thomas marked his place in his book.

Alesander shrugged as if irritated with himself. "Oh, maybe it's the change that makes me uneasy; as it is in dreams when a familiar place has strange dimensions and doors that open onto unknown places. This is home but not home, familiarity breeds complacency, which is shattered by unanticipated change."

"Everything changes. At least Tarsia is still Tarsia. That's less to get used to than the Grand Duchy of Madaria."

"You should have expected some such development. Whoever heard of a glorified town council ruling a nation?"

"Why not? We did the job well enough in my time."

"Over a smaller area."

"Not that much smaller."

Alesander shook his head deprecatingly, "A committee can't rule a large area. Someone must make the decisions."

This was an old argument. Thomas started to explain about majorities and consensus; Alesander cut him short. "You show me a normal animal with many heads, and I'll concede the point. It's unnatural." He changed the subject. "I've been thinking about our callers. Even acknowledging that some were spies, there was a broad cross section of the nobility here today, and talking disloyalty if not treason. Some should be the king's councilors. Who does advise the king anyway? Has anyone in particular been mentioned?"

"From what I overheard this afternoon, Rozer listened to Chancellor Erdevan, but he died about two years ago. Now Rozer agrees with the last man he's spoken with, which doesn't lead to any stability of policy. The council has fallen into factions, but none has attained any lasting hold on the king."

"Meanwhile," Alesander said, "the country drifts rudderless, and these men stand by and talk and watch the wreck."

"Perhaps they just came to gossip."

Alesander raised an eyebrow. "Perhaps, but would you wager on the number of spies' reports now speeding to Arin?"

Thomas shook his head.

"I would bet five hundred kytels," Alesander continued, "that couriers are hurrying south. Consider this: while we had several grand dukes here, none were descendants of Companions of the Conqueror. There are only four left; of those Juhel Rimoc is the Ambassador to Canjitrin, and Selvanian Pirit is on his estates, as is Feracher." Alesander's voice changed. "She is betrothed to Feracher. Why didn't she tell us?"

"Probably the Lady Richenza thought that it did not concern our task. From what I've overheard, Robert Feracher has been a laggardly suitor."

"He won't be now that she is sole heiress to Indes."

"When we—you, rather—win her brother's cause?"

"Yes, dammit. Bad enough in its way to fight in a traitor's cause."

Thomas smiled.

"But even worse to have another profit by it. You're smiling. Did I pass some test?"

"I wondered if you had noticed it *was* treason. It's an odd legal system you have in Tarsia when a man may be found innocent in spite of the evidence."

"Only if he is a descendant of a Companion of the Conqueror and, Haldan be praised, there are only four such houses left."

"Of which you have mentioned three."

"The fourth is headed by Petric Chuskis, who resides in the city and whose chief occupations are dissipation and roistering. The only one who concerns himself with his country is Rimoc."

"Perhaps he prefers the sea air."

"I wouldn't be surprised. So far as we know, the rest were not concerned enough to send a spy, let alone a representative, to see what we did today.'' Alesander rose, stretched, and turned to leave.

"Wait a moment. I found something you might appreciate.'' He rummaged through the pile of books and documents he had collected and held out a small roughly bound volume to Alesander. "*A Secret History of the Life of Anelhar, Son of Ricver, Grand Duke of Maldrin, Lord this that and the other*, etc., etc. by his steward, bound with a list of rentals from the honor of Mesunton, which is why it's in the steward's papers rather than the library.''

Alesander leafed through the book. "I knew Anelhar. Did you read it?''

"In that handwriting? I'm having enough trouble with your bookhand.''

"Our hands are as crooked as our politics,'' quoted Alesander. "Thank you. This should fill some nights when I am too well known to wander abroad.''

7

Fifth Day

"Do you think I should take my lute?" Reynard asked Hamon as he shoved the third bolt of changeable taffeta onto the highest shelf on the north side of the shop. It was the day after the king's audience, and they were setting up shop in a rented four-story building fronting the Temple Way. They had found a merchant from Lin'Var willing to sell his stock. They had also acquired the merchant's nephew Alvord until they paid in full. The man could tend shop when they were absent on more esoteric business.

"I thought you were supposed to juggle." Hamon handed up another bolt. "Unless you and that sleek palace official had more to say after I left."

"I am supposed to. Anything else go on this shelf?"

"Nothing that's unpacked. Tuft taffeta next, on the shelf to the right."

"What's that?" Reynard moved the ladder over, scrambled back up and Hamon handed him a bolt of pile-figured silk. "Oh. The stuff with the fuzzy flowers." He pushed it to the far end of the shelf. "I mean," he reverted to his former line of thought, "people get more intimate with their musicians than their jugglers. They say

more in front of them; keep them around more." He was
rapidly filling the shelf with the cloth Hamon handed him.
"Didn't you?"

"I never became intimate with either. But then *I* never
said I was normal."

"I used to overhear the most personal conversations
when I sang on street corners. When you juggle, people
just hold their breath. Randy and Ekata had me learn to
play so I could overhear conversations in case anyone mentioned something worth lifting, and, besides, I made more
money singing, too, especially from the women. Being a
juggler lacks stability somehow."

"*You* lack stability." The bolts Reynard was no longer
attending to plopped sideways.

Reynard grabbed the last as it slid from the shelf and
returned it to its place. "Taking the lute would be too obvious, wouldn't it?"

"A bit. Come down before you bury us both in a shroud
of southern silks. I've no doubt that you can create an opportunity to display any talent you wish them to know
about."

Reynard slid down the ladder.

"If you can't keep your mind on business," Hamon continued, "do you think you could keep it on sport? I'd hate
to be stabbed by accident. 'Terribly sorry, I was thinking
of something else.' "

Reynard brightened. "A fencing lesson?"

"After lunch. Run down to the pie shop on Pinner's Lane
and bring back three pies. Not mutton. After we eat, Alvord
can keep shop alone for an hour."

Reynard did run, banging out the side door into the
courtyard. He was already into the alley before the door
swung closed. Not exactly courtly manners. Hamon smiled
to himself. *I don't think I was ever that young.* If fencing
didn't calm him down, Reynard would probably burst with
anticipation.

The sound of horses in the street and the trill of feminine
laughter roused him from his thoughts. Some sixth sense
warned him that this was not just any noble lady and her
entourage even before he heard Alvord say, "Your Majesty."

Hamon finger combed his hair and straightened his jacket and his shirtsleeve frills in preparation for his entrance.

"Your Majesty honors my shop." He bowed from the doorway. Queen Betrissa stood halfway down the shop opposite Alvord at the long counter. She had a lapdog in her arms and another pawed at the skirt of her riding dress. Behind her five ladies-in-waiting clustered at the far end of the counter exclaiming over a mixed pile of blue silks not yet returned to their shelves. Through the open front of the shop, Hamon could see grooms in palace livery holding horses and disrupting the traffic on the Temple Way. "How may I serve you?"

"Need you ask after the delights you displayed yesterday?" Betrissa had a husky voice made distinctive by the slightest of lisps. "And those pale before what I see here. Such sheen! Such colors! They make stark autumn bloom like spring."

That was his cue to say, "No, it is your presence that makes the day seem springlike," returning compliment for compliment in a game at which he was a master. So was she; her throaty laughter encouraged him to further extravagances. He dared to suggest that the best silks were not unpacked. Would she care to see? She set her maids the task of choosing fabric for their masquerade costumes and followed him into the back room of the shop, where he spread a silken seat for her upon a packing case and showed her velvets and shimmering gold and silver brocades and the tenor of his mind.

"Green to complement your eyes. Nothing could match them."

"I shall have to trust your judgment."

She looked young sitting there, petting the little long-haired dog in her lap. A foot encased in a fine cordovan boot swung in and out of view beneath the tawny wool of her wide skirts. The tight-fitting gown with its high fur-trimmed collar hid any sign of an aging body. Her face, flushed with laughter, was girlish beneath the sable-brimmed hat perched on her coronet of braided hair.

It isn't going to be a distasteful task, after all. He caught her eye and held it for a long moment. She leaned forward.

Bang. The side door slammed.

"Do you want to eat here or upstairs? I had to get lamb, but Alvord can have that one," Reynard said all on one breath as he rushed around the corner. He stopped abruptly as he realized what he had interrupted. His burden did not and, though he grabbed desperately for it, the upper of the three pies arced through the air to splatter on the floor. The queen's two lapdogs strayed over to sniff, then turned away in scorn of such plebeian provender.

"Excuse my graceless apprentice, Your Majesty. He juggles other things much better."

Reynard flushed as he stooped to clean the mess.

Betrissa slid down from her improvised throne. "It is time that we went. Send what my ladies chose to the palace today and, for me, the red baudekin." His eyes must have betrayed surprise; she had shown no lack of knowledge before of what would or would not become her. "For Ewets's silly masquerade. We're supposed to come as we're not. I think I shall wear a black wig and a stiff loose gown and go as the Dowager Queen of Canjitrin."

Her eyes lingered on the pile of green and blue and silver cloths. "As for the other, you don't know how I am tempted. Bring them to the palace tomorrow afternoon. The king and court hunt then, and we shall not be interrupted."

Hamon leaned against the doorframe, watching as Betrissa swept through the shop gathering her ladies in a flurry of chatter. In moments they were gone, clattering up the Temple Way toward the palace, leaving behind a stunned Alvord and a shop which looked as though a troop of inquisitive monkeys had gone through, unfurling the bright cloths like banners in the breeze of their passing.

"I'm sorry I barged in." Reynard crouched on the floor to clean up the shattered pie. "I hope I didn't ruin everything."

Hamon turned. "I think your precipitate arrival may work out for the best." Reynard relaxed. "I wouldn't make a habit of it, though. Is it too much to hope that that was the lamb pie? No? I'll tend shop while you eat, then the two of you can restore order while I go out to eat and hire a porter. We have a delivery to make at the palace. If you're quick, maybe we can still work in some fencing."

* * *

Twilight shrouded the lane when Hamon rapped on the postern gate of Indes's town house, and the guardroom where he waited reeked not just of sweat and armor grease but also of the guards' dinner. The man-at-arms who admitted him returned to his post, but Hamon, seated on the bench by the door, sensed the covert attention of his comrades dicing in the corner.

Soon Thomas entered, sleek, well-fed, and smug. "Master Haroc, you wished to see Sir Walter?"

"It's about the livery cloth." He followed Thomas past the now-indifferent guards through another room—an office it seemed—to a great hall in which the servants were clearing the trestles from dinner.

Thomas dropped the pretense of normalcy. "Where's Reynard? Has something gone wrong already?"

Hamon helped himself from the table scraps before answering. "Not that I know. Reynard's busy, so I came to report. Where's Walter?"

"With the Lady Richenza. He'll be along in a moment."

"Still trying to keep the girl in the dark?" Hamon neatly stripped a chicken leg. "Have you ever watched royalty dine in state? It ought to be a statutory punishment like the stocks or the pillory. I've just come from watching Rozer and Betrissa dine; it seemed interminable. Twelve courses served with all ceremony and sauced with verse—pedestrian verse, anything else might overheat the digestion. The verse was the only thing where feet mattered; the courses were served kneeling. Which guarantees not being looked down on by your servitors, I suppose, but you never eat a warm dinner and the bills for hose cloth must be enormous. They do it weekly, too; a fine old southern custom adopted recently to enhance their majesty. I only did it once a year and only because it was considered sacrilegious not to. Anyway, Rozer would take the cover off each dish—" Hamon demonstrated—"and look it over carefully—for mold perhaps—then gobble it down quickly and fiddle with the tableware while the queen ate slowly and gracefully and deliberately as though she expected to be applauded for the regality with which she chewed. She does dote on being queen. But I wonder if it makes up for Rozer's—" Walter entered.

"Where's Reynard?"

"Singing for the king's supper or rather juggling for it. I doubt that he will be free till late."

"What's this about livery cloth?"

"What else would you see a cloth merchant about? The boy can come on minor errands; it takes more to bring his master."

"That's true. What do you have to report?"

Hamon told about his own day, from the queen's visit to his encounter with the queen's chamberlain at the palace. "So, we have a private meeting in her chambers at the palace tomorrow. The first, we hope, of many."

"Very well, although . . ."

"Yes?"

"Perhaps it goes too fast."

"Why?"

"If the queen dies too soon, it might put them on their guard, and can you be sure she won't tire of you once she has you?"

"It'll be the first time." Walter looked at him coldly, and Hamon felt his anger rising. "Don't worry," he said silkily. "If I can't hold her interest, I promise you I'll kill them all myself and you won't get your hands bloody."

"Hamon . . ." Walter's tone was a reprimand.

"Except Leot. We don't want the little lady to suffer any material deprivations, do we? He's Alesander's meat, not mine." Hamon said flatly, "I'll send Reynard to report from now on," and walked out the door.

The cool night air told him he had blundered, made a dramatic exit through the wrong door. *What a perfect farce. I won't go back in there and let them look down on me if I have to climb the damned garden wall to get out.* He studied the formal gardens and the walls that surrounded them. *There must be another way out.* He sat on the stone bench against the arcaded wall that separated the kitchen courtyard from the garden.

Why let Walter anger him so? Surely by now he could control himself better. *Do I need his approval? Do I want it? Even if I were still the man I was, what right has he to judge? I might as well ask a statue to weep as to ask Walter to change his mind about me. And yet, and yet, I do want that. So what do I do? I betray myself again and again in childish scenes like that. Forget it and find another way out.*

A door opened and a woman muffled in a cloak stepped out. She walked along the path toward him; he sat still, hidden in the dark.

She stopped in front of him. "What was that about?" asked the Lady Richenza.

"That was a report about a wooing, my lady." He rose to bow.

She stepped back. "Oh, it's you. I thought—"

"I was someone else. Who I wonder? Do you walk alone in your dark garden with someone? Walter? Thomas? That would be dull. Al—"

"Walter," she cut in. "I was looking for Walter, and surely I am safe with him."

He looked down at her, his eyes mocking, "Oh, yes. You're certainly safe with Walter. 'I shall keep thee safe, love, like a bird on her nest, like a jewel in its casket . . . ' "

"Why quote that? It's just a song the country people sing at weddings."

"But it's about Walter. Once it had a great many verses and that was just the refrain, 'I shall keep thee safe,' but he didn't, and so they wrote songs about it. It's quite a romance really, shall I tell you?"

"Go on."

"Once upon a time," his voice mocked the words he spoke, "two hundred and fifty years or so after the fall of Reasalyn, when the grand dukes of the Sueve were slaughtering—no, that's too stark and truthful a word for a romance—hunting the remnants of the Rensel from the valley of the Kelsary, one of those grand dukes had a faithful servant—a black wolf, shall we say—that led his hunting pack for him. A man of a family that, while not of Sueve blood, had been true vassals to him and his fathers for a hundred years. A loyal, trusted servant.

"But one day this trusted servant flushed a covey of Rensel peasants and a girl who was not of their flock. No that's not a good enough metaphor. Shall we say that the black wolf found a pack of mastiffs with a greyhound in their midst? A white bitch so delicate you could break her in your hands. And, though they swore that she was one of them, he knew of what blood she sprang. He let them go.

"He did not tell his master. He hunted her alone. She haunted him waking and sleeping. In the end, he found her and persuaded her guardians that he would, could, keep her safe, and she a Rensel princess, the last of the House of Morcaston. He did not tell his master. No, he would have his lady and his honor, both. He had a castle, gift of his lord, in a remote part of the valley, and there they lived undisturbed for eight years. They had a promising son, and it seemed the world would pass them by.

"But as such things will, the choice he had avoided caught up with him. The grand duke summoned his men to war and he must go. And while he was away a traveler came on business of the duke's and saw the wife and son and knew them for what they were. He told the duke. What was the duke to think but treason? And so they dragged the black wolf back in chains to face his angry master, to find his castle destroyed, his wife and son killed."

"Who cursed him?" Richenza whispered.

"Who cursed him indeed? His loving wife? His betrayed master? That's the melodramatic part, my lady. He cursed himself. Before his master's court but by his lady's gods, he cursed himself. A pretty story for the poets, no?"

Silence was no answer, so she answered softly, "How sad. Why are you so bitter about it?"

"Bitter? I?"

"Yes."

He rose, "You mistake me."

"Is it because . . . ?"

He cut her off. "They'll write no pretty stories about me. Oh, no, they'll write no pretty stories of my life. You asked the wrong question, my lady. You should have asked if you were safe with *me*." He turned on his heel and left her alone in the dark.

Brian brooded into his flagon; even pretending to be destitute was depressing, especially when the innful of people around him seemed to have coin and goodwill without limit. But not for an anonymous Canjitard.

Payne seemed cheerful enough, though, when he collapsed onto the bench next to Brian.

"Any luck?" Brian asked.

"Not a bit. I take it you've had the same?"

Brian nodded and looked around him. The sun was setting; workmen were coming into the common room, and the nobility were lounging in their gallery to watch.

By accident and design the inn had a natural border between the two stations. What had once been two buildings was now joined by the removal of a common wall. The northern building, formerly a private residence, had a floor a few feet higher than that of the original inn. That problem had been solved by putting in a few steps and a railing, thus providing an area where the upper-class patrons could safely watch the brawls of the commoners and vice versa.

Both levels of patrons were becoming noisy.

Payne eyed the crowd. "I've at least found out why we're not being overwhelmed with offers of employment."

Brian smiled crookedly. "I could have had six jobs elsewhere."

"It seems that young men of good family—from Canjitrin or elsewhere—are no longer being taken on at the palace in any capacity."

Brian had heard the same rumor and finished for him, "Because of the queen. Now what? Do we tell Walter that we need to be fat and forty, or maybe eunuchs to get into the palace?"

"Eunuchs." Payne shook his head to get the thought out of it. "No, what we do now, since there isn't a place ready for us, is to make one. The princes and the palace upper servants all come here for recreation, so we'll create an opportunity."

The loud noise had become several degrees louder. Brian turned and saw two Tarseans trying to sit on a third man, who, from his long, fair hair, was a Selinian. Another Tarsean stood nearby, fingering the blade of his knife.

"I see," Payne said, "that they still play that game."

"Game?" It did not look playful to Brian.

"Barber-the-Selinian. Don't they play it in Canjitrin?"

"Not in my circle, anyway."

"Well, unless the rules have changed since I last helped

Ellis, the Selinian won't get hurt. His hair will just be cropped.''

"Two kytels on the Selinian." A voice over his head made Brian jump. A young man with curly red hair was egging the fighters on. He wore bright blue and gold, and on his left shoulder Brian could just make out a gold badge displaying an annulet embattled counterembattled. Brian had always thought the badge looked like a millwork.

Brian nudged Payne's arm so hard he almost spilled Payne's ale.

"That's royal livery on the redhead."

"Him or her?" Payne asked. The man had been joined by a red-haired woman who, from the way she clung to the man and the way her saffron yellow gown clung to her, was undoubtedly a whore.

The fight was spreading like a gleeful plague. Two more Selinians had come to aid their countrymen, but a larger number of Tarseans had joined the fight. A man emerged from the kitchen area. He was well over six feet tall, and seemingly as broad. The crowd must have known him, for it parted quickly to let him pass.

The liveried man let out a howl of indignation as the giant hurled his Selinian out the door. Something cut him off, and Brian looked up.

The whore had put a hand over his mouth. "Please, Jevon, not so loud. He might notice me."

"Who might?" Jevon slipped an arm around her waist.

"Azo."

"Azo, the walking mountain? The innkeep's son?"

Her eyes were wide. "He's very jealous, and I—oh, he's finished!"

Brian turned to look and saw that most of the combatants had been thrown out or had given up and were trying to blend into the crowd. Azo was still holding on to one last man, preparing to send him out the door, but the victim started talking frantically and waving his arms in the direction of the stairs. Azo dropped him and began searching the crowd for something.

The woman disentangled herself from Jevon, gasped, "I knew I shouldn't have come here," and darted down the stairs into the common room. There was only one way out of the inn from there, and she picked her way cautiously through the crowd. She had almost reached the door when her bright yellow dress caught Azo's eye. She was light on her feet, however, and was out the door before he could get to her.

Azo glowered after her, then, ignoring the sniggering patrons near him, started toward the steps.

The man in livery sat down at his table, trying to appear unconcerned. Brian saw that a cloak—a saffron yellow cloak, a match to the whore's dress—was draped across the settle next to Jevon. Jevon saw it, too, and looked about, seeking a place to hide the garment.

Azo stopped at the table next to Payne and Brian's, leaned over, and asked a nervous patron, "Who was Tilda with?"

"I didn't see."

Azo caught the man's cote front. "I want to know who she was with."

Out of the corner of his eye, Brian saw Jevon stand up. The saffron cloak was visible under the settle.

Payne spoke up, "She was with some young buck in livery."

Azo let go of the unlucky patron and squinted at Payne.

"Whose livery?" The man above them put a wary hand on a dagger which looked as if it wouldn't damage Azo more than a hatpin.

Payne shrugged with elaborate unconcern. "How should I know? I'm from Canjitrin."

The liveried man used the reprieve to move away from the table hiding the incriminating cloak.

"What colors were they?"

"Green and gold. I didn't see a badge."

The redhead was staring at Payne as if he were mad; Brian was trying not to. Azo muttered "green and gold" to himself. No one in those colors was in sight, and he turned to Payne.

"You sure it wasn't blue?"

The man in blue-and-gold livery looked trapped, but Payne shook his head.

"Green. I may be from out of town, but I do know blue from green."

Before Azo could look farther someone grabbed his arm. A middle-aged woman half his height, but resembling him in face and expression, threatened him with a ladle.

"Azo Dron," she said. "Why are you threatening customers over a two-riom whore?"

"But, Mama, she charges more than that. . . ."

She herded him back to the kitchen, leaving a wake of convulsed customers too careful of their own safety to laugh out loud.

Brian laughed when it was safe. "I pity anyone in that livery who shows up here."

"Not our problem."

"Neither was that."

Payne smiled into his ale.

"You, Canjitard!" a voice above them said. Payne and Brian looked up. "It would seem that I owe you a drink, at least." Jevon, the man in palace livery, gestured to the settle beside him.

As they climbed the stairs, what Payne had accomplished struck Brian. They had found their foothold into the palace.

8

Sixth and Seventh Day

"Come in." Michel inspected the hang of his velvet cote in the cramped reflection of the hand mirror propped on the cupboard. "Sit down," he said to the well-dressed young man who hesitantly entered, "I'll be with you in a moment."

With his ivory comb he carefully worked at his curly hair. After Bertz's heavy-handed barbering he'd had it properly trimmed in Manreth, but he wasn't quite satisfied. Should he part it on the left or not at all? He was distracted by movement behind him, reflected in the mirror.

"Sit still, Revnal! You make me nervous."

The thin brown-haired man clasped his hands tightly between his knees and sat quietly. Michel returned to the mirror.

Revnal shifted, crossed and recrossed his legs.

Michel laid the mirror flat. "You'd think I proposed to torture you. All I want are a few introductions. Cheer up. We're going to a party, not a funeral."

"I wish I'd never gotten involved. Why don't you go to your ambassador for introductions?"

"I told you in Manreth, ambassadors introduce you to the people your parents would want you to know. That's not the world I want to see. The worthy this and the famous that don't interest me.

79

I want to see the best 'worst' places and do the highest, fastest living available. Why travel any other way?''

"Your father won't like it."

"Why, Jolan Revnal, are you lecturing me?"

"Haldan forbid! I just wish . . ."

"You'd never met me. If you're going to play, you'd best be able to pay. I don't think I'm asking much—a few introductions, and in return I don't go to your father with your IOUs, not to mention any stories of how his son cheats."

"You were cheating, yourself. You had to be."

"Because I won? Don't be crude. I'm letting you off lightly.'' Revnal shifted uncomfortably. "What are you afraid of? That I'll make some dreadful social error, and they'll wonder where you found the barbarian? I think my manners are adequate to the company—after all, they find you acceptable.''

Revnal swallowed hard and looked away.

"Now that that's clear, we can go. Tell me, do they play as high here at the Three Queens as I hear? They say Lord Loventor lost a thousand kytels in a single hour.''

Within an hour Michel had been introduced not only to the notorious Loventor but also to the other leading lights of Tarsit's fast society: the Duke of Ivil, Lords Chollerford, Garrigall, and Ronhale, not to mention the infamous Jon Burward of Slindon—who, it was whispered, once entertained his cronies to a match race between his wife and his mistress when a horse race had been rained out. But Michel had not yet been introduced to any of the princes. Wendis was expected. So Michel discussed badger-baiting with Burward and Ivil and discreetly watched the door.

Chollerford had rented the best private room in the inn for his party, the reception hall on the second floor. It was large, overheated, and gaudy. Its gilded frieze of heraldic lions and ferrets, commemorating a long-ago owner's marriage into the mighty house of Feracher, seemed to shimmer in the fumes of wine and crowded bodies. Michel wondered idly how nightmarish those golden, oversize, snarling ferrets might look to the cup-shotten mind. He himself was sober—self-interestedly sober.

There was dicing at three tables crowded about with men

calling their bets, while gambling more discreet, if no less reckless, went on at smaller tables at the edges of the room. At the far end of the room a sideboard heaped with food and well supplied with drink fed other appetites.

Michel drank, ate, bet enough to be inconspicuous—neither winning nor losing much—talked and watched. In the end, he was rewarded. After midnight, Wendis arrived, to be greeted boisterously and shown to a place of honor at the highest-playing table. Michel drifted over and observed the play. The prince wasn't a bad gambler. He won until, emboldened by the wine, he bet more recklessly, and even then his losses built up slowly. He talked steadily, cheerfully, and joked at his own bad luck. Men drifted over to the table to watch the play. Michel edged in to insert himself among the players awaiting his chance.

Attention was so fixed upon the table that few looked up when five men entered surrounded by an aura of wine. Their leader forced his way through the crowd to lean on the table next to Prince Wendis. His weight borne on massive hands splayed open on the table, the man leaned forward. "Now, who's going to give me a seat?" His face was so red with drink it matched his curly pinkish hair.

Everyone held his breath, and no one moved. The man's attention fixed on Wendis, who gave him stare for stare.

"Come on, little brother," Leot said in patently false cajolery.

"No."

Leot grabbed Wendis by the nape of the neck, pinching till his brother gave an involuntary gasp. "Get up, pygmy, your elders want your chair." His hand compelled Wendis to rise. "Go home to bed, baby, you're up past your bedtime."

He pushed Wendis aside and sat in his vacated chair, oblivious to his brother's anger. "My turn for the dice, I think."

Wendis stood heaving with anger, while the crowd prudently ignored him. Then he whirled and walked blindly through the door.

Michel followed. He caught up with Wendis four buildings up Golden Street. The prince leaned against the jutting building front, shaking with dry sobs.

"I'll kill him. Someday I'll kill him."

Michel cleared his throat loudly.

"Go 'way, Jerram," ordered Wendis.

"It isn't Jerram, Your Highness. You forgot your cloak. It's a cold night to be without one."

Wendis turned to take the cloak. "I don't know you, do I?"

"We were introduced, but there's no reason you should remember. I'm Michel Tazelar of Haelam in Canjitrin."

"Well, Tazelar, thank you for the cloak. Don't let me keep you. Go back to the party."

"Somehow, Your Highness, I think that's going be a very dull party from now on. Everyone walking on eggshells so as not to attract the wrong attention."

"You're talking about my brother, you know. Aren't you afraid I'll be offended?"

"Quaking in my boots. I'd gathered he was Prince Leot, but it's hardly your fault he's your brother. These things occur in the best of families."

Wendis laughed. "Tazelar, you're drunk to speak so."

"Sober as a lord. Or should I say sober as a prince?"

"As sober as this prince. And that is too damn sober. You fit for a lively party? There's a place I know near the tourneyfield where the fun has hardly started."

"Why not? The moon has scarcely risen, and it's a long time till morning. You must tell me what else I'm likely to miss. The ambassador's recommendations all sounded improving."

"Well, there's the Fly in Amber—you been there? They have a girl who dances." He demonstrated with his hands. "Then there's the Golden Pen, you can get any kind of girl there if your purse is deep enough. Or maybe you'd prefer . . . ?" And as they walked up Golden Street he gave a verbal tour of the attractions of the city least likely to be recommended by an ambassador to a young noble.

It was many, many drinks and three dives later when the moon sailed high in the sky, and after they had persuaded a tipsy waterman to ferry them across the Marre to the still-roaring inns and brothels of Mordrum on the other shore, that Wendis returned to the topic of his brother.

"Oh, it's Wendis, fetch this and Wendis, do that and

Wendis, go home, you're not wanted. He treats me like I was still unbreeched. One of these days he's going to get a surprise. One of these days I'll . . ." Wendis smiled at the pictures he conjured in the fire.

"You have another brother, don't you, Your Highness? I seem to recall . . ."

"Oh, Ewets. You don't want to know him. He sits and eats and talks and eats and sleeps and eats. And you know what's worse?" He leaned forward to whisper conspiratorially. "He writes poetry. Really! Someday he's going to eat so much he'll burst, and all that will be left are lavender-and-purple splotches of his putrid poetry. Haldan. I'm beginning to talk like him. I'm drunk. You're lucky, you know. No brothers, no bothers. No one tells you what to do." Wendis rose unsteadily. "I'm drunk. Party's over. Time to go home."

Michel rose, too, and they navigated through the tables to the door.

"You're wrong about one thing there," Michel argued, "My father's worse than twenty brothers when it comes to orders. Do this, do that, apologize for this, beg. You've got no reason to envy me—I swear it."

"Fathers!" Wendis cut in. "That's the same story. Beg for money—there's never enough money. He has all the revenues of Tarsia and you know what I have? Nine hundred kytels a year. It's true. Supposed to keep up appearances on nine hundred paltry kytels a year. Ask for more, and you know what he says? Goes all pious and says it's the will of Anderad. Man's been dead seven hundred years and father's afraid to disobey him. Some king! You know what I have to do? I have to go to a stinking moneylender. Me! A royal prince. What's the world coming to, anyway?"

Michel steered him down to the river and loaded him onto a barge for the return trip.

"A stinking moneylender," Wendis repeated for the edification of the waterman. "Me. You've got plenty of money," he stated to Michel. "How come your father lets you loose with it?"

"Well, Your Highness, there was this girl."

"Yes?"

"This girl I didn't marry."

"Oh." Wendis nodded knowingly and went off into waves of giggles. "Of course."

At the palace river gate Wendis climbed ashore and staggered off still laughing. To Michel's surprise he called back over his shoulder, "Don't forget. I'm showing you the bear-baiting ring up at Grudyke in the morning. Be there."

"Thank you, Your Highness. I shan't forget." Michel wondered when morning was as the sky was already lightening in the east and they were not yet in bed.

It was late morning when Michel arrived at the palace but he was not surprised when he was told to wait and shown to a long and surprisingly empty gallery on the domestic side of the palace. He wandered its length and, hearing voices through a closed door, edged closer to see what he could learn.

"No! No! No! Not sing-song. Do it again," ordered a man's voice, high-pitched and exasperated.

"I can't," said a female voice tightly.

Footsteps approached the door, which was thrown open, and a girl in a revealingly filmy pleated dress rushed out to collide with Michel. She blushed in confusion.

"Yes, you can. Come back here."

She was followed by a paunchy, pale-haired man who grabbed her by the wrist.

"Just say it with *feeling*. You are consoling a queen." He took a deep breath and declaimed,

> *"Despite the dark o'ersmothering gloom*
> *I think I see respite from doom!*
> *The heroes come! The foeman's steel*
> *Runs red, but yet the foeman reels*
> *Back from the valor of true Rensel blades*
> *Take heart . . ."*

The girl burst into tears.

"Exquisite," said Michel, who was ogling the girl.

"Do you really think so?" asked Ewets. "It's just a little piece I wrote as an interlude for my masquerade. 'On the Relief of Carados from the Sueve,' you know."

"I've never heard anything like it."

"You don't have to flatter me just because I'm a prince."

"I assure you, it wasn't flattery. Besides, what has a stranger to your court to gain from flattery?"

"I didn't think I remembered you. You are?"

"Michel Tazelar of Haelam in Canjitrin."

"Canjitrin. What do you think of Fulk Aysham's masques for King Daimiron?"

"Unfortunately, I've never heard them. Haelam is in the south near Onsalm, and I have never been to court."

"Onsalm! I have always meant to write a verse epic on the fall of Onsalm. You must let me pick your brains for local color. This afternoon after the rehearsal? Such a colorful subject! Such sweep!"

"So I've been told. But I cannot come this afternoon." He nodded to where Wendis had appeared in the far doorway. "I have a previous engagement."

"With Wendis? You don't want to waste your time with him. An unlicked cub."

"Still, one must keep one's word. Some other time, I hope."

"I'll hold you to that." Ewets dragged the reluctant girl into the rehearsal room with him.

Wendis sauntered down the gallery. "I warned you he writes poetry."

"Verse. Yes, you did. Still, I wish he'd finished the line. It's going to haunt me. 'Back from the valor of true Rensel blades. Take heart' ta tum ta tum ta raids? Shades?"

"Glades. It's one of his favorite words. Trust me."

"Renegades?"

"Five to one it's glades."

"Done."

"Sucker bet. You shouldn't have taken it."

"Maybe." Michel turned the subject to a more important issue. "Who was the girl?"

"Selvina Salpersey, one of my sister's ladies."

"Very pretty."

"Virtuous."

"That could be remedied, surely?"

"Dangerous. She's like a Selinian woman in more than looks."

"Oh?"

"Man that fools with her is likely to get an arrow in the gut."

"Waste."

"Yes, isn't it? Oh well, the girls at Grudyke are worth three of her. Let's go. Why waste time talking?"

9

Eighth Day—Last Quarter

Ellis surveyed the fruits of a week's digging.
They had unearthed a dozen coins, a headless
statue of a Rensel ruling empress, a nearly intact
painted urn, a pitted and hiltless sword blade, and
two snarling stone cats once used as, he thought,
doorstops. Garrett looked as disenchanted as he
with the lot, but Ulick was fascinated with the
artwork, running his fingers over the carvings and
closely inspecting every inch of the urn. He reminded Ellis of a Selinian woman looking over
a prospective husband.

"Well," Ellis asked. "What do we sell to His
Highness? The image of Empress—oh, say, Malasdrina? The burial urn of a High Priest? The
magical guard cats of the Rensel Emperor's palace? Or the formerly flashing blade of a long-
fallen defender of Reasalyn?"

"The blade," Ulick said positively, "is
Sueve."

"Ewets doesn't know that."

"Do you think even Ewets will buy any of this
junk?" Garrett inspected the more vicious-
looking of the two cats dubiously.

"I hope so. It doesn't look likely."

"But the work is very fine," Ulick protested.

87

"You're joking," Garrett returned. "And most of it's broken."

"That won't matter to Ewets," Ellis told him.

"And the urn," Ulick said, "though defaced and too fragile to carry easily, was painted by a master. See how delicately the Goddesses are done? Who is the man?" He pointed to the fourth figure on the urn, a male and the most damaged of the group.

"The god Orien, brother to the Ladies."

"Ah. I thought that the Rensel worshiped only women?"

"No, Orien governs air." Ellis continued at Garrett's raised eyebrow. "Sailors in Onsalm still called on him in my time. He was always more popular with them than his sisters." Ellis shrugged. "Well, lacking other expertise, I suppose we take the urn."

"It's light, anyway. That"—Garrett poked a finger at the foot-high royal statue—"weighs a ton. How do you know she was an empress, anyway?"

Ellis, looking through his saddlebags for something to wrap the urn in, said over his shoulder, "Because she's carrying the Scepter."

"You mean that thing?"

"The rod, yes."

"It doesn't look like a Scepter to me, it looks like a—"

"It was meant to. The Rensel may have let their daughters rule if they were eldest, but their symbol of rulership was definitely male."

"I'd say so."

"We'd better bury this stuff again in case anyone notices that we've been digging." Ellis scowled at the stone cats.

He didn't relish moving them again.

"Was there really a Scepter, or was it just something they put on statues?"

"Yes, there was. It was ivory, set with rubies; I've heard that Tarses broke it after he razed Reasalyn, but my mother always insisted that they buried it with him."

He looked hard at the little statue.

"Something with an aura of magic and power . . ." Walter had said.

Ellis smiled, contemplating the statue.

"Bad luck, Garrett. We're taking it anyway."

"That thing?"

"I know how we're going to trap Ewets—and right in Tarsit, too." He smiled a little more broadly. "And Walter's not going to like it at all."

Geoffry riding too fast toward the trip wire, laughing as he rode, looking back over his shoulder making a jest at Brian's expense; Geoffry riding toward the wire and toward it and never seeming to reach it. . . .

Brian dragged his thoughts back from that day. It was autumn, but not that autumn, and he was on foot leading a horse in slow circles, not riding after his brother, pulling back just enough so Geoffry could win the race.

Still, it might have been the same. The sky and the trees beyond the tourneyfield were just as vivid. Certainly the whispering and laughing of the ladies and gentlemen of the court were just as grating. The gods knew that the contempt of the princess Meriel, above him on her horse, was just as blatant as Geoffry's had been.

He wished for some further curse he could put on Payne for accepting Jevon's first offer of employment at the palace—riding instructors to the Princess Meriel. On the surface it was the perfect situation: it was work for which they were both suited, it got them out of that filthy inn and into relatively comfortable quarters above the royal stables, it gave them a source of palace gossip, and gave them perfect access to the princess.

Brian could not be as enthusiastic for the work as Payne. He was reminded too much of that other ride, the one with Geoffry. To make matters worse, Payne had admitted that he had only seen the southern ladies' riding style once very briefly, so Brian had to do most of the work.

Brian hated the stupid style, anyway. It was a fashion his mother had introduced into Canjitrin.

He wondered, as he judiciously eyed the princess's seat, what whimsy had prompted her to learn this absurd side-wise perch? Not that he could imagine this princess having anything so undignified as a whim, she was as stiff as a

block of granite—no, granite was too coarse; as stiff as a
block of translucent Marclarian marble.

She had spoken the polite phrases of greeting when
Payne and he had been presented to her. Other than that
she had responded to his teaching with only an occasional
curt nod.

Brian eyed the princess critically. She was keeping her
balance well enough, and she seemed to have control of
her horse.

He cleared his throat. "Your Highness, I think that
you're ready for a short ride in the park." He waved toward
the wooded area just beyond the tourneyfield. He and Payne
had checked the area early that morning for easy riding
paths and secluded spots for murder.

The princess surveyed the woods loftily.

Without looking at Brian she said, "If you think I am
ready."

Payne, who had been watching Brian and keeping one
ear on the courtiers' gossip, brought his and Brian's horses.
Flanking the princess closely, and followed by the train of
ladies and gentlemen, the party set off. They would have
to get rid of the baggage if the plan was to succeed.

Trees of autumn surrounded him; they even smelled
right. And the voices sounded the same, and Geoffry was
dead two years and this princess soon would be, so find
something else to think about.

Ahead of them came the sound of laughing voices and
galloping hooves. Just what they needed to make the day
perfect—high-spirited riders to make the princess and her
mount nervous.

Two riders burst into sight, the lead rider a flushed youth
with golden hair and behind him was—oh, Haldan!—
Michel. That meant, judging from his dress, demeanor, and
resemblance to the princess, that the lead rider was Prince
Wendis.

The princess stiffened. Couldn't she at least try to hide
her contempt in front of all these people? She—or was it
really distaste? Something began to nag at the back of
Brian's mind. Her actions reminded him of something—
what?

Wendis and Michel had pulled up their horses at the sight of the party, and Michel was chortling, "You said you'd be first to the tourneyfield—you forfeit the bet, Your Highness!"

Brian jumped at the address; there were too many "Highnesses" about today.

Wendis waved petty monetary considerations aside. He had found better sport. He saluted his sister with elaborate and mocking courtesy.

"My very dear sister, how are you this morning?"

"Well enough." Her voice would have frozen fire, but it did not faze her brother. Wendis rode in a circle about her, grinning.

"*Just* like the queen of Canjitrin." She did not deign to look at him. He rode up beside her, nudging Payne out of his place. She became, if possible, more aloof. Or . . . ?

"You seem to have picked this new fashion up rather quickly, sister." Wendis laughed too loudly and had to steady himself with a hand on his sister's horse. The horse moved uneasily, and the princess shifted quickly to regain her balance. Brian reached over to catch the reins. The princess pursed her lips; she was not allowing herself to show anger. No, that wasn't right, either.

"Shall we go for a gallop now, little Meriel?"

No, it was not distaste that stiffened her back. Brian looked at her face and remembered another ride with Geoffry. Going too fast over uneven ground and a hedge ahead of him. Brian hadn't known what was on the other side, and he was afraid to jump, but he was more afraid of not making the jump with Geoff watching.

This princess was terrified and was too proud to show it. Now that he saw that, all her actions became clearer.

"I am afraid, Your Highness," Payne was saying, "that thanks to my assistant's poor teaching, Her Highness is not ready for a gallop."

Wendis shot Payne a furious glance, but before he could say anything, Michel spoke up.

"Your Highness, we've two gold kytels riding on the race."

Wendis, reminded of his money or his pride or trying to

find a way out of a game that was no longer sport, turned to Michel, who continued, "But I think I'd have a better chance to win if my saddle doesn't slide off." Michel pointed at Payne. "You, redhead, my girth needs tightening."

Payne, as stony-faced as the princess, dismounted and did as he was bidden while Michel smirked down at him.

"Make sure you get it right, man, I intend to win this race." Payne did not look up until he had finished the job.

"Does that suit, Your Lordship?" he asked coolly enough, though Brian could sense the heat of his anger.

"It will have to do." Michel tossed Payne a copper coin. "Now, Your Highness, I think I can win this race." The two set off at top speed, and their laughter faded into the distance.

The rest of the ride was uneventful, and the party eventually returned to the palace. After a groom had helped the Princess Meriel dismount, Payne bowed and addressed the princess.

"Your Highness, may I suggest that if we rode very early in the morning, say an hour or two after sunrise, we might find fewer distractions?"

Brian watched the princess. What others might take for a moment spent considering proprieties was actually a second of stunned relief.

"I think that would be possible."

Later in their quarters above the stables Payne sat on his pallet and cursed Michel fluently.

At length he scowled at Brian, who sat watching him. "And what are you staring at?"

"I'm memorizing," Brian replied solemnly.

Payne roared. "I admit to waxing ridiculous, but one of these days I'll take this riom"—he held up the copper coin that Michel had tossed him—"and insert it in Michel's anatomy."

"Why do you hate each other?"

"Michel hates anyone he perceives as being superior to himself. He had influence and fortune and could have done anything he wanted, but wasted it on gambling, whoring, and drinking. Do you know why he sold Iskandroc to the

Sueve? He was piqued because his father refused to pay his gambling debts anymore.''

"Charming."

"He was cursed by a whore to whom he boasted. Forget Michel. Did you enjoy your first day of gainful employment?"

"No. Did you find out why she wants to learn to ride sidesaddle?"

"Yes. She's to marry King Daimiron of Canjitrin."

Brian's heart seemed to stop as it had when his mother had cursed him. *Daimiron, king*? Then . . .

"Yes," Payne said. "We were lucky for once. We might have let it slip that we haven't been in Canjitrin since King Aleyne died six months ago."

"Six months ago." That explained everything: the conversation at the inn, the discontent of the merchants. Daimiron—his cousin, king! Why Daimiron was such a weakling little fool his mother would run him like a trained monkey.

And Brian's father dead—dead six months.

Payne had seen his distress. "Don't worry about it. We know now, and no harm was done." Brian stared at him. "Just think, we're going to rescue the new King of Canjitrin from marrying that stick of a Princess."

Brian gathered his thoughts. There was no use making Payne any more suspicious than he was.

"No. No harm done at all."

His father was dead. Brian could not hurt him now. His father was dead.

Walter gazed out the leaded windows over the garden and the inky Marre to the lights that glimmered on the far bank. He felt oppressed, as though the winking lights of the stews symbolized the work he was organizing. A dirty business, shut out from the city of man and alien to the beasts of the countryside. He pushed the thought aside. No use in being fanciful. Think of it as controlled surgery. Or would pruning be the best analogy? Diseased branches cut off. . . .

His glance focused; a man was walking up through the garden from the river, taking his time but not skulking either. The man let himself in the garden door. He had expected a report earlier from Reynard, but not this late-night visit from Hamon.

By the time Hamon rapped on the chamber door, Walter had seated himself in his accustomed chair, buttressed for the interview.

"Come in."

Hamon entered. He was dressed in the style of Tarsit, yet he still looked exotic—foreign to this place. It must be the combination of colors, Walter thought: dark purple and moss green. Dark, discreet, and yet, remarkable. Too becoming.

He did not ask Hamon to sit. "Well? No problems have developed, that you come calling yourself?"

"Reynard was busy, and I was delayed in the way of business." Hamon seated himself. "As Reynard reported yesterday, the queen arranged for me to meet with her tonight. I just came from the palace."

"You didn't let yourself be followed?"

"I know my business better than that."

"You've had enough practice."

Hamon's eyes flashed at that, challenged by the thought that Walter might be picking a quarrel, but Hamon rejected the bait and said lightly, "Indeed I have. Walls are no obstacle nor jealous husbands. Love is a fine locksmith. . . ."

"Did you get the ring?" Walter cut him off.

Hamon reached into the breast of his cote and detached something from a thin gold chain. "One emerald ring from a green-eyed lady." He held the ring between thumb and forefinger, considering it. "A pretty token, is it not? The stone is set in a true lovers' knot. Quite recognizable. The king gave it to her at the end of their honeymoon, and she gave it to me with very little persuasion on my part."

"Stop boasting."

"I'm not boasting. The king gave her this ring; he gave her little else. Anyone who was willing to give her the slightest show of affection could have her. Why, even you could have her." He looked up from the ring to meet Walter's icy stare. "Why don't you take her?" Malice honeyed his voice. "Just once, do the dirty job yourself? Mix the poison, knife the sentry, seduce the maiden or the wife from her duty, instead of giving orders, keeping your hands lily-white, and sitting in judgment of our failings and our failures. I'm tired of it; we're all tired of it, and Justin is sick of alchemy.''

"Don't hide behind Justin.''

"Don't dodge the issue.''

Walter took a deep breath. "If I performed the alchemy, we should surely fail. I allot the tasks to those best fitted to succeed at them. That way we will not fail again.''

"I felt that failure, too. I think that you're not so afraid of failure as of being conspicuous. You like things neat, clean, and unnoticed. The gods only know if we're conspicuous, it's possible we might be summoned more often. It's only been three hundred years. Next time will it be five hundred? A millennium? Or will it all just stop for us? I think that's what you want—no more crimes but no more chances. Amloth would never . . .''

"You didn't know Amloth.''

"Because you knew him four moons, and I knew him two? He had no scruples about an obvious murder. He was too much the barbarian to be sick at the smell of blood.''

"He didn't relish it either.''

"You think I do? He didn't shirk it. Even if the summonses had taught him restraint, he was still a Sueve barbarian at heart.''

"He was not a barbarian.''

"Does it matter what term we use? You've got this rosy picture that because he was the great Tarses's son, he was special. You see the rank and not the man. You'd toady to Ellis if he'd let you. You defer to Alesander. Bis, you'd toady to me if I hadn't done the unforgivable. Anything to escape the dreadful responsibility.''

"And what are you responsible for?''

"A lot of deaths,'' Hamon said levelly, "but I don't tell lies to myself about why I killed, or hide behind any showy front of morality. And I know exactly what I'm doing when I kill.''

"Are you quite finished?''

"For all the attention you pay, I have to be.''

"Then I suggest we get back to business. How soon can you set up the assignation with the queen?"

"Soon. Do you want me to report in person?"

"The boy will do."

Hamon gave a mock bow and left, leaving the door ajar. Walter took a deep breath and consciously relaxed. He could hear voices in the corridor; Hamon's, then Thomas's concerned tones, then, clearly, Hamon's again.

"Are you his nursemaid? You'd better shake Walter out of his prejudices before he destroys us all."

A moment later Thomas entered the room, his eyebrows lifted in a silent question.

Walter told him shortly about the interview, then continued, "I didn't think he cared what he might have to do. He never seemed to before. Do you think he might be developing a conscience?"

If he is, it's a damned inconvenient time to do it, Thomas thought, but he said, ignoring the question, "Bertz says that Justin is progressing with the poison."

10

Ninth Day

Richenza nodded to Thomas as he held the door to the small parlor for her. Alesander was staring out into the garden and did not move as she entered. She surveyed the chessboard critically; white had lost badly.

Alesander still did not acknowledge her.

"Has Sir Walter awakened yet? He did not break fast."

Alesander turned smoothly to her, as if her presence were not a surprise. "No, he may be occupied."

She began to place the chess pieces on their proper squares. One of the white pawns was missing, and she saw that Alesander was idly rolling it in his fingers.

"It was a stupid question. You don't sleep, do you? None of you do." Before he could deny or make light of her words she met his eyes. "I've heard you come in very late at night and pace the floor, but you're always about before the servants, and you never seem to miss the sleep. Annet says that the servants hear Bertz's and Justin's voices all night."

"If my pacing disturbs you, my lady, I shall be more quiet."

"It does not bother me—" She stopped; that

97

was an absurd admission. "And that was not an answer to my question."

"No, it wasn't. No, my lady, we do not sleep. It is a problem and concealing it has so often been worth our lives we try to pretend otherwise."

"I see." She set the ivory queen on its square. "Would you care to play?"

"If you wish." He put the pawn in place.

They played in silence, but Alesander's mind was not on the game, for he hardly seemed to notice her queen's frequent vulnerability, nor her knight's steady advance.

Finally, Alesander looked hard at the board as if it had just mysteriously appeared, then he smiled and moved his high priest to cover his queen.

"I'm afraid I'm poor company this morning."

"Perhaps I shouldn't begin conversations with uncomfortable questions."

"May I ask an uncomfortable question in return?"

"That would be fair."

Alesander leaned back in his chair, his eyes abruptly somber. "Why do you fear Firmin Tredgett?"

It was a bolt shot too close to be tolerated. Richenza rose, scattering the pieces she had taken.

"Why must everyone ask me about that man? He's nothing but one of Leot's parasites."

"If we thought that, Lady Richenza, we would not need to ask." Alesander was being resolutely reasonable, and Richenza sat again. "Tredgett is no fool, and he obviously has influence with Leot. Now, you've told us that Leot is cunning but is neither subtle nor particularly quick and, from what we've seen, that's true."

Richenza grudgingly nodded.

"Walter's plans are as carefully laid as he can make them, but they must move quickly—six people dead in less than thirty days. If anyone is going to realize that there is one large conspiracy rather than many little ones, it will quite likely be Tredgett."

"You're right, of course."

Alesander leaned forward, "So, tell me, why do you fear him?"

"Because if Leot gets what he wants, it will be because

of Tredgett, and Leot hates me.'' Alesander said nothing.
''Leot breaks things that he hates. As a boy he destroyed
anything that angered him. He killed a brachet once for
snapping at his ankles. In a rage he threw it in the fire.
Then he wouldn't let anyone pull it out to kill it cleanly.
No one dared to try until I brought Father. Leot hates me
far more than he hated that brachet. That was why he
wanted Nele dead—that and a kind of belated revenge on
Father. Now that Nele is gone Leot has intimated that he
has plans for me as well.''

''So you fear Leot, not Tredgett.''

''No. You don't fear a danger you know. I know how
Leot thinks. I know what to expect from him. Eventually I
should have married Robert Feracher and left Tarsit, and
Leot would have forgotten me.''

Alesander nodded. ''But Tredgett changed things.''

''All the rules are gone—I don't know how Leot will
move now that he does what Tredgett advises. I—I don't
know how much Tredgett had to do with Nele's murder. I
don't think he would have left loose ends. Now, with Indes's fortune at stake, Tredgett will advise Leot on every
detail. If nothing else, he might learn from his foreign contacts that Hamon and the others posing as foreigners aren't
who they claim to be. As for you and Sir Walter, he has
spies all over Tarsia, and half the city is in his debt or his
pay.''

''That much I know.'' Alesander smiled thinly. ''Tredgett has someone spying on me.''

''Have you told Sir Walter?''

''No,'' said Walter from the doorway, ''he hasn't. Forgive me, my lady, I did not intend to eavesdrop, but I heard
Tredgett mentioned, and, as Alesander has told you, he is
one of our chief worries.'' He closed the door and pulled
up a chair. ''Now, how do you know that Tredgett is having
you watched?''

''Yesterday and the day before at the tourneyfield I noticed a limping, red-haired man watching me. I marked him
especially because he watched only my practice—no one
else's. I was told that he was Jon Bolson, a former professional jouster who still trains young men. I didn't worry
much as I was being inept enough that he might be looking

for a fee to help me train. But last night—I went out late—I saw that someone was following me from the time I left this house. I—''

Angry voices from the hall made Alesander break off.

''You can't disturb Walter now.'' That was Thomas.

''I damn well have to. That—'' Payne, his color high, burst into the room followed by Thomas.

''Walter, I—'' Payne began.

Walter raised a silencing hand. ''It can wait until Alesander finishes.''

''But—'' Before Payne could speak another word he recoiled as if he had been struck, but all that Richenza saw was an impatient flicker of Walter's eyebrows.

''Continue,'' Walter said to Alesander.

''I stopped at an inn and wasted some time to give a reason for my being out at that hour. Eventually I left, and taking care to look a little worse for my wine, I came toward this house so that he would assume I was going home, then shook him. I circled and switched roles and watched him watch this house. After it was quiet he headed straight to Master Tredgett.''

''And—'' Walter prompted.

''As I watched, someone else left the house—Bolson.''

''What do you think Bolson has guessed?''

''Hard to say. My style is different—out of fashion— it's been remarked on. I had hoped that that would be marked up to my 'country' training and lack of skill. If Bolson is as good as they say, he may have realized I'm holding back.''

''We'll discuss that later. Meanwhile, practice as usual, keep an eye out for your spies, and play your part as before. Improve a little if it seems wise.'' He turned to Thomas. ''Do you think anyone else saw Payne?''

''Unless Tredgett has the house watched day and night, I think not. He came in by the south courtyard, and I saw him before any of the servants.''

''Now, Payne, what is so urgent you must come here at this hour?''

Lips tight with fury, Payne replied, ''It's your whey-faced little liar.''

''Brian?''

"Yes, Brian. It seems he's the rightful King of Canjitrin." Walter's eyes narrowed. "We've been riding in the early morning. Brian is a competent teacher, though he hadn't much to say apart from the lessons for the last couple of days." Payne thought for a second, then admitted sourly, "Since I told him that King Aleyne had died.

"The ride today went without incident until we were joined by someone the princess greeted as Lord Abethell, and a young couple whom I took to be his son and daughter. The man chattered to the princess about Haldan-knows-what. Brian fell back and rode just ahead of the grooms. He'd pulled up his hood and kept his head down.

"I knew something must be wrong, but most of my attention had to be on the princess. I thought that the problem wasn't worth our jobs.

"Then a pack of dogs flushed a rabbit just in front of us. The princess's horse shied, and I had my hands full keeping her from being thrown. When the princess was secure I looked for Brian and saw Abethell's daughter on the ground. The idiot grooms had gone after her horse, so Brian had had to dismount and was leaning over her. She looked up at him and—" Payne stopped and rubbed his forehead briefly before he continued.

"She said, 'Prince Brian! Papa, it's Prince Brian!' Abethell and his son, who were riding back to the girl, must have recognized him, too. Abethell said, 'Your Highness, we thought you were dead.' And his son chimed in, 'Or cursed!' I think he was joking, though; he seemed to be laughing.

"Abethell immediately hustled Brian back onto his horse and down the path. I think that I heard Brian say something about me, but Abethell and his family weren't going to let him get away. I had to continue with the princess on that damned circuit of the park. When I got back to the stables, I was greeted by a groom, who wanted to know where I'd picked up the heir to Canjitrin."

"And you had no prior hint?"

"Oh, any number of hints—but I was too stupid to see them. When I told him King Aleyne was dead he looked like I'd kicked him. I thought he'd just realized that we might have given ourselves away—oh, Haldan!"

"What?"

"He even told me that he and his brother had been named after the king's sons."

"In case you connected the names. He said his family name was Hassart." Walter looked to Alesander and Richenza.

"Canjit was still part of Tarsia in my time," Alesander said.

Richenza shrugged. "The name is not uncommon either here or in Canjitrin. Hassart was the name of one of Tarses's uncles. One of his supposed descendants married Brian I's—Brian the Rebel's—great-great-granddaughter, who was the heiress."

"Well," Thomas said, "you can't say you weren't warned." Richenza wasn't sure whether he spoke to Walter or to Payne. "The question is: what does this do to the rest of our plans?"

"Changes them." Walter contemplated the chessboard.

He said at last, "I'll call a meeting for late tonight." He turned to Richenza, "Can you contrive to keep the servants in their quarters, my lady? I must have the whole Hunt here." She nodded. "Excellent. Now I must speak to Brian at once."

"Now, suppose you tell me where you've really been the past two years." Abethell followed Brian into the bedchamber.

"I already told you," said Brian, his back to the bed.

Abethell raised one eyebrow.

"Then I'll tell you again." Brian sat down on the chest at the foot of the bed. "When I got back from Geoffry's funeral I found a note in my chamber. It said it was urgent that I meet the sender in the Fountain Garden after the change of the watch. My safety depended upon it."

"Did you recognize the handwriting?" asked Abethell, who had seated himself judiciously in the chair by the fireplace.

"No, it was a typical chancery hand."

"What did you do with the note?"

"Crumpled it up and threw it in the fireplace." Abethell gave the smallest of involuntary nods. The note must have been found. The note was the one point of truth in his whole story. The one item that he had to allow for.

"So you went alone to see what he wanted?"

"Yes. Stupid of me under the circumstances, wasn't it?" said Brian, who had not, in fact, gone. "Because there wasn't one man, there were four, and they hadn't come to talk. The last thing I remember is trying to fight them off. I had only my dagger, and I didn't dare yell.

"I don't remember anything clearly after that till early the following spring when I woke to find myself in a strange bed in a strange house among people I did not recognize, but then I didn't know my own name either. They told me that I was their nephew and that I had had a terrible accident and a brain fever. That last I believed for I was weak as a cat, but the first, that I was their nephew, just didn't seem right. However, I didn't have the strength to protest it then.

"Luckily, my memory returned more quickly than my strength, so I was cautious about showing it. I played along with them. 'Yes, Uncle Jon.' 'Yes, Aunt Margit.' Meanwhile, I kept my eyes and ears open. About once a month they had a visitor, and I was carefully kept out of sight. Naturally, I wondered if it was someone I knew who might help me to escape. So I plotted some way to spy upon their meeting in spite of the two hulking grooms they'd assigned to follow me.

"I finally discovered that voices from the parlor carried up the chimney to the chamber above it. One night after I had retired I heard a rider in the yard, so I slipped from my chamber to theirs to listen."

"What did you learn?"

Brian suppressed a smile. Abethell was caught up in his story enough to lose some of his skepticism.

"Not as much as I'd hoped. I could only hear clearly when they stood quite near the fireplace. You could tell from the beginning though that the visitor was angry and 'Uncle Jon' smug. They were arguing about money. I finally made out that the visitor was offering five thousand kytels to have me handed over to him and that 'Uncle Jon' was insisting that he continue to pay him four hundred kytels a month to keep me there. So the visitor upped his offer to six thousand, and Jon just laughed. The visitor left, muttering threats.

"I had, as you might imagine, quite a bit to think about. I hadn't recognized the visitor's voice, but I did recognize his accent—pure Yesacroth. I definitely didn't want to fall into his hands. If his threats meant anything, I didn't have time to wait for my full strength to return, nor did I want to rely on 'Uncle's' greed. Two nights later I shinnied out a window and headed for the hills.''

"Why didn't you return to Canjit?"

"That's what I thought they'd expect me to do. Besides, what was there for me in Canjit? My disappearance so soon after Geoffry's death and my mother's denunciation branded me as his murderer.''

"But your father . . .''

"They'd already told me of the king's attack—as a test, perhaps—and my return could only bring him more pain. The best thing was to disappear. I'd have my life at least.''

"But you were the heir.''

"Who everyone thought had killed his brother. I only went to see that man in the garden because I'd hoped that he was a witness and could say I didn't do it. Why else would I go?''

To shut him up forever, was the answer Brian read in Abethell's eyes. So, Abethell believed that he had killed Geoffry and thought the better of Brian for it. What an insane world. Brian walked over to the window and leaned his head against the cold glass.

"Besides,'' Brian said, "Daimiron's a good boy; he'll make a splendid king with no stain of suspicion on him.''

"A splendid king! He does everything your mother tells him.'' Abethell paced in front of the fire. "I never did approve of your father's keeping you so uninformed of politics. I had hoped when Geoffry died. . . . Listen, do you want Canjitrin to be a pawn of the southern kingdoms?''

"Of course not. But—''

"But nothing. That's what will happen if you don't do your duty and become king. Daimiron will do what the old queen tells him, and she will do what her brother the king of Yesacroth tells her. He and the king of Arin have a treaty, and they plan to attack Tarsia next year. Arin is to get Iskandroc and anything else it can conquer. Canjitrin is to be confirmed in its possession of Merscelun. And Yes-acroth''—he paused for emphasis—''is to receive Binon-salm.''

''But that's Canjitrin's territory!''

''Precisely.''

''How do you know?''

''I have my informants,'' Abethell said.

''Merscelun was to be the Princess Meriel's dowry, any-way. It's only marsh, heath, and moor and for that we give up one of our richest southern provinces!'' He was begin-ning to be angry.

''You see, Your Highness, that something must be done.''

''I fail to see what good starting a civil war will do, and that's what my reappearance would cause.''

''Last year, perhaps, but now people are heartily sick of the queen and her southern parasites. And as you say Dai-miron is a 'good boy;' he'll probably step aside when he finds you're alive. That is, if we present the choice in the proper light. If you had a princess for your wife, for in-stance.''

''What!''

''Think. You marry the Princess Meriel. You get her dowry and her father's support. Daimiron's partiality for Arin has made this government queasy—I had a hard time getting the marriage treaty signed—they'd be pleased to support a different candidate for king in Canjitrin. You'd have Merscelun whichever side wins the coming war, and since you haven't a treaty with Arin and Yesacroth, you keep Binonsalm.''

Brian felt the earth slip from under his feet. Abethell made it all sound so logical, except . . . Except Brian rode with the Wild Hunt, and he would be gone with the next full moon. And there wouldn't be any Royal House of Tar-sia to support him. He said, ''It hardly seems fair to the girl.''

''She's a princess, she'll do as she's told. Besides, I don't think she'd be happy long with Daimiron. They are already negotiating a marriage alliance with Arin's sister, and I doubt that they had divorce in mind to end the first marriage."

Death on every doorstep. He changed the subject. "Abethell, you've been very kind, but I really must get word to Payne."

"Payne? Oh, the man you were traveling with. We'll do something for him, never fear."

"I had in mind giving him a job with me. He saved my life and taught me how to get on. They don't teach princes many practical skills, you know."

Abethell humphed. "What did you say his name was?"

"Payne Fulmere."

"Fulmere? I don't recognize the name. He's from Canjitrin?"

"He says so."

"If he were of good family, I'd know his name. You don't want someone disreputable about you."

Brian tried to recover lost ground. "I've sometimes wondered if he wasn't from the south. . . ."

"That's even worse. We can't favor southerners—too much like Daimiron. We'll just give him some money and send him along."

I walked into that one.

Walter was summoning him. He leaned against the window and tried to resist, as he had the other times this terrible day, the powerful pull he felt.

I'll come as soon as I can. He tried to throw the thought into space. Abethell's reflection frowned at him from the glass. Brian opened the window and looked down at the cobbled street a floor below. Why not jump and break his neck? No one could expect anything of him if he were dead. Except he couldn't die. Only suffer. Perhaps if he could think, there would be a way out of this web. He shut the window. Abethell was talking, but he couldn't grasp the argument against the turmoil in his mind. Brian yawned ostentatiously.

"I hope you didn't do anything while you were with Fulmere that he could expect to be paid to forget," Abethell was saying.

Brian yawned again, "I'm too sleepy to remember clearly. Perhaps tomorrow?"

Abethell gave up. "Yes, Your Highness, we shall speak of it in the morning." He closed the door behind him.

Brian sighed and opened the window. Give Abethell time to retire and then climb down. He wished he had the experience at that trick that he'd given himself in his story.

"I wish," Alesander said, "that *I* could sleep through this, my lady." Richenza started out of her near doze. No one else was near where she sat on a shadowed window seat. Eleven other Huntsmen were scattered about her summer parlor, their voices low as they gathered in small groups, talking. She was reminded uncannily of the reception after her father's funeral.

She surveyed the roomful of men. Hamon, garbed in red and gold and black, lounged at his insolent ease near the fire. Sitting there talking to Thomas, he looked like the master of the house. For a moment he turned to look in her direction, his glance flickering from her to Alesander then back to Thomas. In contrast to Hamon, Walter looked the servingman, sober in his grey and black. But there was an unservile stiffness about him as he stood looking out into the garden.

"Walter is angry," she said.

"As angry as I have ever known him to be."

Sleepy enough to be rash, she asked, "How long has that been?"

His smile was bitter. "My time or yours?"

"What is 'your time'?"

"I live a month, the space of one full moon to the next, at a time. You live year by year."

She shook her head in bewilderment.

"I have known Walter for two months and ten days. Just barely seventy days. But if you had been born the day I was cursed and lived a full life you would be dead almost four centuries. For me there has been no time between summonings."

"Four hundred years—" Who did that make him? What Prince of Tarsia had disappeared then?

Hamon smiled a mocking smile at her across the room.

"Yes," Alesander said, and she hastily looked back to him. "Tarsia has grown so much w—" He broke off. Walter had turned abruptly from the window to the door. Like flowers following the sun, everyone turned with him.

The door opened, and Brian halted in the doorway as if the wall of variously hostile eyes held him there.

He found Walter in that sea of eyes, swallowed, and said, "I-I'd have been here sooner, but I don't think anyone ever sleeps in Abethell's house, either."

It was a feeble joke, but it eased some of the tension. Walter finally settled into the chair he had ignored all evening. "Do you think anyone saw you when you left Abethell's?"

"The rooms were all dark, and I didn't hear anyone moving about. I don't think so."

Walter waved to a faldstool placed in a conspicuously central area before him. Brian, as pale and shaken as a man contemplating the rack, took his seat.

"The first time I spoke to you," Walter said, "you told me that your name was Brian Hassart and that you were from Canjitrin. What you did not tell me has done a great deal of damage. There are ten Huntsmen's lives hanging on your answers now. We would appreciate the full truth this time."

Brian nodded, chewing on his lip.

Walter continued, "From what I understand, you are a Prince of Canjitrin?"

"If—if what Abethell says is correct, I am all but King of Canjitrin."

"Why didn't you tell me?"

Brian lifted his chin defiantly. "I thought my father was alive, and I didn't want his name dragged into this. He could have been hurt. But that doesn't matter now."

Walter was silent; when he spoke again his voice was less accusing. "Why did your mother curse you?"

Brian hunched his shoulders "I've already told you that."

"Not all of it." Walter's voice was inexorable. "How did your brother die?"

"I told you we were riding, but . . ." He groped for words. "Geoffry was fond of jests. He always seemed to make them at my expense. I think he was jealous because

Father preferred me. I learned to be careful when I was with him; he often set little traps for me.

"We were riding, and I saw metal gleaming ahead of me in the leaves. Whomever Geoff had had hide the trip wire hadn't done it very well. I was angry. My horse—a gift from Father—could have broken a leg. I pulled back."

"Geoff either didn't know where the wire had been set, or had forgotten. We were racing, and he was intent on winning, so he didn't see it. I realized that if I let him win, he would fall into his own stupid trap. I meant him only to be the butt of the joke for once, but he went flying over his horse's head when he hit the wire. He broke his neck, and he was dead when I got to him."

"And your mother?" Walter prompted, as the boy showed signs of not going on with his story.

"I don't know whether she thought I killed him or not. There weren't any witnesses close enough to see what had really happened, and we were never able to find out who had set the trip wire. Whoever it was was probably afraid he'd be accused of treason.

"Mother was livid. Geoff always did what she told him. He was her key to getting her way in the future. So, during the funeral she cursed me."

Alesander, who was standing beside Richenza, grew very still. She looked up at his drawn face. Something in Brian's story had touched him. Who had cursed Alesander?

"The strange thing is," Brian continued, "I don't think she believed in the curse. The night of the full moon I found an unsigned note asking me to go to the garden after the change of the watch. I think she intended to have me disappear, so everyone would attribute it to her 'curse.' She knew, you see, that Daimiron was next in line after me, and that he'd do exactly what she told him.

"It all turned out better than she hoped. My father had a stroke when he heard I'd disappeared, and I'm told she had taken control by the time he died six months ago."

Walter put his fingertips together.

"What did you tell Abethell about your disappearance?"

Brian recounted his story quickly, and Walter was not quite smiling when he finished.

"It was fortunate that the note was found. Does Abethell believe your story?"

"I think he thinks I deliberately killed Geoffry, but he doesn't count that against me. As for the rest, I think he believes me, or he's willing to pretend to believe it if it suits his purpose."

"Could this help you to get near the princess?"

Brian sighed. "Abethell wants me to marry her."

There was a bark of laughter from Garrett, and even Thomas covered his mouth and coughed.

"Explain," Walter said, unfazed. The political explanation that followed shocked Richenza. War with Arin had been spoken of, yes, but Canjitrin allied with Arin?

Alesander's fists were clenched. Did he still feel so very strongly about Tarsia after all this time? But he'd just said that to him the time seemed two months.

Walter asked a few questions to be sure of various points. Then he said, "You will go along with Abethell's recommendations."

Brian looked stunned.

"We've been looking for a way to get someone alone with the princess," Walter explained. "The current plan assumes that Payne and you could get rid of her grooms and her ladies, which might prove impossible. Her fiancé or her husband, however, should find any number of chances to be alone with her.

"Tell Abethell that you agree with him, but stress that the situation in Canjitrin is such that you must get there before the weather closes the roads until spring. I think that the war between Arin and Tarsia will spur him to the speed we need. The wedding must take place within a few weeks, or you will have to return to Canjit before it can be performed."

Brian nodded reluctantly.

"Can you find a place for Payne in your household?"

"I don't think Abethell will accept anyone into my service that he can't control."

"It's not an insurmountable difficulty. What did you tell Abethell about the time between your 'escape' and now?"

"Nothing; the conversation turned to other things."

"Excellent. You told Abethell you were still weak when

you escaped. Payne, how did you reply to the grooms who asked you about Brian this morning?''

"I was too angry to give a civil answer."

"For once that works to our advantage. Payne, you found Brian delirious. He told you who he was and asked for help in getting away. You decided that you had finally found a means of getting a good position and nursed him back to health, only to discover that Brian had no intention of returning to Canjit. Since then you've stayed with him, taught him how to survive. . . ."

"Why?" Brian asked. "He hardly looks as if he'd do it out of love."

The acid comment took Walter by surprise. He shot Brian a dark look from under his brows. "Payne planned to wait and see what would do him the most good—selling you if the chance came up, or convincing you to go home to your throne. Now, Brian's going to be king after all, and Payne wants to be a great man in Canjitrin."

"I'll try, but Abethell plans to pay him off and send him on his way."

"I want a position in the new king's household." Payne turned to Walter. "Am I an obscure Canjitard or a Yescovian, by the way?"

"Be vague. If necessary, hint that Fulmere is an alias and that your real name would surprise him."

"I'd wager that it would, too." Walter gave him a quelling look.

"Don't, either of you, come to this house again. It would be too compromising if you're seen. Meet Thomas in the marketplace or send word through someone else. Michel, you had better stay away from Abethell." Walter paused. "Who is Abethell, by the way?"

"He is the Canjitard ambassador. My father trusted him, but he is not one of Mother's favorites. She probably sent him here to get him out from underfoot. The whole family are in and out of the palace."

"Michel, get descriptions of the family from Brian. We don't want them recognizing you for an impostor."

"I'll be careful," Michel drawled.

"Hamon." Walter turned his attention away from Brian, who visibly relaxed. "We may need your services in this."

"The queen and the princess both? Come now, Brian's marrying her—let him seduce her. The boy deserves some reward."

"How soon can you be finished with your part?"

"You know what we have accomplished. We have the ring. Reynard is to juggle for the king in two nights. I can arrange to see the queen that night. Reynard will wear the ring, tell His Majesty where he acquired it, and it's done."

"Are you sure of your escape? If I need you later, I don't want you incapacitated."

"Nor do I wish to be. I find it boring. I have been in the palace, and I've planned a route from the queen's chambers. Where do you wish me to go from there—the princess's chambers?"

"Return here as soon as you are sure you are not followed."

Walter surveyed the room, and his gaze rested on Michel. "How are you progressing with Wendis and Ewets?"

"Wendis and I have toured all the most entertaining places in town: the Gold Quill, the Bird in Hand, the Red—"

"Spare us a list of every disreputable dive in Tarsit. Could Wendis be induced to kill his father, his brothers?"

"He'd kill Leot tomorrow, and Ewets as well, given a very small push."

"And his father?"

"Maybe, but his brothers first. Once he's the only surviving son, he'll have what he wants."

"Ewets?"

"I've spoken to him—a verse-writing fool. I doubt if he sees past his poetry."

"And Leot?"

"He doesn't care whom he offends. He bullies everyone, and no one does anything about it."

Walter considered this. "Encourage Wendis. Point out conspiracies, and suggest plots. Bring up the idea of poison."

"Justin," Walter went on. The alchemist looked up warily from his place by the fire. "We will need another poison. Nothing exotic—something easily acquired from a disreputable apothecary. Enough for two."

Disgust plain in his voice, Justin replied, "Will you need the other as well?"

"Yes, but not until later."

"And this?"

"As soon as you can make it."

"Three or four days if I get the supplies I need."

Michel interruped, "If Ewets is poisoned, Wendis will likely say I did it. I'm supposed to be a Canjitard and would be a likely scapegoat. I won't spend half the moon locked in a miserable cell or worse!"

"It strikes me," Walter said dryly, "that once Wendis has poisoned his brother, His Highness could have an attack of conscience. I trust that your forgery is up to writing a suicide note?" Michel smiled. "Make your plans as best suits you. Notify Thomas as before."

Eleylin, who had been standing nearest the door, spoke up, "Does this mean that you won't be using my plan?"

Plan? Richenza looked sharply at Walter. She hadn't been told of this.

Walter shook his head at Eleylin. "Too obviously the work of an outside agency. Our plan for Ewets puts the blame on his brother."

Eleylin scowled. "What if your games with poison don't work?"

Thomas cut in. "Ellis's idea could be kept in mind in case others go awry."

Walter nodded reluctantly. "Very well. Eleylin, sell your coins where they will be noticed."

"Is that all?"

"No. I have another job for the three of you. Keep an eye on Master Firmin Tredgett."

"The moneylender?"

"You know of him?"

Eleylin smiled wryly. "Moneylenders are a favorite subject of mercenaries. I have heard of him."

"Keep a watch on him and who visits him. He has someone watching this house. Find out who and when. Report as before."

Walter surveyed the room. His mind was weary. "Those of you who have reason to visit this house should be very careful to avoid being seen since we know that Tredgett, at least, has this house watched. Unless someone has further business to discuss, you may all go.''

The Lady Richenza was approaching.

"My lady?"

"What is this plan of Eleylin's and why wasn't I told of it?''

"It was not worth mentioning. Too obviously the plan of some assassin and might point to someone in your pay.''

"Walter?" Alesander had joined them. He had a paper in his hand. "I saw no reason to bring this up in front of everyone." He handed it to Walter. "I think you should read this.''

It was a note written in a firm black hand requesting that Alesander come to dine at the Three Queens the following evening. The note was signed by Firmin Tredgett.

"When did you receive this?"

"At supper. It was under my plate."

"Did you finish your supper?" Thomas, reading over Walter's shoulder, asked.

"Not without hesitation, but it doesn't seem a prelude to poison.''

Richenza looked up angrily from the note. "You realize that this means Tredgett has a spy in my house?"

"We expected that."

"I'll see if Annet can find out who delivered this."

"Alesander, keep this appointment. See what he wants and be vague.'' Walter rose.

"Everyone meets Tredgett except me," Thomas said forlornly as he followed Walter up the stairs to Walter's chamber. "But it was obliging of him to come to us.''

Walter sat heavily on the bed and rubbed his eyes.

"I've been doing this too long."

"We all have. Why does it occur to you now?"

"When I spoke to Brian that first night and asked him what he had done, he said he had done nothing. I sensed no lie in his words, but I didn't believe him. Now I learn that he told me the truth—he had done nothing. Have I been at this so long I no longer believe anyone even when I know they are speaking truth?''

"But he had lied in a sense—his 'nothing' killed his brother.''

"He meant no harm, and he was not feigning remorse. He should not be here with the likes of Hamon or Michel or me."

"Not you, Walter. You are less to blame than—"

"No!" Walter commanded him to stop with the full force of his will. "I am guilty. I foresaw the consequences of my actions, but I chose what pleased me. That boy was condemned for a moment's hesitation in a situation where other consequences were much more likely than death. He should not be with us."

"Nevertheless, he lied to you."

"He lied to protect his father; it was an honorable lie."

"The gods protect us, then, from an honorable fool," Thomas quoted acidly.

"He will learn, Thomas. We have all learned to be dishonorable."

"Some of us faster than others, Walter. He has no loyalties here. At least be sure Payne keeps a tight rein on him. I don't trust his instincts. He has too much conscience for his good or ours."

Walter nodded wearily. "You are right, of course." Too numb to argue any further, he changed the subject. "What have you learned about those Tarsean guardianship laws?"

Tenth Day

Firmin Tredgett waited in the entry of the Three Queens Inn. He knew that Fiskin Dron had received his orders for a private room for dinner, and he knew that the innkeeper knew that he knew it. Let the man have his moment of superiority; why offend a man who had known him from his youth to assert his present status? If only Dron would hurry with his paper-shuffling, for above the din of the common room Tredgett could hear men descending the stairs from the rooms above, any one of whom might carry tales to Prince Leot of Master Tredgett's whereabouts this evening. At least the Lady Richenza's champion had not yet arrived.

"Oh yes, here it is. Had it all the time," said Dron. "The small room with the fireplace right across the hall." He gestured for Tredgett to follow, but it was too late. The crowd on the stairs debouched into the entry hall, joking with laughing curses on the whims of fortune. Most of them Tredgett knew as debtors. Most of them were well-known at court, and any of them might speak to Leot. Most of them walked past him uncaring and departed. One remained.

"Master Tredgett! Just the man I need to see,"

the man said, a note of false joviality warming his voice.

"Yes, my lord," said Tredgett, impassive.

"Just the man," the man repeated to restore the momentum of his speech. "Couldn't time it better. Remember the loan I asked you about? 'Fraid I need an answer sooner than I thought."

"Yes?"

"Need it now." He draped an arm around Tredgett's shoulders.

Tredgett shrugged him off and started across the hall. "See me at my house tomorrow." He paused in the doorway, "Unless . . ."

"Yes?"

"Did you speak to the other councilors about the Canjitard marriage?"

The other man shifted and looked down at the slate of the floor. "No, I didn't get the chance, but now that this new pretender has shown up I don't think it'll take much talk to stop it as you wished. The Princess Meriel will never be Queen of Canjitrin now, in spite of Abethell's silver tongue."

"Who is he wielding it for?"

"This new pretender, Prince Brian. Wants him to marry the princess. He's buttonholing everyone with influence with a story about some treaty Daimiron has with Arin."

Tredgett's eyes flickered, and he turned and walked back. "Two percent off on the interest—if . . ."

"Yes, yes." The man was pumping his hand.

"If you support this new marriage in the council."

"Yes, but—?"

"We'll draw up the papers tomorrow. I'll outline the position you should take. Midmorning?"

The man nodded as if dazed. Tredgett left him standing in the hallway.

So Abethell also knew of the Arin-Canjitrin treaty and was doing what he could to counter it. Tredgett poured himself a cup of the newly delivered wine and leaned against the mantel. What if there were no danger of a flank attack when Arin moved in the spring?

The rap on the door, when it came, found him deep in thought. He composed his voice. "Come in."

"You sent for me, Master Tredgett," said the young man he had last seen at Indes's town house.

"Sir Alesander"—Tredgett bowed him in—"I wasn't sure you'd dare come."

"Dare?" Alesander looked faintly puzzled. "What should I fear from such a well-written and signed invitation? Such formality hardly suggests nefarious purposes. What could you propose?"

"Only dinner." Tredgett smiled and gestured toward the table. "And talk afterward. Some wine?"

Alesander took the cup that Tredgett poured.

After they had eaten, Tredgett studied Alesander across the rim of his cup. A decorative young man—on the surface. Golden wavy hair, deep blue eyes, features regular enough that women would think him handsome. Not perfect. Narrow face, long sharp nose, eyes set too close together.

He looks like someone I've seen before, Tredgett thought, *or a drawing or a sculpture I've seen, for I don't remember coloring. The sketches of the spies from Arin? No, not that recently, and his accent doesn't hint of the south.*

Tredgett guided the conversation to talk about the city. "For I've heard you've been seeing all the sights." *He's not as tall as Leot, or as broadly built, but he's no weakling. He doesn't dress to emphasize his muscle as Leot does. On purpose? The same purpose that Bolson suspects in his jousting?*

Not unintelligent, either. Tredgett weighed the conversation. *Might as well get down to business.*

"Have you been long in Sir Walter's household?"

"A few months. Why?"

"It must be a shock to be so suddenly thrust into the middle of great affairs. I wondered if Sir Walter chose you after he received word from the Lady Richenza. It must have been quite a scramble to get here so quickly from Ulvidia."

"Memorz," corrected Alesander. "But we were already in Hersin when we crossed paths with her messenger."

"How convenient. I wonder that you didn't miss him."

"It's difficult to miss livery as gaudy as Indes's red and gold."

"Sir Walter uses black and silver for his colors, I notice, and yet he is of the House of Indes."

"True. But he uses the colors of his maternal grandmother from whom he inherited the bulk of his lands. In Mentorz that counts more than a distant connection with a lowland Grand Duke. We're a very self-contained and self-content society, I fear."

"And yet you were on your way to Tarsit."

"Did I give that impression? Sorry. No, we were going to Manreth and, if the weather permitted, to the baths at Credom."

"No serious illness, I hope?"

"Oh no, just the bane of the fighting man—sore back and rheumatism."

"You seem a little young for that."

Alesander laughed. "Not me—Sir Walter. He was a very bonny jouster in his youth. I just came along to see the sights and maybe—"

"Yes?"

"Make a few connections. I'm a second son, and Father'd be hard put to provide for me. So when I heard that Sir Walter was to travel west I had my father find me a place in his household. Can't pass up a chance like that."

"So you came west to make your fortune."

"An old story, isn't it?"

"You'll make a name for yourself in a hurry. Too bad you won't be around to enjoy your fame."

"I haven't lost a joust in years."

"Forgive me, Sir Alesander, if I suggest that Mentorz is not Tarsit," said Tredgett gently.

Alesander continued the thought, "And my style is provincial and old-fashioned. So I've been told, but I don't think that all this flash and novelty will count against honest skill."

"You haven't seen Prince Leot joust, have you?"

Alesander shook his head.

"I thought not. He hasn't lost since he was sixteen."

"Yes, but then one must remember, after all, that he's a prince."

"Meaning?"

"Meaning," Alesander said gently in his turn, "there are many who profit more by letting him win."

"A point you might keep in mind."

"Why? He'll be dead."

"His father and brothers won't be. How far do you think you could rise in Tarsia against their displeasure?"

Alesander looked up and then down into the wine he swirled in his cup. "There are other places."

"Where you would be a foreigner with all the attendant disadvantages. Perhaps the king of Arin might reward you for your disloyal actions since they are so convenient for him." Tredgett noted a brief frown at the mention of Arin. *Interesting, I wonder why that touched him.* "But Arin will keep the best rewards for his own subjects."

"I want nothing from Arin."

"But you want a great deal from life. You're a young man graced with good looks, good health, skill and—I judge—intelligence. You should go far. But you have not thought through the consequences of your present course. You could lose your life in the joust. Leot really is very good."

"I'm not afraid of him," Alesander muttered.

"*I* would be. And should you win, what can the Lady Richenza give you that outweighs the enmity of the Royal House?"

Alesander stared down into the cup, refusing to meet his eyes. "What can I do? I gave my word. I stand by it."

What's his word worth, I wonder, Tredgett thought. He said, "Very honorable. But how honorable is it to support such a treasonable cause? The Grand Duke of Maldrin was surprised armed in ambush in the king's chambers."

"I know. I've heard the story."

"Do you really want to stake your life and honor in his cause?"

Alesander hesitated, then said, as if half-convinced, "I gave my word to Sir Walter and Lady Richenza."

"What can they do for you? A girl you've scarcely met and a man you've not served a year. Would you profit from treason? Think. I can do more for you than they can. What do you want? Name a place, I can get it for you. I can help you advance more than they ever could. Don't waste yourself in a questionable cause.''

"Master Tredgett." Alesander rose and went to the door. "I want a great deal, but I won't sell my honor for it. You can tell Prince Leot, if he put you up to this, that I stand by my word."

Tredgett rose to face him. "I speak for myself, not for Leot, and I tell you this: if you withdraw from the combat, I will reward you in every way that I can, but if you persist in your challenge, I will do everything in my power to stop you. I warn you—I am no gentleman and I will not let honor constrain me. I give you three days to think it over. You're not stupid, and I am sure that when we meet here again you will have a more pleasing answer. If you doubt my power to carry out my promises or my threats, I am sure that there are people who will tell you otherwise."

"I don't doubt it. When young Russoc first pointed out how provincial my jousting was I thought that I might hire Jon Bolson to smooth out the roughnesses of my style. But I soon found he had another paymaster." Alesander bowed and left, closing the door behind him.

Tredgett set his cup down on the table with a click. *What a waste. What a damnable waste.*

12

Eleventh Day

Brian, trapped between Rozer and Ewets at the banquet table, took advantage of their momentary self-absorption to contemplate the previous two days. Abethell had been busy. On the afternoon of the day Walter had told him to play along with Abethell's plan, Abethell had called on the most politically useful men in Tarsit. By the morning of the next day he had arranged a semiofficial reception by the royal family and now tonight this invitation to a "family" dinner from King Rozer. Family being not only the king, queen, princes and princess, but thirty of Rozer's usual dinner cronies and Abethell.

Brian wished the dinner over. He thought his face would crack from smiling and his mind go numb from presenting the agreeable and noncommittal comments that Abethell wished of him.

But there were limits to any man's patience, especially when dealing with the House of Thaiter. Rozer hadn't been too bad at the reception—just called him "my boy" patronizingly and nodded monotonously as he listened to Abethell. The princes were another matter. They had carried him off in a group, competing for his company. Leot had attempted to talk simpleminded politics, to his brothers' disgust and Brian's feigned bewilderment. After Leot's departure, Brian had been subject to a tug-of-war for his attention between Ewets and Wendis. Wendis had wanted to discuss horses and hadn't shut up until Brian had promised him stock from the Hassart stud at Coliram.

If this were real, I'd send him geldings, the cheeky beggar.

He had not escaped from Ewets until he had spent three hours admiring his antique collection and, by a display of ineptitude unlikely and unbecoming in a person trained to public appearance, escaped being forced to play a part in the masque for Ewets's upcoming masquerade. Attending the masquerade itself was inescapable.

He had seen the Princess Meriel for only a formal greeting. Her greetings had been addressed to a point over his left shoulder; he hadn't even been able to catch her eye.

She was present tonight with three chairs between them. Brian glanced past the king, past the queen's empty chair, past Leot, who stared into his plate, to Meriel's clear-cut profile. She was the only woman still at the table. The queen had left during a lay set in the shrill Sartherian mode, clutching a wetted handkerchief to her temples. No one seemed surprised.

On Brian's other side Prince Wendis had left after the second course, pleading an earlier engagement. His father dismissed him all the more eagerly to end his cracking nuts during the recitation of the "Elegy of Lycus." Brian wished he dare do the same before Ewets asked his opinion again on some point for his masque or Rozer, having finished the fruit course, took up his tedious explanations of each act in the evening's entertainment. As if Brian had never heard a lutenist before!

The next act was a trio of recorders, and before they had even started to play Prince Leot said, "Oh, ye gods!" and left without his father's permission. Rozer frowned momentarily, then busied himself explaining to Brian the history of the piece, the performers, and the instrument while Brian made polite noises of interest. Luckily when they were finished, the next course had been served and Rozer put his full attention to eating. On Brian's other side Ewets came out of his self-absorption to say, "Fades."

"What!"

"Glory fades. A line for my masque. I was going to use 'leafy glades' but someone pointed out it was too pastoral an image for a martial subject. It could be thought a piquant contrast. What do you think of 'glory fades'?"

"It's more metaphysical, surely." Brian fought the urge to noisily pulverize a walnut.

"Hmmmm. . . ." Ewets returned to his meditations.

Brian turned to Rozer to find that the king had commanded the table to close up, so the princess now sat in the queen's chair. Maybe he could manage a word with her. He leaned forward but so did the king.

"Now we'll have something special," said Rozer. "Something different with the final course."

Brian stifled a sigh. What was special about the platters piled with cakes and pastries and flagons of spiced wine? The music for once was subdued and unobtrusive. You could have made decent conversation, if your neighbors were conversable. Since his were not, Brian reached for a cake, then noticed the red-haired young man bowing from the end of the tables.

Theyad Haldan, that *banquet*. Brian had been lulled by the classicality of the evening's entertainment.

Reynard bowed again, coming forward to stand in the middle of the "U" of linen-draped tables. The boy began to juggle: balls, then blocks, mixed objects, Brian scarcely noticed what; all he could see was the flashing gold and green of the ring on Reynard's right hand. He could scarcely look away to steal a glance when Rozer gasped. But the king had not noticed, he only clasped his hands together at some intricate maneuver. How could he not see? For now Reynard was juggling, still skillfully, but in the more awkward position that keeping the backs of his hands toward the king entailed. It seemed to Brian that the green light from the emerald played about the room like a mischievous spirit, yet Rozer sat oblivious. Reynard, his bearing tauter now, stepped forward to stand directly before Rozer and slowed the speed of his circle of balls.

Rozer looked down, stuffed a honeycake in his mouth like a greedy child, then looked back to Reynard's moving hands. His gaze focused, and he choked on his indrawn breath.

"Father?" The princess started to rise, but a grey-haired man seated beyond her pushed back his chair and hurried to the king.

Rozer coughed till he was red-faced and teary-eyed but gestured away the goblet Meriel offered. "Come here, boy." He beckoned Reynard forward.

Reynard bowed and smiled as though he expected a reward, but, at Rozer's sharp demand, "Where did you get the ring?" he glanced nervously about.

"What—?" Reynard broke off and twisted the ring on his finger.

"Where did you get the ring?"

The princess looked from her excited father to the boy who now had the ring turned into his fist to show only a plain gold band. "Father . . ."

Rozer ignored her. "Let me see the ring."

Reynard took it off as though it burned him and held it out glittering on his palm. The emerald winked green sparks from its intricate setting. The princess gasped.

"Claverdon, call the guard," Rozer commanded the man hovering at his shoulder. He turned to Reynard. "For the last time, where did you get the ring?"

"I . . . I borrowed it."

"A likely story," said Claverdon.

"All right—I stole it."

The king relaxed.

Reynard went on rapidly, "But I thought I could return it if he noticed it was gone. He left it lying about just begging to be taken. I—"

"Who is 'he'?" the king demanded.

Reynard seemed surprised. "Why, Master Haroc, of course."

"Do you know where he got it?" Rozer leaned forward.

"From a lady, as usual. He didn't say which one. Please, don't tell him. Promise. He'll beat me this time. Take it." Reynard seemed genuinely terrified as he threw himself to his knees before the king.

Rozer ignored the ring. "What do you know about this woman?" His face was screwed into a mask of calculation.

"He doesn't tell me about his conquests."

"Surely you know something. Tell me who she is, and you can keep the ring."

"But I don't know! All I know is that when I said that he was dressing with unusual care tonight he said that it was to please a lady, but I don't know if it's the same one."

Rozer turned to his hovering steward. "Claverdon, tell off twenty guardsmen and surround the queen's chambers. Arrest anyone going in or out. Have another twenty assembled but wait for me." His eyes glittering above a fixed smile, Rozer turned back to the kneeling Reynard. "Keep the ring, boy. You have, perhaps, done me a service that none of my court has been able to do, and if you haven't, if your master subverts fidelity, he can't expect it in return."

Reynard clutched the ring and retreated, his proper bows hardly slowing his escape.

The king clasped his hands across his belly as though he savored some fine dish. "Let us have some dance music to end the banquet. Play 'Hunt's End.' "

"Father, no!" Meriel protested, "Not that."

"Why not? Years ago she killed my honor and has mocked its corpse ever since. Let her bleed this time. It's a quicker death I'm giving her than she has given my manhood."

"You should divorce her. Don't demean yourself to her level. Just because she has mistreated you, should—"

Rozer cut her off. "Don't be any more of a fool than you have to be." Her slight opposition had changed his mood to open anger.

"Father, I beg you." Meriel slipped to her knees beside his chair. "Don't kill her. Won't a divorce be humiliation enough? As the injured party you'll keep most of her lands."

"You women always stick together." Rozer got to his feet and pushed her aside. "Meek and pure on the outside and inside ravening leeches. All of you." His voice rose to hysteria. "Except your mother. I thought once that you were like her. But you're just like the rest. Did you and Betrissa make a bargain to deceive me? Do you compare notes, laughing at me in private?"

Meriel was white-faced with shock, but persisted with her plea. "Papa! How can you accuse me of such things? What reason have I given you? It's your reputation and welfare I think of when I beg you to spare her life."

"What reason?" Her father struck aside her clutching hands. "What reason? You lying, sneaking bitch! Why was Nele Indes found in your chamber the very morning he tried to murder me?"

"Papa!" Meriel sank back on her heels as Rozer hurried from the room. Fighting back her tears, she turned to Ewets, who had been a bored observer. "Please, stop him." Ewets stretched his legs but made no move to rise. "Try to stop him."

"Why? I never did like Betrissa."

Meriel looked wildly about, but there was no one left but Brian.

He, trapped in an ugly scene, fell back on formal manners and offered his arm to help her rise. "Shall I summon your ladies, Your Highness?"

The caress of the queen's silk chemise across his bare leg roused Hamon from his lethargy. Evading Betrissa's clutching hands, he slipped from the bed and padded barefoot to the window. He moved the jug of wine set there to cool and swung the window open just enough to admit the night air and a snatch of song. The banquet still went on, but for how long?

"Come back to bed. It's cold." Betrissa pulled her chemise to order about her legs. "Why did you get up? It's not near time for you to go."

"I'll come gladly, my love. But don't you want the wine?" Hamon skillfully balanced jug, goblets, and tray. "My blood certainly needs cooling after the taste of you."

"Oh, well . . . bring it here." She settled back on the mussed coverlet. "But close the window."

He shut the window, making sure the latch worked smoothly and glanced to the shadowed garden half a story below. Not a bad drop and the garden seemed deserted. He carried the tray back across the tiled floor and presented it with a flourish. She laughed, leaning forward to take her goblet. He sat on the edge of the bed and drank and studied her. How long ago had she taken to wearing a chemise to bed? It was not a northern custom, especially not such as she wore—thin silk in shirred fullness that both concealed and flaunted.

Does she wear such for Rozer, he wondered and nearly choked on the wine. Betrissa turned knowing green eyes on him as if they shared the secret in his thoughts and stretched catlike, snuggling deeper into the folds of the crumpled coverlet.

Emboldened by that seeming intimacy, Hamon asked, "Why do you stay with him?"

She stared at him uncomprehending.

"You don't have to stay. You could leave him."

"Why should I go? I manage Rozer well enough."

"Why bother? There is a world beyond Tarsit."

"Is there indeed?" She caught hold of the dangling ties of his shirt and pulled him toward her. "Tell me."

"Places that would be a fitter setting for you. Villas on the Bay of Merith of white stone set in green cypress groves warmed by the sun and cooled by the breeze from the sea. The only wear is silk; the only thought is love. Come away with me."

"With a merchant?"

"You would live like a queen."

"But I would not be queen." She pulled him back down as he started to pull away. She guided his hand to the curve of her hip. "Men!" she said almost to herself as his hands roamed her body. "Always so serious." Her hands were busy in his shirt and hair. "Run away with you indeed." The laughter in her voice tickled his ear. "You're not *that* good in bed, my dear."

He set himself to prove otherwise, so intent upon that self-imposed task that he was unaware of the crescendo of music from the banquet hall or the silence that followed it.

The crash of the antechamber doors being flung open and the tramp of many feet across the floor to the locked doors of the queen's chamber finally awakened him to danger.

"In there!" Rozer ordered shrilly.

The doors shook under repeated blows, then flew open, shattered. Men-at-arms erupted into the room, spears ready. Hamon rolled off the side of the bed nearest the window.

Betrissa pulled at her shift as she rose to her knees on the crumpled bed. All motion stopped as Rozer stared at his wife. Then, his voice breaking, Rozer screamed, "Kill them! What are you waiting for? Kill them!" The men-at-arms leaped forward.

A spear took Betrissa full in the chest, and she fell back on the bed, blood soaking her white chemise and spreading across the sea-green coverlet.

Hamon, sheltered by the bed hangings, threw the tray at the nearest attackers and, as they stumbled over jug and goblets and slipped on the spreading pool of wine, wrenched the window open and jumped out.

The garden was full of men. He rose from his landing squat and dove for the shadow of an outjutting wall.

A company of guardsmen searched the gardens. *Guardsmen.* He set his mind to recalling their uniform. *Yes, that should do.* He stepped out of his hiding place to mingle with them just as someone thrust a lantern through the window above. Rozer leaned out, shouting, his voice still rough with emotion, "Catch him, for Haldan's sake! I want his head!"

Hamon worked his way quickly and unobtrusively toward the river gate. He gained it with a sigh of relief and a sardonic thought, *I doubt that it's my head he's after.*

Richenza looked at the small bloodstain that marred the white silk of her sewing. This was the third time she had pricked her finger tonight, and she was afraid she couldn't hide this stain as she had the others.

Plainly, she couldn't concentrate on this any more than she could on reading. She turned to the door of her withdrawing room, willing it to open.

There was still no sign of Hamon. Reynard had come hours ago to say that his part had been successful. Walter had given him orders and sent him off.

No one had come since, though Reynard had said that Rozer had been on the verge of discovering the queen with Hamon when he had left. Richenza had expected news within the hour, but the night that had swallowed up Reynard showed no sign of giving forth Hamon. So long was the wait, even Annet, as fiercely as she had resisted leaving

Richenza alone, had had to fight off sleep. Richenza had finally allowed herself to be helped into her nightclothes and had sent the protesting Annet to bed.

What could keep Hamon so long? He had had an escape route planned, but what if he hadn't been able to get out of the palace?

Someone tapped lightly at the door; Thomas looked a little surprised to see her still awake when Richenza answered.

"What is it?"

"Michel has arrived with news."

The boy waited in the parlor, impatient to tell his story. He and Wendis, whose rooms were a floor above and across the courtyard from Betrissa's, had seen enough to know that the queen was dead.

". . . there was blood everywhere. I thought Wendis was going to toss his supper! Hamon dived out the window in nothing but his shirt. Then someone came and told us that the queen had died of a sudden illness. No one will believe that! I've already heard—"

"Enough. I'm not interested in gossip," Walter said. "What happened to Hamon after he went out the window?"

Michel shrugged. "Didn't see him again."

After all the elaborate scheming the result had been so simple, exactly as planned. Curiously, she found that she felt no triumph, merely disgust that Betrissa's end had been so tawdry.

Thomas and Michel were gone, and Walter stood looking out into the night, oblivious to her presence and to the rain that beat on the windowpanes.

They were alone together perhaps a quarter of an hour, before a bedraggled Hamon straggled in. With his black hair soaked and plastered to his face, and wearing a disreputable green cloak that had done nothing to keep him dry, he did not in the least resemble the exotic southern merchant Haroc. He went straight to the fire and stood with his back to the room, cradling one arm as he warmed himself.

When Walter finally spoke he was more brusque than

Richenza thought Hamon's condition warranted—the man looked half-dead.

"Well?" Walter inquired. "Michel reported nearly an hour ago. Where have you been?"

"Across the river, hiding. Did you want me to lead Rozer here?"

"What happened?"

"She's dead."

"Michel told us that much."

"I'm sure Michel gave you all the details."

"What happened after you went out the window?"

"Everything went as planned, until I tried to cross the river. The boatman I hired tried to come back to this side when he heard the guards hailing him. They must have realized that I'd try to leave the city that way. The boatman wouldn't take a bribe to continue, so I had to kill him."

"Is that what happened to your arm?" Hamon's shirt was torn and bloodied.

"He had a knife. I took his cloak and dumped the body."

"You remember where to meet Thomas for further instructions?"

"Of course. When do I forget anything?"

Walter seemed on the verge of replying, when Thomas appeared in the doorway.

"Michel has been upstairs regaling Justin with details of the queen's death. Bertz has thrown Michel out, but if you want the poison finished. . . ."

Hamon gave Walter a taut smile, and Walter turned abruptly away from him. He seemed surprised to face Richenza.

"My lady"—he held the door for her—"I am sorry that this has gone so late." He escorted her up the stairs and left her at the door to her chamber.

Richenza was in bed when she remembered Hamon's injury needed to be tended to.

Thomas and Walter were dealing with Justin; Annet was asleep, and no one else could be trusted with knowledge of Hamon's presence.

Hamon had not seemed bothered by the wound, but she knew her duty. He had been injured in her service. Reluctantly she rose and pulled her bedgown over her nightshift.

She had half hoped that Hamon had left, but he still stood by the fire, too lost in thought to glance up when she entered.

Feeling foolish and unsure of what to do for him, she hesitated.

"Do you—do you need anything for your arm?"

He did not look up. "I need nothing, my lady."

"You're bleeding."

"It will mend."

From the way he held his arm it was more than a scratch. She crossed the room.

"At least let me see it."

His shoulders tightened as he drew himself up and pulled her hand away before it touched him.

"Leave it." He faced her, his attention on her at last.

"Is there anything you need?"

He brought her hand down, but did not let it go.

"No, there is nothing I need." His eyes narrowed. "But I know what you want." Before his words could take on meaning, he kissed her.

Hamon stopped as soon as she pulled away, but he did not let her go.

"Still pretending to be untouchable?" He shrugged off the cloak. "Why did you come back?"

She shook her head and moved away, but he did not free her.

"Are you afraid of being found out? Don't worry, I'm a dead man—I can never tell anyone." He plucked at the knot she had so hastily tied in the sash of her bedgown.

"Let go of me!"

"What do you want? Flattery? You are prettier than she—and younger." Angry at his mockery, she tried to break his hold.

Hamon's grip on her wrist became painfully tight.

"It was you who asked what I needed, my lady." Bolder now, or more indifferent, he pushed open her bedgown. "After all, Betrissa's dead." He pulled her closer. "She found me to be a good lover." He whispered in her ear as one whispers an endearment, "So did my sister."

With her fist she struck his injured forearm. He let her go, but she saw that he was laughing.

"Am I to take it that you prefer older lovers?" Hamon asked. "Or fair-haired ones?"

Richenza fled the room and Hamon did not follow.

The rest of that night sleep was as elusive to Richenza as to the men she had summoned. In her few, uneasy dreams Hamon and Leot seemed to blend into a looming shadow which pursued her through her own passageways, waiting for her even as she thought she escaped them.

Mostly, though, small sounds started her from a state that was neither waking nor sleeping. When Alesander's closing door signaled his return, she sat up in her bed and gave up all pretense at sleep.

She was being a fool, but she could not keep from jumping at every sound. And Alesander's presence in the next room, which should have been reassuring, merely led her down other unpleasant paths of thought.

It was Hamon—only Hamon. Hadn't he warned her against himself? She should have known better than to go alone—in her nightclothes, no less!—to tend to him. The stories she had heard of him should have warned her away.

Hamon of Saroth—he'd seduced his own sister and murdered her; that was why he had been cursed. No one was safe with him. It had been the height of folly to trust him.

She tried again to sleep.

A board creaked in the next room.

It's Alesander in the next room. Alesander is a gentleman. Alesander is—fair-haired.

What could have made Hamon think . . . ?

He did know Alesander. Perhaps he had cause.

13

Twelfth Day

Morning drove away Richenza's night terrors, but they were replaced by a feeling of embarrassment as if her stupidity could be read on her face. In the daytime, with all the Huntsmen busy in their various roles, she found it easy to be alone.

She wanted something to occupy her mind. The library was the only room that none of the men except Thomas used, and he was out on errands.

The only book that caught her eye was Jesper Donnit's *The Grand Chronicles of the Most Noble Kings of Tarsia.*

No need to look in the first volume—the kings before Anderad were only names whose reigns gave chronology to the grand dukes' achievements, each king elected to give a formal center to the Sueve and their expansion.

She leafed quickly through the second volume. Donnit spent a lot of space on Anderad—Anderad the first king after Tarses to truly rule. The grand dukes had misjudged their man in electing him, mistaking a weak body for a weak will, and Anderad had never given them the chance to right their error. By the time Anderad died sixty years after his election, he had so cowed the remaining grand dukes that they had obediently confirmed his chosen successor, his great-nephew Alesander I.

Alesander—the name was southern—had in turn chosen his cousin Marald, great-grandson of a king before Anderad, to succeed him. The qualification for election was the same as to be elected chief of the Sueve: being within the fourth degree descended from a reigning king. After Anderad each king forced the election of his designated successor and the grand dukes merely confirmed it. Donnit called it a Golden Age. Her father had called it something more pungent.

She scanned for Alesanders. The second Alesander, grandson of Marald, succeeded Vitaut, Anderad's great-grandson.

The third Alesander had been the king who had finally established himself in 742, "the year of three kings," at the height of the civil wars. He had been killed with all his sons six years later.

That had left only the House of Vitaut to claim the throne and her Alesander—*Alesander,* she rejected the possessive—was of the House of Vitaut.

Donnit could waste another volume before getting to Thaiter I. She remembered the scroll that showed the genealogy of the Royal House from Tarses through the children of Laidoin III, illustrated by stiff portraits and, where imagination failed, by coats of arms. It had been a wedding present to her paternal grandparents from Queen Meriel, Wendis III's young widow. The bride had been the queen's sister-in-law, Princess Leoda, Laidoin III's youngest daughter. Richenza frowned, preferring not to remember that common ancestry.

She unrolled the scroll gingerly. The early sections were unimportant, a well-pruned descent from Amloth to Anderad to Vitaut. The artist had used the statue of Anderad in the Great Square as the basis for both Anderad and Vitaut and, checking ahead, Laidoin I, who her father had told her had been the model for it. Those little portraits, at least, had some vitality. The rest were conventional and wooden.

She went back up to Vitaut's arms—barry wavy azure and argent, a lion rampant, countercharged—and searched for Alesanders. Vitaut's grandson Colwin had married a daughter of Alesander II. Colias, King Laidoin . . . Laidoin had had a son named Alesander who died in 776, but he'd been only twenty—too young. She checked the year in Donnit. Prince Alesander had been killed in battle near Rayln fighting an incursion of the Sueve. Except for the prince's death it had been a great victory. His brother Mascelin had named his newborn son in his brother's honor.

She turned back to the scroll. There it was: Laidoin's three sons, Mascelin, Alesander, and Thaiter. In the next generation Mascelin's four sons and single daughter. Richenza noted that Mascelin's wife had been Hersinda, Princess of Saroth.

Richenza studied the bland little portraits. The four sons were portrayed as variously blond and the daughter Lescina, "Dark as you, no, darker, for she had brown eyes."

Harmund and Colias had both died in 800. Which had Alesander murdered? Both? No death date was given for Alesander. Anselm, the remaining son, succeeded his father in 805 and died in the following year. In the same year Lescina had married her uncle Thaiter. Before or after Anselm had died?

Richenza turned back to the book. It said that Alesander had stabbed Harmund after Colias had "died mysteriously." Donnit either had no imagination or a very close mouth, for he said that Alesander had then fled.

His family must have kept the fact of his cursing a secret. He'd said that he had only been with the Hunt for two summonings; no wonder she'd never heard of him.

Anselm had been murdered by a group of discontented nobles who had been, in turn, executed by his uncle and heir Thaiter I, aided by nobles still loyal to the throne. Richenza noted the name Indes among the list of loyalist nobles: Anelhar, who had built this House. Anselm's wife had been implicated in the conspiracy, and she had fled to her father the Lord of Wolves' Hold, where no one, even the new king, could have fetched her without a great deal of trouble. Some also said she was pregnant at the time, Donnit reported noncommittally.

Thaiter had married his niece Lescina as the genealogy showed, and proclaimed a new constitution. The throne would henceforth descend to the eldest son. No more shadow of a hint of election. The throne would descend in a civilized manner by strict inheritance. Donnit made a pretty speech of it, Richenza noted with a sardonic smile. "Civilized" like Arin and Canjitrin. She looked down the scroll and remembered another royal genealogy that had the name of each member murdered inscribed in red. Few generations of Tarsia's Royal House had escaped that telltale scarlet.

Her champion came of a fine old line. . . .

A lover? She'd as soon bed a leper; at least that contagion was involuntary.

"Well, what do you think of her?" Wendis's voice was muffled as he tried to pull the tunic of his masque costume off over his head.

"I think she's too skinny for the costume," Michel said.

"Dunce! Not my sister—Lady Marika."

"Oh. Very eye-filling, not to mention costume-filling."

"Isn't she though?" Wendis pulled his tunic back down with a jerk. "Almost makes this farce worthwhile, rehearsing with her. Got a melting smile, too. Have you noticed?"

"She hasn't turned it on me."

"See that she does not," said Wendis in mock severity.

"No, Your Highness." Michel bowed. "I know better than to poach on a royal preserve."

"Too bad that southern merchant didn't." Wendis's fingers trembled on the intricate laces of the tunic. "Haldan! All that blood."

"Here, let me help." Michel worked at the recalcitrant knots.

Wendis, his voice steadier, said, "Do you think people ever really wore such clothes?"

Michel let him turn the subject. "So the histories say. But no wonder the Rensel lost; it must have taken all day to get dressed."

"Just think of them on the battlefield getting all hung up on their panes."

"Oh, no, Your Highness, the panes are camouflage so it can't be told that the Rensel have already been cut to ribbons. It's a wonder they didn't sew bells on the end of each streamer and look like proper fools.''

"It's a wonder Ewets didn't. He's got enough gold braid on mine to clank. Just think—great Rensel war maneuver: two bells on every pane to make the enemy think they've twice the men.'' He threw down the despised costume and turned to put on his own clothes.

Michel, already changed, looked it over carefully as he folded it and put it beside his own similar but less trimmed costume on the tiring-room shelf. "It's only for the masque.''

"No. Ewets's latest edict—we're to stay in costume the whole masquerade.''

"Prince Leot should love that. A whole evening as the hero.''

"His chance to strut.'' Wendis snickered as he pulled on his shoes. "I don't understand Ewets. Why are the Rensel the heroes? I think it's soft-headed; as though it were ennobling to lose. If I had my choice, I'd play the Sueve general. That's the man's part.'' He declaimed a few of Zeris's lines. "But no, Ewets says, 'You're blond; you're Renselian,' and then he makes me wear a wig because my hair's too short! Dolt! Do you know that he would have given Zeris's part to this Prince Brian just because he had black hair?''

"Why didn't he?''

"The man was too simple to learn his lines.''

"But not to eliminate his brother.''

"Come on. That was an accident. They don't do that in Canjitrin.''

"Too provincial? Why I'm even reliably informed that they do such things in Arin. It really was cleverly done. Prince Geoffry was popular, he has an 'accident'; his mother raises suspicion; Brian disappears; the next heir, Daimiron, and the queen make themselves very unpopular with a servile foreign policy, and Brian returns as a second 'Liberator.' I wouldn't underestimate him.''

"You think he's dangerous?''

"To Daimiron, surely.'' Michel paused as though lost in thought. "Although . . .''

"Although what?''

"No, it's just a coincidence."

"What is?"

"Queen Betrissa's death."

"That would have happened sooner or later. Father tried to catch her for years."

"Yes, but he did it now."

Wendis thought for a moment. Michel continued. "Brian has been seen with Ewets recently, and Ewets hated the queen. She's dead. . . ."

"What's that to do with me? Leot should look behind him if Ewets is getting ideas. Leot's the one who is always treading on his tail, and, if the rumors about the Maldrin business are right, Ewets has every right to worry."

"Maybe. But what if he wants some practice first? I have read that with the sons of King Mascelin it was the youngest who died first."

"Ancient history." Wendis frowned, and Michel noted his continuing preoccupation.

14

Thirteenth Day

The passing of another night and half a day
helped quiet Richenza's mind, but her reading
had left her with little taste for the company of
her guests. Determined to find a task with abso-
lutely no relationship to any of the thoughts
which disturbed her, Richenza picked up long-
neglected embroidery. The rhythm of her stitch-
ing was soothing, and the weather fine enough to
cheer anyone. She found herself listening expectantly whenever someone walked past her door.

As she threaded her needle she admired the
autumn-bright garden outside the parlor window.
After the cold and rain had come this day of
warmth and sunshine.

This was likely to be the last fine weather of
the year.

Richenza smiled; Nele always said that.

He won't say it again.

She stared at her work as if she had stitched
some answer there. Her anger was gone. She felt
as hollow as one of the corn maidens that the
peasants raised at harvest. Her mourning was an
affront to the fine weather; this was a day to be
riding, to be laughing.

Tears, the first since the morning he'd died,
blurred the blue sky and the foolish bright leaves.

She wiped the wetness away, but could not stop it. Turning in the window seat, she buried her face in her arms and gave way to her grief.

She was alone; Nele was dead, her father Rychart was dead. Who was left who knew her? Annet? No, no matter how long Annet had been in her service she would always call Richenza "my lady." Who would know her again?

She would not be anyone but "my lady" anymore. She would not be Richenza, and never, never Ric'a as she had been to her father and Nele.

"My lady?" She knew the voice—Alesander's.

"What is it?" She wished he were anyone else.

"I didn't know you were in here." Richenza struggled to master herself as he cast about the room searching for something. He had found whatever it was when she let out an undignified sniff.

Only then did he look at her and see her distress.

"Are you ill?"

"No." She didn't sound convincing, even to herself.

"Is there anything I might do, my lady?"

Stop calling me that!

"I said I was fine."

He turned her face to him. "You're not ill." His voice was kind against her harshness. "You've been crying." For a moment she looked into his worried face. He seemed to want to help her.

She pushed his hand away sharply and found all her anger welling back into her. "Of course I'm crying. Nele is dead." The understanding she didn't want from him was in his eyes. He started to say something, and she cut off his commonplace. "*I* didn't want my brother dead."

"What?" He had caught the venom, but not the intent.

"You know very well what I mean. Someone else murdered *my* brother."

Slowly, very slowly, he drew back. Her attack had bewildered him, but he had realized that it *was* an attack.

"I know your House much too well," she pushed harder. "Thaiter may have been your uncle, but his wife was your sister and it is your nephews who squabble over the throne. After all your family has done they have the gall to call my blood corrupt!"

She had succeeded in angering him; she could see him fight to master himself, and she drove home again. "Perhaps Leot *is* true kind—fratricide does run in your family."

She had underestimated him; he was angry, but he kept himself under control as he answered, "What would you have had me do, my lady? Wait my turn to be killed? I did not begin the killing."

"You did not stop it, either."

Alesander closed his eyes; she had found an open wound. Doggedly, he kept his voice even. "I thought that I had. At least I brought it into the open. Harmund had Colias poisoned. Colias was sixteen—the youngest, the weakest."

"And Harmund's death left only one brother between you and the throne. It was undoubtedly justice disguised."

That finished it. She had finally broken his reserve. He searched for a reply and found one.

"You might consider your blood in the matter, my lady." It was a small book he had found in this room; he held it up. "It seems that my sister's son was probably not Thaiter's. She had a lover—Anelhar Indes, Grand Duke of Maldrin. From whose blood does the treachery come, my lady of Indes? *My* brothers, at least, did not try to murder a king in his bed."

He flung the book down next to her. "Here, Thomas found this. I suggest that you study it."

He left her.

When he was gone, she wiped her eyes and began to read.

Firmin Tredgett sighed as he unfolded the next dispatch from the stack that waited piled beside the candlestick. He hadn't expected Indes's champion to appear, but he had hoped. It was long past suppertime, and Alesander Scelin had not come. Tredgett glanced up to the rain-splashed window. His hand reached toward the candlestick; he might as well give the signal to the men who waited across the street, hidden from the fitful, flickering torchlight spotting Golden Street.

His hand fell. No, there was still time. Scelin might come. He might agree. Tredgett turned back to the reports. Four porters who had worked for Haroc of Lin'Merith had been questioned. Their depositions would be sent tomorrow. Haroc's suspiciously talented apprentice had been questioned by the king and hired at the palace. His associate Alvord had left for the south the day before the queen's death but should be captured soon. Haroc himself had been seen at Gressly on the Utran Road. Other reports placed him on the road to Morthrell.

The commander of Iskandroc was secretly receiving envoys from Arin. *Better speak to Leot about having him replaced.* Tredgett put that dispatch aside.

What else was there from the south? He searched through the pile. A report from one of the men he had sent to check on Walter Martling's story. The story checked out from the Indes hunting lodge at Sulby. Esden also reported that the old Indes family tomb there showed signs of disturbance. Should he wait for further orders?

"Dunce!" At least by now the order should have caught up with him to turn east toward Hersin. Tredgett put the report down. He must remember to show that report to Leot.

· He slumped and rubbed his eyes. If only he could have put Audwin on that search, but he was gone on some mission for Leot. *I shouldn't have put him in Leot's service, but I needed someone I could trust to watch him. So, of course, now Audwin's gone when I need him. Strange he hasn't found some way to report. I wonder if his wife knows anything. I'll have to find out tomorrow.*

Tredgett reread Esden's report. It was odd that he didn't mention Indes's messenger. Esden wouldn't ignore a side issue in pursuit of his quarry. Indes's livery was difficult to miss.

A rap on the door distracted his thoughts.

"Come in."

"I came to give you my answer, Master Tredgett."

But Tredgett already knew it even as he went through the motions of courtesy. Indes's livery was, indeed, hard to miss. Under his thrown-back black cloak Alesander wore a golden cote brocaded in scarlet and hose of deep red. Even the wide hip-belt and the dagger sheath it supported were scarlet leather, plentifully embellished with gold—very different from the discreet richness of Alesander's clothes at

their earlier interview. Even his manner differed. Before he
had carried himself with an easy assurance that was not at
all provincial. Now he was as taut as an unslacked bow-
string.

"Sit and have some wine?" Tredgett stalled the answer.

"I came on business."

"No reason not to be gentlemanly about it."

"You admitted you were not a gentleman."

Tredgett looked up sharply. Alesander was deliberately
being offensive. Because he didn't like the answer he was
to give? *Somewhere there is an argument I could use to
change his mind if I had the time and the wit to find it.*

Alesander hooked his thumbs insolently in his red-and-
gold belt. "No reason to waste your time and mine. My
answer is 'no.' "

Tredgett sighed. He set down the goblet and grasped the
candlestick on the table. "I'm sorry that is your answer."

"Put that down." Alesander's dagger glittered un-
sheathed in his hand.

Tredgett continued to hold the candlestick. "Why?"

"That's to be your signal to the men hiding in the street.
Some movement of the candle."

"And if it is?"

"Put it down."

"Or what? You'll knife me? Plenty of people know you
came here to see me. I made sure of that. If I turn up dead
or wounded, they'll know who did it. If you're in jail for
assault or murder you can't act as Indes's champion."

For a long moment their eyes locked, then Tredgett deliberately turned and put the candlestick on the window
ledge. Behind him he heard the door close.

Alesander considered his next move. Tredgett had signaled
to his men on Golden Street, so they would be waiting
there. No doubt men waited in the common room, too, and
there was no way to reach the rear of the inn without going
through the common room. Not on the ground floor.

Alesander strolled across the entry and went up the stair.
On the next story a cross-corridor separated what had been
the main reception rooms when this part of the inn had been
a private residence. An open arch led to a passageway

which ultimately led onto the gallery of the innyard.

He dropped his cloak as a red herring and changed his clothing into the obscure garb of a Tarsean townsman. He pulled up the hood of his shoulder cape and sauntered along the gallery to descend the spiral staircase nearest the stable entrance on the alley.

He hoped they followed the false trail or waited in the street as he plunged into the noisome darkness of the alleyway.

The light of the torches at the Three Queens' stables was lost with the first twist of the alleyway. Light glimmered from the south, silhouetting a man to his stalker or his prey even as it furnished his only guide through the maze of sheds and hoardings, fenced yards and building backs left graceless and unadorned since they were never seen by any man who mattered.

The hunters would expect him to turn north toward Indes's town house, so he turned south, searching for a passage that would take him to the Temple Way before he reached the well-lighted square around the castle.

A whistled snatch of song sounded behind him and was echoed before him to the left where the alley narrowed. He must find a passage to the Temple Way or the river soon. He heard a faint splash and a swallowed curse as someone behind him stepped into a puddle left by the evening rain.

The alley's boundary was no longer wall but rough board beneath his hand. He stretched to find the top. By straining he could grasp it. He pulled himself up to balance momentarily like a prowling cat upon the splintery edge. Beyond was blackness.

He reversed his hold and, praying, let himself down into the muddy yard. Miraculously no dog barked and no stray object fell to raise a clamor in the night.

He held his breath and listened for the sound of footsteps in the alley. The man, unknowing and unseen, passed the yard where Alesander stood.

He considered the alternatives and liked neither: no time to double back and no exit visible from this yard to the street. He looked at the solid mass of building that filled the street side of the lot.

A far-off shout of, "Bring a lantern," spurred Alesander

to move, groping along the fence until a stone wall forced him to turn at the side of the yard. The faint glow of approaching lanternlight struck the upper story of the building, revealing no openings but shuttered third-story windows. There had to be a door. But he couldn't wait for his pursuers' light to reveal it.

His groping hand touched plank again—the fence to the neighboring yard, where the stone building at the rear would shield him from view from the alley. He hauled himself to the top and dropped onto the side of a woodpile that gave way under him, tumbling and clattering loud in the night. A shout came from the alley behind him as he scrambled to his feet.

Ahead he could see the faint glow of light reflected on a building side from the torches which lit the Temple Way.

He ran, heedless of noise, across the yard and into a narrow passage between buildings blocked at the street end by a tall iron gate. The gate was chained shut, but its ornamental filigree gave hand- and footholds enough to reach the spiked top.

Behind him wood clattered, and men cursed their footing as his pursuers dropped into the yard he had left.

The rusty spikes tore at Alesander's hands as he pulled himself atop the gate. He twisted and dropped into the street beyond. Late passersby stared. No way to mingle with the traffic, marked as he was with mud and rust and blood. His pursuers pounded down the passageway, to be brought up by the gate.

Alesander ran across the Temple Way, ducking into one of the narrow ill-lit lanes that led to the Great Square. He slowed to a fast walk at the square and paused in the shadow of the statue of Anderad in front of the Guildhall to rid his clothes of stains. Unfortunately the public fountain was in the circle of light thrown by the torches at Tredgett's door, and Fortune was too fickle to tempt audaciously.

He added gloves to his outfit and hoped that he had not carelessly rubbed mud or blood on his face. He shrugged, straightened his shoulders, and walked boldly across the square to the lane which connected with Old Wall Street. Just as he reached it he heard a whistle behind him, again a snatch of song. He kept walking, and the whistle echoed faintly from the north, the same phrase repeated.

Alesander crossed Old Wall Street and plunged into the maze of lanes to the west, an area crammed with small shops, taverns, and artisan's cottages. It was poorly lit. Only the taverns showed a torch or lantern against the night.

He worked north. The next test was to cross the lighted street that led to the Utran Gate. No whistle had sounded since Old Wall Street and, thinking back, he grasped part of their system. The first melody they had whistled was different from the rest—part of the refrain of "Heart's Ease"—and the man that had whistled that, Alesander knew, had seen him. But the other tune—did those whistlers only signal their positions to each other? He might have lost them. Best not let them pick up the trail again.

He swerved into the shadow of an ill-built shed and concentrated on changing the entire silhouette of his appearance. *Too bad I can't change my build.* He slumped deliberately under the weight of a homespun cloak and managed a shuffle to his gait as he stepped out again to the north.

He crossed the lighted street with no signal sounded west or east and continued north. *Tredgett must not have expected me to come this far east, but he will have men posted farther north. He knows I must pass a gate, and soon. There are fewer honest passersby as the night goes on, and any traveler will be conspicuous.*

The street turned west, paralleling the city wall. Alesander ducked into the dark arch of a recessed doorway as a party escorted by link-boys lit the otherwise ill-lighted street. The sooner he escaped the walled part of the city the better—best try the Tourneyfield Gate. The unregulated inns and taverns beyond it should keep a steady flow of traffic going through that gate no matter how late the hour.

He skulked in the shadows of a block of houses, waiting for a large enough crowd of would-be revelers to confuse any of Tredgett's men who might be waiting. Soon his watch was rewarded. He followed in the wake of a group of tipsy carolers, joining a badly sung chorus as the gate watch waved them through. He left the group hastily at the first lane west, heading for the Temple Way.

One more corner to turn and he would be in sight of Richenza's town house. Even Tredgett wouldn't have him attacked on the well-lighted and patrolled Outer Temple Way. He relaxed into a more normal gait.

Richenza.

What could he say to her when he saw her in the morning?

Why the attack that afternoon? He couldn't remember doing anything to cause it.

I don't understand it; I thought she liked me. You thought, a bitter inner voice reminded him, *that Lescina liked you, too.*

Someone whistled and suddenly many footsteps sounded up and down the cobbled lane. Alesander drew his dagger, unfastened his cloak, and put his back to the solid wall, cursing his inattention. He wasn't on the Temple Way yet; this was still a neighborhood where a body found in the morning street was little cause for comment.

Three men surrounded him, knives drawn. More were coming, silhouetted against the glow from the Temple Way. Alesander parried the thrust of the biggest man's knife, catching the blade in the folds of his cloak, then slashed out with his dagger at the knife hand of the man to the left. The man jumped back as Alesander edged along the wall.

The big man thrust again and grabbed for the cloak. Alesander pivoted to the right and slashed at the left-hand man. This time the man moved too late and Alesander's dagger cut him across the knife hand; he howled and dropped his knife.

Alesander backed up to the wall. One down, but two more coming. Alesander swung the cloak at his attackers' eye level. They retreated, still circling, while the third man groped left-handed for his knife.

The big man tired of waiting first and closed in with a roar, as his companion awaited the opportunity to thrust. Alesander tried to keep the big man's body in his partner's way while avoiding his knife. But the big man grabbed at his arm above the cloak and spun him around.

Alesander slashed at him, expecting a blow in his now-unprotected back. Instead there was the thud of a blow, and a body smashed into his. Alesander used the impact to drive a thrust into the big man's chest and spun around to face the new arrivals.

"Did they hurt you?" Garrett cleaned his dagger.

"No." Alesander started to shake.

Ulick returned from chasing the third attacker and dropped to his knees to search the bodies.

"Best if it looks like a robbery." Ulick took their purses and shook the contents of one into his hand. "Well, well, another of those pierced coins." He looked in the other purse. "And yet another."

"How did you turn up so opportunely?"

"We were watching Tredgett and saw you go into the Three Queens. There were a bunch of Tredgett's men skulking in the neighborhood, so Ellis thought it best to shepherd you home."

"So you were there all the time."

"No, we lost you somewhere near the Great Square. But since you had to pass one of the northern gates, Ellis set up watch there."

"Where is Ellis?" They started along the lane to the east.

"A bunch of Manrefians decided to play barber-the-Selinian with the wrong man and got their points cut instead." Garrett said.

"He wasn't hurt?"

Ulick continued the story. "No, it's not easy to fight someone with your breeks 'round your ankles. But they had Ellis down in an unpaved lane, and he was in no more fit condition to be seen in the street than you are." He took a look at Alesander in the light from an inn they passed. "In his case, though, it was mud. Come along."

They hurried him along, protesting, to a disreputable bathhouse and left him alone with a tub of hot water. A bronze mirror nailed to the wall confirmed Ulick's estimate of his appearance, and he quickly stripped and washed.

Garrett returned with a tankard of ale. "Ellis wants to talk to you. Wait here so as few people as possible see us together."

Alesander sat down, drank the ale, and contemplated the barren room. Time to think was the last thing he wanted. *Why did she act like that?* From an adjoining room came the smack of a hand on bare flesh and a woman's laugh.

I don't understand women. Alesander dropped his head on his hands. *Lessa smiled, she looked at me with wide brown eyes and said that it was nonsense.*

"I wouldn't have helped her if I didn't think the words were nonsense, 'Sander. It seemed to settle her mind. You know how much these killings have upset Mother. It was nonsense, wasn't it?" And Lessa had laughed and he with her although his heart had still been cold.

Two women's voices heard across a graveyard. Two women draped in black. Mumbled words. And his heart had stopped. *Nonsense, Gods, nonsense. Had she lied even then? Did she have a plan, she and Anelhar? Or did she take her chances as they came along?*

Did Lessa alone curse me? She, my twin, whom I trusted with my inmost thoughts? I should compare notes with Hamon on how it feels to be betrayed.

He looked up, startled from his thoughts as Ellis entered the room, his still-wet hair tied back.

"Quite a night for rescues." Ellis sat down. "I thought I could give you my report rather than rendezvous with Thomas." Garrett returned with ale. "Tell Walter that I've gotten a nibble from the palace. Two nibbles, in fact. One from Ewets and one from the king. The king of Arin is presenting himself as the true heir of the Rensel, and someone has advised Rozer to do the same. They can't get enough Rensel artifacts. I could even sell Garrett's chamber pot." He stretched his legs under the table. "All I need is the go-ahead from Walter. How are you going to get home?"

Alesander shrugged. "Walk in, in the morning."

"Tredgett's men might still be waiting. They seemed well organized and determined."

"You three can't risk being seen with me. I'll have to take the chance."

Ellis conferred with Garrett and Ulick. A moment later Garrett could be heard yelling, "Free ale for all!"

In the early-dawn light Alesander was escorted to Richenza's town house by thirty drunken singing revelers; the other Huntsmen inconspicuous in their midst. He had drunk enough himself that he didn't care at all.

*   *   *

Thomas moved a chess piece and smiled, as Walter considered it sourly. The rain had lowered Walter's mood.

"My game," Thomas said, "in two moves."

Walter pushed himself away from the table. "I wonder what's keeping Alesander."

"The rain, I imagine. From what we've heard the Three Queens is as congenial a place as any for waiting out foul weather."

"True. He hasn't shown much inclination to stay here of an evening."

Thomas, too wise to tell Walter what he thought really drove Alesander from the Lady Richenza's house, shrugged.

"Tarsit was his home; he likes to explore it. He still feels proprietary."

Someone was on the stairs.

"Michel," Walter told Thomas.

Michel dropped his sopping cloak. "We've been practicing Ewets's perishing masque all evening. The damned thing's to be presented tomorrow night, and he can't make up his mind what he wants us to say. Not that it matters; it's so bad no one's going to listen."

"I trust you haven't come just to complain about Ewets's literary failures."

"No, but I think I know how to keep him from committing any others."

Walter raised a skeptical eyebrow. "Explain."

"This masquerade is being held in honor of Ewets's birthday."

"So?"

"Gifts are in order." Michel perched on the arm of a chair and grinned. "Ewets is very fond of sweetmeats. We could give him some of Justin's very special ones."

"The masquerade is tomorrow night. Justin may not be ready."

"He is," Thomas interjected, "or he will be. I spoke with him this afternoon."

"It's very soon after the queen's death . . ."

"And it's only two nights until the new moon. Time is

too short for niceties. You've four people besides Leot to
kill.''

"True. But I still want to be sure of Justin. Shall we go
and find out?''

"Yes''—Justin didn't look up from his work, at Walter's
question—"it will be ready long before morning—if I'm
left alone.'' Thomas wondered if he referred to Walter and
Michel or to Bertz, who stood silently watching Justin's
every move. "You'll have to put it in something strongly
flavored.''

"Lasteel,'' Michel suggested. "Ewets is fond of it, and
it's got enough ginger in it to peel your tongue. Besides,
it's sticky already, so a little more liquid on top won't be
noticed. I'll put it in an antique box.''

"We had planned to make it look like Wendis's work,''
Walter pointed out.

"I've worked that out, too. As long as Justin's done as
told''—the alchemist ignored him, and Michel continued—
"and made two doses.''

They began to discuss details, and Thomas relaxed. Walter had apparently lost his doubts. Justin, Michel, and Walter could work out the rest themselves.

He decided that this was as good a time as any to perform
a small task of his own. He left Walter and Michel arguing
in the long gallery and went to the room where he ostensibly
slept and fetched something he had carefully hidden.
It was a sash—deep blue, with gold weights on the end, a
match to the bedgown that the Lady Richenza had worn
the night the queen was killed.

Without the sash her bedgown would have fallen open,
and he did not recall it so as she had followed Walter and
him upstairs that night. But he had found it in a corner of
one of the parlors, hours later, as if tossed aside and forgotten. By whom? Not Alesander; Thomas didn't think his
infatuation had gone that far. Not Walter, nor anyone else
in the house.

Shielding his candle Thomas peered out his bedroom
door, then crossed to Lady Richenza's drawing room and
sought an inconspicuous place to put the sash. His light or

some small sound must have betrayed him, for Richenza's door opened a crack.

"What is it? Has something—" She saw what he carried and her face reddened. "Annet has been looking for this. Where did you find it?"

"In the winter parlor. It was Hamon, of course. Did he hurt you?"

She shook her head, and, blushing again, blurted out, "I only went back because he was hurt. But he seemed to think . . ."

"I doubt that." Before she could misunderstand him, he explained, "I mean, Hamon sometimes feels more than he wants to, and he resents it. He meant to make you suffer as well. Walter depends too much on Hamon's not caring, but it seems to me that Hamon is like a man whose hands and feet have been frozen. At first he feels nothing, but when feeling returns it is all pain."

He shook his head. "I don't believe he was ever quite what Walter believes him to be. It was said in Amaroc, in my time, that he killed his sister because she plotted to kill him and his son, not because they had been lovers. At any rate, no harm was done to you?"

"No, I ran away."

He let you run away. Even if he had had only one good arm this girl was no match for Hamon. Hamon had acted, as he had thought, more to frighten her than out of any real desire to hurt.

"Don't dwell on it. Hamon should have no more business here."

15

Fourteenth Day—
The New Moon

Brian closed the door and breathed a sigh of relief. The morning spent helping Leot practice his lines for Ewets's masque had been nearly unbearable. Giving Leot the hero's part had merely served to invigorate Leot's already-robust self-opinion.

Perhaps Ewets hopes Leot will explode from an overinflated ego. Brian tried to recall where in this maze of a palace Abethell had said he'd be.

"Your Highness?" someone said, and Brian turned to find Reynard, in palace livery and carrying a lute, bowing to him.

"Your Highness, you said you'd hear me play when you had a moment free."

Walter sent messages as best he could.

"Of course." Brian turned to Martin, the omnipresent manservant that Abethell had set on him. "Find Lord Abethell, will you? I'll be—"

"There's a small withdrawing room, Your Highness," Reynard said. Send a cheeky boy to play a cheeky boy.

"There, I suppose."

When they were alone Reynard began to play. Brian listened critically for a few moments. Reynard played the classical piece surprisingly well.

Reynard spoke low enough to be covered by the music, "I've a message from Walter."

"I assumed as much." They both paused as Reynard executed a particularly intricate passage. "But I hadn't expected to see you here."

Reynard grinned without looking up. "When the king's guards went to search Haroc's shop they found me hiding there. They took me to the king, who questioned me and decided I was telling the truth when I said I'd not seen Haroc since before the banquet. The king was so pleased at what I'd helped him find out about the queen that he decided to keep me around. Besides, good jugglers are hard to find." The door opened, and Reynard raised his voice. "Do you like this piece or should I play another, Your Highness?" he asked as a servant passed through the room.

"Keep on." When they were alone again, he added, "What does Walter say?"

"Just a warning. Ewets is to be given a box of poisoned sweetmeats at the masquerade. It'll be in an antique wooden box. Don't eat any by mistake, or let anyone besides Ewets get them—especially before Ewets."

Brian marveled at Walter's dispatch—Queen Betrissa wasn't cold in her grave. Reynard continued playing.

"Where did you learn to play?"

"In Rayln. It was easier than cutting purses, more interesting than juggling, and I was getting too old to earn much begging."

"You're very good. Why steal when you could do better playing?"

Reynard met his eyes with adolescent contempt. "It just wasn't that easy."

"Easier than being hanged."

Reynard's concentration strayed long enough to cause a discord. "I suppose. But I wasn't the one who got hung—hanged."

"Apparently not."

Reynard played for a while, then cast Brian a sidelong glance. "You told Abethell that Payne had saved your life. Has anybody ever really saved you?"

Brian shook his head.

"Well, Randy and Ekata saved me. My parents died during Anderad's siege of Rayln, when I was barely old enough to walk. They took me in—they were beggars, players, thieves, whatever was easiest. I was little enough at first to get extra coins begging, and later I crawled in windows to unlock doors. When I got too big for that they made me lookout.

"I'd be dead if it weren't for them, and they wouldn't have wound up gallows-meat if they hadn't saved me, because I didn't keep watch well enough. That's why I'm here."

Brian thought about Abethell and what he himself was doing, and he didn't even have the excuse of gratitude—merely expediency.

He started to speak, but Martin returned with Abethell. Brian and Reynard rose, Reynard bowing.

"Keep up with your playing. I think it has gotten you much farther than the other."

He was gratified to see a quick flash of laughter in Reynard's eyes.

Brian could not have slept through Ewets's masque, but even had he been able to, he would have found the verse grating enough and the damned flapping trousers he wore distracting enough to keep him awake. But it was a relief not to be the center of attention; he felt silly in his costume, with its short jacket and full trousers.

Still, no matter how silly he felt, the players in Ewets's masque must feel more so. Their paned cotes with fluttering panels and dagged edges looked more like fools' motley than fancy dress. The ordinary Rensel soldiers looked ludicrous enough, but the Rensel royalty wore their cotes trimmed with enough bullion to sink a ship. To heighten the chaos the Rensel were green-clad, and the Sueve wore red so that the two armies clashed in color as well as battle.

The Rensel queen made her entrance, and Brian sat up and forgot about his trousers.

She was a slender woman with long, fair hair and a white pleated dress, transparent enough to reveal her bare arms. The woman from his dream; the one who had spoken to him!

He recalled the style of dress, too; that was the way the

Goddess Elun was always shown. That meant the woman in his dreams had been . . .

The woman onstage spoke, and Brian was disappointed, for the stilted, stumbling voice was certainly not the Goddess Elun's.

On closer scrutiny, this woman was much too thin, her cheekbones were too wide, and she was altogether too stiff to resemble a Rensel goddess. Even then it was several moments before Brian realized that the queen was played by the Princess Meriel.

He crossed his arms and paid attention to the masque with an even more critical ear. Yes, poisoning Ewets would be a service to the art of poetry.

If Brian had thought the Rensel queen's lines were bad, her lady-in-waiting's lines were even worse:

> "... the foeman reels
> Back from the valor of true Rensel Blades.
> Take heart, for from our leafy glades
> Come warriors of our vaunted blood
> And victory. . . ."

Michel, among the Rensel men, looked disgusted. The princess was dignified as usual when she wasn't speaking, but the red tinge to her cheeks told Brian that the revealing Rensel dress and unbound hair embarrassed her.

The masque ended, its smug moral intact. Since that moral concerned the nature of true nobility, its being written by a descendent of the ultimate conqueror of the Rensel made it more than a little ambiguous.

The performers had begun the closing dance. Brian found entertainment in his neighbors' attempts to find something good to say about Ewets's verse. He supposed he would have to be polite about it eventually, but he, at least, was not trying to curry favor with Ewets.

Brian realized that all Ewets's cronies were dressed in varying shades of the "Rensel" green, and in his red and blue he felt conspicuous. Worse, he found the similarity between his costume and that of the Sueve disconcerting.

Be patient, and don't eat the sweetmeats.

The players broke their couples to draw partners from

the audience. They still wore their stage garb, but had donned the required masks. Ewets's was a copy of an antique drama mask and Wendis's was as gaudy as his costume—a floriate beast mask with a lolling tongue. Only Leot went bare-faced.

Brian looked for Meriel. She was apart from the others. He suspected that she had been instructed to look for him, but held back from presenting himself. He would be obliged to make some comment on the masque, and she must know how wretched both it and her performance had been.

Ewets, still basking in literary glory, saw Brian and abandoned the simpering girl he was dancing with.

He clapped Brian on the shoulder. "Well, what did you think of my masque?"

"It was unique."

Ewets smiled, and Brian wondered if Ewets could be as stupid as he seemed, or did he save the half-truths and concealed insults, biding his time until he was king?

"Let's leave this press," the prince said. "I've a bottle of excellent wine waiting." Brian could find no polite way to refuse.

At the door, still in his beast mask, Wendis met them. The youngest prince did not speak, trying to preserve the facade of anonymity. He bowed with a flourish and handed Ewets a box.

Ewets thanked his brother without looking away from the present, a box carved with roses and fylfots. Ewets did not notice as Wendis straightened up.

Brian began to comment on the gift and then he met the eyes behind the mask—green eyes, not blue. Michel, not Wendis. Those green eyes narrowed with amusement, acknowledging Brian's recognition, then Michel disappeared into the crowd.

Brian looked at the box in Ewets's hands, a carved antique wooden box, as Reynard had warned him. Ewets opened the box to reveal that it was full of sticky, little lumps of nuts and spices and poison.

I seem to have incredibly bad timing.

Before he could think of a plausible excuse for abandon-

ing Ewets before he ate any of the lasteel, Brian was ushered into the passageway.

"I must know," Ewets babbled, "what you thought of
the imagery in Althiel's speech just before the final battle.
I was trying to echo—" He broke off to peer at a white-
gowned figure ahead of them.

"Meriel," he called, an edge to his voice, and his sister,
with obvious reluctance, turned to him.

"I was just going to—"

"To what? I *did* order you not to change after the
masque." A fool might think the bantering note in Ewets's
voice teasing, but Brian heard something less amusing.

So did Meriel, but she did not protest as Ewets caught
her elbow tightly. "Come, have a little wine with us, sister.
Shall I send for Wendis and Leot?"

She paled and shook her head. "No, please."

"Come along then." He gave her a push and guided her
roughly to his parlor, with its tapestries of scenes from Rensel myth.

In a moment Ewets's mood changed; he was chortling
over his masque, his past poetry, and his future plans, but
every so often he would look at his sister as he spoke, and
she would shrink farther into her chair. She was frightened
and silent, her hands twisting nervously.

Brian found himself trying not to look anywhere, simul-
taneously maintaining an air of interest in what Ewets was
saying, and pretending total ignorance of what passed between the princess and her brother. He tried to avoid looking at the sweetmeats. Instead, he stared fixedly at Ewets,
the lapdogs, and the tapestries. To leave too abruptly would
cast suspicion on himself when Ewets did finally eat the
lasteel.

". . . Eighty-six stanzas. You must read it sometime,"
Ewets beckoned to the hovering servant. "Pour the wine."

Brian started to refuse; he did not want to drink with this
man, then thought better of it. It had better be plain that
the sweetmeats were poisoned, not the wine, since the
blame was to be laid on Wendis.

"Meriel?" Ewets offered a goblet to his sister.

"N-no, thank you, Ewets. I should go back." She started
to rise, but Ewets pushed her into the chair.

"Have something to drink, little sister." Ewets waved the goblet at her, the dangerous edge back in his voice. Her shaking hand fumbled, and she splashed Ewets's satin sleeve.

Everyone froze like the figures in the tapestries—the terrified girl in Rensel dress, the livid and somehow triumphant Ewets in his antique garb. The wine was red as blood, and Brian was reminded of some old tale of murder.

"You stupid bitch." Ewets spoke deliberately, as if he had been awaiting the opportunity. Meriel lifted her arm as if to ward off a blow.

Ewets dragged her out of the chair, shrilly screaming at her, "You stupid little bitch, can't you do anything right?"

He slapped her, and Meriel tried to fend off the blows. "Ewets, please, not now—not while—"

Ewets shook her sharply. "Shut up. You can't do anything. You ruined my masque, you couldn't remember your lines, you couldn't even say them right." His eyes narrowed maliciously. "You can't even wear the dress right—skinny little bitch."

Unbelievable. Brian tried to decide what to do. No wonder Meriel quailed every time she saw any of her brothers.

"Prince Ewets," he began, but Ewets wouldn't be distracted.

"Yes, you're just too scrawny." Ewets looked down at the box of sweetmeats and smiled. Brian stiffened, guessing what he planned. Ewets twisted Meriel's arm behind her back. She gasped in pain as Ewets grabbed a fistful of the sticky lasteel.

"Little sister, we need to fatten you up."

"Don't let anyone but Ewets get the sweetmeats," Walter had ordered, as if the princess's expression was not reason enough to end this.

"Stop that!" Brian knocked the sweetmeats from Ewets's hand to the floor.

Ewets turned on him. "How dare you?"

"How dare you, you fat slug! She's your sister—a princess. Not even you have the right—"

"I have any right I please," Ewets spluttered, and having squared off against Brian, heedlessly let go of Meriel.

"And, if you expect me to support any alliance with us, you'd better mind your own business."

"That's not your place to say. You aren't King of Tarsia yet."

"Neither are you—yet."

Presumably, Ewets meant that Brian was not yet King of Canjitrin; Brian was struck by the urge to laugh. Standing there, fists clenched, they were too much like young boys starting a brawl, even to the customary boasting and belittling.

A strange, small noise made them look under the table.

One of the lapdogs was being sick; it stood stiff-legged in the midst of the scattered lasteel. Beside it, its mate lay still, dead or nearly so.

Justin does his work well.

"Haldan's Shield!" said Ewets, as what had happened slowly dawned on him, "Wendis tried to kill me."

Meriel made a small sound much like the dog, and, ashen-faced, fled the room.

Two princes stared at one dead dog and the final twitching of a second. Ewets sat heavily in a chair.

"Do you want me to get someone?"

Ewets shook his head. "No. Wendis won't go anywhere, and it won't do to start a scandal now."

That's right. Beating your sister in front of strangers is acceptable, but it won't do to accuse your brother of murder during a party.

Brian shrugged; let Ewets deal with the mess.

"I shall go back to the others."

"As you wish. Gods. Wendis," he muttered to himself. "Leot—but Wendis?"

Brian paused in the passageway to regain his scattered wits. That plan had failed. He should pass word to Michel—no, this was too public, and Michel might be suspect. Word would get out soon enough.

At least he'd saved the plan from total disaster. The princess might have been fed the poison by mistake, and if she had—

Theyad Haldan! She'd be dead, and dead with no possible blame on anyone but Wendis. Brian almost groaned aloud. The perfect chance, and he had lost it. If he had kept his hands to himself, his part would be painlessly over.

First he'd let himself be recognized, now this. Walter would have his hide if he found out.

Which he might not. Ewets would undoubtedly tell someone about the poisoning, but would he admit that he had found out while force-feeding his sister? No, Walter needn't find out yet. Maybe sometime Brian would mention it in passing. "You remember that princess I was supposed to murder in Tarsit . . . ?"

Brian stopped himself; he was letting his thoughts run wild. He straightened, took his blue-velvet mask from his belt, smoothed his rumpled scarlet sleeves, and started into the ballroom.

"Your Highness?" a familiar voice called to him; a young boy stood in the shadows. Brian almost addressed him as Reynard, before he realized that it couldn't be; this boy was shorter, and thinner, with a triangular, solemn face, and brown hair peeking from under his cap. The boy came farther into the light before Brian knew who it was.

"Princess Meriel?" She smiled just a little. "I didn't expect you to return." "Come as you aren't" had been the theme, and she had taken it literally, even to hiding her light hair under a short wig.

"I-I wanted to thank you." She bit her lip. "If you hadn't stopped Ewets . . . I should have before, but—but when I thought what almost happened I—"

"Believe me, I fled that room as soon as I could myself."

She shook her head once as if angry with herself. "No, it was no excuse—you were kind." She frowned as if the word were unfamiliar.

Kind? He'd just been kicking himself because he hadn't let her die, and here she was thanking him. Where had he ever got the idea that he was becoming accustomed to this new life of his?

Nevertheless, he inclined his head courteously, acknowledging her thanks, and she automatically held out a thin pale hand. He kissed it lightly, and, still holding it, turned to look into the ballroom. Musicians were playing "When Spring is crowned with love all blooming," a basse dance.

"How much gossip would there be, I wonder, if the visiting prince were seen dancing with a young boy?"

Her eyes widened, and then for the first time in a long time, he thought, she laughed.

16

Fifteenth Day

". . . Four hundred bales of pelts at Treloum waiting to be shipped to Morthrell.'' The clerk went down the list. ''Of which forty bales are beaver, six stoat, four sable, and ten lynx. The rest are medium grade; mainly mink and other weasels. Some fox . . .'' He broke off as Prince Leot entered.

''Don't stop for me,'' Leot said to Tredgett, who had risen and started to dismiss his clerk. Leot wandered over to the cupboard to examine the plate displayed there.

Tredgett and his clerk exchanged startled glances. Usually the prince demanded immediate attention. Tredgett finished his business quickly. ''Have all the bales brought to the main warehouse in Tarsit. Tell Peason to select the best pelts for sale here and have the rest shipped upriver for the winter season. The fox might sell well at Rayln. See what Peason thinks.''

The clerk bowed his way out.

Tredgett studied Leot, who was hefting a gilt ewer as though estimating its worth. Tredgett finally prompted, ''Yes, Your Highness.'' Let him broach the subject, there was no accepted way to commiserate about an attempt to poison one's brother. Especially when the attempt had failed.

164

Leot put the ewer down. "Now I understand why you were so upset about Wendis's absence during the Maldrin business. You needed him here for your alternate plan."

Tredgett hesitated, then said nothing.

Leot smiled and shook his head. "You really think up some good ones. Poisoning Ewets and letting Wendis take the blame. You were right; the plot with Nele was crude. I bow to a master. Too bad the lapdogs got it instead."

"These little accidents happen," said Tredgett, feeling his way through the pitfalls of Leot's temper.

But Leot was not setting traps. "What do we try next?"

"I hadn't quite decided, Your Highness." Tredgett changed the subject to give himself time to think. "I assume that things are in a uproar at the palace?"

"Haldan! They act like a flock of geese; Ewets squawking more than any. He has a food taster now. You'll have to use a poison that takes longer next time." Leot perched on the edge of the desk and gave a detailed account of affairs at the palace, chortling over his brothers' actions.

Tredgett half listened. If Leot hadn't done it, who had? It was so much in his interest. Who else would it help? Arin? Possibly, if it sowed distrust and discord in Tarsia. Neither Ewets nor Wendis had enemies rabid enough for murder.

"Next time . . ." Leot was saying. *Next time*! Tredgett cut in. "Your Highness, have you heard anything from your cousins of Wolves' Hold?"

"They asked me to the boar hunting as usual. Pity I can't go, but the combat should be as enjoyable. Why?"

"I just wondered. No rumors of unrest? No feuds or riots?"

"No. Should there be?"

"No. This Sir Walter Martling from Mentorz has me worried. So convenient that he should show up. And his secretary has a southern accent. I wondered if Arin was stirring up separatist feeling in Irkeldra. That's easy enough to do. Though nothing serious has erupted since your parents' marriage, it could happen again."

Leot snorted. "It won't while I'm alive. Why put up a pretender when they can have a true heir of Wolves' Hold on the throne? You see Arinese plots everywhere."

"Perhaps. But all Arinese plots are not phantoms. Read this." Tredgett rescued a report from the pile Leot had been idly riffling.

Leot reddened as he read. "He ought to be impaled for the deserter he is! Receiving envoys from Arin! Wait till Father hears about this."

"I want you to speak to your father. Unfortunately, since Lord Spurstow was raised with him, the king won't let himself be convinced that any treason was intended."

"Senile fool."

"I think the quickest, surest way to get a reliable governor at Iskandroc is to promote Spurstow elsewhere. Rayln, perhaps. He's unlikely to plot with Feracher; he's never forgiven him for the third of the Vekin inheritance he lost. I think you can persuade your father to promote his old friend to *High* Governor of Rayln."

"It should be. But who do we put in at Iskandroc?"

"Dorenton?" Tredgett suggested, then continued as Leot frowned. "No, what about the younger Chuskis, Karlinian? He's a fine soldier, and he hates Arin. King Ludvik humiliated him in a tournament fifteen years ago."

Leot considered. "He's not the man to forget a grudge. And he's as scrupulous as an old virgin about his honor." He slid from his perch on the desk. "I think I can get Father to agree."

"As soon as possible."

"He can announce it at the betrothal banquet. He's going to hand out less deserved honors."

Leot turned at the door. "Pity, that means we'll have to put off our other plans till then."

Only a frail sliver of moon had set last night, and tonight even that was gone.

Rensel legend said that when the moon was in Anchytel's charge it was gone from the sky because Anchytel, being Goddess of the Earth, walked there rather than above.

But to Walter the moon's hidden face seemed a reproach and a warning. Half his time was gone, and half his task should have been finished. But it wasn't, and his carefully constructed plans were threatened as a tower is by undermining.

First, Alesander had been attacked in the street by men who carried Firmin Tredgett's token. That attack had failed, but Tredgett would try again. If Alesander were injured, who would fight Leot? A number of Huntsmen were capable jousters, but almost all were accounted for in this.

Well, I can fight the combat, if necessary.

But that was not the worst; before dawn Reynard had brought word from Michel. The attempt to poison Ewets had failed; Reynard knew little more. It was plain that some upset had occurred; the king and his sons had been closeted together after the masque. Reynard hadn't learned any details—those few who had attended on the Royal Family were close-mouthed.

The day passed slowly, newslessly. He sent men to the marketplace, to taverns, to shops, to anywhere gossip about a crisis in the palace might be heard. But whatever had happened in the palace had not spread beyond its walls. All, seemingly, was serene in Tarsit.

And Michel, the only one of his men who could answer his questions, had not shown his face outside those unspeaking palace walls.

The sun was long set, and Walter, frustrated almost beyond bearing, sent Michel a mental summons that should have brought him from his grave. He tried to reason the problem out, to plan around the gaping nothing of "What happened?"

A stir in the palace had been carefully concealed. Rozer had tried to conceal the manner of his wife's death; was it possible that family honor would have him try to hide one son's attempt to murder another? Was Wendis locked up somewhere in the palace to discreetly die of another "sudden illness"?

And Michel, did his absence mean he was suspected? No, Reynard heard no hint of suspicion, and if Michel did nothing else, he'd meticulously assure his own safety.

Damn it, where was he? How had he failed to kill Ewets?

Gods, maybe Hamon was right—go in, do what you're ordered. Never mind subterfuge. Leave whatever havoc you've wrought to be dealt with by the survivors.

Walter rubbed his eyes. If only it could be that simple.

How could they, by quick violent means, have forced a

duke to prosecute his favorite? That had been the task last
time, and there had been no simple solution. How could
they have recovered the Talisman of Facry that way or—

Even now it wouldn't work. How could they lure Leot
into the judicial combat after his family had been slaughtered? Put in those terms it was ludicrous.

Poison had gone astray before. It seemed so easy; have
Justin add a little of this to a little of that and the job was
done. Except when it wasn't. And Justin always drank more
then. Maybe it was better not to trust poison; maybe that
would let Justin heal. The man was only five months from
his nightmare. Walter himself, had he been prone to excess,
might—

He could almost feel the clap of Amloth's hand on his
shoulder. "You think too much."

How could he succeed if he didn't think? He wasn't Amloth—never could be.

Walter tried to fit the few pieces he had together in another way, knowing he needed more information.

Where was Michel?

On the stairs, Walter knew, at last.

"I nearly spilled wine in Ewets's precious lap with that
last call." Michel dropped into the chair nearest the fire.

"Where have you been?"

"At the palace; I was with Wendis when everything
broke loose, and I couldn't get away at first; later I thought
I'd better stay."

"Explain from the beginning."

Thomas had followed Michel into the small withdrawing
room and sat in an inconspicuous corner as Michel began
to speak.

"I delivered the poisoned lasteel as we'd arranged—I
changed into Wendis's costume, and presented the box to
Ewets. Everything seemed to be working. Brian and three
or four of Ewets's toadies were right there to see 'Wendis'
give Ewets the box. To get Wendis out of the way I'd bet
him that he wouldn't disobey Ewets's express orders to
remain in his masque dress. So when I saw him slip out of
the ballroom before I did my act with the box, I thought
that everything was set, but I should have known better
when I saw Wendis again. He hadn't changed clothes. But

Ewets didn't come back to his precious party, and that boded well. I tried to catch Brian's eye to find out what happened after he and Ewets left, but I couldn't.'' Michel grinned knowingly. ''Do you want to know why that was now or later?''

''Later.''

''I went to Wendis's rooms with him when everyone had cleared out. But about the time I was thinking of dosing his wine a servant came and said that His Majesty requested Prince Wendis to attend on him. That sounded good—I was sure then that Ewets had been found. Then everything fell apart.''

''How?''

''After he chased the man out Wendis said, 'You know when I left the party just after the dancing started? I was off with Lady Marika, and I'm afraid that her husband's found out and complained to Father.'

''That meant that he had a witness who could swear that he hadn't been the one who'd given Ewets the box, so I told him that I'd go with him and say I'd been with him all evening. That way I could find out what happened, and if there were any chance that Wendis still might be blamed for the poisoning I would be with him and might have an opportunity to give him the poison.'' He looked brightly at Walter, expecting praise, but Walter merely nodded.

''Well, we get there and there sits Rozer and next to him sits Ewets, looking like a cat who's cornered the wrong mouse. It's pretty plain that Wendis is in trouble; Rozer looks like he's on his way to all his grandfathers' funerals.

''Wendis takes one look at Rozer and Ewets, and says, 'Whatever you think I did, Tazelar here was with me all evening.' Of course they knew then that he had done *something*, and Ewets turns bright red and makes noises like he's choking. Rozer, meanwhile looks at me bowing and scraping, and asks, 'Young man, were you with my son when he presented a box of sweetmeats to His Highness?' 'Sweetmeats?' I say, all curls and big eyes. 'Sweetmeats,' Ewets says. 'The ones he tried to poison me with.' 'Poison?' Wendis squeaks. He looks at Ewets, then at Leot— did I tell you Leot was there?''

''No. Go on.''

"Wendis says he doesn't know anything about any poison, then he turns to me. 'Tazelar, tell them you were with me the whole time.' But I thought that even if Ewets was still alive it might be possible to pin the blame on Wendis anyway, so I back off and say, 'Your Highness, I can't lie for you if it's murder. Your Majesty, he wasn't with me for about an hour just after the masque.' Rozer looks down at Wendis, who was squirming by then. 'Well?' he asks, and Wendis confesses that he'd been with the Lady Marika. Somebody goes looking for her and eventually comes back with her and her husband.

, "When the king asks her if she'd been alone with Prince Wendis that evening she goes all virtuous and says she's a married woman and how could she have possibly done anything like that? Wendis goes dead white and Leot is snickering.

"Just then Claverdon, the king's steward who's hanging around in the background, clears his throat. Claverdon says he'd be more inclined to believe the lady if he hadn't caught her in a 'compromising' position with one of the liveried gentlemen not a week ago. At this point both Lady Marika and her husband are the same shade of red. The lady looks down at the floor and admits she'd been 'conversing' with Wendis at the time everyone saw Ewets given the box."

"That accounts for last night, what kept you today?"

"I'm not finished with last night. Rozer is obviously relieved, and starts to dismiss everyone, until Ewets howls, 'Someone just tried to poison me.' Rozer tells him not to worry, they'll get to the bottom of this. Ewets doesn't like that, and goes on whining, 'And what am I to do in the meantime—starve?' He keeps this up for a while until Claverdon butts in again. 'Why don't you appoint someone to be your food taster?' Ewets likes this idea, and he looks around, trying to think of someone. I'm trying to blend in with the paneling; Rozer doesn't like family squabbles spread abroad. But Ewets lights on me, and says, "Tazelar, you'll do.' So I'm food taster to His Royal Highness. Since he's stuffing his face most of the time, that's where I've been all day. I had to wait until he had his bedtime tipple."

Regrettably both targets had survived, but a new plan

presented itself. It was easy to have the taster do the poisoning; the trick was making it look as if another had done it.

"You've done well insinuating yourself."

Michel was beaming. "The food is excellent, and I get served first. All through supper everyone watched me—even Rozer. I'm to move into the palace. Will it do?"

Walter regretted the impulsive compliment. "What about Wendis? Have you alienated him?"

"Nothing I can't mend. I'll say that I took the position to discover Ewets's plans."

"Have you any inkling of how Ewets found out about the poison?"

"I asked Ewets's man and he stiffened up, but finally admitted that the lapdogs had eaten the lasteel before Ewets."

Walter scowled. "Does that mean that Ewets suspected something and tested his sweetmeats on them first?"

"No, it means that Ewets spoiled the damned dogs. They were almost better fed than I am."

"I see. Thomas, go and—"

As always when he had gossip to impart Michel was impatient. "Don't you want to hear about Brian?"

"All right." He'd get no peace until Michel had purged himself of news.

"Everyone at the palace is still chattering about it. I told you that Brian went out of the ballroom with Ewets? Well, when he came back he wasn't alone. He was escorting a pretty young boy he danced with the entire evening!"

Walter raised one eyebrow.

"You could hear the whispering over the music, then it came time to unmask. The boy didn't want to at first, but Brian said something and the boy took off his mask and wig and turned out to be the Princess Meriel."

Very very good. The Prince of Canjitrin was managing his affair well.

"There's more. I spent the whole day in Ewets's wake, and this afternoon he waited on Rozer. The king said he'd summoned him to tell him that he had agreed to the betrothal of Brian and Meriel.

"Ewets didn't like the idea. He mentioned the princess's

betrothal to Daimiron; that it wasn't certain that Brian could reclaim his throne, and I forget what all. None of his arguments held water, even Rozer saw that. Eventually Rozer got irritated with Ewets, and Ewets was obliged to shut up. Anyway Brian had been sent for, and Rozer said that Abethell had said that Prince Brian desired to start for Canjitrin within two weeks, before the snows closed the faster route. So, Rozer was planning the betrothal banquet for two or three days from now, and the wedding a few days later."

Michel grinned. "I know another reason Rozer's in such a hurry." Walter didn't like encouraging Michel's gossip, but sometimes valuable information could be gleaned from it.

"After Ewets had buttered him up, Rozer started to get maudlin. He kept talking about how lonely it was being a widower. Then he finally cheered up and admitted that he had decided not to remain unmarried for the rest of his life—'the few years remaining to me' is how he phrased it. Ewets didn't like that idea any better than the other marriage plan, but he scraped up enough tact to be polite about it. He asked who Rozer had in mind, but the king got coy. He said Ewets would learn soon enough. He had to make arrangements before he made any announcements."

"So you've no idea who he's considering?"

"No, his wedding plans haven't even become gossip. Does it matter? He's not likely to get that far."

"Keep your ears open."

After a day of no news this glut was overwhelming. Walter tried to digest it all.

Poison had proved as undependable a tool as Eleylin had declared, but luck had offered them as foolproof a method of administering it as could be imagined. The failure had done damage, though, but how much?

"Michel, does the king share Ewets's fear of being poisoned?"

"He doesn't eat until after I do. I don't know whether he's got someone sampling his food when I'm not around, but I think he's nervous."

After Ewets and Wendis died, poison was not going to work a third time.

He considered the problem for a few more minutes, then looked up. Michel had left.

"Thomas, you'll have to tell Justin that we need the same amount of the poison we just used and an antidote if one can be contrived."

"And if it can't?"

"Then have him make something for which it can. Whatever it is it needs to be done quickly, in two or three days."

"The betrothal banquet?"

"Easier to forget a person's movements when he's in a crowd, and many convenient things can be remembered after a suicide. Go after Michel and tell him to send word when the date for the betrothal banquet is set."

Thomas could hear Justin's rarely raised voice halfway down the hall. Walter had neglected to keep sufficient track of Michel, who had taken the opportunity to visit his gossip on the apothecary.

"What do you mean," Justin said, "the poison failed? It should have been more than sufficient for Ewets and half his household!"

"Well, it wasn't," Michel said as Thomas came into the stillroom. Arms folded, Bertz stood between Michel and Justin as if to forestall violence.

Thomas judged it wise to break in. "It seems that the poison went astray before Ewets took any of the sweetmeats."

Justin regarded him blankly for a second, then shrugged. "I can't help that." He picked up a flask, then stopped. "Who did take it?" His knuckles were white around the neck of the flask.

Before Michel could answer and make the problem worse, Thomas intervened. "Lapdogs. Ewets fed them some of the lasteel."

Justin relaxed, put the flask down, and took up another. "If Michel can't carry out orders better than that, I can't be held responsible."

Michel started to protest but stopped as Bertz's hand tightened on his shoulder.

"I'm afraid," Thomas said as offhandedly as he could

manage, "that Walter needs you to make more of the same."

Justin snorted. "Naturally. What guarantee is there that this plan won't fail, too?"

Thomas had almost forgotten what speaking to a sober Justin was like.

"Well, it seems that Michel has gotten himself in a good position to administer the poison so it won't go astray—he's become Ewets's food taster."

Michel shrugged off Bertz's restraining hand, displeased that Thomas had given away his news.

Justin said, "So the brat'll have to take the poison with the prince, or does Walter want him beheaded for treason?"

Michel, unable to stay silent longer, burst out, "Walter says you're to have an antidote."

"Well, there's none that I know of, if he insists on the same as before."

"He said not."

"That's the soonest prepared for his purposes. How much time have I for concocting it?"

"Two or three days."

"No more?" Justin scowled. "There is always oil taken beforehand as we used in Saroth."

"No!" Michel exploded. "I won't drink that stuff again. It makes me ill, and they'll get suspicious if I'm sick before Ewets takes his wine."

"Well"—Justin didn't sound concerned—"the poison doesn't work quickly. You won't develop symptoms until Ewets has finished his wine. You'll just be another victim of the prince's assassin."

Michel went rigid. "I won't do it!"

Justin turned on him with the impatience characteristic of his sober moments. "Well, little man, would you rather burn? It's no matter to me!"

Michel's face was scarlet, so Thomas stepped in. "Walter needs him healthy. He's an excellent spy, and he has to be well enough to forge the note from Wendis and slip him the extra poison."

"Then he'll have to try to dose Ewets's wine or food unseen." Justin searched his worktable. "That's not my problem."

"A ring?" Thomas suggested.

"No." Michel nervously straightened his cote and pulled at the sleeves. "Too common. Even Rozer'd suspect me if I'm seen wearing a ring. Besides, I've never seen a poison ring that would stand up to scrutiny. And Rozer'll want to find an outside assassin."

The room was silent, except for the noise of Justin's work. Bertz, almost forgotten, broke the silence.

"Is that what you'll be wearing when Walter wishes the poison administered?"

Strange question; Bertz's indifference to fashion was a joke.

"This? No. It'll likely be livery for me by then. I don't fancy myself in blue, but—"

"Will it have these buttons? The ones on the sleeves?" Michel's dark green sleeves each had a couple of dozen gold buttons marching down the forearm.

"Buttons?"

"Yes, buttons." Bertz caught Michel's arm. "These foolish things."

"Of course." Michel pulled away. "They're fashionable."

"Couldn't the poison be concealed in one or two of these? No one would notice; he constantly plays with them." Michel stopped fingering the buttons as if they had grown red-hot. "It took very little poison for the sweetmeats. Would not one, or perhaps two, hold enough?"

Justin considered the buttons.

"Yes, two, or four if you want enough to use that method on both princes."

"It won't work," Michel said. "How am I to get them open and closed?"

"Let me see one." Ignoring Michel's protests, Bertz wrenched a button off. "It would be simple." He studied them a few minutes. "They are only two half spheres, already hollow. All that needs to be done is to break the button apart, and fill it with poison. It would be no work to pull apart one that is not sealed, and just as simple to squeeze it back together if we used wax on the edges. I could prepare them easily." He looked up at Thomas. "Do you think Walter would approve?"

Thomas was already nodding. "There shouldn't be any problem."

As he left Justin and Bertz discussing ways and means he breathed a small sigh of relief. That was one less burden on Walter, who was beginning to stagger under the load.

17

Sixteenth Day

In fourteen nights he would disappear. Brian anticipated the event with impatience. The king of Tarsia, having decided to permit the king of Canjitrin—Rozer and Abethell had agreed that Brian's assumption of that title was essential to the negotiations—to marry his only daughter, had summoned his relations and retainers to hear the great news. The formal betrothal would take place in two days, but the informal fuss had begun; it made Brian nervous.

The princess was not the problem. She was as silent and aloof as she had ever been except for the night of the masque. No, the reason for Brian's discomfort was everyone else.

They kept calling him "Your Majesty," which made him jump, and usually made him think that Rozer was being addressed. Rozer doted on him like an old hen with one chick. Abethell was more discreet, as befitted his station, but he preened like a peacock. Ewets glowered. Leot managed to seem both uninterested and calculating. Wendis's boredom was a relief. The various lesser nobles and retainers were a source of embarrassment merely by their presence.

After half an hour of dubious revelry Rozer rose from his place. "I think that although the betrothal isn't official, it is permissible to leave the young couple alone together. I'm sure they have much to discuss.''

Haldan! The man is simpering!

But, as the last retainer filed out of the room, Brian relaxed. His almost-betrothed retreated even farther into herself. Before, the princess had kept her gaze confined to a spot on the wall. Now she looked down at her hands, as if afraid Brian might insinuate himself into her line of sight.

A few nights ago she had danced with him, and, disguised and unrecognized, she had been a shy but charming companion. Now she resembled a chastised serving girl.

Conversely, she was almost pretty today. On their other encounters her clothes had been maddeningly wrong—either cut to emphasize her thinness, or of a color which made her look paler and more sallow than she was. Today she was delicate in a gown of cream satin embroidered in gold under a rose-silk overgown dagged at the bottom like the petals of a flower.

She would not look at him; expecting her to speak first was out of the question.

''Do you dislike the idea of this marriage?''

The less than tactful query startled her into looking at him. How could such golden brown eyes look panicked?

''Oh, no!'' she began, ''I—not at all.'' She stopped, then began again with an effort. ''You—you see, Canjitrin is very far away from Tarsia.'' The countries bordered each other, but Brian understood. ''It is you who have cause to regret this marriage.''

''I think not,'' Brian answered quietly, puzzled.

She started to look at her hands again but resolutely met his eyes instead. ''After—after what Father said, you must have some doubts about—about me.''

''When?'' Brian asked.

''The night that Betrissa—When he spoke of Nele Indes.''

The name Indes raised a panic in Brian, until he recalled the words of which she spoke.

''Your father was angry. I do not count anything he said that night.''

''But it was true, you will hear it from someone else—

Nele Indes was in my rooms that morning.''

He began to protest, but she shook her head to stop him. Whatever this story was she was determined to tell it.

She summoned the fortitude to continue looking at him. ''It was just past dawn; the noise he made running into my rooms woke me. So many guards had been diverted to ambush Nele in Father's rooms that no one was outside mine. Nele came running in; I'd never seen anyone so frightened.'' Her knuckles were white where she clenched her hands together. ''He begged me to hide him. I could already hear the guards in the hall. Armed as he was I knew he must have done something terrible. Leot and Father had been close about something for days, and I knew that it must have been about what they were doing to Nele.

''I couldn't hide him. Leot and Father—Leot's no better than Ewets, worse, and some days Father suspects everyone. I knew''—she paused to swallow—''I knew they'd find Nele whatever I did and if they realized I'd hidden him, they'd kill me as well. So I called the guards. Leot had them behead Nele in the courtyard outside my rooms, to be sure I was there to—to see.''

She closed her eyes. ''I liked him. He wasn't like Leot's other friends. I didn't want him to die, but I was so afraid . . .'' Her voice trailed off in shame, and she looked at her hands again.

''Surely you don't blame yourself—''

''I should have helped him.''

''And died? I've seen your father and brothers at work. I believe they would have killed you.''

It didn't matter that she hadn't helped Indes. She was to be killed for not aiding him as surely as if she had.

I wish all this were over and done with. I wish the bloody moon were full.

But that wasn't true; day by day, it was the Hunt that seemed unreal, not this betrothal. He looked out the window and saw the moon, pale as Meriel in the day sky, and realized that it had begun its waxing.

He began talking to his almost-wife quickly about the weather, the wedding, and little things to make her laugh.

* * *

"I told you." Eleylin sat down opposite Walter. "Poison doesn't work."

"I should think," Thomas interjected, "that the problem was that it worked too well."

Walter shook his head. "That's not the point."

"What is the point?" Eleylin demanded.

"I want to discuss your plan."

"This hasn't just been a study of comparative antiquities markets?"

"I think your plan might work—but not as you envisioned it. I've told you my reasons for rejecting it." Eleylin nodded, his eyes less accusing. "Alesander told me that you have two buyers—Ewets and Rozer." Eleylin made no comment. "We have a plan which should dispose of Ewets. We still have two men, possibly three, in the palace and well placed to ensure success one way or another."

"So you want me to make Rozer the target," Eleylin finished impatiently. "Isn't he a little old to take the bait?"

"On the contrary, he is considering remarrying and having had one wife stray because of his—" He groped for a word.

"Inattention?" Thomas supplied.

"I should think," Eleylin put in, "the problem was too much attention."

Walter ignored them. "At any rate, Rozer should be all the more eager to 'take the bait.'"

"Reikos! He's got three sons already. How many more does he want?"

"He won't have three sons by then. Our plans for Ewets and Wendis should be put into effect in two nights. Approach him as soon as you think he will be responsive."

"In other words, give him time to realize that he has but one son left."

"A son who is committed to a judicial combat with unrebated weapons."

"Yes, it should work, providing your plans for Ewets and Wendis are successful. When do you want the final killing to take place?"

"Late, as late as possible, so that Leot cannot cancel the judicial combat." Walter steeled himself; Eleylin wouldn't be as amenable to the next change as to the last. "The subject of Leot leads me to the main objection to the plan. Namely, that Rozer's murder would obviously be the work of an outside assassin.''

"We might establish a trail to Arin or Canjit. In that case it would be logical to expect an outside assassin.''

"No, we don't have the time. However, I have a possible alternative. Instead of assassinating Rozer yourself, I want you to lure Leot into doing it.''

Eleylin drew himself up. "I can think of a dozen ways that that could go wrong. Why bother? Once the stupid combat is over the Lady Richenza won't have to worry about being arrested for treason. Whoever takes Rozer's place after we're through isn't likely to hold his crown past the spring. Just finish the job quickly—we've already lost half the month.''

Less vehemence than Walter had expected. "I don't intend to leave the Lady Richenza in any danger. If you don't think you're capable of handling Leot, I shall have to go back to the original plan for Rozer.''

"Which involved poison." Eleylin scowled out of the window, then turned to Walter. "Do you have any notion as to how this seduction of Leot into the ranks of parricides should be handled?''

"The plan involving the urn and the statue should go on as you first conceived it, but the three of you should be as conspicuous as possible.''

Eleylin was amused. "A Selinian, a Sueve, and a beanpole? The only problem we've had so far is being inconspicuous.''

"I'll have Michel make sure Leot gets wind of something which complicates his status as only son.''

Eleylin nodded. He had accepted the plan.

When Eleylin had gone Walter turned to Thomas, who sat smiling to himself in the corner. "You were right. Poisoning Rozer was the only argument that would sway him.''

"I thought it would. Do you have any idea whom Rozer intends to marry?''

"Michel had no idea when he came this evening. But the possibilities are rather limited if he intends to marry another Tarsean. The Lord of Wolves' Hold has several eligible kinswomen, but Rozer's choice seems to be someone immediately available. Not that it matters.''

"My curiosity has been aroused." Thomas stood up. "Where is the Lady Richenza tonight?"

"She was exhausted; she spent the day with her dressmakers. Didn't you hear the great news?"

"I was with Justin and Bertz playing with sleeve buttons. What news?"

"The Lady Richenza, Alesander, and I have been commanded to attend the betrothal banquet of Brian, King of Canjitrin, and Princess Meriel."

"Is that wise?"

"Wiser than staying away. Besides, it *is* a command."

"Do you have any idea why?"

"The Lady Richenza thinks this might be Leot's doing."

"Be careful. The House of Thaiter doesn't strike me as the type to let the laws of hospitality keep them from murder.''

"I have thought of that," Walter said, "and I plan to be careful.

"See that you do. I don't want to have to clean up after you."

18

Seventeenth Day

Leot's messenger didn't knock; Leot's men never bothered to knock. He strode into the counting room, and announced, "Tredgett, His Highness wants you." When Tredgett finished checking the page instead of moving, he prodded, "Now."

Tredgett sighed and shut the ledger. What had upset Leot? There had been no rumor of any disturbance at the palace. The king had announced the Princess Meriel's betrothal, but Leot had been talked around to wanting that.

Tredgett glanced sideways at the messenger as they hurried through the streets. Gauging from the man's manner, Leot must be furious. Most of Leot's servitors, taking their manners from their master, showed little respect for anyone below the rank of lord. This man showed none whatsoever. He also showed no disposition for talk, and Tredgett gave up his attempt to draw him out.

To Tredgett's surprise, their destination was not the palace. They continued west across the Temple Way and threaded down a lane to enter the Three Queens Inn. The messenger pushed through the crowded entry and plunged into the upper level of the common room. Leot was hunched over a tankard at the far end of a bench,

nearly concealed by two or three of his drinking companions and a couple of liveried gentlemen who perched on
the rail beyond. The splatters of ale on the table testified to
an earlier contest at riom flipping, but no such childish
games now occupied the prince's companions. They fiddled
with their tankards, stealing glances at the silent prince.
Leot was smoldering, waiting for the spark to ignite his
volatile temper. Tredgett knew better than to supply it, but
the messenger, less used to the prince or less astute, loudly
cleared his throat. Leot erupted to his feet; his companions
jerked to attention.

"It's about time!"

His companions fell over each other getting out of Leot's
way as he edged down the bench to the aisle. They formed
a traffic-disrupting clot at the top of the stairs, blocking the
aisle and earning curses from the other patrons. Tredgett
couldn't have said just when he became aware that they
were not the only obstacle to free passage. Perhaps it was
the sharp exclamation in East Suevarna.

"*Tiat Altan!*" said an unmistakable Sueve, who was sitting near the rail on the lower level. "We haven't got the
money yet."

"And we never will if we let him handle it." His companion lurched to his feet and into the aisle, unfolding to a
remarkable height. "I never met a Selinian you could
trust."

"Nor I a northerner with more brains than a cow-
cabbage." The fair-haired man on the opposite bench, as
plainly Selinian as the other had been Sueve, remained
seated.

"More brains than to trust you after *we* did the hard
work!"

The Sueve was making ineffectual comments to soften
his companions' anger when Tredgett's attention was
claimed by a sharp shove. He swung around and stifled his
protest when he found Prince Leot beside him.

"Find us a private room."

Before they could move from the head of the steps the
argument below became more than a sideshow. The tall
man's voice rose—*Tributary Lordships,* Tredgett assessed
his accent—and the fair man said something that Tredgett

couldn't hear. The tall man paled and grabbed a full tankard from a tray carried by a passing barmaid. The Sueve grabbed at his arm as he started to throw it, deflecting his aim.

Taros and Enath! Tredgett realized its new trajectory and pushed Leot aside. The tankard struck Tredgett's leg before bouncing down the steps, and the ale splashed his hose, cote, and gown. Tredgett met the man's eyes, an odd light green, before the tall man spun away. *He's not angry; he's amused.* Then Leot, who had been hit only by a few splatters, exclaimed sharply and started to push down the stairs. Tredgett pulled him back; the tall man was already at the door, the Sueve following him, gesturing and expostulating. Leot subsided and glared after them.

"You said something about a private room, Your Highness?"

Later, when they were ensconced in a room on the second floor, Tredgett waited less patiently than usual for Leot to tire of recriminations and get down to business. He shifted from one soaked shoe to the other, feeling the drying hose cloth's stickiness on his leg. At least Leot had dismissed his sniggering companions, sending them on the trail of the tall man who had thrown the ale.

Leot roamed the room, pacing and cursing. Tredgett shrugged and moved to the window, where a small table held a wine pitcher and pewter goblets. Better wine within than ale without.

"Your Highness?" He handed Leot a goblet.

Leot dropped into a leather chair and drank. "Are there none but fools in the world? First my father, then that dolt."

So it was something that Rozer had done. "Did the king refuse to transfer Spurstow?" Tredgett didn't think that that was the reason for Leot's displeasure.

"What? Oh no, that went well enough. He'll announce it at the betrothal banquet, but do you know what nonsense he's got in his feeble mind now? He's going to marry again."

"It seems a bit soon, but there are advantages to having a Queen in Tarsia if he doesn't make too large a settlement on her. It would depend on whether she brought useful allies and a rich dowry.''

''Do you think Father'd think of that? No, he intends to marry that paragon of nobility, *Richenza Indes*. What do we do?''

''Are you sure?''

''He told Ewets and Ewets, all atwitter, rushed off to tell me.''

Tredgett swirled the wine in his goblet, watching its redness veil the silvery pewter. His discomfort made him less cautious than usual. ''You could marry her yourself.''

''No!'' Leot hurled his goblet at Tredgett's head.

Tredgett ducked, and the goblet struck the window frame behind him. ''Why not? She has a rich inheritance. If you marry her, you would control it; if you win the judicial combat, it only escheats to the crown.''

''I won't honor that bitch with my name.''

''It needn't be for long.''

''A day would be too long. No, I have other plans for Richenza Indes, and they don't include marriage. So, what do we do, Master Trickster?''

''Change his mind.''

''Why not kill him as well as Ewets?''

''I've explained that before. We can't afford an obvious murder while Arin remains a threat. If Ewets dies, no one is going to think much about it. No one likes him, and no one respects him. If the king dies, that's another matter; people respect the office if not the man. We don't have Nele Indes's impetuosity to blame it on anymore. And it would give Arin fine grist for its propaganda mill. No, we must remove Ewets before the campaigning season starts, but we don't dare touch the king.''

''And I'm to call that bitch 'Mother.' ''

''If you won't call her 'Wife' and can't change the king's mind. We must have control of her Duchy of Maldrin; it's too strategically placed. Better that than have it controlled by Arin or even by Feracher. It wouldn't be for long,'' he coaxed. ''We should have Arin defeated by late summer. After that we won't need Rozer, and as king you could do as you please with her.''

Leot had calmed enough to listen. He grunted. ''And what have you done about Ewets?''

''I have men placed as servitors at the palace now. The trick will be getting past the food taster. A slow poison would work best.''

Leot lurched out of his chair and poured himself an ample goblet of wine. ''Is that all you've accomplished?'' he mocked. ''I shouldn't keep you from your labors. Get out.''

Tredgett bowed and left the inn, passing Leot's smirking companions in the entry. The cool night air felt clean on his face, and he straightened and started briskly home.

I wish that Wendis were a few years older. But he knew that he deceived himself. Leot was the only possible choice. Who else of his family made a passable show as a warrior? Not Ewets, not Rozer. And a warrior was vitally necessary.

Gods help Tarsia now. Haldan, give us strength in war; Taros, the fruits of peace. We need all the help we can get with that for a Royal Family.

19

Eighteenth Day

A passing servant proffered wine, but Walter shook his head. He had accepted only one cup, and that sat untouched before him. He wondered if those who watched had noted his abstinence. In the royal palace of Tarsia, the heir to Lady Richenza of Indes was the subject of no little interest; avoiding speculative eyes was impossible, and Walter had comported himself carefully.

Walter took the opportunity to observe the Royal House, an activity which even the most critically minded observer could not deem suspicious in a man who had spent his entire life in Mentorz.

The members of the House of Thaiter were much as Lady Richenza had described them. Having seen them for himself, he was less troubled by his task than he had been since the lady's declaring of it. No country could prosper under such a ruling house: Rozer looked simple, Ewets arrogant and foolish, Leot sullen and boorish by turns, and Wendis a drunkard in the making.

In their midst Richenza was like a vessel of gold shelved with the brass. She could not flaunt her mourning in this company, but her plain silk gown of dark red stood out among the brocades and velvets as surely as black would have.

She had been seated only three places away from His Majesty, ignored by Ewets and Leot, who sat on either side of her. The Lady Richenza took no notice of the less than chivalrous treatment and behaved with decorum.

On the king's right sat the betrothed couple. On their right, either for symmetry's sake or to keep him away from his brothers, was Prince Wendis. Such wine as Walter had refused had found a home with the youngest prince; he was of little interest.

King Brian and Princess Meriel were quiet, exchanging few words. Rozer seemed to claim more of Brian's attention than his betrothed. Walter had not had any contact with Brian since the Hunt had gathered at Richenza's house, but the boy seemed confident and had managed to do exactly what he had been told to do.

Only the princess gave him a moment's pause; she was not what he had envisioned. She was aloof, not speaking to her brother or to Brian save when he spoke to her. But something did not jibe with what he had been told about her. She had a—he groped for the word—vulnerability he had not expected. And once, when all eyes were on Rozer making an announcement, Walter thought he had seen her look at Brian and that look was—

He shook his head sharply. *Walter, you're getting old, and sentimental. She helped lure Nele Indes to his death.*

It would be best if her part of the business were finished soon. The wedding was to be in four days, a hurried affair because of her husband's need to return to Canjitrin. Walter must find out from Michel what the couple had planned following the wedding.

That would leave Rozer and Leot.

The high table was served the last course. On the dais Michel was watched by Ewets and those near him with expressions varying from concern to amusement to contempt as he ostentatiously sampled the tart.

Five hours of feasting interspersed with entertainments, Richenza carefully shredded a piece of bread into her plate. *At least it's almost over.*

She'd been seated entirely too high. The head of the House of Indes, Companion of the Conqueror, was entitled to sit with the highest, but a less correct seat farther down the table would have been more diplomatic than this ridiculous place between Ewets and Leot.

On the other hand, this wasn't much more uncomfortable than meals with Alesander. She sought again to find where he sat, but could not see him. She had read the book he'd forced on her and understood much she hadn't before. The volume had hinted that Queen Lescina's ascension to the throne had been carefully planned.

Did that mean that the first murders and Alesander's cursing had been Lescina's doing? That Anelhar had been her coconspirator all the time? The book made no bones about his having been her lover, but did not go so far as to claim that Lescina's son, who became Rozer I, was Anelhar's. Considering Thaiter I's general incompetence, it was a very real possibility.

Which meant that the Royal House she was having eliminated was not that of Thaiter, but a bastard, inglorious branch of Indes.

It doesn't matter. They call themselves Thaiter; it is the name I want to end.

I might have been unfair to Alesander. Just because Hamon made some foolish insinuations doesn't mean that they were true. Alesander has never acted other than as one of breeding should. *Not until I provoked him.* She should apologize, explain. But how to apologize to a man who is frigidly polite and quits your company as rapidly as he can?

Besides, a complete explanation to Alesander must, if she were honest, include what had upset her, and the memory of those minutes with Hamon still shamed her.

"My lady?" Leot's voice broke into her thoughts. This was the first time he had addressed her all evening.

"Your Highness?" Foolish game—pretending he hadn't had her brother murdered; pretending he didn't want to break her neck.

His eyes were insolent. "I recall that you dance well. You will dance with me later."

She had hoped to leave discreetly early; that is, before Ewets was poisoned.

"As you wish. Which dance?"

"A set piece for two—I believe you know 'Her tears to me are brighter than diamonds'? "

Oh, Gods, just with him and before the entire court.

The king rose and the company followed. The banquet was officially ended. Richenza breathed a sigh of relief. For a little while she could blend into the crowd and find Sir Walter.

A liveried man bowed to her.

"His Majesty commands you to wait on him at once."

Haldan! For what?

"Where does His Majesty wish to see me?"

"I am to escort you, my lady."

Her mind full of questions, and fear in the pit of her stomach, she followed him through the passageway. They traveled only a little ways until stopping before a door. But *anyplace is remote when no one knows where you are.*

She straightened her shoulders as he opened the door. Rozer would not find her cowed. She was bowed into one of the small parlors. A second door, though closed, showed light, and she heard musicians beginning to play. This room was just off the great hall. The room was empty, and the liveried man, as if under orders, left, closing the door behind him.

The room was warm; a fire had been lit; wine and cakes had been set out. The signs were of a social call, not an interrogation. But it was possible that Walter's plans had been discovered. Had one of the spies Tredgett had set in her house learned more than Walter thought? Michel had made no slip. He had been at her elbow all evening, tasting Ewets's food.

The door into the great hall opened, and Rozer entered, followed by a silent, hovering Claverdon.

She faced the king.

He beamed at her with the face of a happy baby. "That feast dragged on far longer than I expected." He sat down suddenly, and only luck seemed to have placed a chair behind him when he did. He waved a plump, pink hand at her, "Don't just stand there, sit."

"I should rather stand, Your Majesty."

Rozer's face hardened, and she could see the resemblance to his sons. Claverdon moved from behind the king to behind Richenza. He moved a chair closer to her. "I should sit, my lady," the steward said almost inaudibly.

Wordlessly, she sat.

Rozer smiled again. "Now, isn't this friendlier?" He settled back into his chair as Claverdon, as if on cue, poured wine.

"Your father and I were good friends."

That is nonsense. Father despised you, and you barely tolerated him.

"He was an excellent governor to my sons. The best they had."

That was true.

"It was a bad decision of Betrissa's to remove them from his care. I often questioned it."

She dismissed him because she couldn't seduce him. Richenza was finding it difficult to sit silent. When would he get to the point?

"And now your father is gone and Betrissa is gone."

And Nele, her thoughts fairly screamed. *Why did you bring me here?*

"When your father was alive a match was suggested between our two houses. You were a little girl."

Yes, she remembered her father mentioning it. Queen Kamilka had favored the idea.

"Now that we are both alone, I think it would be suitable if we were to honor those wishes."

He can't possibly mean that he wants to resume that ancient betrothal to Ewets.

Rozer rose and began to pace. "You're unmarried with no one to protect you."

She started to protest, but he waved her into silence. "Don't speak of that guardian of yours! I cannot think that anyone who could coerce you into agreeing to that foolish challenge to my son could be a fit guardian."

One does not contradict the king of Tarsia, especially when he's gone mad.

He turned abruptly. "We are both alone in the world. I am asking you to be my wife, Richenza Indes."

Richenza, who had fought to school herself to silence till now, was bereft of speech.

She licked her lips; Claverdon was watching her narrowly. *Does he expect me to pull a dagger from my bosom and stab Rozer?*

"Your Majesty, this is very—very sudden," she began cautiously, "and I am betrothed."

Rozer's brow puckered; he had forgotten that. He sat down again. "To whom?"

"Robert Feracher, Your Majesty."

Rozer frowned.

"Feracher! Where was he when your brother caused you all this trouble? He is no better than your guardian." He took one of her hands and patted it comfortingly. "No, no, my lady. These are minor details. I am the king, after all, and to me they are nothing. Merely say you will marry me, and all petty problems will disappear."

She looked down at the hand that held hers. What would the woman he thought her to be reply?

She did not meet his eyes. "Your Majesty, it is a very great honor you do me, but"—she seemed to gather enough modest courage to look up at him from beneath her lashes—"but I cannot make so important a decision without consulting my guardian."

Rozer sighed, but sounded only mildly peeved as he replied, "He is your kinsman, and I suppose it is only reasonable to want his advice. I shall give you time then to speak to him before I require an answer." Then, half to himself, he muttered, "And that will give me time to speak to Leot about this pointless combat."

He mustn't stop the combat! She had to tell Sir Walter, so he could find a way to stall Rozer.

The music from the next room became louder; the dancing had begun. Rozer half turned toward the great-hall door.

"Ah yes, we must return before we are missed. Claverdon, escort her back for me. I need to recover a little from all this excitement." He belched softly. "Long feasts always give me indigestion."

In the great hall, she scanned the crowd, looking for Walter, but found only Alesander, who was critically watching Brian and Meriel dance. He frowned as he caught sight of Richenza, and he came toward her.

She dismissed Claverdon with a fiction about having promised to dance with Alesander.

When they were alone Alesander said quietly but with distinct disapproval, "You do not make it easy for a body-guard, my lady. Please, let me know when you go off alone."

"The king commanded me to wait on him, and I had no chance to tell you." Alesander raised a questioning eye-brow. "But I can't tell you any more now. Where is Sir Walter?"

"I haven't seen him since before the banquet. Do you want me to find him for you?"

"Please! You have no idea—"

Alesander looked past her, his expression belligerent. Leot stood a few feet away looking from Richenza to Ale-sander then back, implying a thousand insults. *Filthy minds dwell in the same sewers.*

"My Lady, you had promised *me* this dance."

"Of course, Your Highness." She gave Alesander the briefest of glances as she allowed herself to be led away.

The Lady Richenza did the first reverence and strove for composure. Leot looked like a cat in the buttery—sleek and much too pleased.

He left her in suspense for the first few measures. Then as she came up to brush palms and exchange places he spoke in a low voice.

"Did you have a pleasant visit with my father?"

"Tolerable," she replied as she turned to face him. "Shall you call me 'Mother?' "

Something was wrong. The jibe should have infuriated him, but he maintained his smug half smile through the next few measures, until he passed her again.

"As queen you should not be bothered by thieves."

"Thieves?"

He permitted himself another small smile.

"No one would dare break into the tomb of the queen's ancestors."

She tried not to look confused as she performed the small curtsy that came next. Smiling blandly at her Leot contin-ued, "Even as isolated a spot as the tomb near Sulby would be left alone."

Sulby was where she had taken Nele's body.

"Considering the circumstances," Leot purred, "Father

or I would be glad to send someone to see if anyone had taken anything away from the tomb that should be there, or put in anything that shouldn't be.''

Damn him, he knows!

''Don't trouble yourself.''

He was silent for a few more measures.

''I might be convinced not to.''

''What do you want?''

''Come to the parlor where you met Father in half an hour.'' The dance required them to advance toward each other. ''But be very circumspect. We don't want to start rumors.''

He bowed with elaborate courtesy as the dance ended.

The waiting was not easy; Leot was watching so she could not tell Walter or Alesander. She did not know whether to count as luck that neither was in sight until she left the hall when the time was up.

Leot was waiting for her alone.

Richenza, who had maintained a façade of calmness until then, found herself having to fight to keep it.

''How pleasant; you came. Close the door,'' Leot said, and she realized that she had been standing frozen in the doorway.

He stared at her silently for some time, enjoying her discomfort. ''Father's taste in women was never very good, but I hadn't expected it to descend this far—to the sister of a traitor.''

''That is not proven.''

''Oh, but it will be. I'll have no trouble with that bumpkin you've hired.''

''That remains to be seen.''

''How did you answer my father?''

''That is between His Majesty and me.''

He caught her wrist and pulled her to him. ''I'm in no mood for polite little games. Answer me!''

''I repeat, it is not your business.''

''But your brother's body is. Father wasn't pleased that I'd sent it to you, and it's taken long enough to find it. If you want it left undisturbed, answer me.''

''Your father won't like his brother-in-law's head displayed on the city walls. Do you think His Majesty still wants Nele found?''

''And do you think I give a damn about what Father thinks? I'll do it without his leave.''

''You wouldn't do that to your stepmother, would you?''
He slapped her. ''Answer me!''

He had changed the rules; she had seen him angry before, but he had never dared more than bluster. He raised his hand, and she edged away and answered before she thought. ''I said nothing one way or another.''

''Then you've shown more sense than I expected.'' He let go of her. ''I'm willing to bargain. What would you say if I offered to drop the combat and any threat to the good reputation of the House of Indes and your brother?''

''I'd want to know what you wanted in exchange.''

''Why, only the same as Father—Maldrin and those beautifully placed lands and''—he put his hands on her shoulders and smiled, looking from her face to her body—''all that goes with them.''

She started to pull away, but Leot tightened his grip, his thumbs digging painfully into her arms.

''Let go of me!''

Leot knew that he had frightened her. ''Come now, my lady, I am proposing; don't you have a better answer?''

She strove for a tone of mock decorum and knew that she failed. ''As I told your father, I must consult my guardian.''

''Oh yes, the old man. I wouldn't count too much on the old man. Old men die suddenly.''

The pressure of his thumbs tightened until, at last, she cried out in pain.

''Don't be so distressed. I'll make it very quick.'' Then he dropped the mockery and shook her sharply. ''Do you think I'll let you marry my father, or Feracher, for that matter? Either agree to marry me, or I'll make very sure you have nothing left to offer any man. Do you understand me?'' She nodded, trying to hold back her tears.

Smiling, he let her go. She stepped back.

''May I have leave to go, Your Highness?''

''No, you may not. Come here.'' She moved away.
Not again. Elun, please, not again.

"I'm going to be your husband," Leot coaxed. "Why run away from me?" She remembered the door to the hall, but he caught her before she could run to it.

"If you're going to be my wife, you're going to have to learn to do as you're told." He pulled her against him, his hands moving up from her waist.

"Let go of me, you've no right to touch me."

He laughed at her. "You *are* as stupid as your brother." Then he bent to kiss her; with both hands she pushed his face away.

His eyes narrowed with icy fury. "If you won't learn one way—" He caught one of her flailing wrists, and viciously and dexterously wrenched it behind her. "Now, are you going to cooperate?" She tried to kick him; he avoided her, and gave her arm a sharp twist. She gasped with the unexpected pain.

"See? I can do anything I want with you." He twisted her arm harder and just as she thought it would break or she must scream, or both, he let her go.

She drew in a ragged breath and backed away from him, then realized gratefully that voices outside the door had shifted his attention. As the door opened she retreated into the shadows. Two men, supporting a third, entered the parlor. For a moment she thought the third man was drunk, but then he doubled over in a sudden spasm and vomited. She saw his face as he did. It was Ewets.

The poison! Michel had given Ewets the poison!

Leot's attention fastened on his brother; she had time to get away. She fled, and no one stopped her.

In the passageway she caught her breath and touched her cheek gingerly. He had not struck her hard enough to bruise, and she didn't think that the redness would show in torchlight. Her arm was more seriously hurt; she could not raise it to shoulder height without pain, but that would not be apparent. Besides, there was no reason not to leave at once. Under the circumstances her departure would be considered discreet.

She entered the great hall, and, as she had expected, Ewets's sudden illness had brought a halt to the festivities. The party had become a rout, as if someone had yelled "Fire!"

Richenza looked anxiously for Alesander or Walter. She

did not find them at once, her attention arrested by the couple on the dais. King Brian was helping his betrothed down, and for once Meriel had lost her composure; she was pale and shaken. Brian, by contrast, looked thunderously angry.

"My lady?" she spun to face Alesander. "Sir Walter—"

"We must leave at once. I was just—Ewets—I saw—" She took a breath to steady herself. "Where is Sir Walter?"

"Waiting for you, my lady. He also suggests that we leave."

The short journey to Richenza's home passed in silence; Walter deep in thought, and Alesander unspeaking and reeking of disapproval.

Neither quitting the palace nor arriving in her own house put distance between her and what had happened. She had opened too many doors to anger and fear and shame. If Walter had questions, he held them. She accepted his polite dismissal and escaped to her chamber.

Annet, on the other hand, saw that she was injured and had a dozen questions. Richenza promised to explain in the morning and escaped to her bed, where physical exhaustion temporarily won over mental distress and she slept. But she woke crying out from a nightmare more frightening than any caused by Hamon, because this one was real.

Shaking, she lay back down and realized that she was afraid to sleep again. Richenza reassured herself that she was merely overtired, that morning would chase away these phantasms as it had the others, but she could not convince herself.

A childhood memory rose in her—light would drive away her fears.

The fire in her chamber had burnt out, and a candle would be too bright. Perhaps the fire in the withdrawing room was still lit.

She wondered at herself as she sat before the fire, only a few bright embers against the dark wood. An old man whose death was already arranged had proposed to her, as had his son, who would not outlive his father more than a few days. Why should these proposals concern her so much? They were nothing, a story to relate to her children.

But when she closed her eyes she could see Leot's smile, and knew that her mind was not set to reason in this. She pulled her bedgown tighter around her and huddled into her chair.

"Would you like me to bank the fire, my lady?" Alesander asked, startling her. "I heard you cry out, and came to see that you were safe."

But it had been several minutes since she had cried out. If he had responded at once what had he been doing since then? Watching her?

"You can see I am safe." She looked back at the fire. "I can't sleep, that's all." He shrugged and started back to his room, but then turned to her.

"I would not have thought that this would distress you so much. It was your own doing."

"What?" She started up from her chair.

"Ewets's death, my lady, You commanded it."

"Ewets! You think that I—I wish it were Ewets!" She covered her face with her hands.

He touched her arm, and, without thinking, she pulled away. Pain shot through her injured shoulder, and she cried out again.

Alesander's voice sounded very far away. "I've hurt you. Tell me what I've done?" He meant more, she knew, than just her arm.

"It's not you. He hurt me."

"Rozer?" he asked. "You told me you spoke with him this evening."

"No, not Rozer." She couldn't meet Alesander's eyes, "Leot."

She told him what had happened, omitting nothing of Leot's bullying and her own cowardice. And as the words poured out, so did the weak, unbidden tears. She never remembered at what point he touched her, but when she finally finished he was holding both of her hands.

"Your hands are like ice," was all he said, when she stopped talking and stood with her head lowered in shame. He guided her to the nearly dead fire and pulled her down to sit with him before it. "How badly did he hurt you?" Alesander began to feed the fire.

"My shoulder, a few bruises, not enough to account for letting Leot see I was afraid of him, and"—she forced herself to a further admission—"I am still afraid of him."

His hand tightened on the wood he held, and he threw it on the fire with more force than was necessary.

"You've nothing to be afraid of, my lady." When she looked up at him his face was cold with anger. "I will kill him for you."

His features blurred and she looked at the flames. It gave her no more warmth than the fire on the altar at Reasalyn, and she shivered.

His hand tentatively brushed her face, urging her to look at him. "You don't have to be afraid. I won't let him near you."

"I'll have to see him, and, oh Haldan, I almost begged him—he—" She was close to breaking down again.

"You won't be alone with him again. Walter set me to guard you, and I won't leave your side if there is even a chance he'll set eyes on you." He ran his finger down the side of her face to her chin and turned her face up to his. "Only tell me one thing."

"W-what?"

"Why are you angry with me?"

"I-I'm not." His eyes were skeptical. "I was just angry."

"That is a child's answer—'just because.' "

"It was a child's anger. Don't ask more; it was unforgivable of me to attack you for something someone else said."

"Who said?"

"It doesn't matter."

"Yes, it does. I am the injured party. Tell me."

He was right. "Hamon."

"What did he say?"

"He asked me about fair-haired lovers." Richenza hoped that that would end Alesander's curiosity.

He was silent, then he said ruefully, "I can't kill Hamon for you, but I can make sure that neither he nor anyone else has reason to make such insinuations again."

He started to rise, but she stopped him, "I don't want you to leave."

"But, my lady—"

"You said you'd guard me."

He had to laugh at her determination, but he sat beside her again. "It seems that my family causes you grief one way or another."

"Some less than others." She smiled at him.

"Since you've told me your story, I should tell you that I, too, had an encounter with the Royal House this evening. . . ."

The hour grew early before he helped her to her feet and escorted her the few feet to her bedchamber door. Neither of them noticed that as Richenza closed her door, Annet closed hers.

When a Prince of Tarsia dies there is a certain amount of fuss. When a Prince of Tarsia is poisoned with the entire court watching at his sister's betrothal banquet there is a great deal of fuss. At such times it is not difficult for the lowliest, most recently hired musician-juggler to make himself unnoticed in the uproar. Reynard sat in a corner of the withdrawing chamber just outside Rozer's apartment. It was the obvious route for anyone entering those rooms, and if asked why he was there, Reynard could have said, truthfully, that Rozer had not yet dismissed him.

Everyone knew he had been in attendance on Rozer earlier, while the king had waited for word of his son's condition. It seemed to Reynard that the old man had been trying to drive death away with music.

He found his current post interesting and informative.

All the servants, Michel included, who had waited on the head table had been summoned before the king, then, just as abruptly, set free, except for two men.

Reynard fingered his lute and kept an ear cocked to listen to the gossiping courtiers. He'd already learned most of what had happened during the questioning.

Michel was here, too, still looking greenish. He must have swallowed a lot of salt water to feign being poisoned. Michel met his glance and nodded toward the door.

Reynard sighed, went out into the passageway, and waited a discreet distance from the door. A few minutes later Michel joined him.

"What is it?" Reynard asked.

"I've got to get into Wendis's room. I've been locked out."

"Going to pour poison down Wendis's throat?"

"No." Michel's voice was shrill as it always was when he was scared, and Reynard signaled him to silence, then looked around a corner to be sure no one was eavesdropping.

"Why do you need to get into Wendis's chambers?"

"Because right after I put the poison in Wendis's wine two great hulking guardsmen hauled me away. Taros! They were searching everyone they questioned. I don't think they'd have found the buttons. I was sick myself by then, but I still had—have—the note I'm supposed to plant on Wendis."

"Hard to explain. Are you sure that Wendis drank the wine?"

"He was half-finished when I left."

"It doesn't matter who they think poisoned him as long as he's dead."

"Idiot! Do you have any idea what they'd do to me if they found out that I'd poisoned two royal princes?"

"Nothing permanent. Everything'll be fine when the moon is full." Reynard couldn't suppress a small smirk.

Michel clenched his fists, then thought better of it; Reynard had made it clear long ago who would win a fistfight. Michel was soft.

"I've got to get into that room and leave that note!" Michel's voice rose. "Otherwise, they'll figure out I'm the only one who could have poisoned the wine."

"Oh, all right." They passed few people in the passageway.

Michel jumped at every sound. "I wish I knew why they let me go so soon. It might be a trick."

"You didn't hear? They found two other servingmen carrying poison. Their stuff was slow-acting, so you wouldn't notice till too late."

"Oh ho, that exp—" It hit Michel then. "You mean I could really have been poisoned!"

"Just think of the trouble you would have been saved!"

"Dolt! That would have been ten times worse than the

salt water.'' He realized that Reynard had caught him again.
''Who sent them?''

''They *said* the king of Arin.''

''Aren't you sure?''

''Anyway, knowing that another group of poisoners was
after Ewets would have saved Walter a lot of trouble.''

''And I wouldn't have had to risk my neck.''

''And mine. If we get caught, don't forget I'm helping
you and won't *that* look suspicious?''

''They'll just think you're a thief.''

''And what would that make you if you're with me?''

''But I won't be.'' Michel fumbled in his purse and
brought out a folded sheet. ''Here's the note. Walter won't
want us both endangered.''

''And, naturally, you're too lazy to learn anything as
useful as lock picking.''

''So? You can barely read your own name. I had to forge
the note.''

''At least I'm learning.''

''Now who's making too much noise?''

Reynard scowled and listened at the door to the outer
chamber. He heard no snores nor heavy breathing, so Wendis's man wasn't there.

This door was unlocked, and Reynard slipped silently
into the room. A footstep in the passageway made him peer
back out the door; Michel had started to leave. Reynard
grabbed his arm.

''At least keep watch. You can find some excuse to make
noise if anyone comes.''

Shaking his head in disgust, Reynard went back into the
withdrawing room. Michel's devotion to his own skin was
more inconvenient than usual. If Reynard stumbled over
something in here or in Wendis's chambers, he'd have the
guard down on him in no time. Fortunately the withdrawing
room was relatively bare. Before Reynard knelt to his task,
before he even felt for his lock picks, he checked to see
that the door was really locked. Michel, when scared, had
made unbelievably stupid mistakes before. Not this time; it
was locked.

The room was dark, but Reynard had learned early to
pick locks by feel.

"The thief who needs a light to work is a dead thief," Randy had often said. Thinking about Randy gave Reynard a hollow feeling in the pit of his stomach; Randy was the dead thief now. Fortunately the lock on Wendis's door was designed less to keep out thieves than intrusive servants, and Reynard opened it handily.

So far so good. Reynard listened intently at the door before opening it. No sound, not even breathing. He carefully nudged the door open.

Reynard swallowed, and wished for the light he hadn't needed earlier. He had no idea where Wendis would be. How quickly had the poison worked? Would Wendis have had time to go to bed, or would he be where he had drunk the poison?

When Reynard's eyes had adjusted he saw that Wendis was on the bed. Better be sure he was dead rather than in a deep sleep. Gingerly the boy touched the back of the prince's outflung hand—it was cold.

Michel had finally done something right. Of course, if the poison had gone wrong, it would have been fun if Michel had gotten it.

One summons Ellis had twice wound up taking poison intended for someone else. That was why Ellis hated poison so much. Ellis hadn't really been well the rest of that moon.

Never mind, Reynard thought. *Where should I put the note?*

An empty goblet sat on a table next to the bed. If Wendis had really committed suicide, he'd have put the note where it would be found easily. Reynard put it under the goblet. One of the servants would find it if no one else did.

Then, as if death followed him, Reynard left the room and closed the door.

20

Nineteenth Day

Sometimes the nights without sleep passed quickly; sometimes Walter of Jacin found them useful.

He had half expected this plan to fail as the other had. Perhaps some of Eleylin's mistrust of poison had taken root in his mind. Now with the problem settled, he had been able to grapple with the new problem King Rozer had handed him. No wonder the Lady Richenza had seemed distraught on the ride home last night. To receive a proposal of marriage from one of the men responsible for your brother's death must be very distressing.

He heard Richenza laugh as the door opened, and she and Alesander entered. As he rose, Walter struggled to hide his own unexpected disapproval. He should, he knew, find her raised spirits a relief; he needed her cooperation. But should she be so pleased today of all days—the day after two men had died at her command?

It was not his place to judge her. He greeted her with courtesy as Alesander helped her to a chair. But a smile still lingered in her eyes as she faced him.

"Doubtless you have heard that Ewets and Wendis are dead." His tone was sharper than intended. Alesander must have recognized the note; he raised a questioning eyebrow from where he stood behind her chair.

Walter mastered his voice. "So they are no longer a concern. We can go on to other matters." He folded his hands before him, "Last night after he had spoken to you, my lady, King Rozer summoned me. He tried to enlist my help in your decision to marry him. So you see, I know of his proposal." He paused to let his words sink in. "And it is my need that you accept him.

"Before you say anything, let me explain. Certain of my plans require that Rozer should believe it necessary to ensure the succession. A marriage to you, or the possibility of one, would be the incentive we need. It would also guarantee your safety."

"Not necessarily," Richenza said. Alesander looked down at her, his grip on the back of her chair tightening. "Rozer's was not the only proposal made to me last night. Leot also made me an offer. He was less gentle about it than his father." She told the details tersely. As she finished Walter looked at Alesander and found his anger mirrored in the prince's face.

"All the more reason to see you safe from the son in a betrothal to the father. Will you agree to this betrothal? It won't go any farther."

"If I must." She sounded staunch enough, but she was pale. Alesander scowled as he watched her.

Why should that bother me?

"I think that this betrothal will drive a wedge between Rozer and Leot. And with enough encouragement on your part, my lady, this could force Leot to defy his father and insist on the judicial combat—which Rozer told me he intends to stop."

"I know."

"Then you shall write a letter accepting. Tell Rozer that Leot has threatened you."

She nodded and rose to leave.

Marry Rozer, Richenza thought. *My father did not raise me for that. But it's only a betrothal. It will never come to pass.* But she still had a hollow feeling in the pit of her stomach.

She buried her face in her hands. She had forgotten Alesander, who had followed her.

"Lady Richenza, are you all right?"

"Yes." She straightened. "It must be that I haven't eaten. Annet let me sleep late and woke me with the news that Sir Walter wanted to see me. I went straight to him."

"And your Annet didn't scold?"

"My Annet, indeed! She barely spoke a word."

"Now that *is* unusual, but her neglect means that you have had all this bad news on an empty stomach. Come." He escorted her to the great hall and imperiously commanded someone to bring her food.

While they waited he talked to turn her mind from the troubling decision she had just made. She let him speak until he ran out of things to say.

She smiled. "It's not really so bad. It's just pretending to want to be queen that bothers me."

His smile was rueful. "You don't want to be queen?"

She hadn't thought of it that way. "Not Rozer's queen, anyway. Whom would you have married?"

Alesander was taken aback, "I never—" he began, "I never found a suitable candidate." He paused to let the subject die. "Feeling better?"

"Yes, but I have to go write that . . . letter Walter wants and I've no idea what to say."

"I'd help you, but I've got to practice."

Richenza said wistfully, "I wish I could go out."

"Come watch me, then. I am, after all, your champion; it would only be proper."

"The letter could wait a few hours." She beckoned a liveried man. "Tell Annet to get my riding cloak ready. And tell the grooms to have my horse waiting for me—when?"

"Half an hour—I shall have to fetch Bertz. Walter insists that your bodyguard have a bodyguard."

She laughed as she sent the man off, and followed Alesander as he went to fetch Bertz.

When she reached her own chamber she was braced to face an irate Annet. It looked as if it were going to storm, and Annet never believed that Richenza knew enough to come in out of the rain.

But Richenza's bedchamber was empty. Her black riding cloak was thrown across the bed, but there was no one to give her an admonition to keep its hood up. Bewildered, Richenza could not escape the feeling that Annet's absence, like her silence that morning, was an accusation. Of what, Richenza could not imagine.

The lowering clouds, with their promise of rain, had kept the tourneyfield unpeopled that day. And with no potential spies, Alesander felt free to truly practice his tilting. To be precise, he preened like a smitten squire. It amused Richenza to watch him, for he was a fine jouster. He could defeat Leot—perhaps not as easily as Leot deserved—but she had no doubt who would emerge the victor.

She was disappointed when the clouds kept their promise and the rain fell.

Alesander smiled at her as she waited beneath the canopy of the pavilion that stood at the edge of the field.

"Are you enjoying your outing, my lady?" he asked after he dismounted.

"We should hurry home. I have a letter to write."

"As you wish, my lady." He waved away Bertz, who had begun to accompany him into the pavilion. "No, stay with Lady Richenza. Aylmer can help me."

Bertz surveyed the tourneyfield. The only other signs of life were Richenza's servingmen waiting across the field with the riding horses. The pavilion had only one entrance—Bertz found no objection to waiting outside.

She stood listening to the rain and watching Bertz guard her.

Poor Alesander, to be constantly bodyguarded by a Stros. She did not wonder that Alesander preferred to be squired by Aylmer. Bertz had made a name for himself in her household for an arrogance far above his station. He also excited no little curiosity in the servants' quarter. From the first it had been impossible to explain why a Stros was in Sir Walter's service, and after much debate, it was decided that no explanation would be given. Let there be a small mystery to keep the servants and spies from noticing the larger irregularities of Sir Walter's household.

So far only one servant had dared broach Bertz on the subject, and she had been quickly sent about her business. Annet had told Richenza it was one of the younger serving-women, and at first Richenza had been surprised, but, on closer inspection, she could understand. He was certainly not bad-looking—tall and a little thin, but his gaunt features were not harsh, only the sternness of his bearing gave that impression. He had red hair and fine grey eyes. He moved well, too, with an unstudied grace Richenza might have wished for Nele. He even, Richenza had to suppress a smile at the thought, turned an excellent leg. He spoke like a northern peasant, of course, as all the Stros did, but his voice was pleasant.

Altogether Bertz was a very handsome man and completely unaware of it.

You are getting as bad as Betrissa.

The wind and rain grew stronger. Bertz looked into the tent and spoke to Alesander, then beckoned Richenza inside. Alesander, in hose and shirt, his armor off, sent Aylmer to fetch the horses.

When the man was gone, Alesander said, "Let's hurry. I'm not sure that this eyesore won't blow over." The tent billowed ominously.

Bertz began to put the odds and ends of armor in the chest, but Alesander stared bemusedly out the door. Richenza wondered for a moment at his idleness; he was the one in a hurry. Then, as she watched, his body—no, the clothes on it—seemed to blur and shift. The sensation made her dizzy, and she had to look away. When she turned back he was wearing a brown cote rather than a white shirt. And hadn't there been an instant just before she looked away that he had been clad in black?

Suddenly she understood why none of the Hunt had seemed concerned about buying clothes, and now that she thought of it, Alesander had been fashionably dressed ever since they had come to Tarsit.

"Alesander, have you decided what arms you will display for the tourney? They need to be painted on the side of the pavilion you will be using on Haldan's Day."

"I think the annulets and lance," he said. "Their argent

and azure will help explain all the blue and silver I've been wearing.''

"Good, I'll make sure that Hildebert tells them. Do you—''

The sound of men and horses approaching forestalled any further conversation. Bertz finished his task, exited, and Alesander turned to call after him. He stopped, drew his sword, snapped, "Stay here!" and dashed out.

Peering after him, Richenza saw Alesander and Bertz, weapons drawn, facing five of her own grooms and men-at-arms.

No. These were strangers dressed as her servants, and they, too, had drawn steel. Tredgett had sent his men after Alesander here. Where were Aylmer and the others?

Alesander and Bertz seemed to be holding their own— apparently Tredgett's men had not expected the liveried Stros to be skillful with a weapon. Even as she watched, Bertz struck one of his foes, who lost his footing and fell heavily against one of the two poles supporting the canopy. His weight broke the first pole and the other toppled after it.

She started to push the canvas aside, then jumped back as a knife blade ripped through the fabric. If she ran out the door, she would be in the middle of the fight.

The only other escape was to cut her way through the side, but with what? A tilting lance was no use, and Alesander had his knife and sword with him. Would there be something sharp in the arming chest? She sank to her knees and pushed at the heavy lid.

The sound of the canopy ripping away from the door made her look up, hoping wildly that Alesander or Bertz had won clear. But it was one of the attackers who stood in the doorway, knife in hand, and she scrambled frantically to her feet.

If she moved off to the side, she could trick him into letting her sidle toward the door where she could escape. For a moment she thought it might work, but he he stayed between her and the way out. Richenza could hear fighting outside. There was still hope of rescue.

She backed away. He stalked toward her, clearing the

door. She backed a little farther. He followed until she had her back to the center pole.

Run now! She dodged to one side and dashed for the door, but the man caught her arm as she passed and threw her to the ground.

But as his arm drew back to strike, his look of triumph disappeared. Something flung him around, and Alesander, who had entered behind him, dispatched him with one efficient thrust.

She was up again and flying out of the stifling pavilion. She tripped over the black-clad legs of a man on the ground.

Black hose . . . She looked again. It was Bertz she had tripped over, and his was no flesh wound. His belly was ripped open, blood and worse than blood spilling out, reddening the white of his cote. But more horrible still, he was alive. Not even mercifully unconscious, his body was convulsed, his long hands clutching to hold himself in.

But he made no sound.

Frozen, she fought nausea, until Alesander caught her shoulders.

"My lady, you must ride home and get help."

"But—" She shook her head to clear it—he was right. Four men besides Bertz lay sprawled on the ground and no sign of her men anywhere.

Alesander helped her mount her horse, then he bent over Bertz.

She had almost recovered by the time she rode into her gate and wanted to go back with the men Walter sent, but he forbade her to leave, and for once she was too stunned to disobey. But he could not stop her waiting in the courtyard, heedless of the soaking rain.

What if Alesander had been attacked? He was alone. He could be terribly injured or killed. For the first time she wondered what became of a Huntsman who died. None of Annet's tales ever mentioned a Huntsman dead. How could Bertz live with such a wound?

What was taking so long?

The party returned, finally, with Alesander riding in the lead. As Richenza started to run to him a familiar hand was laid upon her shoulder. Annet had come.

"That one," she said, gesturing at Alesander, "can wait until you've dry clothes on." Richenza realized she was numb with cold. So, with a backward glance at Alesander, she allowed herself to be led inside.

Alesander, his hair straight and dark with rain, was warming himself by the fire in her withdrawing room when she came out.

"Are you hurt?"

He shook his head. "Nothing happened after you left. Tredgett seems to have run out of assassins."

"And Aylmer and the others?" She dreaded the answer.

"Aylmer was merely knocked out. The others must have been taken from behind. They were all dead and their bodies dumped out of sight."

She looked down; too many of hers had died at Leot's orders.

"And Bertz?"

"He is as you saw him. Justin is doing what he can."

"How long can he live with a wound like that?"

"How long?" Alesander looked up and sudden anger lit his face. "How long? Forever—unless we fail. He will not be allowed to die any more than he will be allowed unconsciousness—despite all of Justin's poppy juice—only the dubious escape of delirium when his wound begins to fester and grow purulent. The Ladies made their punishment very thorough. We have not the fear of death. Neither do we have its blessing." He flung himself into a chair. "Is it not marvelous? We cannot die! We have nothing to fear save failure! Some fool wrote that about us—envied our immortality! I could wish on him a belly wound where he must linger for eleven days, or the pleasure of being tortured, knowing that whatever is done to you will not end until the moon has made its circuit. One of us was beheaded—imagine surviving that—and buried as well. He could not lose consciousness.

"Oh, the Ladies knew well that death—final death—was not the thing we would find most horrible. Some among us would welcome it. Oh, we are very fortunate in our immortality. You need fear nothing for us!"

"Alesander!" Walter spoke sharply as he entered the room. Alesander drew himself up as if he would turn his anger on Walter, but then he remembered himself.

"I am sorry, my lady. I was too long alone with Bertz."

But Walter was still tight-lipped with anger. "I need to hear what happened. Tell me."

They told him—Alesander first, then Richenza. When they finished he neither replied nor dismissed them but sat looking into the fire.

"My lady, have you begun your letter to His Majesty?"

"No." Richenza had all but forgotten it. "I planned to write it this afternoon."

"Just as well. You should not find it difficult to explain to the king that you fear for your life from his son."

"No, it should not be difficult."

"Then I—we—shall leave you to your task. Come, Alesander."

Feeling as if she were being abandoned, she watched them leave. Once alone, she marshaled her wits and called for Annet to bring her writing things.

21

Twentieth Day

Earlier in the day the antechamber to the king's apartments had bustled and buzzed with the crowd of would-be petitioners hoping for an audience with the king. The ushers had cleared them away and now only the late-afternoon sun enlivened the carvings and the tapestries which formed the long room's decorations. The tapestries, a set which narrated the deeds of Alesander I, were hung with the four small pieces between the window alcoves and on the narrow end walls of the room above the doors. The three large pieces had been hung on the long wall of the room opposite the windows. So hung, they covered two rarely used doors. Doors recessed just enough, Michel had discovered, for the width of a man's shoulders. In one of those recesses Michel now sat hugging his knees. He wished Ellis would arrive for his interview with the king.

A door at the end of the room opened and shut, causing a breeze that riffled the hangings and stirred the dust on the floor. Michel stifled a sneeze. Moving carefully so as not to crackle the petition stuck in his belt, which was his excuse for being there, Michel looked through the slit where two tapestries met. Rozer and one of the ushers walked into his line of vision. Rozer went to the window and stood looking out with his hands clasped behind him. The usher continued down the room. The door at the far end of the room opened.

"Ellis Meilhoc," the usher announced.

The king turned and stood rocking back and forth on his toes as the two men walked up the room toward him. Ellis bowed as formally as is possible when carrying a bulky, heavy bundle. Rozer dismissed the usher.

When he had gone, Rozer said, "Well, let's see what's so special that I had to see it myself."

Ellis looked for a place to put his burden and, locating a table near the window alcove, set the bundle down with a thud. Michel smiled to himself; he'd thought that they would need that table. Too bad the light was behind them; he couldn't see as much as he'd like.

Ellis untied the knots that held the bundle together as the king edged closer. "This, although a good enough piece, is not the something special I told your agent Brydson about." He pulled off the outer cloth and the padding to reveal a foot-high statue. "This, you might say, is the appetizer."

Rozer circled the little statue, his hands behind him. "Middle period Rensel isn't it? Too bad it's broken. Do you have any idea of the subject?" His hand caressed a fold of carved drapery.

"A ruling empress. See, she is holding the Scepter of Reas against her breast." Ellis pointed to the front of the seated figure. "Probably Malasdrina from the style."

Rozer touched the rod the little figure grasped. "I'd heard about the Scepter." His hand stroked the statue. "Too bad it's broken."

"It's difficult to find anything that old that isn't."

Rozer continued to look at the statue. "How much do you want for it?"

"I told Brydson when I showed it to him, four hundred kytels."

"Steep for a headless statue. I'll give you three hundred."

"Three hundred sixty. I have two partners to satisfy."

"Done." Rozer touched the statue, running his hand across its breast. "What was the 'something special' you had to sell?"

Ellis shifted as though embarrassed. "This is on my own, my partners mustn't hear about it. It's got to be a secret."

"That could be arranged."

"I hear in the market gossip that the king of Arin is putting it about that Arin is the true successor state to the Rensel, to cause trouble in Iskandroc."

"Go on," the king urged, puzzled.

"I can help you scotch those rumors. I can get you the Scepter of Reas."

Rozer touched its sculpted replica. "Do you have it? What do you want for it?"

"I don't have it now. But I can get it. I know where it is."

"Ivory and rubies. . . . I always heard that Tarses broke it. Is it true that . . . ?" He dropped his voice so low that Michel couldn't hear.

"Well, it *was* hung above the marriage bed of every heir to the Rensel Empire, and they never lacked for children. And Tarses when he died left two pregnant concubines even though he was over sixty."

"Why are you, a Selinian, selling it to me? I'd think you'd want it for your own people."

"Damned if I'll give it to the priestesses after the way they treated me."

"Why don't you offer it to Ludvik then?"

"Because he can't give me the revenge I want."

"Revenge? I'm not likely to stir up war in the Selin hills when we already face war with Arin. Not even for the Scepter. Name another price."

"I had no violence in mind, Your Majesty. I want the grant of a manor in Scandron, one that's in sight of Limare in the Selin hills, and that's something King Ludvik can't give me."

"I don't understand; I thought you people were wedded to your stony hills."

"I've been a mercenary for fourteen years, since I was sixteen. Last year I finally had enough money together for bride-price and bride-gifts, and I had the girl all picked out. I'd known her since we were children. So I paid the bride-price at the temple and I took my gifts to Laneta at Limare and she took them and she looked them over and she turned me down. And when I went to the temple to get the bride-price back, the priestesses just laughed at me and said they weren't responsible if the girl wouldn't take me and there I was with my money all gone. So I said to myself, 'Maloc swallow them and their secret lore' and I set out to make another stake. When I heard about the war and King Ludvik's propaganda I thought, 'Now's my chance. The king'll want the information I can give him, and one manor's a small price to pay for it. I'll get a no-nonsense Tarsean wife and we'll raise fine horses and strong sons and Laneta can look down from her rocky fields and choke on it.' "

"But how do you know where the Scepter is?"

"I overheard the old women talking at night when I was a boy and supposedly too young to understand. They all know, but Tarses cursed any Rensel who touched it. But that wouldn't harm you, his descendant. Is it a bargain?"

"How soon can you get it?"

"*We*, Your Majesty. I'm not keen on facing Tarses's curse. You grant me my manor, and I'll show you how to get the Scepter."

"How soon can *we* get it?"

"As soon as I can shake my partners. I needed help digging up the 'appetizer,' and their greed might be harder to sate than mine if they knew I had another sale in mind. A few days, perhaps a week. They shouldn't be suspicious after I pay their shares on the statue although that damn Sueve, Ulick, is as persistent as a fly on honey. I'll get word through Brydson when it's safe."

"Won't you tell me more?" Rozer looked down at the statue.

"Not till I get the grant. After the priestesses I don't trust anyone."

Nervy of him, Michel thought, *but Selinians are nervy.*

Rozer sighed and dismissed Ellis. He stood contemplating the little sculpture, while Michel fidgeted in his hiding place. He had overheard what he was supposed to. Why didn't the king leave and give him an opportunity to tell Leot? Someone raised his voice outside the door, Michel settled back with an exasperated sigh, the door banged open, and Rozer swung around.

Leot's voice came from the doorway. "Fool! The king

sent for me!" Leot stalked into Michel's line of vision. He made a sketchy bow. "You wanted to see me, Father."

"I sent for you this morning. I have received a most disturbing letter from Richenza Indes."

"Turned you down, did she?"

"She did not," Rozer bristled.

"That *is* disturbing."

"She graciously agreed to be my wife." Rozer refused to be baited.

Leot changed his tone. "Tell me, Father, why do you want another wife and why, in Haldan's name, did you pick Richenza Indes?"

"Why not? She's wellborn, well-bred, and young enough to be a comfort to me in my old age just as Ricvorna Indes was to Ewets II. She might even bear me a son as Ricvorna did." Rozer stroked the statue.

"Unlike Ewets II, you already have a son—you don't need another." Rozer smiled a secretive smile, and Leot went on more sharply. "What makes you think you'd be any more successful with her than you were with Betrissa or your first wife, Lovisa of Arin? She's a bitch like them, and what did you ever get on them?"

Rozer continued to smile and stroke. "You know nothing about it. Besides, if I marry the heiress of Indes, I get the lands of Maldrin, and you don't have to fight her champion."

"But I want to fight Scelin. My honor has been impugned."

"You want to fight so much that you had Scelin attacked on the tourneyfield by five hired murderers and you weren't careful enough to keep the girl out of it even though you know of my interest in her. Or did you want her dead, too, as she believes? Her letter pleaded for my protection."

"She lies. I had no one attacked yesterday or any other day."

"They have ten bodies that say otherwise. Why not stop playacting and admit you're relieved. I'll marry the girl, and the whole thing will be forgotten."

Leot growled and paced across the room and back. "I did *not* have Scelin attacked. I did *not* have the girl attacked." He stopped in front of his father. "You're a fool to believe a word that harpy says. I will fight that combat, and I will win. It's gone too far for you to stop, and you'll look worse than a fool with your dowerless, traitorous bride. You thought this whole thing up to shame me, didn't you? Well, the shame will rebound on you, you senile, impotent old fool.''

Rozer clutched the statue, and his voice was shrill. ''I could stop you, but I won't, you insolent puppy! Get out and go to your room. And stay out of my sight or you'll spend a night in the dungeon. Win the combat''—Rozer managed a laugh—''I hope he breaks your neck.'' Rozer gathered the cloth about the statue and, cradling it in his arms, carefully carried it from the room.

''Then you'll have no sons at all!'' Leot yelled after him.

What an embarrassing conversation to overhear. Michel considered his situation. It was going to be very difficult to bring up the earlier interview without betraying his knowledge of this one. He coughed delicately. Leot swung round and flung back the tapestry.

''How long have you been there?''

''Since this morning, Your Highness. There wasn't anyplace to sit, it was so crowded, and I must have fallen asleep . . . Now I'll never get to present my petition.''

''How much did you hear?''

''Everything, it was impossible not to.''

''And you'll blab it to the rooftrees, no doubt.''

''Oh, no! Why would anyone be interested in where the king buys his antiquities even if he is buying Reas's Scepter? I'd think there'd be a limited market for that information even if it will guarantee him sons.''

''What?'' Leot pulled Michel out of the antechamber and toward his own rooms.

''Guarantee him sons.'' Michel summarized what he had overheard. ''The Selinian said that they could get it in a few days after he had paid off his partners. Funny, he said one of them was a Sueve.''

They had reached Leot's rooms, and Leot paused in the doorway. ''Tazelar, what did you want from the king?''

''My petition? Well, you know I've lost my position, and the truth is I've spent all my money. So I was asking for a new job or money to get home. I wrote my father, but he'll only send money if I continue my tour on to Rayln or some such other dull place. Ugh, and with winter coming, too.''

''Do you know where Firmin Tredgett lives?''

''On the Great Square?''

''Yes. You go tell him I want to see him right now, tell him what you overheard between the king and the Selinian, and tell him to give you fifty kytels. Got that?''

Michel nodded.

''Then go home to Canjitrin. I don't ever want to see your face again.''

''But will Tredgett believe me when I tell him to give me fifty kytels?''

Leot stifled an oath and pulled off the ring he was wearing. ''Give him that. He'll believe you.''

Michel looked at the ring as he walked toward Tredgett's house. A ruby set in gold—easily worth two hundred kytels. He debated whether it would be necessary to turn it over to Tredgett.

No one seeing Firmin Tredgett's unperturbed face or steady gait would have guessed his disquiet. He closed the door to Leot's rooms behind him, nodded at acquaintances in the corridors, and unhurriedly left the palace. Inside he felt as though daemons pursued him. He had known from Tazelar's story that he would have to face Leot's wrath about the botched assassination attempt on Alesander Scelin, but he had not anticipated that winning the combat had become the centerpiece of Leot's pride. The way of showing his father and the world who was the better man. Tredgett had weathered that storm by letting the waves of Leot's anger break over him, letting Leot feel superior to him—how could a commoner be supposed to understand the importance of a gentleman's honor? He had even weaned Leot away, he hoped, from any attempts on Rozer's life; easing the prince's fears by ridiculing the idea of fertility amulets and finally pointing out that even if Rozer had another son, it would be years before he could threaten Leot's position. And children die. . . . they die every day.

Leot had finally swallowed it. But Tredgett had had to allow the prince some victim for his venom. Tredgett repressed a shudder, remembering Leot playing with the poison devices that had been taken from the "Arinese conspirators." Leot's hands pressing the spring on an intricate belt buckle and liquid poison, gold and smooth as honey, forming a droplet on the buckle's tongue. Leot's voice, falsely sweet, congratulating him on Ewets's and Wendis's deaths.

How tempted he had been to shock Leot from his smug invulnerability by telling him that it was not their poison that had done the trick. But he had held his tongue. With Wendis dead he must seem fully in charge lest Leot decide that he had lost his usefulness. He had let Leot divert himself in planning a different death than the king's. Richenza Indes's guardian no longer had a necessary role to play in the present comedy, reasoned Leot. Tredgett was in no position to deny it. He had diverted Leot's mind with murder plots and left him pondering the merits of poison or knives, of the effectiveness of murder in public or private, in Richenza's own house or the publicity of the palace. Tredgett had had to tell Leot much, too much, about who worked for him and where.

When he shivered, it was not from the chill in the air. He had better find the man who proposed selling Rozer the Scepter of Reas. The Selinian who had a Sueve for a partner. It would be too convenient if they had been the pair in the Three Queens a few nights before; his life had not been that simple lately. Would it ever be again? He hunched his shoulders into the late-autumn wind.

Halfway across the Great Square he decided that his was a mood he did not want to go home with and turned aside, intending to go to a tavern near the law courts, but at the foot of a steep staircase by the City Hall he changed his mind and clambered up. Conversation cleansed the soul better than wine.

The door at the head of the stairs stood open. The room beyond was lined with shelves and lit by narrow, small-paned windows facing the street. Every table and flat surface was piled with rolls, registers, ledgers, or notaries' books. The floor was clogged with baskets overflowing with papers filed or tied in bundles.

The old man who was the room's only occupant pushed his coif back from his eyes and came forward, bony hand extended. "Firmin! It's been too long since you visited me. Come in and have some ale."

Tredgett eased his way across the room while Master Philemon cleared a stool for him and produced a pitcher and two tankards from under a table. "I can't thank you enough for getting me this job with the city. It's the perfect situation for a historian, and I really am making some progress sorting out this confusion." Tredgett glanced round at the welter of documents. "I can set my hand to any record you might want within two hours. It took my predecessor days even if you bribed him and weeks if you didn't."

"Enough about me. How is my star pupil doing? I never thought that the pupil who I taught for free would repay me more in the end. Is your boy as good at languages as you are?"

They spent the last hour of sunlight reminiscing until a laggardly law clerk clattered up the stair to search out the copy of a writ. While the old man assisted the clerk, Tredgett's thoughts reverted unwillingly to his conversation with Leot. When the old man finally shut the door on the departing clerk, Tredgett asked, "You're a historian—after Prince Leot, who is the next heir to the throne?"

The old man looked up from lighting a candle. "There isn't one that I know of. Unless you believe in fairy tales like descendants of Queen Cassandra's supposed son or that King Mascelin's son rides with the Wild Hunt."

"Are you sure there aren't any heirs? No man, however obscure, who has a claim to the throne?"

"The last pretender was hanged a hundred years ago, but I could see what I can find in the records if it means that much to you."

Tredgett looked up from swirling the dregs of ale in his tankard. "In two hours?" he teased.

The old man looked down his nose at him. "It isn't a *city* record, but I should have an answer in a day or two." Then his expression softened. "Firmin, is it important? One can't help but hear rumors."

Tredgett looked at him soberly. "Vitally important. There is something going on that I don't understand, some thread I haven't grasped, and maybe that's a part of it."

22

Twenty-first Day

"Do what you can," Walter told Justin, "I know it can't be much."

On his pallet Bertz couldn't have been aware of either of them. He groaned, and said, "Minka?" He had said that name before, almost as often as he had babbled not quite incoherently about children and blood. Walter, knowing why Bertz had been cursed, had had to steel himself to remain in the room.

"He's almost better off this way." Justin put a damp cloth on Bertz's head. "If only he'd shut up about the damned brats!"

Walter looked at Justin. The alchemist had been in Bertz's room for three days.

"I'll see that Thomas relieves you this evening."

Justin looked surprised. "I can just see the lawyer trying to be a nurse, but send him up anyway. I need a drink."

Downstairs in his own chamber, Walter opened the window overlooking the bare garden and tried to drive the stench of the sickroom from his nostrils and the waking nightmare from his head.

He could understand a just punishment, but this bordered on—no, surpassed—torture.

"If you can't let the man die," he flung his prayer to
the Ladies defiantly, "then let him rest."

The plea went unanswered as always.

He closed his eyes, but the smells still lingered in his
mind and sent his unwilling thoughts to Jacin. He had never
heard the details of Cassimara's and his son's deaths. Had
they died easily or fought against death, making it harder?
A hundred songs told what had happened to Walter of Jacin, but not one voiced the fate of his wife and son.

The door behind him opened, and Walter turned to see
Annet regarding him sourly.

"I need to talk to you."

"Not now." He looked out the window.

"Now. It won't wait."

Better this than pointless brooding. He pulled the window to and turned to the woman.

"What is it? We've moved the injured man upstairs so
he won't disturb anyone. We can't do more."

"That is not the problem. It's that boy you have guarding
my lady."

"Do you mean Prince Alesander?"

"You'd better keep him away from Lady Richenza."

"Why? Because of the attack at the tourneyfield? He
couldn't have known about that beforehand, and he saved
Lady Richenza's life."

"I don't mean that. After you are gone, my lady will
still be betrothed and with no father or brother to take care
of her, she will need a husband."

"I still don't understand. What would prevent her marriage?"

Annet stood taller. "If that one has his way, she'll not
be a fit bride for anyone!"

Walter stared at her, hoping he had misunderstood.

"You can't think that Prince Alesander would try to seduce the Lady Richenza?"

"I saw them together the night after the betrothal banquet." She told him the story.

Walter shook his head, "She was distraught—Prince
Leot had threatened her. Alesander was trying to calm
her." But he remembered how she had looked at Alesander
that next morning, how they had acted together. He had

seen her face when Alesander returned from the tourney-field. Annet's idea was not so unlikely.

Annet saw the flicker of doubt cross Walter's face. "You've put him in the room next to hers. Move him elsewhere."

"I can't do that. Lady Richenza's life has been threatened, and Tredgett has at least one agent in the house."

"Have someone else guard her."

"With Bertz injured there is no one else."

"Then I'll guard her!"

Walter closed his eyes.

"No," he said finally. "Even you must admit that Alesander is well qualified as a bodyguard. I'll speak to him." Annet looked obstinately unbelieving. Walter put a hand on her shoulder. "Don't worry, we'll keep your lady safe."

Then he realized what he had said.

"You promised that once before." She pulled away. "Didn't you?"

Ellis stretched his legs and crossed them. "Well?" he asked Ulick and Garrett.

Garrett, astride the only chair in the private room at the Three Queens, grinned widely. "How does it feel to be a fine landowning Tarsean gentleman?"

"You mean that landlocked rock field Rozer's granted to Ellis Meilhoc? *Meilhoc* may be Rensel for rustic, but I'm not so great a fool as to think the land will be of any real worth. Did you get here without being seen?"

"Now who's a fool—?" Garrett began, but Ulick broke in.

"I believe so. We seemed drunk as we left the common room. Tredgett paid us well."

"Besides," Garrett said, "we're supposed to be watching you."

"Not this close, I'll wager."

Ulick shrugged. "Only if we were careful."

"I see. What did you think of Master Tredgett?"

Both men paused.

Garrett answered first. "He asked me all the right questions. He had done some checking on us before he asked

to see us. Still, he seemed a typical merchant—his mind
forever on gold.''

Ellis turned to Ulick.

''Tredgett speaks Suevarna very well, and he seemed satisfied with my answers.''

''You told him what we agreed?''

Garrett waved his hand impatiently. ''Of course.''

Ulick said, ''We told him that we had served with Captain Beswic. That we had been busy on the Sueve border
and that you'd gotten tired of dealing with Rayln winters
and would-be barbers and decided to head south, and that
Garrett owed money to half the garrison. I was vague as to
why I joined you.''

Garrett, bored by the recital, interrupted, ''And I told him
that Ulick was afraid his mother-in-law would send her
sons after him for deserting his wife, and that you had had
us dig around some old ruins, and that we had sold the junk
we had found.''

''And,'' Ulick finished, ''we made sure he knew that you
kept away from other Selinians and, when drunk, spoke ill
of Selinian women.''

''Good,'' Ellis said. ''But did Tredgett believe you?''

''What else would he believe?'' Garrett snorted. ''Anyway, our stories matched, didn't they?''

''He seemed convinced,'' Ulick said.

''Seemed convinced!'' Garrett looked offended. ''We
did it right! He couldn't possibly have thought we were
lying.''

''I'll report to Thomas.'' Ellis stood up. ''We agreed not
to meet again until it is time, so . . .'' He strode to the door
and threw it open. ''I should have known you two could
smell money clear across the Marre,'' he shouted. ''Get
out!''

Garrett got up, spinning his chair against the wall as he
did. ''I should have known that you're as stingy as any
other beardless longhair.''

He left the room, nearly slamming into a man and a
blond whore in the passage. Ulick followed silently.

Tredgett reread his clerk's neat transcript of the afternoon's
interrogations. The Selinian Meilhoc's companions corrob-

orated his story and each other's. They fitted together flawlessly. Clear and guileless as the tall northerner's eyes. Exactly what you would expect him to be: countrified, rough, gawking at the sights, overwhelmed but gratified to be the center of attention. But he had been *amused* at the Three Queens the other day. The Sueve, on the other hand, was not what one would expect him to be, not unless you had dealt with many of them: cool, reserved, serene, and in command of himself. But he had been the one who lied.

That I know lied, Tredgett corrected himself.

The Sueve had said he had served in Mauger Beswic's company, but Peason, who knew Beswic, said that under no circumstances would he have allowed a Sueve in his company; he was violently prejudiced against them.

One lie and an uneasy feeling. What shall I tell Leot? That I think the scuffle in the Three Queens was staged to get our attention? Why? So the Selinian could get a better price if he had another bidder? Too elaborate a scheme for so little gain; Leot would never believe it. Tredgett raked a hand through his hair and sighed. Finally, he noted the single discrepancy in the transcript's margin and said no more about it. Let Leot make of that what he would.

He folded the papers together, tied the string, sealed it, and went to the door to give it to the waiting messenger. He frowned after the boy. Should he have told Leot more?

He returned to his desk with its unruly pile of letters and reports. He dropped his head in his hands and closed his eyes to shut out the clutter. He ought to sort the papers out into their accustomed order. He ought to sort his thoughts, but that was harder than mere papers. Papers stayed put; they didn't scurry about screaming, "Why?"

Why should a Selinian and a Sueve go into partnership to deceive a prince and—or a king? Arin was the enemy and a Selinian might possibly work for Arin. The Selinians were mercenaries. But a Sueve and a rustic from the Lordships? Not likely.

A northern conspiracy? The Stros didn't use outsiders; the Lordships were proverbially disorganized; and the Sueve had been engaged in intertribal warfare. Who was left? Feracher? But Feracher wouldn't soil his hands with commoners. He might raise his vassals and defy the king with banners displayed, but he wouldn't demean himself with petty plots.

Feracher was betrothed to Richenza Indes. But this odd lot of mercenaries had arrived in Tarsit before news of Nele Indes's death could have reached Feracher.

He pushed aside a report from the south that had tumbled into the candlelight, then unfolded it and reread it. Walter Martling's party had not been seen at Hersin or any place to the east. Nor had any messenger of Indes's. Another lie. Scelin lied. Where had Martling's party come from?

Tredgett rifled through reports. They hadn't been seen in Hersin or any place to the east. Nor had they been seen to the south or west. No mention of them at Iskandroc, and if they came from the south, they had to pass the fortress. To get to Sulby from the west they would have had to cross the Magnary by ferry, but none of the ferrymen remembered them. The ferryman on the Queen's Road between Hersin and Manreth did report a large party of night riders soon after Nele Indes's burial—but on the east side of the river.

If they didn't come through Iskandroc, they can't be from Arin, Tredgett argued with himself, *but they could work for Arin even if they came from Canjitrin.* Daimiron was Arin's ally. No one in Indes's party had an Arinese accent. Sir Walter's was faintly western, Sir Alesander's and the nondescript servingman's were central Tarsean. The other servingman was a northerner; Tredgett's spies said he was Stros, but that was unlikely. The secretary's accent was southern, but it was Madarian—educated Madarian. Another odd lot of people. Was the absence of Arinese—or Canjitard—accents more suspicious than their presence?

The only combination of Arinese and Canjitard accents brought to his notice lately were the Canjitard king and his bear-leader. But King Brian's reappearance didn't help Arin. Arin lost an ally this year whether or not Brian was successful in claiming his throne. Canjitrin would be in internal uproar, and Tarsia's flank would be safe.

Odd that King Brian should reappear now, after two years' disappearance. There was some queer story he had been told about the king, but Tredgett couldn't recall it.

The food taster from Canjitrin, who had tried to abscond

with Leot's ring, had a central accent—but the gentry of Salmidia prided themselves on the purity of their speech. He hadn't been an effective food taster, or had he been lucky? Or in league with Wendis? Or working for someone else? *My men didn't poison Ewets. Wendis could have—his note was circumstantial enough about means to be believable. But from what I know of Wendis, it's Leot he would try to kill, and he had as much—better—opportunity to kill him as to kill Ewets. Unless someone nudged him along.*

The food taster was reported to be very close to Wendis. Could he have prompted his actions? For whom did the food taster work? Arin? Arin profited. So did Leot. Leot had sent the food taster to him to be paid off. Paid for what? Just for telling about the Selinian?

He started to put the report he had just read away, then stopped and reread it. Martling's party wasn't the only one that hadn't passed Iskandroc. Alvord the silk merchant had been there, but not with Master Haroc. And there was no juggler with the party. *A juggler with a northern accent.* Another odd lot. But, on the other hand, jugglers got around. This one had made a home for himself with the king.

Haroc had made a home for himself with the queen.

She was dead.

Dead like Ewets and Wendis.

Years had gone by with the same tensions in the Royal Family, but nothing had happened. They had been frozen like insects in amber and now within the moon all was movement. Who profited? Arin? Not from the queen's death.

Leot says I see Arinese plots everywhere. But who else profited? Who could predict where the king's fancy might alight? The Selinian mercenary profited; he sold Rozer a story about a legendary fertility charm. Rozer had chosen Richenza Indes. Could she have predicted that? Could she have expected to be queen? She had challenged Leot; Leot might lose. Had she and her brother planned this as a second string to their bow?

Tredgett's small acquaintance with Nele Indes, who had treated social inferiors like furniture, led him to think that

Indes didn't have the flexibility for such a risky scheme. The grand duke had been very straightforward and very easy to lead. But what about the sister? Her guardian and his ill-assorted entourage—who appeared from where?—so soon after her brother's death. Could she . . .

"Firmin?"

He looked up, startled, to find his wife Karina standing, candleholder in hand, beside his desk. He had been so pre-occupied that he hadn't heard her approach.

"Aren't you ever coming to bed?"

He made the usual excuses about the time and realized they were true. The candles had burned down; some were only pools of wax. It would be dawn soon.

"Surely some of these papers can wait." She came 'round the desk to look over his shoulder. "My father always said that no profit was worthwhile if you had no time to enjoy it. And these"—the short hairs that escaped her braids tickled his cheek as she leaned forward—"don't even look like business."

He turned in his chair and pulled her down in his lap. "I haven't been the best of husbands lately."

She laughed and started to pull away. "I'll forgive you but in bed, not in the parlor."

"I've got to finish this."

She sat back with her cheek against his shoulder. There was a long moment of stillness, then she sighed. His arm tightened around her. He looked at her, the sweet curves of her face, the first grey showing against her brown hair, and he was afraid.

"Perhaps we need some time away, just as a family. You and Nick could go to the country house, and I could join you as soon as this combat nonsense is finished. I don't want to leave the house unprotected to such crowds."

"But, Firmin, it would break Nick's heart to miss the combat. He's had all his school friends over to see that he, and those he's asked to share it, will have the best view in the city. And I would worry more if I were at Meton if there is rioting. It's the not knowing that's worse, and I'm sure with all the men you've hired that we would be just as safe in town. Let's wait till we can go together."

He sighed and acquiesced. They probably were as safe in the city as out of it.

She slid from his lap and picked up the candleholder.

"If I'm going to supervise the maids as they deserve, I need to get *some* sleep even if you"—she kissed him lightly—"don't need any to supervise your clerks. Do, at least, come to breakfast."

He looked after the fading light of her candle, surprised at the sharpness of the fear he had felt earlier. Fear of Leot. Leot, who was sliding out of his control. *What would Leot do if he thought me no longer necessary?* Tredgett pushed himself up from his chair and paced the floor working the stiffness from his bones. Karina's father had also said that the wise man leaves politics to his betters.

Betters in what way? Why let a fool make life-and-death decisions about you because he had the right father? The right blood? But it wasn't easy to do otherwise. He stopped at the window. It wasn't easy at all.

Nick was right about the view. These second-story windows would overlook the grandstands built along this side for the less important spectators. The stands for the Royal Family and for the appellor, Richenza Indes, would be built opposite and the combatants' pavilions would be at the ends of the square. The fighting would take place directly opposite his windows at the foot of the statue of Anderad.

Ironic that Anderad might preside dispassionately at the end of his line as dispassionately as he presided over the stalls of the victual merchants at the weekday markets. *What, after all, could make a statue frown, a stone eye weep?*

Tredgett's gaze sharpened, and he frowned as he stared at the serene sculpted face. *That's who Scelin looks like! Long face, long nose, eyes set too close together. No wonder I didn't remember coloring.*

He tried to remember everything he knew about the statue. It didn't date back to Anderad, but a king had posed for it. One of the kings after the Civil War had posed for it as a way of asserting the legitimacy of his claim to the throne.

Tredgett remembered Master Philemon's acid commentary on using your ancestors for prestige and profit. Phile-

mon had told him that story when he was ten—no, eleven.
Mascelin had posed for it. No, his father Laidoin—practically his first act after killing his rival, Alesander III, and
securing the throne.

Alesander. . . . Alesander III had been Alesander Marald.
This was Alesander Scelin. For Mascelin? There were tales
of Mascelin's family. Philemon had mentioned them just
the other day: "Fairy tales like Queen Cassandra's son or
that Mascelin's son rides with the Wild Hunt." Ridiculous.

But what if you were trying to set up a conspiracy? A
pretender? You might use a chance resemblance, an evocative name. But it was chancy, tenuous and chancy. And
no claim had been made. Yet. There had been pretenders
off and on these four hundred years claiming to be descendants of Anselm and Cassandra. Vitaut, they said, bred
true—but not that true. No rational man would believe it.

*No rational man could swallow the alternative. And that
seems to be the claim they're setting up. Scelin for Mascelin. I bet I'll find that the cursed son's name was Alesander. Who are the conspirators? Richenza Indes,
"Alesander Scelin," her guardian, and his party and who
else? If I were going to set up a claim, what would I do?
What do the stories tell about the Wild Hunt? I've got to
talk to Philemon.*

The Wild Hunt had to be summoned. The tales from his
childhood had emphasized the great temples of the Goddesses.

Tredgett crossed the room to unroll one of the maps
stored in the sideboard. The greatest of all the temples had
been at Reasalyn, and that, he checked, was a short journey
from the Indes lodge at Sulby, where all his queries deadended.

What would I find in Reasalyn? He shivered. *Nonsense,
it doesn't have to be true. Anyone can use some names.
Remember the story you heard about the Grand Duke of
Yesacroth, "The Wild Hunt made me do it!"* It was a wonderful excuse; a way out of an intolerable situation. *Just a
clever imposture*, Tredgett reassured himself.

But, another part of his mind pointed out, *if it is an imposture, it would take a long time to plan, and Richenza
Indes didn't have time.*

He sent two men to search the ruins of Reasalyn.

23

Twenty-second Day—
First Quarter

One would think, Thomas mused, *that after twelve hundred years the people of Tarsit would have seen enough of kings and their assorted kin.* But the crowds at the Palace Gate seemed as impressed at the wedding procession of Princess Meriel and her new husband as they must have been all those centuries ago when Tarses set up his winter camp here after razing Reasalyn. It was natural enough, he supposed, to want to see the people who governed you, though Thomas couldn't recall crowds lining the streets to see *him* pass. The royal House of Tarsia made a more impressive show.

The procession from the palace to the Temple of Haldan gave him an excuse to finally see the people he was helping Walter destroy, and to attend to other business as well. He could tell little enough about the Royal Family, save that they were presentable in public. Brian looked worried, but that could have been Thomas's imagination. The important part of this excursion was still to be discharged.

As the procession passed and the crowds around the gate began to move, someone bumped Thomas, causing him to drop the papers he carried. Both men bent to gather them before the precious parchment was trampled in the mud.

"What does Walter want?" Payne handed Thomas the sheets.

"Reynard says that Brian and his wife will leave tomorrow for one of the royal estates to the north."

"Yes. I'm to go with them."

"How did you manage that?"

"I switched Brian's horse with mine and thereby made myself indispensable as the only man who can handle His Majesty's mount. Since I'm acting as groom, it'll be no problem changing them back for tomorrow's journey."

Thomas nodded. Payne could not command Brian's horse, but he could command his own not to allow itself to be handled by anyone else, and he could change the appearance of either or both horses as easily as he could his own dress.

"Good. Hamon has been told where you are going, and you are to let him in tomorrow night to finish the girl."

"I don't need Hamon for that."

Thomas frowned as he brushed mud off one of the pages. "Walter doesn't trust Brian. You can't count on his co-operation, and it is possible that he'll try to stop you."

Payne handed him the last of the papers. "Will Walter need me after that?"

"No. You, Hamon, and the boy should get away, as far and as fast as you can."

"Aye." Payne disappeared into the crowd, and Thomas was on his way a moment later.

King Rozer's wine was good, Walter thought as he emptied his cup, the best he had drunk in nineteen moons and more. Or was his memory poor?

He had to drink the wedding toasts. It would be rude not to.

"Long life!" he had drunk.

"Many children!" He had drunk that lying wish, too.

"Prosperity!"

"Happiness!"

Guests had made these same toasts at every wedding he had ever attended—including his own. He put his cup down abruptly, and a servingman refilled it.

No, his memory was not poor. He suspected that the wine made it better. If that were true, why did Justin drink so much?

Not that he could equate this wedding with his own. The only guests at his wedding had been Rensel peasants. He had made his promise to them, to himself, to her and to her Three Goddesses.

He took another drink.

Walter had never liked weddings.

The high table was less symmetrical with two kings, one queen, one prince, and the Lady Richenza. The lady didn't seem as composed as she had been at the betrothal banquet. What was Rozer saying to her that made her so uncomfortable? She tried to hide her unease, but Walter had come to know her too well.

Much too well.

The first few days after she had summoned them he had watched her, studied her, deceiving himself that he needed to know her to help her. But now, with the illumination provided by Rozer's wine, he understood. He had been indulging himself, grasping the chance to be near this dark-haired substitute for Cassimara. But it had become too bitter a study. Even the differences between the lady and his wife made him recall Cassimara in more detail than had been safe for his peace of mind. So he had withdrawn from Richenza's disturbing presence, telling himself he had no right to interfere in her life.

It seemed that he should have watched her more closely or trusted someone other than Alesander with her safety—if Alesander was guilty of what Annet feared. Walter tried to remember when he had had Alesander with him at night and when Thomas had said Alesander was out wandering. Walter was certain he had detected hostility toward Alesander on the part of the lady. Had that been real or an attempt to hide a clandestine love affair? If they were lovers, which Walter could not quite bring himself to believe.

This was not the time to think about that. He returned to the only distraction he had—the high table.

The princess—no, she was Queen Meriel now—was speaking to her new husband. She was one of the few brides Walter had seen who looked good in bridal scarlet.

Brian did not look like a man at his wedding; he looked
worried. Because the plan might fail, or because it might
succeed? Payne should have been able to keep a closer
watch on him.

I don't trust his instincts. He is too young.

Rozer claimed Brian's attention but, even as he turned
to her father, Queen Meriel kept her gaze on her husband
as if he might disappear.

Walter did not like that at all.

The discreet music ended, and an announcement was
made; rare Sartherian Kemtar wine was being served for
the final salute—the one to Haldan that was always last to
be given at Tarsean banquets.

To pass the time while the guests were being served, a
lutenist came to play—a young player, red-haired, a boy of
fifteen or sixteen. Reynard's playing was good enough and
the king's favoritism blatant enough that the hall quieted
for him.

Walter drank more wine. One of the reasons he hated
weddings was the music.

Music had been different when he was young. He had
quieted when his lord asked silence for the bard but otherwise had had no opinion of it. Cassimara had made it
different. She had shown it to him as something to think
about and had even taught him to dance. Now it was another reminder of her fate, another stroke of the lash.

He deserved the pain, didn't he? Arrogance had always
been his strongest failing. Plain arrogance had made him
decide that he could protect Cassimara better than those
who had devoted their lives to the task. She could have
been smuggled to Madaria in time, could have lived her
life safely and happily there. But he had been too arrogant
to give up his station, too sure that he could protect her.

*She was so close to safety, and I carried her away from
it.*

The servingman brought the small goblets of Sartherian
wine. Walter had never tasted Kemtar. In his day Saroth
had laws, so Hamon said, against exporting it, and even
now it was so rare as to be almost mythical in the north.
Its quality was so legendary that Sartherians swore by it.

He raised the small goblet curiously to sniff the wine,

and as he did so, a small warning went off in his mind like the warning that sounded when he was lied to; the Kemtar was poisoned.

So Leot had decided Walter was expendable. Richenza had told him that the prince had threatened him. Well, that young man would be in for a surprise. The Ladies had decreed that the Leader of the Wild Hunt should be given protection from the common threats of the life he led: he knew no illness; he was warned of lies and of poison. More importantly, in the case of poison he was given the power to avoid it. All he need do now was mentally gather the poison and roll it into a ball until nothing was left but a small amber bead at the bottom of the cup. Rozer's serv-ingmen would find a reward in the goblet.

Before Walter could perform this small task, a ripple of conversation among the people seated near him made him look up. Reynard was shaking his head at the king. The king made some remark, but the boy seemed to refuse him. Walter recognized his stance; Reynard was being stubborn.

With Michel dismissed, Walter needed a spy in the pal-ace. This was no time to displease the king. Walter sent Reynard a warning.

The boy paused, then bowed in acquiescence. As he seated himself he cast a quick glance in Walter's direction and began to play.

The first few notes were familiar, but it was not until Reynard began to sing that Walter's heart went as cold as it had when he was cursed.

> *"I shall keep thee safe, love,*
> *Like a bird on her nest,"*

This was a song that peasants sang at weddings.

> *"Like a jewel in its casket,*
> *Like a doe at her rest."*

It had once had a great many verses. Walter remembered them all.

> *"No harm shall befall thee,*
> *While I still draw breath,"*

A commonplace song, but Walter noticed that it seemed
to please the new queen. She placed her hand on her husband's and smiled as she listened.

> *"For now, for all morrows,*
> *Until my own death."*

But I am still alive, and she is dead—dead nine hundred
years because of my conceit.

The song ended everywhere but in Walter's head.

He looked into his goblet and remembered the poison.

The toast was made to Haldan, and Walter drained his
goblet without tasting the rare wine of Saroth.

No servant that night had the fortune to find an amber
bead in a goblet.

Brian looked ruefully at his bride, who slept nestled against
his side. Even in the dim candlelight her painful thinness
was too obvious, unsoftened and unhidden by her unbound
hair. Her hair relaxed into waves and tendrils and, as Brian
idly curled a stray lock around a finger of his free hand, he
realized that Meriel, too, was relaxed as he had never seen
her before. His wedding night had been surprisingly enjoyable, and he had not expected to enjoy it at all. He had
gone into it with a chivalric little speech about waiting until
she was ready. Meriel had been panic-stricken at the
thought that anything might leave their marriage incomplete
and dissolvable and presented a brave little speech of her
own about understanding his repugnance. Somewhere in his
efforts to disabuse her, the whole thing had become very
natural and right.

He couldn't go through with it, he acknowledged finally.
She trusted him, and he could not betray that trust. Not for
his own life, not for anybody's. He tried to justify the price
of the Hunt's failure—they deserved it, didn't they? And
then he thought about his conversation with Reynard. No,
not all of them.

Walter must have guessed that he would have second

thoughts. His part in this was so easy—open a door, stand aside and let others do the bloodletting. Simple and clean. But he couldn't stand aside. He couldn't tell her the truth either. He owed the Hunt something, and he felt no regrets for Rozer or Leot.

Would she even believe the truth: "The Wild Hunt was summoned to exterminate your entire family?" Not likely, and not likely to lead to action that would truly protect her. No, for once he would have to use his well-practiced talent for lying to save a skin other than his own. What would she believe and what could he do to keep her safe? He hadn't much time, especially if Walter suspected that he might not cooperate.

He had invented and discarded several stories before the tickle of her hair on his arm made him aware that Meriel was awake and watching him.

"Lady Marika told me that men always fell asleep afterward." She reached up to smooth the frown from his forehead. "Or is it possible that *you* have a headache?"

"If only that were all."

Meriel pulled herself up beside him on the pillows. "Would it help if you talked about it?"

Brian looked at Meriel sitting beside him, her head tilted with wifely concern. He'd not get a better chance, so he'd best try the story he had just worked out.

"I'm worried about Abethell. It seems that he is trying to control me, much as my mother controls Daimiron."

He talked in this vein, offering examples of Abethell's supposed high-handedness as her interjected comments became more and more distressed.

"I don't wish to be ungrateful. I owe Abethell a great deal, but I don't want to be anyone's puppet king."

"What can you do?"

"I can make sure that I don't owe my throne solely to him. There are other lords willing to depose Daimiron. I must approach them on my own, not through Abethell. And that won't be easy since he's packed my household with his spies." He paused, but she had no comments. "I'll have to slip away." Her face fell. "No, *we'll* have to slip away. It wouldn't be safe to leave you in Abethell's hands. He could use you as a hostage."

"Oh, yes." She brightened. "Take me with you."

"Of course, I couldn't take you all the way to Canjit. It's too hard a journey at this time of year." Meriel shook her head in protest. "Don't you have some trusted friend away from Tarsit with whom you could stay without anyone knowing?"

"No." Her head dropped, then she looked up, tears in her eyes. "I wouldn't be a burden, truly. I'm much stronger than I look. Please"—she swallowed hard—"take me with you."

"But, Meriel, it has to be a fast journey; could you keep up? It's not a trip for a woman. We'd have to travel light and with no servants, because I don't know whom to trust."

"I'm not helpless, and I still have the boy's clothing from the masquerade." Her tears were gone; she was caught up in the excitement of planning. "I could cut my hair."

Brian winced but said nothing.

"No one would know I was a girl. For once there would be an advantage to my being so skinny."

Brian doubted her enthusiasm would last very many days on the road. She would think of some refuge soon enough, but now her eagerness was useful.

"The trick will be to escape our household. Especially since time is so short. I wish we could go in the morning, but there are too many people around. We'll have to wait till everyone is asleep tomorrow night and slip away. But I hate to lose the time and distance."

Meriel's eyes lit up. "Rosara's sleeping potion! I'll ask her for some." She reached for her bedgown. Brian caught her hand.

"You can't tell her you're going to run away. She'll . . ."

"Of course not." Meriel smiled. "I'll say that I desperately want time alone with my husband without everyone gawking. I'll suggest to the steward that we stop midday to rest and dine. There's a beautiful glade near Ainshurst, with a pond in its center. My governess taught me to swim there."

Brian raised an eyebrow. Few noblemen, let alone noblewomen, of his acquaintance swam of anything but necessity.

Meriel answered his look. "It was such a good way to escape my brothers. Ewets didn't swim at all, and Leot swam badly. In the water I was free of them. Anyway, it is a beautiful place where anyone would want to tarry, and after everyone eats I'll share the comfits the Madarian ambassador gave me yesterday. They're fruit preserved in sweet wine—Rosara's potion has a sweet taste—and sufficiently rare and foreign that people won't know what they're supposed to taste like."

"How long does it take the potion to work?"

"It's quite fast—less than a candle inch the time I had the toothache."

Brian considered. "The fewer people involved the better. We could send part of our households on ahead. The guard could be posted on the road, leaving just a select party of nobles. After the potion does its work we'll slip off through the forest. Do you know the area?"

"My governess's family had lands in the Lordship. I stayed there often as a child. I could find my way." She leaned over and kissed him lightly, then slid from the bed. "It's almost dawn. I've got to get my costume out and packed in my cloak bag before the maids wake up."

24

Twenty-third Day

Walter couldn't die, Thomas reassured himself, and Justin said he was on the mend.

The night of the wedding banquet had been uncomfortable from the moment Alesander had deposited Walter with Thomas, saying, "He's drunk."

Thomas hadn't known whether to believe Alesander. Walter had stood quietly looking out the windows, drumming his fingers on the ledge. Thomas had seen him do the same for hours on end, but there had been something different about it last night. He seemed to be waiting, not thinking.

Finally Thomas had ventured a question. "Why did you come home so early?"

Walter had looked around. "I'm going to be sick." Then he was.

Thomas had fetched a chamber pot and a cloth and had waited for the vomiting to end. But it hadn't, and Thomas had realized that besides his glazed expression and clumsiness Walter was straining for each breath. When Walter had doubled over, pain writ clear on his face, Thomas had run to fetch Justin.

Walter had barely noticed when Justin examined him, though Thomas had expected him to object. Justin had been bitterly amused when told Walter was ill, but had grown grim as Walter had cried out against the pain. When the spasm had passed Justin had taken a candle and moved it slowly back and forth in front of Walter's eyes.

"This isn't drink," Justin had said. "If I didn't know better, I'd say he'd been poisoned."

They had helped Walter to bed and Justin administered what help he could. But Walter was weak, very weak. The dose would have killed him had he been anything other than what he was. And even now, after a full night and day, the slightest effort left him weak and shaking. And he could not, or would not, speak more than a few words. Thomas had to force himself not to hover in the bedroom asking questions.

Where were they in Walter's labyrinthine plan? Hamon and Payne should have killed Princess Meriel by now. Rozer seemed to have taken Ellis's bait about the Scepter. Michel had reported that Leot, too, had acted according to plan. Alesander said that he was ready for the combat—those were the only plans which might be endangered now. What could go wrong? How could he prepare for mishaps?

From Michel's report of the conversation between Rozer and Leot, Alesander was safe. But Thomas wished he had Walter's ability to summon the others at will.

Oh well. I'll have to manage without it.

Raised voices from the passage were followed by the thud of a large object falling and the crash of metal against stone. Thomas hurried across the room and opened the door a crack.

Hamon lay on the stone paving, surrounded by scattered plates knocked from an overturned sideboard. Alesander stood over him saying, "And if I see you in the same room with—"

Hamon spun a plate into Alesander's face and launched himself across the space between them before Alesander could recover. Tackled at knee level, Alesander hit the wall and slid to the floor, the wind knocked out of him.

Thomas judged it time to intervene. He grabbed Hamon by the neck of his cote, pulled him off Alesander, and planted himself between them. "I don't know what this is

about''—but in a sudden flash of insight he did know—
''but this schoolboy nonsense could not be more ill timed.''

Eyeing each other, both men scrambled up. Alesander
kicked a plate at Hamon's shins, and Hamon sidestepped
Thomas to throw a punch at Alesander's midsection. Exasperated, Thomas shoved Hamon down into a chair and
pivoted to face Alesander.

''Alesander, look after Bertz. Now,'' he prompted, when
Alesander did not move. ''You've made your point. Go.''

Alesander scowled at Hamon and stalked off.

When he was gone, Thomas let Hamon get to his feet.
Hamon rubbed what was going to be a nice bruise on his
left cheekbone. ''I'll be damned. She told him. I'd have
wagered—''

''What are you doing here?'' Thomas pulled him into
the withdrawing room. ''It's almost dawn, you might have
been seen.''

''I need to see Walter.''

''You can't.''

''Then you can tell him that his two birds have flown
the coop.''

''What?''

''Payne let me in about midnight as planned. Only Their
Majesties were nowhere to be found. It seems when Brian
and Meriel stopped to eat they sent most of the train, including Payne, ahead. Late in the afternoon everyone but
Brian and the girl turned up. According to Payne, one of
the maids-in-waiting was bawling about having helped
them 'spend some time alone' together and that she had
lent the princess her sleeping potion. All any of the rest of
them knew was that they ate and fell asleep. When they
woke, Brian and the girl were gone.''

Thomas glanced toward the bedroom door. ''Walter
thought that Brian couldn't be trusted.''

''*Now* can I see Walter?''

''No.''

''Damn it—''

''You can't see Walter because it wouldn't be any use.''
Getting angry at Hamon was useless; he had to think. ''He
chose to take poison at the wedding banquet. He's barely

able to speak, and it'll be days before he's strong enough to deal with this.''

Even Hamon took a moment to digest that news. ''Well, someone's got to do something. If the girl isn't killed—''

''Then kill her. Brian can't bring her back here, there'd be too many questions. The only other place he can take her is Canjit.''

''And there are only two roads he can take,'' Hamon said slowly. ''North through Morthrell or south through Manreth.''

''Unless he goes straight west through Merscelun.''

''I don't think so. Between the lake, the hills, and the swamp they'd never make it in five days. And the damned fool isn't likely to abandon the girl in the wilderness.''

''Take Payne. One of you go north, the other south. Kill the girl.''

''What if he does go west?''

''If they don't turn up on the roads to Manreth or Morthrell within a reasonable time—you and Payne work that out—then meet somewhere and look west. There can't be that many well-dressed young couples riding through the swamp this time of year.''

''Only two of us?''

''Do you want Michel? I have no way of sending for him.''

''We'll do better without him. Bertz?''

Briefly, Thomas told him of the attack on Alesander and Richenza, and of Bertz's injury.

''Dropping like flies, aren't we? Let's hope that it doesn't get worse.''

Thomas could think of no fitting reply except to echo him.

25

Twenty-fourth Day

"It'll be much easier for you, Annet." Richenza felt every sort of dissembler. "Another woman can wait on me, but who else can safely nurse Bertz while Justin is with Walter?"

Annet pursed her lips and brushed Richenza's hair. "I don't think it's safe to leave you alone."

"With Thomas and Justin directly across the passageway?" This was not the time to mention Alesander.

"I don't like it."

"Nothing will happen. I'll see that Gunnora sleeps in your room, if you're so worried. I don't want you running up and down stairs all the time to tend to me."

"Why Gunnora?"

"She did well enough last year when your son was sick. Besides, I just wouldn't feel right if that poor man didn't have you nursing him." Annet's only vanity was of her skill as a nurse. "And you'll be distracted if you rush from me to him."

Annet didn't speak until she'd finished putting Richenza's hair in its nighttime plaits. "I'll go if you promise not to leave the house until the tournament."

"I'll not leave these rooms."

And after Gunnora had been summoned and

given a long recital of all the things she must not forget, all the things she must watch out for, and all the things she had done wrong the last time she had waited on Richenza, Annet departed.

Richenza sighed with relief and turned to the nervous servant girl. She had chosen her not for her skills, but for her timidity. Gunnora wouldn't say a word about anything she saw out of the ordinary, and would not disobey any orders.

"I can put myself to bed, Gunnora." Annet had already helped her change for the night. "You may go. Don't come until I summon you in the morning."

When the girl had gone she sat at the windows overlooking her garden and waited for Alesander to return from helping Thomas.

Waiting was not helpful; she thought too much.

I am about to behave like a common tavern wench. Or worse, like Betrissa. That's not true. She slept with many men. I only want one. And only now because I can't have him any other way.

She saw the gibbous moon that had forced her decision and totted up the time left—counting tonight that left five or six days. Not enough to make up for a lifetime.

She wasn't sure Alesander would let her do this. *If I want to behave like a tavern wench, what is it I want him to behave like?*

The moon seemed to fill the whole sky. A three-quarters and more moon; who ruled that? Poets and storytellers had told her that Anchytel ruled the new moon, Enath ruled the half, and Elun the full. Who ruled when the moon was between phases? Richenza supposed that the Rensel philosophers must have argued about that.

Enath, Elun, she prayed, *whichever it is, please help me. Let me have Alesander until the full moon. You'll have him forever after that. Let me have him until you do.*

The unblinking gaze of the moon was cold and unfeeling. In her mind she could see the Three Goddesses depicted on the wall at Reasalyn, with their serenely secretive countenances and their long hair flowing as if they were brides.

Richenza's hair was in clumsy plaits, and she went to comb them out.

She had no more than finished when she heard the door from the withdrawing room to the passage open and shut, and then heard sounds in Alesander's chamber.

She slowly made the last long stroke with the comb, looking at the door between her room and the next. Walter had had Annet move so that Alesander could be next door in case of assassins. Annet had been scandalized, but once the necessity had been impressed upon her she had suffered the change to be made.

It wasn't bolted.

Richenza put down the comb very quietly. She wore the blue bedgown—the one she had worn the night she had gone to Hamon.

She wanted nothing to remind her of Hamon's hands. The bedgown dropped to the floor, leaving her only in a nightshift embroidered with black hummingbirds.

The door opened silently to her touch. Alesander was sprawled on the bed, gazing into the fire. He did not move until she reached his bed. Then he turned quickly as if expecting an attacker. He froze in disbelief.

The only light in the room was that of the fire, and it fell full on her as she sat across the bed from him. She saw him take in her tumbling obsidian hair and her night shift.

"You should not be here, my lady."

"In five days the moon will be full again."

He shook his head and started to back off the bed, but Richenza lightly touched his shoulder.

"Stay. I want you to."

Without looking at her he said, "When the moon is full I will have to leave you. I will be gone forever."

"I know."

"And you still came to me?"

"Yes."

He reached out to brush her hair back from her face.

"My lady, we are both about to do something very unwise."

She smiled. "I know that, too."

He laughed, then kissed her.

Ellis knew the footsteps in the passageway meant he was about to have visitors. Who would stump about the pas-

sageways of this inn three hours before dawn but Ulick and
Garrett, who would be quieter, or someone come to haul
him off? He'd been marking time waiting for Prince Leot
to make his move. He gave the plump, blond whore next
to him a quick shake to wake her, rolled out of bed, and
began to lace his hose. If he were going to be arrested, he
was damned well going to be dressed.

The question was, were they Leot's men or Rozer's arguing in front of his door? Rozer could have decided that
he had to have the bloody Scepter tonight—wouldn't that
make Walter happy? It could be Tredgett trying to save the
king—another pleasant thought. Or—the door flew open.

"His Highness wishes to see you." Even if he hadn't
seen the leopard's mask badges, how many "Highnesses"
were left in Tarsia?

This, at least, was according to plan. Ellis reached round
the gaping whore to grab his shirt.

He wasn't able to keep track of where they took him,
nor did he recognize the house.

Leot looked puffy and sour; he must have been dozing
while he waited. Looking at him, Ellis could understand
why—given the choice between them—Richenza had chosen the king. Leot looked stupid and vicious, as opposed
to just stupid.

Putting on his best Selinian manner, Ellis lifted his chin
and spoke before he was addressed.

"Well? Why have I been brought here?"

"Mind your tongue," Leot said, as one of his men
handed him a goblet of wine. Then he seemed to notice
that there were more people about than he wanted. "Get
out," he ordered his hangers-on, "I've private business."

*That's right, Your Highness, make sure they know what
you're doing.*

Leot eyed him. "You've been granted a manor by my
father. Why?"

"I sold him a Rensel statue he fancied."

"Brydson has sold him dozens of statues he fancied, and
he's never granted him a 'thank-you,' let alone a manor.
You promised to sell him something else, didn't you?"

"You're telling this story, Your Highness. What did I
sell him?"

"The Scepter of Reas."

"That's been missing for twelve hundred years."

"You know where it is."

"How would I know that?"

"You were overheard, man. Don't play with me."

"And if I did say such a thing?"

Leot leaned back in his chair. "I'd have you killed right now." He paused to let his words sink in. "Of course, since I know you're lying, I will probably get rid of you, anyway."

Even if Ellis hadn't expected Leot to make a further proposition, the purring tone in Leot's voice would have given it away, so he stood impassive, waiting.

"On the other hand, you might do me a service."

"Such as?"

"Where is the Scepter?" Before Ellis could deny knowledge, Leot stopped him. "Your only chance to get out of here alive is to answer me truthfully."

"In Tarses's tomb. Buried with him."

Leot thought about it. He took a drink of his wine and nodded, his mood improved.

"Good. It's an isolated place—especially if Father dismisses the guards, as he surely will." Leot got up. "You can have your manor, and your life, if you'll take him to the tomb and kill him."

"No."

"Are you out of your mind, man? I said—"

"And what would my life be worth if I killed one of Tarses's descendants—a king at that—in his presence? There's a curse on the Scepter as it is. Do you think I'd get away unscathed?"

"Surely you don't believe that—"

"And then, Your Highness, there is the matter of the guards. His Majesty may dismiss them, but they won't go far. As soon as they see me leave alone they'll look to see what's become of the king. Dying here and now would be a damned sight easier than the penalties for high treason. Thank you, Your Highness, I'll pass."

Leot's face flushed with anger, and he started to call someone, but he reconsidered.

Come on, Your Highness. Work it out. Save me having to feed it to you.

"There are ways around those problems," Leot said.

"If you can think of any, I'll be grateful."

"I could send someone . . . No, that would mean . . ."

Someone else to blackmail you, Just a little more thought.

But that little bit of thought was beyond him. Leot continued staring at an uninspired fresco depicting some early Sueve slaughter.

"Your Highness, if I might suggest. . . ."

"What?"

"King Tarses might not be so vindictive if the . . . deed . . . were done by one of his descendants."

A puzzled crease appeared between Leot's brows.

"But I am the only . . ." He thought the matter over, then nodded. "The guards could be bribed. And afterward no one would dare ask what had happened. I'd be all but crowned."

He looked to Ellis. "When?"

"I've made arrangements to go with His Majesty the night before the Feast of Haldan."

This seemed to take Leot aback, then he grinned. "It'll be a fine way to start my reign. I'll make that arrogant bitch understand who the king is."

Very well done, Your Highness. Very well done, indeed. Welcome to the ranks.

26

Twenty-fifth Day

Richenza woke from a light doze and sat up suddenly. Dim light came through the window; she'd slept longer than she'd intended. She turned to look at the man lying beside her. He was watching her lazily, his head resting on his folded arms.

She wasn't sure what to say.

"Good morning," she ventured.

He smiled. "Very good—so far."

Richenza blushed, and laughed back at him.

Alesander rolled over and stretched. "At least I won't think I dreamed this." He sat up. "Your servants are beginning to stir, my lady."

"I know, I shouldn't have slept." She caught up her night shift and pulled it on hastily. "Will you dine with me tonight?"

"Is that all?"

"What else should there be?" she asked, wide-eyed. Alesander caught her for a final kiss. Pushing away from him at last, she rushed into her own room.

Annet stood holding the discarded bedgown.

Without expression she turned to look at Richenza. "I came down because—because I knew Gunnora couldn't do your hair. . . ."

"Annet—"

She dropped the bedgown. "I shouldn't have come at all."

"Annet, please."

The woman turned without answering and went through the door.

"Annet!" The door closed firmly, and Richenza stood looking at it, not knowing what to do.

Richenza paced the floor of her drawing room. Alesander would not arrive for an hour, yet. She felt more alone than she had felt in her life—except for the night she'd gone to Reasalyn. That night she'd been shielded by her own cold anger. Now she felt less shielded than imprisoned. Was it because Annet had not come back after her catastrophic appearance in Richenza's rooms this morning, or was it because, with Alesander off with Thomas, Richenza had nothing to distract her thoughts from what would happen in five nights?

She had to face it; at the full moon she was going to lose Alesander. He was cursed. He had to go back—didn't he? She searched her memory again. Only one story she could recall ended with someone escaping the Hunt—Amloth, Tarses's son.

You could never trust any story with Amloth in it, they contradicted each other. In one story Amloth was a savage, and in the next he was as courteous and gently behaved as—as Walter. Did the stories confuse the two or had they been changed and twisted down the years? Had Amloth changed?

Worse, she had heard several versions of the fall of Onsalm, when Amloth escaped the curse. Annet's story said he was unable to join his men because he was trapped in a burning building. A poem written half a century ago, which her father had been fond of, ended with his being freed by the Ladies for his nobility of heart—an unlikely idea, considering the man had just set fire to Onsalm. And wasn't there a play in which he was freed at the behest of a Rensel princess?

"How did Amloth get free?" she asked the fire.

"Bad luck, likely," said a harsh voice from the passage

door. Richenza turned. Justin stood there, barely supporting himself against the doorpost. He held a goblet in one hand and a bottle in the other.

"What are you doing away from Sir Walter?"

"Oh, I've not abandoned him, Your Ladyship. Thomas has given me time off. Trouble is I've nowhere to go. Thomas doesn't want me in there"—he pointed down the passage with his chin—"and your woman won't have me upstairs."

He took Richenza's lack of action as a welcome. He pushed himself into the room and collapsed into a chair.

"This isn't all drink," he assured her, pouring wine into his goblet. "We get tired, too."

"How is Sir Walter?"

Justin grinned sardonically over the edge of his cup. "He'll live." He lowered the goblet. "He'll force himself up when he wants to. He should be almost back to normal by the time we go back."

Back to what? She studied Justin as he studied the fire and his bottle. She'd never spoken to him before, but the things she wanted to ask weren't things you asked a stranger.

Or were they? He'd be gone at the full moon like the rest of them, so there'd be no encounters raising embarrassing memories. Why not ask him?

"You don't know how Amloth was freed?"

Justin shrugged. "Who cares? Freed or not, what difference does it make?"

Alesander had said he was a confirmed drunkard, but he showed no signs of it; his eyes were clear, and, when he was sober, his hands were steady. Were the ills of heavy drinking cured like all the other hurts and illnesses at the full moon?

His cloudy grey eyes fell under her gaze, and he shrugged again. "I suppose Walter or someone has mentioned it, Your Ladyship, but I really don't remember."

Silence fell. His bottle was nearly empty.

She had another question.

"What happens to you between summonings?"

"That I wish I *could* forget." He refilled his goblet. "You don't want to know, Your Ladyship."

"But I do. Very much."

He eyed his bottle, then her. "Another bottle's worth?"

"If you wish." Richenza rose and pulled the bell. She gave orders to the liveried man, and Justin was soon settling back in his chair with a fresh supply of drink.

"There isn't much between times, but it's all bad." He took a long draught. "For a moment or two we just wait— to learn if we've failed or not. At least I think it's a short time. We've no way of judging how long it is."

He was silent for a moment. "After that we sleep." He gave her the skull-like rictus that passed for his smile. "Think of the worst nightmare you've ever had. Think of it three hundred years long, and you can't wake up. That's how it is between summonings."

He leaned forward. "These aren't the foolish nightmares children have of being chased by even more foolish monsters. No, Your Ladyship, these are real—where everyone you loved dies horribly because you didn't care. Only in these dreams you *do* care because now you know what you did, but you can't stop it happening. Over and over and over." His voice dropped. "And do you know what the worst is?" His eyes almost burned her they were so intense. "Do you know?"

She shook her head.

"When you wake up you have to do it again to someone else."

He wasn't drunk, she decided, he was mad.

"Do you still want to set us free, Your Ladyship?" He forced himself to his feet. "None of us should be let loose on the world. There's a reason we're here." He made it to the doorway and looked back over his shoulder. "Thank you for the bottle."

"Alesander," Richenza said as they dined that night, "tell me about Justin."

Alesander, who had been silent except when spoken to throughout the meal, scowled. "Why would you want to know about him?"

She shrugged. "I spoke to him today, and it seems unlikely that an apothecary should have been cursed."

"No more so than a Stros or a Sueve. . . ." It was left unsaid that for a Prince of Tarsia, such a fate might be considered natural.

"But Bertz and Ulick were warriors, you said. They had enemies."

Alesander looked at his plate. "Neither Walter nor Justin has given any details. I gather it was some accident involving his wife and children. Since Walter lets him drink when he isn't needed, it must have been something grim."

"Only now you know what you did," he'd said, "but you can't stop it happening. Over and over and over. . . ." Very grim, indeed.

Richenza looked at Alesander. She'd had to hold up the entire conversation herself. He didn't seem abstracted, precisely, but it was as if he was trying not to say something. He only looked at her when he thought she wasn't looking at him.

"And Sir Walter, how is he?"

"It's hard to say, my lady." Alesander paused as if seeking words. "Justin says he should be able to sit up and to speak. But he doesn't seem . . . interested."

She was reminded of her father. When Betrissa had stripped him of his office as governor to the princes he had just given up and died within a year.

Walter couldn't die, but among the things left unsaid was that there was still no word of Brian and Meriel.

Later Richenza sat on a bench near the fire and watched Alesander pretend to look at the garden.

This was getting them nowhere. She might as well get the problem out in the open.

"Alesander." His hands pressed hard against the window ledge. "Alesander, what have I done wrong?"

Alesander slumped forward. "It isn't what—" He paused to collect his thoughts. "My lady, I am not a fool. Nor am I, I think, overly vain." He straightened and turned to face her.

Richenza knew what he wanted to know, but she waited for him to ask.

"I've had women in my bed because I'm a prince, because I'm handsome, because they wanted to be there, and because I paid them." He took a deep ragged breath. "My lady, why were you there?"

"Because I wanted to be. Isn't that enough?"

"I told you, I'm not that vain. You have too much to lose to give in to a moment's whim."

She pulled her knees up and rested her chin on them. "What have I to lose?"

"You're betrothed to Feracher, and he—"

"He'd jump at the chance to marry into Indes's lands if I were selling myself on street corners."

"So you still plan to wed him."

"After being betrothed to the king? I don't think I could settle for a mere grand duke."

"Then you're not?"

She closed her eyes. "I honestly don't know. It might be safe, it might be intolerable. I can't think of it just now."

Alesander repeated his first question, "Why?"

Richenza rose and faced him. "Because I love you." He lifted one hand, ready to protest—not her love, but her actions. "And in a few nights you'll be lost to me." She caught the half-raised hand. "If I had left it at that—'I love you, good-bye'—you would have faded into a pleasant but distant memory, like a childhood holiday. I wanted more than that of you."

"You may have more than memories."

"I know. I hope so." She looked out at the fat, threatening moon. "That's why I don't know if I'll marry. I doubt you'd want your child raised as a Feracher."

She'd made him smile. "Feracher has always been a far more recalcitrant House than Indes."

She smiled at him. "But you must admit that Indes has always been more persistent."

"Much more."

A little later she said, "My father and brother always called me Ric'a. Please, I am not 'your lady.' "

"Oh, but you are. . . ."

Brian looked back at Meriel, riding a dozen or so yards behind him. She was wobbling with exhaustion. He had bought her a few hours' uneasy rest on the ground the night before, a mile or two off the main road in a copse, but it had been little enough. Her mount was nearly spent, too, even though the uncanny beast he rode seemed not to notice the miles of hard riding.

She pulled up beside him. "Are you . . ." Her voice faded. She closed her eyes and mustered strength to try again. "Are you all right?"

"Yes." She looked tense in spite of her exhaustion, and he wondered if his own fear had communicated itself. The boy's clothing disguised her well, but a costume designed for a masquerade was not very warm outdoors at night when it was nearly winter. And they traveled north; it would get colder.

"Are you sure you want to continue? It smells like snow."

She sat up straighter. "Of course I can go on." It was a brave show, and utterly unconvincing.

"There's an inn a few miles north, and I've a little coin money."

He saw relief in her eyes as she nodded. He'd hoped to wear her down to the point where she'd name some safe place where she could be protected, but he was afraid now that she'd collapse before she would admit weakness. Canjit was more than five days hard ride away on the road—but they might reach the border. Over the border he would have to leave her with someone he could trust.

And for the rest of her life she can wonder why I abandoned Canjitrin and her.

As they rode side by side at a slower pace, he watched his wife covertly. How many women, especially sheltered women of high birth, would not only have agreed to make this journey but helped to plan it to the last detail, and would pretend not to notice that it was half killing her? Offhand the only two he could think of were his mother and the Tarsean lady who had summoned the Hunt, and he doubted that either of them would be so charming about the situation.

The inn was the one where he and Payne had stayed on the trip to Tarsit. The common room was full of travelers trying to make the most of the last weeks, or days, before snows closed the shorter of the two feasible roads to Canjit. He pulled Meriel down beside him at one of the tables; she was trembling with exhaustion, and her collapse would make them conspicuous.

He looked at her in the hazy light. She looked both exhausted and elated. In spite of the hardships she was still eager for the journey. Why? Because it was the only adventure she was likely to have in her sheltered life—ah, but she hadn't dealt with his mother yet!—or because inexplicably she felt she was doing something for him?

That was a frightening thought. How could he ever explain abandoning her when it was time to go back?

"Hungry?" he asked.

"A little." She looked around. "Isn't that your man, Payne?"

Brian looked where she pointed. It wasn't his man, but it was certainly Payne.

"Could he help us? You said he helped you before."

"No," he said sharply. She looked surprised. "I don't know whose pay he's in now." He was lying again—oh, he knew who had directed Payne to chase them. "Abethell may have sent him after us."

"What should we do?"

Payne was talking to the little tapster who "wouldn't forget" him last time. Brian could tell by the girl's pout and the angry toss of her head that he wasn't propositioning her. He must be asking if she'd seen them.

They'd made some luck and fallen into some. He'd spoken to no one at the inn, and Payne would be looking for him with a woman. Or had Walter figured out that Meriel would be disguised? He wouldn't put that past the old man.

"Meriel," he said quietly, "get up and go out to the yard. Get your horse and head south."

"South?"

"Yes. Wait for me where we made the decision to stay here—remember the place where the trees are thick by the road?"

"Hide in the trees?"

"Yes." How to put the fear of the gods into her without telling her the truth?

"I'm afraid that he may be an Arinese spy. He's from the south, and Abethell didn't think he was from Canjitrin at all." She nodded. "He may mean us both harm. If I don't catch up with you by—by the time the moon shows over the horizon, I want you to flee as fast as you can to somewhere you'll be known. Promise me."

"But—"

"Give me your word."

Her face was pale and frightened. "I—I promise."

"I'll probably catch up with you in a few minutes." He hoped he sounded confident. "But be sure it's me before you stop."

She walked out the door, and Payne, arguing with the tapster, barely glanced at Meriel. At least she had a beggar's chance of getting somewhere safe, and since Brian didn't have any idea where she'd go, he couldn't reveal it to Walter no matter what the Huntsman did to him.

A crowd of men argued by the fire. He wouldn't have to pass Payne to get to them as he would the door. He rose casually and joined the men. Payne didn't look his way.

He put the group between himself and Payne. Now what? Payne could see the entrance and the stair to the sleeping rooms. Even the door to the kitchen would be under his eye.

"Hey, you." A red-faced man had noticed him. "Will you fight in the spring, or run like these cowards?"

"Not him," said one of his companions, drunker than the others, who were all far from sober. "He's going to stay warm with Janet. He's been watching her since he came in."

Brian gave them a measuring look. They were past any subtle reasoning. He had an idea.

"Not the woman—I'm watching the man. My employer has heard of an Arinese spy with red hair, riding for Canjitrin."

They were interested now. "And he'd be very grateful if someone questioned that man—who fits the description— and found out where he was from. I can't, of course, because I might be traced to my employer."

They all turned to look at Payne, who was trying something besides money on the tapster.

"Who is this 'employer' of yours?" a dark, skinny man asked suspiciously.

Brian raised one eyebrow at him—a trick he'd taught himself to use on servants when they'd found him embrangled in one of Geoffry's jokes. "Let's just say he has a fair amount of influence—and money."

He smiled deprecatingly. "At any rate, I'll be upstairs in the second room from the left, if one of you would be so kind as to talk to him long enough to find out if he's suspicious. And do it in a way that'll keep him from getting wise to who wants to know."

They were eager to help; the combination of money and patriotism seemed irresistible.

The red-faced man went first; he leaned on the bar, and struck up a conversation with Payne. The other men followed, giving the proceeding the air of an inquisition.

Still, it worked. The crowd around Payne was so thick and so intent on their interrogation, that none of them, and certainly not Payne, noticed him slip out the wrong door and into the cool night air.

Now if he could only convince Meriel to take his cloak and could find a barn for them to sleep in. They would have to take the longer southern route to Canjit. Who could he leave her with on that route in five days? And who else had Walter sent after them?

27

Twenty-sixth Day

Tredgett leaned his shoulders against the stone wall of the loggia that connected the priests' quarters to the Temple of Haldan. Behind those carved doors Alesander Scelin might even now be claiming to be a Prince of Tarsia as he took the preliminary oaths for the judicial combat. Tredgett hoped that whichever priests had witnessed those vows would prove talkative. Gossip could tell him what he needed to know. The knot of guardsmen in Indes's livery waited in the sunlit courtyard, but Tredgett knew that they could not see him hidden in the shadows beyond the grillwork that separated walkway from courtyard. Scelin wouldn't see him unless he moved.

Tredgett fingered the dagger thrust through his belt, the dagger with the arms of Indes that his man had brought from the ruins of Reasalyn along with news of Audwin's body and warm ashes on the altar, and he shivered, but not with the cold of the late-autumn day.

The carved door swung open. Tredgett saw with dismay that Scelin was accompanied by Symond Tierse, the High Priest's confidential secretary. He'd get no gossip from that close-mouthed man. Perhaps he could glean something from Scelin. Tredgett shoved himself away from the wall.

"How can a Prince of Tarsia destroy his country on a woman's whim?"

Alesander looked up, startled. The two men faced each other through the grill.

"If you know that," Alesander said, "you know I cannot change it."

"You can always change things."

"And leave her to Leot?" Alesander turned to join the guardsmen.

Tredgett watched them go, grasping the grillwork so tightly that it cut his hands. *Damn Richenza Indes and all of her kind.*

"I'm tired of making excuses for you," Thomas said sourly to Walter of Jacin. "You've been lying here trying to pretend it will all go away if you don't act, and it won't." Silence. It was hard to wrestle with someone who'd already pinned himself. "I assume this misplaced chivalry is in regard to the princess; Prince Leot wouldn't excite your delicate sensibilities."

Women were always Walter's weakness. It would be easier if he simply chased women as half the others did, but, no, Walter had to protect them. In Thomas's experience, women, when left to it, were capable of taking care of themselves. This Tarsean lady certainly had found a way to avoid the dirty work.

"So you're going to let us all die because she shouldn't? How can you justify so many lives for just one."

He thought he saw Walter's lips tighten, but it was only a momentary flicker.

Thomas turned away from the figure on the bed. He'd thought he'd seen Walter in all his moods, but this was different—akin to the despair Walter must have felt when he had cursed himself. There had to be a way to reach him.

"Maybe," Thomas said over his shoulder, "Hamon was right—you want the Hunt just to stop. Barring that, I suppose, failure will get *you* out of it?"

He stalked to the door, hoping that Walter would call him back. As he searched his mind to find one last argument to fling as he retreated, the door was torn out of his hand.

Lady Richenza's waiting woman pushed past Thomas
before he could catch his balance. She strode over to the
bed to glower at Walter.

"They tell me you're not truly sick. And I haven't time
for children's games." Walter, for a wonder, opened his
eyes to look at her as she spat out the words, "He's done
it, your fine prince. He's taken my lady."

Walter stayed silent, which infuriated the waiting
woman. She raised her voice. "Do you hear me?"

Thomas was halfway to her when he realized that Walter
was speaking.

"Yes," Walter said, his voice weak but sweeter than
music to Thomas. "What do you expect me to do? That is
beyond my power to fix."

The reply enraged her to the point of speechlessness.

"Something has to be done," she finally choked out. "I
found them yesterday morning. You said you would protect
her. Or is that just another of your promises?"

Walter seemed to gather himself; then he sat up and
rubbed his eyes.

"What are you going to do?" the woman demanded.

"Enough!" Walter said, "I'll do what I can!"

*Anchytel, it's taken a woman to do it. I apologize to the
sex.*

But there were limits even to miracles; Thomas half ushered, half pushed the woman out of the room, and closed
the door behind her. When he turned to Walter, Walter had
thrown back the covers and swung his legs over the side
of the bed. Thomas watched the Leader of the Wild Hunt
clothe himself with a thought, then balance tentatively on
his feet.

Thomas was afraid Walter would fall, but when he offered to help he was waved peremptorily away. Walter
managed to walk to the chair nearest the fire and sit. He
leaned his head back and looked into the flames, and Thomas wondered what to do next.

He'd just said things to Walter which were nearly unforgivable, so it was likely that he wasn't wanted, but Thomas was afraid that Walter would lapse into melancholy if
he weren't encouraged.

Before Thomas could decide whether to go or stay, Walter said quietly, "You were right; it is one thing to throw away my own life—but to throw away ten others is unforgivable."

"You—" Thomas began.

"I am sorry," said Walter of Jacin.

A tongue-tied Thomas wanted to ask half a dozen questions, not the least of which concerned some promise made to the waiting woman.

"I think," Walter continued, "I have muddled things beyond repair."

"I've sent Hamon and Payne to catch Brian and the princess."

"In Merscelun?"

"They may meet them on the road."

"Perhaps, but I don't think so. There is more to Brian Hassart than I suspected."

"Surely he won't take the girl where he might have to abandon her in the wilderness."

"Will he have to abandon her?"

Thomas scowled. "Surely that's not likely."

"It has happened before. Amloth and the other one—Lorcan."

"Yes, but—"

"Elun told me after Onsalm that there was a way out."

This was news; he'd never heard Walter more than reluctantly acknowledge the possibility of freedom.

"It depends," Thomas said, "on the princess. How much she knows."

Walter nodded. "I don't know what the Princess Meriel has heard—but I want you to tell the Lady Richenza everything you know about escaping."

"And Alesander—how much should I tell him? I don't know whether it will help or hurt if he conspires to get himself out."

Walter turned to look into the fire. "I doubt that it would make any difference. I don't know what happened when Amloth or Lorcan escaped, but I do know what happened the last time someone tried to hold one of us back, and Alesander rode with us then."

"The priestess who tried to hold Hamon? The one he killed?"

Walter nodded without looking at Thomas. "You know Alesander. Do you think he'd let Richenza try if he thought he might harm her—or kill her?"

"No, he wouldn't."

"But he may be the only one I can save." Walter sat with his elbows on the chair arms, his chin resting on his clasped hands. "Tell the Lady Richenza what you can, but be sure that Alesander suspects nothing."

"What about Brian?"

"We'll see what we can do. A moment—" Walter closed his eyes; when he opened them he said, "Brian is traveling south."

"That means he's still on the road."

"He'll get no more money. That should help Hamon and Payne find him, or slow him down." He looked up at Thomas. "Tell me everything. Has Eleylin reported yet?"

Thomas told him the news.

28

Twenty-seventh Day

Hamon had found half his quarry—the wrong half. The man was Brian Hassart, he was certain, even though he had only seen him twice. But knowing that was no use when Brian rode in a party of twelve people, almost half of them women.

From high ground Hamon had watched a stretch of road five miles north of the ferry beneath the Magnary bridge for two days. He was close enough to the ferry that he could see everyone bound for it and far enough away that his haunting the road wouldn't arouse suspicion. If the fleeing couple were going to go south, they would have to cross here or travel another forty miles to the next ferry.

But which of the five women in the party was Meriel of Tarsia?

He'd seen the princess once—at the audience where he'd caught Betrissa's eye, and all he could recall was that she had been pale, thin, and disapproving.

One of the woman was stout and forty, which eliminated her. The other four were more or less right. One was fair, but she didn't seem thin enough. Two were thin enough, but the first had red hair—though it could have been dyed—and

the second seemed to fit, though her hair was more brown
than fair. But *she* appeared to be attached to the middle-
aged man riding next to her. The last woman was dark and
too young but hair could be dyed black as well as red.

Four possibilities, and Brian was avoiding them all, riding at the head of the party with a stout older man.

If he could get Brian alone, Hamon was sure that he
could extract the information, eventually. But time was the
problem. He had only three days left, and if he caught
Brian, the woman could hide anywhere.

Maybe Brian had stowed her somewhere and was leading
them on a wild-goose chase.

Hamon scowled at the sky and wondered if it were going
to be this blue in two days for Alesander's combat. Not
that it mattered—if Hamon didn't figure out which was the
right woman, there could be a blizzard and it wouldn't
make one bit of difference to the outcome. But Walter
would undoubtedly persist in protecting that fool woman,
anyway.

He didn't know whom he disliked more: Walter for being
a chivalrous ass, Richenza for summoning him for this
pointless orgy of bloodletting, or Brian of Canjitrin for
turning it from a routine task to a perilous one.

*Just my luck that we should fail now when it matters to
me.*

The red-haired woman struck up a conversation with a
boy about Reynard's age. Didn't she seem a little too flir-
tatious with the boy for the little prig the princess was supposed to be? Damn, except for her hair she'd been the most
likely.

Maybe the princess wasn't all she was reputed to be. It
was hard to tell about women.

No, it wasn't. They were all alike.

And all very easy to figure out. "But I wouldn't be
queen," she'd said.

Oh, yes, they were very easy to figure out.

He could see the ferry waiting. Was Brian planning to
remain with them until they stopped at an inn for the night?
If he were with the woman, the chivalrous idiot would
probably stay at the inn so she could rest. If not, he would
likely get farther in what time he had.

Either way Hamon would manage the situation.

What was Brian hoping for anyway? The Tarsean Royal House had never recognized inheritance through the female line; she didn't stand a chance of becoming Queen of Tarsia. And surely Brian didn't expect to get her all the way to Canjit, where he could leave her in safety as his wife?

Maybe Brian hoped to get free of the whole mess while the rest of them burned. Maybe he expected the woman to set him free.

Perhaps he'll do my job for me.

The priestess who'd tried to hold him back had never made another mistake. She'd certainly been dead when he had escaped her. He'd just pushed, and she'd fallen back—or was there more than that? The memory was hazy.

But she'd been dead. "I know what I'm doing when I kill."

Hamon approached the group as they neared the ferry. He was close enough to see that the young boy was blushing at whatever the skinny redhead said to him. The boy looked away, as if to avoid the woman's eyes, and Hamon was the nearest safe thing to look at.

He was surprised to see recognition there. He cursed Rozer's inane jealousy to the nethermost triad of the nine gods of Saroth for having spread his description too far. The man must have known what Betrissa was. She had been a woman, after all.

The boy didn't start an outcry, though. Hamon saw fear in those yellow eyes.

Yellow eyes—but it wasn't until the boy turned away, and edged his horse forward to where Brian of Hassart was riding, that Hamon knew why those eyes had sparked something in his memory. The boy's eyes were the same color as the king's—Betrissa had spoken of them as beasts' eyes.

Hamon had to give the pair credit—no one would have looked at the boy twice. He supposed she just recognized him as Haroc—had Brian bothered to tell her from whom she was running?

They were less than half a mile from the ferry now and once they were across it wouldn't be difficult to get them alone—they could continue on this road or into Merscelun—and he would stay close behind.

The girl was as good as dead.

Like his sister Herlind.

He shoved the thought away. The part of him that fought that pain was very skilled.

Hamon stayed a little behind the party. No need to ride closer as long as he caught the ferry.

Brian looked back, then turned away, and Hamon could see him urging his horse and the girl's ahead of the others.

You can't go any faster than that ferry. I've had four days of worry, boy, and you're going to pay for trying to kill me.

He could feel himself beginning to relax. He hadn't realized how tense he had been. His stomach unknotted, and his shoulders felt less tight.

He kept his eyes on Brian—he hoped the boy could feel his stare: *You almost destroyed ten men, and all for a woman.*

What had the woman said to convince the young fool to run with her? What could *any* woman say? They were all liars and whores—every last one of them.

They'd say sweet things—"You're not *that* good in bed, my dear." Hamon wondered why he thought of that now.

He understood them, women were easy to handle—you led them on. It would have taken only a few foolish words to get her to do what he wanted. To sleep until she wouldn't wake again.

Instead I said, "Come away with me."

He shook the memory away. Brian and Meriel had reached the ferry.

"Come away with me," I said. What would I have done if Betrissa had said "yes?"

The question would not be put aside. *Would I have risked all the others—my own existence—to keep her alive if she'd said that one word?*

At the ferry, the rest of the party were boarding, and the ferryman prepared to cast off. Hamon could join them in a matter of seconds.

But the voice in his head asked the question again. "What would Hamon of Saroth have done?"

He could see the princess looking at him out of terrified eyes. He could face those eyes. He could face Brian's desperate ones. But the ones in his head wouldn't stop staring at him. Herlind's black eyes. The priestess's grey eyes. And Betrissa's green ones, laughing.

The eyes of dead women. Women he'd killed.

What would I have done—and why?

Then it was too late—the ferry was away, and he could see two puzzled faces watching him as he stared back, as uncomprehending as they.

By the time the ferry returned he'd repented, of course, but by then it was too late.

Richenza heard the door open and put out her hand to cover what lay on the table next to her. When she saw that it was Alesander who entered she hesitated, then dropped her hand to reveal a dagger bearing the arms of Indes.

Alesander must have understood by the look on her face and her attempt to conceal the dagger that it was of grave importance.

"Ric'a?" He used the name she had taught him.

She looked from him to the blade.

The note had come this morning. "Master Firmin Tredgett, presents his compliments and desires to meet with you to return the property which you misplaced at Reasalyn."

The mention of Reasalyn had left a cold chill down her spine, so she'd made sure that one of her guards waited outside the summer parlor, She'd thought of Alesander, but he'd been silent last night and had left her alone. Today he had occupied himself at the tourneyfield. So she had marshaled her courage and received Tredgett unaccompanied. Then Tredgett had politely handed her the dagger.

"I had this at Reasalyn," she said, "in case Leot followed me, or—or if nothing happened. I must have left it on the altar. Tredgett brought it."

"So that's how he found out," Alesander said. "What is he going to do?"

"He didn't say."

Tredgett had said enough, though. "I hope you are proud of yourself, Your Ladyship," he'd begun.

And she'd replied, "Of ridding the world of that nest of vermin? Certainly."

"I should tell Walter, or Thomas," Alesander started toward the door.

"No! Please, don't."

"Did Tredgett threaten you?"

Threats. No, there hadn't been threats. "Will you still be proud when Arin comes marching in the spring? Proud that you destroyed your country?"

"Tarsia will be better off without such a king as Rozer is or Leot would be."

"Better either of them than to be ruled by the king of Arin," Tredgett had answered.

"There are always claimants enough to the throne."

"Not this time." Each word an accusation, he had told her where all the lines ended. Besides Thaiter there were no remaining male line descendants from Tarses. Richenza thought of the scroll showing the line of the Royal Family, and she'd nodded in agreement.

"The throne of Tarsia has never passed through the female line," Tredgett had said. "But to find even such a claimant you must go back to King Rozer's great-grandfather Laidoin III's time. Besides his son, Laidoin had two daughters who married and had descendants."

"One married my grandfather," Richenza had said.

"And the elder wed the king of Arin's grandfather. Before that are Wendis II's daughters, who married the Grand Duke of Madaria and the Grand Duke of Yesacroth. Oh, yes, and the youngest married your Robert Feracher's ancestor. Except for Feracher and you, all the heirs are our enemies."

Feracher. There would be civil war before the nobles would allow a man with so many enemies to take the throne. A civil war would do half Arin's job for him.

"Alesander, I have been so very stupid."

"You understand, then? You understand what you are making me do?"

"Would it have been better," she'd demanded of Tredgett, "more patriotic to let Leot use me until he got bored and killed me? You were going to take me to him. You know him."

"You have reason to fear Leot. But Wendis was no threat to you."

She said now to Alesander what she had said to Tredgett, "I cannot stop it."

"No. Nor can I. So in three days' time, I am going to kill the last heir to the throne of Tarsia and ensure that it falls to Arin in the spring."

She couldn't look at him. "Tredgett said that I acted as the Companions' Houses have always acted. I have put my family's feud ahead of everything. He's right."

To her surprise, Alesander bent and turned her face up to him.

"He accosted me at the temple, yesterday—accused me as he accused you."

"That's why you bolted your door last night. You must loathe the sight of me. There is no defense for what I have done."

"You were angry and afraid."

"Not of Wendis. Not of Betrissa or Ewets or even Rozer."

"When I was angry and afraid, I killed my brother. If I hadn't done that . . ."

It did not absolve her. It did not even begin to ease the horror of what she had wrought with her summoning, but at least Alesander didn't hate her.

She wondered what to say now. What to do.

"You have done this, my lady," Tredgett had said. *"You must find a way to undo it."*

As the door closed behind Alesander, Thomas stepped out of the shadows. He'd waited to see what happened when Alesander returned ever since he had realized that it was Firmin Tredgett who had left her parlor that morning. And eavesdropping might not be done in the best of families, but there were times when it was necessary.

So the very proud lady from Tarsia has learned a hard lesson, he thought, as he moved into the room. He had more to teach. That might make the other easier.

Brian rode them both hard until long after dark. He had no idea why they had been delivered, but he was not about to lose the time the miracle had bought. Besides, if he exhausted her, perhaps he could stop the questions he was sure she would ask.

Where could he take her now, with Hamon at their backs and the gods and Walter alone knew who else? She'd not be safe even if he could find a place to stow her in the swamps of Merscelun. And if, by another miracle, he kept her alive for two days, she could die there alone.

Her family was probably dead already, except Leot, and Leot wouldn't survive the full moon. Who would be heir to Tarsia then? Would they welcome Meriel or kill her as a potential source of trouble?

Could he send her to Canjit, to his mother, who was no doubt furious at Brian's reappearance? Tarsia might be safer.

He looked back. Meriel had fallen behind—he kept forgetting that his horse never tired. Hers was visibly spent, as was she.

The moon was low on the horizon. It must be far into the night. Hamon would look for them, but if he wasn't sure where they had turned off the road, he could miss them completely. Exhaustion was as likely to kill her as Hamon.

So, stop for the night and pray to some god—any god but the Three Goddesses he was bound to, to whom Meriel's life was forfeit—that Hamon was on the wrong track.

Brian was rubbing down the horses when Meriel came up behind him. He pretended he didn't notice. She must have recognized Hamon as Haroc. Brian had hoped she would be too exhausted to do anything but sleep.

When she touched his arm, he could feel how cold her hand was through his shirt.

"We can't light a fire," he said quietly. "It might be seen."

"Tell me why we are running from Master Haroc."

Brian leaned his head against the mare's damp, sleek flank. He was too tired.

He turned. She was grave, but it wasn't the innocent excited gravity of their wedding night. She must have caught his fear—must have realized that this was not a game.

His lies had all escaped him; he had nothing left to tell her but the truth.

"We ran because he would have killed you."

"Why would a southern merchant want me dead? I'm not important enough to affect the outcome of the war."

She'd done some thinking about it. Automatically his mind searched for a way of turning this chase into an Arinese plot. He forced himself to stop. Nothing—nothing!—he could say would explain why he'd have to abandon her when the moon was full.

"He's not a southern merchant." Meriel didn't speak. "He's—" How do you explain the impossible? No way but to say it straight. "He's Hamon of Saroth."

She'd believed all his lies so readily, but the truth was not so easily accepted.

"Richenza of Indes summoned him—us—to destroy your House."

Pale as a corpse candle, she stared at him, then swallowed and said, "Because of her brother." Another moment—her lips pursed as she thought, "And they killed Ewets and Wendis, too?"

Brian nodded. "And your father may be dead by now."

"And Leot. How do you know?"

Brian closed his eyes. "Because I am one of them—one of the Wild Hunt. I was to help kill you. I was to let Hamon and Payne into the house the night after we left Tarsit."

"You are one of them," she said levelly, accepting.

"Yes." He laughed mirthlessly. "I doubt my mother even believed what she was doing when she cursed me."

"But you helped me escape."

"I couldn't let them kill you."

Very still, she looked at the ground for what seemed a long time. When she looked at him again, she had changed. He couldn't see fear in her pale eyes.

"I've read— If you don't kill me, the Wild Hunt will fail. They failed at Onsalm." Brian nodded mutely, wondering why she was telling him this. "And they all died for failing. So if you fail—"

She took a deep breath, and said simply, "You must kill me."

At first he could not grasp what she had said. The words

rode on the surface of his mind like a leaf on a pond. Then he understood.

"No!"

"Yes." Meriel remained as still and calm as glass. "If you don't, you will die, and it won't matter whether I am alive or not."

This was horrible. Brian pulled his thoughts together and remembered what Walter had told him.

"No, love." The word came of itself, but it was the right word. "I won't die. Three of us will be left."

"You're sure? You're not just saying that?"

"Who was left after Onsalm? Walter, Hamon, and Eleylin."

Meriel nodded. He could almost see her remembering, but she must have recalled something else.

"You will have to leave me."

"Yes. At the full moon in two nights."

"That's almost worse."

"I know." For the first time since they had halted, almost for the first time since they had begun to run, Brian reached to touch her. "I know." Then he held her very close.

29

Twenty-eighth Day

The stone effigies of Tarses the Conqueror, and Meliora, his mother, were not the work of a master sculptor. Ellis supposed that Rensel artists had not been considered useful chattels by the Sueve, so they'd made do with anyone who had known how to use a chisel.

Next to him, King Rozer shifted impatiently, but Ellis maintained a suitably enigmatic silence. He wanted to be sure that Ulick and Garrett had had time to dispose of the guards and take their places.

"Hurry up!" Rozer whispered. "What are you waiting for?"

"In a moment, Your Majesty. Do you want the guards overhearing?"

"They're long gone."

Ellis looked reluctantly at the coffins. He'd hoped that it wouldn't be necessary to resort to grave robbing.

Not that robbery gave him pause. He'd robbed the dead a time or two before.

No, it was simply that he didn't want to see the Scepter that, had things fallen otherwise, he might have had to bear.

Am I afraid that seeing it will raise my mother's ambitions in me? She'd been the one

277

who had wanted to open this grave and wield the Scepter. *If it had been destroyed, rather than hidden, would she have left·well enough alone?*

He doubted it. She'd been an obstinate woman.

Ellis looked at Rozer. So he wanted the Scepter. Why not grant him that last wish?

He looked at the two sepulchers—the one nearest the entry was Meliora's, the wife of Ortas, mother of Tarses. She'd been a border woman, and more fanatic about the harrying of the Rensel than her son. Amloth had inherited her red hair. Ellis wondered what kind of a life his sister Ozanne had had with him.

Tarses's coffin lid was far too heavy to lift, but it could be pushed. It moved too slowly for Rozer.

"Hurry! I must have it."

The lid fell with a crash, and Ellis crouched behind the coffin. Rozer, not concerned about the guards, stood on tiptoe to peer into the stone box.

"Look! The Scepter!" Ellis rose cautiously, and picked up the discarded lantern. Lying among the rotting silks of his burial robes, Tarses's bones looked like anyone else's.

The Scepter was there, as Ellis's mother had said it would be, lying beside the body. Phallic, it was as big around as a woman's wrist and yellowed with age. A column of dark spots that might be rubies marched up the side.

Why had Tarses—or more likely Meliora, who had out-lived her son—had it buried? To hide it from possible claimants, or to prove that Rensel glory was at an end forever? If that had been the reason, the effort had been in vain. Ellis's mother hadn't believed it. The king of Arin didn't believe it—he claimed to be the true heir of the Rensel. As did this old man. Why didn't they all just—

He heard a rustle from the doorway. Ellis looked up and saw a figure dark against the night sky.

"Good evening, Father." Leot's voice was like raw silk.

Rozer, beaming over the Scepter as if it were the son he hoped it would help him get, started at the sound of his son's voice.

"Look!" he said. "The Scepter of Reas!"

Then he saw that his son's sword was drawn, and the king's eyes widened.

As Leot advanced on his father, Ellis watched warily. There was one thing Rozer could say that Ellis didn't want him to—three names and a curse.

But Rozer, third of that name, King of Tarsia and head of the House of Thaiter, did not utter a word; he held out the Scepter of Reas in front of him, as if hoping it would protect him.

Leot thrust once, and his father looked surprised as he crumpled to the stone floor on top of the Scepter.

Good, I don't have to tell Walter that Leot will be joining us.

Leot wiped his sword on the hem of his father's robe and turned to Ellis.

"You've done a good job, Selinian, but the pay is different than I promised."

"You don't want witnesses."

"If I kill you, I can say I got here just too late to save the king from a murderer in Arin's pay." He advanced toward Ellis.

Leot's expression was as amazed as his father's had been as his knees hit the ground. He toppled onto his face and into the black pool of Rozer's blood—Tarses's blood. Garrett stood in the doorway grinning, the small bag of sand in his hand.

Ellis darted forward. "That sounded too hard." He bent over Leot. "If you've killed him. . . ."

But Leot was breathing and didn't seem to be more than stunned.

Garrett said, "If he has to fight with a headache it'll make it easier for Alesander tomorrow. Besides, how else was I supposed to stop him?"

Ellis grunted and checked the old man. He was dead.

"Let's report to Thomas." He straightened.

"Drinks first?" Ulick suggested as he put aside his helmet.

"Yes," Ellis said. "I think so."

30

Twenty-ninth Day

The king had not yet arrived. The royal stand with its blue-and-gold brocade hangings was deserted. To its left in the crimson-draped stand for the appellor, Richenza Indes and the man who called himself Walter Martling sat talking composedly. They played their parts well. Sir Walter's nondescript secretary stood behind their chairs. Armed liverymen of the House of Indes formed a protective line at the perimeter of their stand. The High Priest of Haldan and his entourage filled the violet-draped stand reserved for them, surrounded by a bodyguard of spearmen in the livery of the temple. At the far end of the lists the azure pavilion of Prince Leot and the crimson-and-gold pavilion of his challenger bustled with activity. The crowd which filled the Square outside the stands and the roped-off lists was increasingly restless, no longer diverted by the mountebanks who sought to turn a penny before the real show began. For once the liverymen noble families had brought into the city might keep the peace instead of breaking it.

Tredgett watched from his place among the crowd as yet another messenger scurried between Leot's pavilion and the High Priest's party. What had happened? Tredgett had a sick feeling in the pit of his stomach. Rozer couldn't come; Rozer was dead. But killed when and by whom? Had Leot ignored all his warnings and advice?

Or was this the real meaning of the Lady Richenza's note that a messenger had delivered last evening? "I will make it right," she had written—nothing more. At the time he had been relieved, but what would she consider "right"?

He had been naive and uncharacteristically indecisive, he chided himself. Even now he could not make up his mind. Should he confront Leot? Should he tell Leot his suspicions about the Wild Hunt?

He looked at the open casements of the second story of his house, where his son and the boy's friends jostled, pointing out distractions below. A flutter of white veil behind them caught his eye, and he remembered what Alesander had said, "And leave her to Leot?" Could he tell Leot? How could he keep his family safe? Keep Tarsia safe? In time of chaos what was "right"? His wife leaned forward, her hand on their son's shoulder. He started to wave, then stopped. A squad of guardsmen came toward him, stern-faced. Tredgett moved forward; if worse had come to worst and Leot had murdered the king, the prince might turn on him as well. The farther from his house they found him, the less excuse they would have to molest his family.

"Firmin Tredgett?" the guardsman asked. Tredgett nodded. "Come with us."

They formed a square around him and hustled him away, pushing through the crowd to Leot's pavilion. Once there, all but the leader and two members of the squad dropped back. The leader shoved him into the tent. That shove had been intended to send him, humiliated, to his knees, but Tredgett had been expecting it and kept his feet.

The pavilion was crowded. Leot, wrapped in a gaudy gold-and-purple robe over his arming doublet, sat on a gilded faldstool surrounded by his squires and cronies. Tredgett had expected them. He was relieved to see that the priests who had administered the final oaths for the combat had not departed and that their leader was Symond Tierse, who would be an intelligent and impartial witness. His presence would restrain Leot's impulsive instincts.

"This is the man I told you of," Leot said. The priests pivoted to stare at him. The table near Leot held not only the Shield of Haldan, on which the oaths were sworn, but also an ivory rod. Ivory set with red stones. The Scepter of Reas.

It had been Leot. *What stupidity.* Tredgett stared at the Scepter as it lay half-hidden among folds of gold brocade. *What incredible stupidity would drive Leot to this?*

A too-familiar shrill whine in Leot's voice roused Tredgett from his bemusement.

"I should have realized before and warned my father, but I didn't grasp the depravity of the conspiracy. This man was my advisor. Who would have thought he was conspiring with our enemies?"

Who would think it indeed? No one would, if Leot couldn't invent more plausible and specific charges. But when there are spears at your back, impatiently awaiting word for action, it didn't much matter what was believed afterward.

"I should have had the story verified by gentlemen." Leot gestured toward his sniggering cronies. "But it seemed so unimportant—the king often bought historical relics—in comparison to preparing for the coming war. How could I have guessed it was a conspiracy to lure the king, my father, to his murder? How could I have guessed my trusted advisor was a part of it?"

"You have proof?" asked Tierse. Tredgett watched the priests' faces as he edged slow inch by careful inch toward the table where the Shield and Scepter lay. Their expressions ranged from rapt belief to incredulity.

"Proof? My word is proof. This man conspired with our enemies. He sent a Selinian mercenary to my father to tempt him to Tarses's tomb. He lulled me into disregarding the danger with false reports of the truthfulness of the Selinian's cohorts. They murdered the king last night. I arrived too late to stop them. I found my father lying dead in his own blood with the Scepter of Reas beside him, mocking him, and the tomb of Tarses, our ancestor, ransacked. I was attacked myself, but I fought them off."

"The tomb and King Rozer's body are as you report,"

said Tierse. "But what proof have you of Master Tredgett's guilt?"

"He has visited the house of my appellor Richenza Indes. He has conversed on numerous occasions with her champion, Scelin. Why, only yesterday she sent a message to him saying she would make things right."

Tredgett was at the table now. Leot had turned his own spies against him to know that last.

"Your Highness, what I did I did in your service. I swear on the Shield of Haldan"—Tredgett reached out to grasp it before the hovering guards could prevent him—"that I had no part in King Rozer's death." He looked at Leot, who was paralyzed between his natural instinct to strike out immediately and violently at those who crossed him and the respect even a prince must show a sacred object.

"I admit that I have spoken with the Lady of Indes and her champion. I did so to convince her of the error of her challenge. Instead she has convinced me. Let me add to the charges of the appeal and join my quarrel to that of Indes." He looked to Symond Tierse, who nodded shortly, his eyes alert.

"I am innocent of King Rozer's death, let the combat prove that. Let the combat also prove that Alesander Scelin has more right to rule in Tarsia than this perjured princeling." Leot lurched forward to strike, but his blow was struck aside by the priest who guarded the relic. "You killed the king, your father. The presence of the Scepter here proves that. You are a parricide, not fit to rule. Let Haldan, God of War, judge your depravity."

Tredgett looked at Symond Tierse, who nodded, and said, "The challenge shall be so amended." Tredgett took his hand off the Shield and was immediately pinioned by two guardsmen, who started to hurry him out.

Tierse said mildly, "The ceremony is not completed."

The guardsmen stopped but did not loosen their grasp.

"Leot, Prince of Tarsia, descendant of Thaiter, King of Tarsia, do you swear to your innocence of the charges brought by Richenza, descendant of Indes, Companion of the Conqueror Tarses, and by Firmin Tredgett, merchant?" The incongruity of station inspired at least one gentleman to titter uneasily; Tierse's stare silenced him.

"I affirm my innocence," declared Leot, his hand upon
the Shield. "I will prove, by the grace of Haldan, the guilt
of my accusers."

"Let Haldan judge," said Tierse, echoed by the other
priests.

The priests gathered up the Shield and its wrappings.
Leot nodded sharply to his guardsmen, who shoved Tredgett toward the pavilion's entrance. As he was forced outside, Tredgett could see Leot whispering with the captain
of the guard. The priests left as they must, to report the
oath-taking to the High Priest. Tredgett tried to judge
whether there was any reaction to their report, any stir, any
commotion, but surrounded as he was by guardsmen,
squires rushing to help Leot arm, grooms, and Leot's res-
tive warhorse, he couldn't be sure what was happening in
the stands. *Enath*, he prayed, *let my words have some effect.*

The captain rejoined his men. "Prince Leot says we're
to hang him as soon as the combat begins."

Finding cord to bind Tredgett's hands behind his back
was simple; finding rope long and strong enough for an
effective halter proved harder and they had just slipped the
noose over his head as Leot, resplendent in gilded armor
and azure surcoat, emerged from his pavilion. Leot smiled
wolfishly at Tredgett's predicament, mounted, and rode toward the center of the lists, to where his challenger awaited
him in front of the High Priest's seat. Leot's squires followed, bearing the weapons he would use in the combat.

Tredgett watched him go; he would have liked to know
the result of the combat but, although the captain sighed
heavily as he looked at the final ceremonies before the
joust, he said to his men, "Let's get on with it."

The public gibbet had been taken down to make room
for the lists, which left the guards at a loss. To Tredgett's
eyes the heavy frames from which the shop signs hung
were strong enough to sling a rope from, but that idea did
not seem to occur to the captain or his men. Tredgett saw
no reason to enlighten them. Instead, the group pushed out-
ward through the crowd, which was clamorously pushing
inward now that the combat was starting.

Tredgett considered breaking free and losing himself in
that unruly mass, but the guards were alert and kept their

hold on him. They pushed through to the outer edge of the square as the drums and trumpets sounded, signaling the beginning of the joust. The captain was tugging straight his rumpled livery and considering the best place to carry out his orders when someone behind them loudly cleared his throat. The captain spun around.

"Captain," said Symond Tierse dryly, "in a case like this, the wise man waits till the combat is over before he does something irreparable."

Tredgett let his breath out in a sigh.

Although the captain protested, Tierse led them along the edge of the crowd and through the gap between the king's and the High Priest's stands. They came out at the side of the lists among the men-at-arms of the temple. The view was excellent as they took a place along the rail. The first course had been run. Fragments of shattered lance were being cleared from the field by scurrying squires as the combatants were armed with their lances for the second run.

An officer in temple livery leaned over to Symond Tierse. "The first course was even. Both lances shattered cleanly, and each kept perfect seat and control of his horse."

Tredgett, still bound and haltered, stood between Tierse on his left and Leot's captain on his right. Four of Leot's guardsmen stood at his back.

Trumpets and drums sounded. The combatants gathered their horses into a gallop. Tredgett barely had time to register that Scelin was bearing not the crimson arms of Indes or the arms he had worn in practice, but the ancient arms of Vitaut—barry wavy argent and azure, a lion rampant countercharged. A claim had been made.

The blue and silver of Vitaut shimmered before him as the fighters met. Not lance leveled on lance this time. Leot's lance lowered below the horizontal to strike Alesander's horse.

"Foul," Tierse said under his breath. But even Tredgett, untutored in arms, knew that in a combat to the death, all blows are fair. Alesander's horse stumbled before righting itself and Alesander's lance passed harmlessly over Leot's shoulder. As the fighters passed, returning to the end of the

list to be armed for the third course, Leot raised his hand
in mocking salute.

This course, Tredgett saw, would not be fought with
equal lances. Leot was handed a war axe. Tredgett remembered stories of his cleaving a helmet with a single blow.
At his end of the field, Alesander took up an iron-reinforced
lance, shorter and lighter than the jousting lance, such as
the Sueve used in battle.

*Haldan, please, let Bolson be right about Alesander's
skill.*

Again the trumpets sounded. The crowd fell silent and
the sound of the horses' gallop echoed off the houses that
walled the square. As the fighters met before the High
Priest's seat Leot kneed his horse to pivot, and rose in the
saddle to deliver a crushing downward blow; but Alesander
had anticipated that tactic, for he ducked under the up-
swung axe and drove his stiff lance through the mail-
protected gap in Leot's plate armor, through his groin, and
into the saddle behind. The force of their charge separated
the fighters. Alesander gathered his mount, turning at the
end of the list. Slowly the axe dropped from Leot's hands.
The lance protruded from his body, and around it arterial
blood poured down, staining the blue and gold of his
horse's barding.

The crowd sighed as one. Tierse ducked under the rail,
signaling some of the temple's men to follow, and ran to
Leot's guideless horse. Leot slumped in the saddle.

Tredgett looked around. The crowd was milling, stunned
and leaderless, but masses of the temple's guardsmen in-
terleaved with nobles' liverymen had formed up at the pe-
riphery of the square. Someone had had the sense to
anticipate what could happen if Leot lost. Leot's own
guardsmen stood stunned, uncomprehending. Tredgett took
advantage of their dazed state to follow Tierse into the lists.
Running awkwardly because of his bound hands, he came
to where Leot lay. They had taken the prince from the saddle, and he lay in a widening circle of his own blood. The
wound was unstaunchable. Tierse knelt beside him. Tredgett leaned over as Leot tried to speak.

Leot mumbled something weakly as Alesander paced his

horse back up the field to dismount before the High Priest. Leot's eyes closed then opened wide.

More clearly now Leot said, "She has not won." He paused for labored breath. "She has . . . not. . . ."

Tredgett looked at Tierse in the lengthening silence. Leot's now-sightless eyes stared at the cloudless sky. Tredgett straightened as Tierse closed the dead prince's eyes.

The world had turned upside down in a few minutes' time. Tredgett prayed to all the gods he knew that he had done the right thing and that justice had prevailed.

Thomas tucked his hands into his sleeves and looked over the square. "No rioting. Someone must have anticipated Leot's losing."

"Perhaps they think they have another king in the offing," Walter said. Walter had made no move to leave Indes's stand, even though the lady of that name had departed long before. The Huntsman wanted to talk to Alesander, who had doubtless received a forceful summons.

"Perhaps that was why Alesander chose to wear the arms of Vitaut, to make the crowd think that this was a dynastic change, not a legally sanctioned assassination? The emendation of the oaths at the last moment to announce Alesander's claim to the throne would support that."

Walter nodded and rested his hands on the carved walking stick he had used since he had risen from his sickbed.

"They will need a king. What will happen if Alesander burns with the rest of us at moonset, I wonder?"

"I've been thinking about that."

Walter turned from the rapidly emptying Great Square to look at Thomas.

"And?"

"Do you remember what the lady's command was, Walter, when she summoned us?"

"I thought I did, but I'm sure you remember it better than I."

"We were summoned to 'avenge her brother and destroy the House of Thaiter as it has destroyed the House of Indes.' "

"We have at least avenged her brother," Walter said.

Leot's body, chastely draped, was being carried away on a litter. "Treason answered with murder."

"Who is left of Indes?"

"No one," Walter frowned. "The Lady Richenza—but . . ."

"And who is left of Thaiter?"

Walter thought before he answered; the words came out slowly as if he was afraid he'd have a second thought.

"The princess—Queen Meriel." He sat looking out, but Thomas didn't think he saw anything.

"It is the letter," Walter said at last, "But it doesn't feel . . . finished."

"But it is the letter."

"It was the letter in Saroth, too. The unfaithful wife? The summoner who wanted the death of every man who had seduced his wife?"

Walter had been right, then.

Someone was hurriedly mounting the steps to the stand; Thomas turned. Alesander at last.

But not Alesander alone, behind was Firmin Tredgett. The merchant's eyes moved past Thomas to rest on Walter. *Facing your legends, merchant?*

Alesander's color was high as he cast quickly about the box.

"Where is she?"

"The Lady Richenza?" Thomas said. "She left as soon as your victory was confirmed."

Walter pushed himself to his feet with the help of the cane. "Alesander, why was the challenge amended, and why did you wear the arms of Vitaut?"

"I amended the challenge," Tredgett said. "It was necessary."

Thomas studied the merchant as he faced Walter. *More than necessary. You know who he is. You want him to be king.*

"And was displaying the arms of Vitaut Master Tredgett's idea, too?"

"No," Alesander replied impatiently. "In all honor I could do nothing else."

Walter did not look pleased, but before he could say more—if indeed he would have said more in front of the merchant—Alesander said quickly, "We don't have time for this. Leot—he's planned something against Ri—Lady Richenza."

"Planned?" Thomas said. "He's dead."

Walter shook his head. "Dead men can kill, too, as you well know. What did he do?"

Tredgett met Walter's gaze with a small frown. "Before the combat, Prince Leot had me arrested. One of his accusations concerned a note the lady had sent me this morning. He not only knew that it had been sent, but what was in it. That means he has suborned at least one person in my employ in the lady's household."

"How would this endanger the lady?"

"I don't know, but just as he died, he said—"

Alesander interrupted. "He said she hadn't won. Don't you see? He made plans to do something to her even if he lost."

"He could have been denying he'd lost," Walter said. "Men have done so before."

Tredgett looked sour. "The prince was too parsimonious to bribe a man for mere information. The note, I think, was luck on his part. He would have bought the man for something more telling."

Alesander turned to the steps. "She's in danger. I need to go to her."

Walter nodded then looked at Thomas. "I was right. If she dies, who will be left of Indes?"

"No one."

"And Thaiter has a living daughter."

Full Moon Again

Brian pulled the saddle from Meriel's horse and turned the animal into the ramshackle pen the boatman maintained. There was no reason to un-saddle his own mount. He would be returning soon, too soon, when he had said good-bye to his wife. He straightened the saddle on the splintery rail and chided himself for wasting time. He could not put it off any longer; he had to assure Meriel's safety and that meant letting her go.

The sun was dropping toward the west, glittering on Elun's lake. By the time the sun set Meriel would be on the other shore in Canjitrin, in a village ruled by a loyal lord who would keep her safe despite pressure from the king of Tarsia or from Daimiron. Safe from his mother, too. He was not leaving Meriel to an easy fate. What else could he do? He had only until the sun overwhelmed the moon, a few hours' time. Time to say good-bye and set her free. Time to guard the lakeshore lest Hamon or Payne come hunting.

He half slid down the bank to the dock where the boat was tied. The sunlight reflecting off the lake reduced Meriel and the boatman, standing close together on the dock, to silhouettes. The boatman leaned forward and grasped Meriel's arm. Meriel shook it off, looked up, and hurried to Brian, hugging her cloak around her as if she were chilled. Her face was flushed as she greeted him, and though she smiled, he knew her too well to be deceived.

"What's wrong?"

"Nothing. I was tired of waiting."

Brian raised an eyebrow.

Her face crumpled. "It's the boatman. I didn't want to be alone with him."

Brian scowled. "What did he do?"

"He guessed I was a woman. He said that. . . . No, it wasn't what he said, it was how he said it." She shivered, looking out over the expanse of the lake. "I know I must, but I don't want to be alone with him."

Brian considered. It would be twilight or later when the boat reached the western shore, but the trip back would have the full moon for light. It could be done. It would be done, even if he had to force the boatman at dagger point. The thought of Meriel alone at some man's mercy was unbearable.

He put his arm around her. "Don't worry. I'll come with you. He won't dare anything if I'm there."

"Thank you."

They walked to the dock hand in hand. The boatman looked up, but his eyes dropped quickly under Brian's gaze. His only comment on learning of his second passenger was a grunt and a demand for a higher fare.

They arranged themselves in the boat; the boatman at the oars, Brian and Meriel seated together at the stern facing him. The boatman kept his eyes on Meriel as he rowed. Brian glared back. The boatman dropped his gaze, but soon his eyes were back on Meriel's body. She shifted, fidgeting with the small bundle of spare clothing and jewelry, her only remaining possessions, in her lap.

They were past the midpoint of the lake, passing a small wooded island on their left. The setting sun made the water golden ahead of them and painfully bright. Meriel shifted, reaching for his hand. Her bundle, entangled in the folds of her cloak, slid onto the seat beside her, then slowly tumbled overboard. She grabbed at it, but it slipped beneath her grasp and hit the water. It bobbed beside the boat as Meriel half rose. She leaned over, reaching for it. The boatman stopped rowing and tried to snag the bundle with an oar.

Voices clashed, bodies collided in confused movement. The boat rocked, and, before Brian's horrified gaze, Meriel overbalanced and followed her bundle into the water.

Brian swore and dove in after her. He wasn't a good swimmer, and it was some minutes later before he and the boatman got Meriel back in the boat, her wet clothes clinging to her, her sodden bundle seeping at her feet. She shivered in the evening air. Brian sighed, his own teeth near to chattering.

He couldn't see it clearly in the dusk, but he could feel the boatman's smile. The man's voice, though, betrayed no trace of amusement. "There's a place on that island that the fisherfolk use where you could build a fire and dry out. Want me to pull in there?"

Brian grunted his agreement.

On the island, Meriel and he stumbled up the bank and followed the directions the boatman shouted after them. A narrow path led not to the hut Brian had expected, but to a stone building with a small paved court centered on an overgrown pool. It must have been a temple once, with its open side and columns, but it had been put to lesser uses since. Someone had built a fire ring, recently used, in a nook against the lee side of the courtyard. There, protected against the night wind, he found a pile of firewood and a flint and steel. By the time he had a fire started, Meriel had stripped her wet clothes off and laid them out across the courtyard to dry. The firelight warmed her nakedness.

He opened his cloak, magically dried, and she came to him, nestling against him, reaching out to unfasten his belt.

Brian started to stop her. It was so late. The moon was almost above the treetops. She reached up and pulled his face to hers and kissed him.

"One last time. Just be with me one last time."

Alesander swore as he dismounted in the courtyard of Indes's town house. The crowds in the street had held him up. The sun was setting, the moon would be rising.

The only person in sight as he entered the great hall was Justin.

"Where is Lady Richenza?" Alesander asked. Walter and Tredgett followed him.

"Isn't she with you?"

"She should have been here an hour ago."

"What's wrong?"

Thomas appeared in the doorway. "Her grooms and her horse are here. They say she went straight to the house."

Alesander was dimly grateful to Thomas; he would never have thought of simply checking the stables.

"Could she have gone to her chamber?" Walter asked. Alesander took a deep breath to calm himself. Fear made him forget that she might be perfectly safe, waiting for him to come and say farewell as they had planned.

But Justin shook his head. "I just came from there. Bertz is begging for water, and I went to the lady's rooms to see if her waiting woman would fetch it so I wouldn't have to leave him alone. No one was there."

"Thomas," Walter said, "search the gardens. I will see to the downstairs. Alesander—"

"The groom could be lying," Thomas ventured.

"Someone check the stables then," Alesander said. "He could have hidden her . . ." But he didn't want to believe that she was already dead.

"The stables," Thomas said, "then the gardens."

"Justin, finish searching the second story. Alesander, that leaves you the third."

She wasn't there, of course. He hadn't thought that she'd have had any reason to go to the least used part of the house, to where the ballroom sat deserted with its tapestries showing the first Indes fighting beside Tarses as they conquered the Rensel lands. Indes was shown as being present at the moment when the heiress to the Rensel throne stood in front of that too-familiar altar and refused Amloth. The ensuing rape had tastefully been omitted, though.

Damn Amloth. If he'd kept his temper, none of us would be here now, Alesander thought as he hurried down the stairs, *and I'd never have met Richenza.*

Would that have been better or worse? To have a taste of something you'd always wanted and never to know it again, or to never have tasted at all?

If she is dead, better, much better, not to have known her.

In the great hall, the servants were beginning to light the candles. The moon must be well up.

Walter stood gazing at the closed doors; the full moon's pull was much greater on him than on the others.

"No sign of her, or Annet," Alesander said.

Walter shook his head without looking at him, "No one has seen them down here either. Not since she returned."

One by one the others came back, Tredgett, who had searched the gatehouse, all four floors of it, the last to straggle in. All reports were negative. Wherever she was, Annet was there, too. No one had seen the servingwoman for most of the day, though she hadn't been at the combat.

"The servants," Tredgett said. "I know which ones we should question." He gave a list of names.

Walter was still distracted; he turned his attention away from the doors only long enough to order Justin and Thomas to fetch those Tredgett named.

"Master Tredgett," he said, "as soon as everyone is here we must return to Reasalyn." Alesander's heart turned cold.

Not yet!

"Reasalyn?" Tredgett said. "That's two days away."

Walter smiled faintly, "For you, perhaps. For us—it will take our mounts no longer than it needs to get from anywhere to the place of the summoning under a full moon."

"I will stay," Alesander said.

Walter looked at him, his face unreadable. "As long as you can. If the Lady Richenza is dead and Princess Meriel is alive, we have failed. Find her."

A hesitant step from the entry made them all turn to look. Bertz stood in the door, half-supporting himself. He looked tired, but the agony was gone from his countenance.

"Do you need me?" he asked.

"See to the horses," Walter said. "But leave Alesander's." The Stros turned; he gained strength every moment the full moon rose.

The men Justin and Thomas ushered into the great hall were silent and wide-eyed when they saw Firmin Tredgett. Alesander surveyed them. Which one or ones had Leot suborned and how loyal would he remain to a dead prince?

A hand fell on his shoulder, and he turned to look at Walter.

"We are leaving. Remember what I said—find her."

He watched the Huntsman leave, unable to shake off the feeling that there had been a meaning deeper than the words in Walter's speech.

"Which of you was paid by Prince Leot to kill the Lady Richenza?" Tredgett asked as the doors closed behind Walter, Justin, and Thomas. None answered, a few looked shocked. "I warn you, he is dead, and—" Tredgett gestured to Alesander—"Sir Alesander has claimed the throne. So it will be better for you if you tell us what happened to the Lady Richenza."

Silence. Either the man was loyal to whoever paid him most or was afraid to speak.

There were twelve of them of varied station in the household: liveried men, footmen, guards, grooms, even a scullion from the kitchens. Aylmer, the man who'd survived the attack at the tourneyfield, was among them.

Impatience rose in Alesander like a bubble about to burst. One of these men knew where Ric'a was, knew if she were dead or alive. He restrained himself—threats would only frighten his quarry.

Tredgett glowered at the row of men, inspecting each in turn as if he thought his look could force a confession. Alesander tried to do the same, meeting the eyes of each of the bought men in turn. Too many eyes fell, too many remained steady; it was impossible to judge.

What if he picked one man out and killed him. Odds were he'd get an innocent man, but it might panic the guilty one.

It was likely to panic the rest of them, too.

Tredgett had finished one slow, painstaking inspection and started again. The men were fidgeting more now. Would this alone be enough to break them?

The merchant went from one man, to another, to the man next to him, then to Aylmer, then, suddenly, back to the man before Aylmer. Alesander watched as his eyes swept the man—one of the footmen—from head to foot and stopped at his waist. Then Tredgett looked him in the face again. The footman bolted.

"Stop him!" Tredgett and Alesander both ordered. He got no more than a few steps before Aylmer and two of the others grabbed him.

"Where is the Lady Richenza?" Tredgett's voice was deep as the deepest temple bell. The footman shook his head and the merchant struck him.

"Where is she?"

The footman was bleeding from a cut on his mouth, but he only glared sullenly at Tredgett. He could hold out for hours, Alesander decided—until the sun rose to overwhelm the moon—and he'd never know if Richenza were safe or not.

"You've tried to poison her." The footman's eyes widened. The merchant's hands went to the prisoner's belt and undid the buckle. Holding the object to the man's face, Tredgett said, "You used this to do it."

The man's eyes fixed on the belt, and Alesander saw that the buckle was a complex design—not a likely thing for a footman to wear. As everyone stared at it, Tredgett pressed a stud in the pattern and a drop of a golden liquid appeared on the tongue.

"This was Prince Leot's," Tredgett continued inexorably. "How did you get it?"

For the first time the footman spoke. "It's too late. She had the wine before you even started looking for her."

Alesander drew his dagger and grabbed the man by his hair.

"If she's dead, so are you." Alesander held the blade to his throat.

The man's eyes bulged. "She might not be dead yet. I didn't see her drink it. . . ."

"Where is she?"

"In the strong room."

"Where?"

Propelled and guarded by the group of men who had held him, the footman conducted them to the small withdrawing room off the gallery. He pointed to a paneled wall.

"The room's behind that. I spent the day helping Mistress Annet rearrange it."

"I see," said Tredgett. "They've sealed off the space under the stairs."

Alesander pushed at the wall, then turned to the guilty footman.

"How does it open?"

"I don't know. It was open when I went into it."

"Who does know?"

"The Lady Richenza and Mistress Annet."

"They are both inside?"

"N-no. Mistress Annet isn't." And he told them where she was.

Walter had searched the kitchen storeroom, but he hadn't looked in every barrel. Alesander found Annet in a flour barrel, trying to pound the lid off from the inside.

Alesander helped her out in a cloud of white that made them both sneeze.

"The lady's wine has been poisoned. Show us how to open the door to the strong room."

Annet ran for the strong room, taking the stairs two at a time. Tredgett was pressing the carved paneling.

She shoved him aside. "You've got it wrong."

She pressed somewhere and somewhere else, and stepped back as the door slid open. As Annet held the door to keep it from closing again, Alesander pushed past her into the narrow, stone-walled room. A branched candlestick sat in the middle of a small table, hiding what was beyond it; all he could see was a still, seated figure.

Richenza's head was lying on her arms at the table. Before her sat a goblet.

He froze in the doorway, afraid of the truth. Before he could make up his mind to move he felt two strong hands—Tredgett's hands—on his back. Alesander was shoved into the strong room and he heard the door close with a soft thud behind him.

The Wild Hunt rode toward Reasalyn, quickly, too quickly for anyone to see, but the wind they raised along the road would be a thing to remember. Walter tried not to wonder what he had left behind in Indes's town house. If Richenza were dead, could Tredgett keep Alesander from coming to him? Did it take a lover to hold a Huntsman?

The nine horsemen turned east toward the temple where this task had begun. The fire on the Ladies' altar was glowing coals now—more bright than they had been for the past twenty-nine days but not fully alight, not until the sun outshone the moon.

Payne and Hamon had not joined them. Walter deemed it best that they continue searching for the last of the House of Thaiter. If she lived and the lady died, they would have failed. If she died and Richenza lived, it would make no difference.

The moon was high now, and Walter drew strength from it and began his summoning.

The light changed. One moment it warmed Meriel's soft face as he leaned down to kiss her. The next moment all was harsh, cold and angular as though she were no longer a woman but a demonic temptress such as the folktales claimed haunted deserted places like this isle. Brian stared. One moment he saw Meriel's pale soft curls; the next long snakelike strands of silver hair fell across her face from over his shoulder. From behind him. He jerked around.

There was no one there.

Meriel moaned, and he looked back. In Meriel's place a cadaver lay.

"No!" Brian scuttled backward, not rising from his crouch till he was stopped by the temple wall.

The body stirred and rose to its knees. Now he could see Meriel again. She wrapped his cloak around her and got to her feet. She didn't seem surprised.

Brian concentrated. He had to go before the moon set. It wasn't possible to stay. Walter would call him. Was the rushing sound of water that filled his head Walter's call? That call had always had meaning before; this was irrational and animal. Overwhelming.

Meriel watched him, silent, waiting. Brian got to his feet and clothed himself.

"I have to go. I'll send the boatman back for you."

"No."

"I must. I don't want to go; I must go." She was blocking his way.

"I know. The boatman's gone."

He sputtered a protest.

"I paid him to leave." She settled the cloak more firmly on her shoulders, planted herself more firmly in his way. "I paid him to strand us here, and I paid him to leave."

Someone was standing in the shadows just beyond sight. The rushing waterfall that filled his head resounded like singing. He had to see. He edged past Meriel.

In the trees something white fluttered. Liquid laughter teased him. Who was that?

Meriel grabbed his arm. "I won't let you go."

He shook her off. He had to follow that tantalizing sound. Meriel stumbled and cried out as she hit the temple wall.

"Ah, gods. I've hurt you," he said.

She smiled and straightened. "It is but a little pain when you are here." She took a step toward him, and he backed away, remembering. *He thinks he killed her.* Walter had said that about Hamon. Meriel reached out to touch his face. *He killed her.*

"No," Brian shook his head, avoiding her caress.

"Yes."

He made a choking noise deep in his throat and turned and ran—ran away from her, from what he might do, not toward the voice that summoned him.

Richenza had planned a seduction, planned her every word, every gesture, planned the meal, the wine, the soft carpets and pillows piled to make a bed before the fire. None had been necessary. From the moment she had felt Alesander's hands on her shoulders, heard him say her name she had not thought. She'd gone into his arms and they had kissed, clung to each other and sunk to the floor, caught in one single overarching desire.

Now, much later, she could think again, could feel the fire's warmth on her bare back. Opposite her, the fire illuminating his face, Alesander finished his narrative.

She glanced at the goblet that sat untasted on the table and shivered as though Leot's dead hand had touched her. "*Tredgett* helped you find the poisoner?"

"Yes, and he pushed me in here, too!"

She shook her head in wonderment, and Alesander smoothed back her loosened hair.

She reached to pull him toward her. A log in the fireplace snapped behind her, and she realized his attention was on the fire, not her. She turned to look. The fire burned high, golden with dazzling motes of red, orange, and hot blue. Alesander shifted beside her. She touched him and felt cloth beneath her hand. He had clothed himself.

He pulled away, rose, and walked to the door. She scrambled to her feet and struggled into her gown as she watched him search for a way to open the door from the inside. Finally he slammed his fist into it. "I give up. How does this work?"

She told the truth. "It doesn't open from this side. My grandfather partitioned it off to be a secret strong room."

"How did you plan to get out?"

"I was to rap, and Annet would open the door."

"But Annet's not there; Tredgett is, and Tredgett won't open it." He hit the door with his fist again, then slumped against it.

The fire flared up behind her, illuminating the room bright as day.

"Is there another . . ?" He stopped and stared at her. "You planned this."

She found no words to deny it.

"You conspired with Tredgett."

"No." She moved forward, reached up to touch his cheek. He shook her hand away and stared grimly down at her.

"Is there another way out?"

She shook her head. He swore and pushed past her.

"I only wanted you—wanted you by my side forever, but I have done great wrong with my summoning, and I must do all I can to make that right."

She crossed the room to where he stood by the fire. "All I wrote to Tredgett is that I would make it right."

"The rest was Tredgett's plan? The oaths? The claim?"

She nodded. "Tredgett wants a king. I want you." She leaned upward to kiss him.

A golden wall of flame shot up between them. Blinded, she retreated. The flames died to a ring around her feet, and beyond them Alesander knelt among the fireplace logs, looking up the chimney.

She screamed, but he did not seem to hear. So she stepped forward and the fire blazed up again.

Oblivious, Alesander began to climb the chimney. She had not thought of that escape. She started forward, and the flames licked at her skirts. She hesitated, then pushed through them to the hearth. Ignoring the heat, she stretched up, but he was beyond her reach. Tears of frustration filled her eyes and fell to hiss in the fire.

She sat back on her heels and tried to think. She'd been so close—there had to be a way. Her hand brushed the soft pile of the carpet where she had stood. It was not burned; it was not even warm.

Spirit fire! Enath's fire! Emboldened, she stepped into the fireplace and looked up. Soot sifted down, and she brushed it away. She might be able to climb up and pull him down. She started to unbutton her encumbering gown.

Soot fell heavily and, coughing, she stepped back. Above her Alesander cursed, and the sound of metal scraping stone reverberated down the chimney. Alesander slid down in an avalanche of soot. He sat on the hearth cursing fluently.

Wordlessly she wrung out a towel in the brass basin by the table and handed it to him.

He wiped his face. "There's a grate about twelve feet up. It jammed when I tried to push it aside." He looked around the stone-walled room. "It'll have to be the door."

She tried to put herself between him and it, but, unseeing, he pushed her aside. His fist hit the door. It did not budge. He hit again high on a panel, and to her eye it jumped. What if he could break through? He would be gone forever.

Alesander kicked the door. Nothing happened. He hit it again, then slumped against it. He cast about, grabbed a chair, and smashed it against the door. The chair shattered, and the door stood firm.

Richenza breathed easier. The door had been built for a strong room; it was not so easily breached.

Alesander eyed the table, tried to lift it, and couldn't, so he upended it and pushed. It moved but it was a clumsy weapon, so he threw his whole weight against one leg. It broke off, and he hefted it, swinging it like a club.

That weapon might be strong enough. Richenza threw herself against the door. Alesander moved forward, swinging his club.

"Get out of the way."

She didn't move. He swung the club back and she closed her eyes and pressed her back to the door, fearing the blow. But instead she felt him grab her arm and fling her out of his way. Unable to check herself she stumbled across the room and collided with the upturned table. She slid to her knees, the wind knocked out of her. She could only watch as Alesander rained blows on the door, but the table leg was splintering and the door stood firm. Perhaps it would be enough.

The firelight threw Alesander's shadow huge on the door and glittered on the dagger on his belt. The dagger. He could use it as a tool. She looked away, afraid her stare would remind him of its existence. If he thought of it, what could she do? She huddled in the shadows, husbanding her strength, watched and planned and waited.

32

Dawn

Meriel pulled the cloak close around her. The breeze had strengthened, blowing off the lake's water and, though she stood sheltered among the trees, it chilled her nakedness through the cloak's woolen folds. Or was it fear that made her shiver? Brian had been afraid. Afraid for her or of her? She did not know which and so she had not followed him but had come here to the lakeshore, facing the boatman's dock, to watch and wait. Brian had said he must go to Walter, to Reasalyn, and that lay to the east beyond that far shore. Sooner or later Brian would come. What would she do then? She didn't know, but she would have to do something.

The enemy moon, Elun's full moon, was sinking toward the western horizon behind her. Its rays made a faint path on the black water of the lake. The weaker stars were disappearing from a sky that no longer was only vivid in the moon's presence. The eastern sky was no longer black but pellucid blue. The sun battled the moon to rule in heaven. But this was Elun's isle and Elun's lake; the Goddess would be a formidable opponent. If she wanted Brian, she would have to fight for him.

The snap of a dry branch breaking alerted her

to Brian's arrival, and she watched unseen among the trees
as he stumbled down the bank to the muddy shore. He
worked his way up and down the shoreline casting back
and forth like a hunting dog that had lost the scent, searching for any way across the water. Brian had worked his
way back up the shore; he stood only yards away, his back
to her, his body straining toward that eastern shore.

With every minute's passage the sky grew brighter,
bluer. Brian's body was silhouetted against that blue sky
and its shattered azure reflection in the lake's water. The
far shore was dark; its ragged line of trees was black against
stillness. Meriel ached to touch him, to soothe him. He was
so close. Unwilled, her hand reached toward him.

Brian cried out. She crouched back, then realized he had
not seen her. His attention was on the far shore, where a
white horse, moon-bright, galloped along the bank. The
horse he had ridden all their journey had been roan, but
Meriel had no doubt this was the same animal. On this
night all the masks came down, and truth was seen in all
its starkness.

The horse was opposite Brian now and it plunged down
the bank and into the water. Brian walked into the lake and
began to swim.

Meriel threw aside her cloak. She had not thought that
Brian, who had proved a poor swimmer the night before,
was capable of swimming to the far shore before dawn. But
if he reached his mount, would he be gone forever?

She scrambled down the bank, dove into the water, and
began to swim. Surfacing for air, she judged the distance.
She had to slow him down.

Meriel swam better than Brian; last night had shown her
that, and she was unencumbered by clothes. Soon she had
caught up with Brian's flailing strokes. She dove, grabbed
his nearer ankle, and pulled.

Brian missed his stroke, his head went under; he flailed
around blindly and bobbed to the surface, momentarily dis-
oriented. Meriel surfaced some distance off. Brian had been
slowed, but the horse swam steadily toward them. Meriel
blinked the water from her eyes. There was not one silver-
shining horse churning the lake's azure water, but three,
and the other mounts had riders. Huntsmen come for Brian

or come to kill her? She could not stop to speculate; Brian had resumed his labored strokes.

She dove again, grabbed, and pulled him under. He fought her, hitting out blindly and ineffectually. She let go, and they both surfaced. He was gasping for air but he immediately started swimming doggedly toward the east.

Horses and riders were nearer. She could see the detail of the horses' gear. She could put names to the riders: Payne and Hamon. Payne saw her, cried out in triumph, drew his sword, and veered his course toward her.

She dove and swam underwater, hoping that the sky's shimmering reflection hid her movements. Eyes open, she could see Brian's dark-clad legs ahead of her. She grabbed his leg and this time did not let go. She clung like a drag anchor, slowing his progress.

Horses' legs churned the water. Brian struggled in her grasp—tried to kick her away. His arm came down to push hard against her shoulder. She tightened her grip, though she thought her lungs would burst. His next blow caught her in the temple. Dazed, her hold loosened; she was unprepared as his arms came down and pushed her away.

They surfaced scant feet apart. Payne was some distance to her left. Brian's horse was only yards away and Hamon the same distance to the right. Hamon saw her, smiled, and drew his sword. The silver morning light ran along the blade. Meriel dove and swam to place herself between Brian and his horse. Their bodies collided and rose to the surface. Hamon's horse was beside them. His sword struck the water inches from her head, sending fountains of diamond-bright water drops into the opalescent sky. Blocked from his target by Hamon and his mount, Brian's horse screamed and kicked. Both mounts shied, circling. The horses' dark wakes marred the lake's silver surface. Meriel dove again as Hamon's eyes found her. He knew she had to stay with Brian. He couldn't think she would flee now.

Brian's scarcely moving legs formed the center of a moving circle. It tightened, focusing ever inward. Meriel swam beneath the surface, trying to keep between him and his riderless mount. She came up for air, and Payne spotted her bobbing head. He kneed his horse, and now they were between Brian and his mount as she had hoped. She smiled and dove.

A sword cleft the water, slicing near her arm. Hamon's sword; he was more observant than she had thought. She collided with Hamon's mount and pushed away, breathless. The hooves were so near her face. She surfaced. Hamon's raised sword was like a black bar against the white-pale sky. Mesmerized, she watched as it swung toward her. Water splashed her face and a dark wall rose before her. Brian's shoulder and arm filled her vision as he pushed her down. Hamon's sword struck, and this time there was red among the fountain's droplets. Brian screamed. His cry was nearly lost against the men's shouts and the horses' screams as they collided. Meriel grabbed Brian's waist and pulled him under. His blood made a trail behind them in the water.

She held them down as long as she could, blinded by his black clothes—when had they changed?—afraid she'd drown him and afraid to surface. Finally, her lungs bursting, she let them rise.

The lake was empty. A faint chop was the only sign of any previous struggle. To the east the sky was rose and gold; the lake was gold and silver around them. For the first time she felt the cold of its water. And now the birds sang. Meriel shifted her grip and floated, cradling Brian's body against her. He was white but breathing. The boatman would come soon as she had paid him to do. She could see him even now on his dock untying his boat.

Soon she would have Brian safe. No Goddess, however cruel, would let such struggle go for nothing.

Tredgett paced, waiting for he knew not what. He could hear naught but muffled voices even if he pressed his ear hard against the secret door. He knew, he'd tried. So he paced and tried to plan. He could see each time he passed the open doors to the gallery, the full moon sinking, oh, so slowly, to the west. To the east the sky was dark above the torchlit courtyard.

He'd organized the men available to guard the house. He'd busied himself with orders, with messages sent and received. He had heard from both Tierse and the High Priest's treasurer that arrangements were in hand for the election of a new king. Musty treatises, no doubt, were being consulted; it had been half a millennium since election had been anything but a meaningless formality. This time when the Electors, the descendants of the Conqueror's Companions, met, they would have a real choice to make.

If the girl did her job and held Alesander, they would have a worthy candidate. A candidate whose victory today made him look divinely appointed. That ought to convince the Electors.

Tredgett's pacing brought him next to the hidden door, and he resisted another try at eavesdropping. He could control Petric Chuskis's vote; the man was credulous and owed him money. Selvanian Pirit was dull and conscientious; he could be convinced. If the girl could vote in Indes's place, that would give Alesander the majority without having to wait for the two other Electors to arrive. Tarsia would have a king in days.

But could she? There was the famous story of the Widow's Vote, but had Darika voted in the place of her dead father or as proxy for her unborn son? There were other tales as well; did they set the precedent he needed? He had sent a messenger to Philemon for information as soon as the voices behind the door had convinced him Richenza was alive. It was the second message he had sent; the first had been to Juhel Rimoc far away in Canjit, telling him the situation and summoning him home.

Rimoc, one of the few noblemen whose judgment he respected, would give them the majority they needed if Richenza could not. Then they wouldn't have to deal with Feracher. Haldan knew what dangerous concessions Feracher would demand.

The sinking moon's rays made a long bright path across the floor; Tredgett altered his pacing to avoid it as though it were a snare. Even masked by the torches' brightness he could see light in the eastern sky. It wouldn't be long until this night was over.

The first thump on the secret door was simultaneous with a scream from the stable. Tredgett hesitated, then went to the windows. The door to the secret room had not budged.

He threw the casement open and looked out. Below all was confusion. Men he had set to guard the outer gate and inner doors rushed toward the stables, whose open doors glowed with fire within.

He could hear the horses' screams, the men's shouts. Tredgett could imagine the shattered wood, the flames, the fear. Horses, some escorted, many loose and terrified, poured out, dark against that radiant door, and spread chaos in the courtyard below.

The next shrill scream was distinctly human, and a groom limped out, closely followed by a white horse—its tail and mane dripping fire. Fire that dissolved into nothingness as it hit the pavement. Alesander's horse—Tredgett knew, feeling sick—the Goddesses' horse come for its rider. The stable door was dark now, and the men and horses below shrank away to the courtyard's farthest corners. Tredgett leaned out; below him two spearmen still guarded the doors. He called to them, warning them to keep their place.

The horse, which had stood head up in the courtyard's center as though searching for a sign, paced forward toward the door. The men-at-arms gripped their spears and formed up before the door. Tredgett shut the window and sped down the stair to warn the men in the entry below. Behind him the pounding on the secret door beat in a steady rhythm.

He was halfway down the stair when the first blow struck the outer door. That dull thud might have been a man's body; the scream that followed was certainly human. Then the double doors to the courtyard shook under repeated blows; their heavy wooden bar jumped with each blow. The men in the entry edged away, eyeing it uneasily. Tredgett called out, encouraging them, and they gripped their spears more resolutely. Tredgett looked around the weapon-decorated room, exasperated. Trust a grand duke to keep no weapon on display that was of real use against aristocratic cavalry. What they needed were the Stros's pikes.

The center panel of the left-hand door split. Then the right-hand door fell inward, held half-up by the bar. Past it, Tredgett could see the morning twilight.

The horse's rear hooves flashed silver as it kicked in the remnants of the doors. Stray bits of fire fell, mingled with the flying splinters. One cut a guardsman's face and, unnerved, he turned and ran. Unnerved by his small wound, Tredgett wondered, or by the sight of his companions lying dead outside, their heads kicked in?

The horse picked its way daintily over the wreckage of the entry doors. The remaining spearmen formed a retreating half circle before it. Tredgett could hear the pounding above him. Would the horse hear it also? Tredgett backed up the stairs, watching. The men still held formation below. He slipped a spear from the display above the stair landing and retreated to the second floor.

He barred the door at the head of the stairs, then pushed a heavy chest in front of it. That done, he walked across the long room to the antechamber where the paneling concealed the secret door. It jumped beneath his hand from steady blows. The sky outside the windows was lavender with increasing light. The sun was gaining.

He walked back to the stair. Putting his head to the door he could hear shouts below. The horse neighed wildly. A man screamed, something crashed, and hooves rang on the floor. Another human scream, and all was silence.

Tredgett waited. He could hear the horse's hooves as it moved slowly, deliberately, across the stone floor below. Then, eerily, the sound changed. Like the change from paved road to drawbridge, the horse was climbing the wooden stair. Tredgett gripped his spear and retreated. It was up to him. If Tarsia was to have a worthy king, he would have to fight.

He watched from the opposite doorway as the doors shook and fell open. There was a pause as the horse turned, then it jumped the debris that blocked the doorway. It seemed to fill the room. Whiter than the early-morning light, it paced toward him. Stray bits of fire spun off its mane and tail or glowed where its hooves struck. Spirit fire—for what they touched did not burn. It came directly toward him, toward the pounding that vibrated the wall behind him.

Holding the spear at the ready, he backed till he was against that pulsing wall. The antechamber was narrow and confined; one spear would have a chance here. Keeping his eyes on the advancing horse, he shifted his grip on the spear. It had been a long time since he had wielded one.

Since an eager sixteen-year-old had run off to enlist as a man-at-arms and learned the ugly futility of war.

The horse came on, and the wall jarred behind him. The horse had kicked the other doors open with its powerful hind legs; he must distract it—keep it facing him. Tredgett feinted forward with the spear. The horse reared. Hooves near his face, Tredgett stepped back, then feinted again toward the horse's eyes as it came down. The horse shied back, its head swinging from side to side. It started forward. Tredgett feinted. The horse backed and started to turn. Tredgett lunged and speared it in the flank. The horse screamed and reared. Blood seeped like rubies down its silvery side.

The horse's front hooves glanced off the wall near his head. Tredgett flattened against the hidden door. The sound of the pounding had changed. Tredgett lunged with the spear, then retreated, back against the door. The horse shied back but only a few feet. Its eyes followed his spearpoint.

The pounding no longer sounded like fists on wood. It sounded like a tool, like metal. Tredgett remembered the long dagger on Alesander's belt. Even as he lunged, forcing the horse back, his mind's eye pictured that dagger blade piercing the wood behind him, piercing his back.

No time for sick fantasies; the horse rushed forward, rearing above him. Its hooves thudded against the wall. Tredgett thrust up into its neck. The horse screamed. A forehoof kicked out, catching Tredgett in the shoulder. He staggered back, clutching the spear one-handed. His head struck the wall, and the room exploded into flame.

He braced himself with the spear to keep from sliding to the floor and shook his head to clear it. He couldn't hear anything. His right shoulder and arm throbbed, useless. Slowly his vision cleared.

Red sunlight streaked the floor of the outer room. The horse was gone. The pounding had ceased behind him. Tredgett pulled himself erect. One-handed, he fumbled at the paneling. *Push here, yes, then here.* The door slowly swung open, and Alesander's body sprawled across the threshold. Tredgett braced himself, then pushed him over. Alesander lay on his back, bruised hands outflung, breathing heavily.

Richenza sank to her knees beside him. She looked up at Tredgett. She was black with what appeared to be soot, and there was a cut on her mouth. She had not come through this unscathed either.

"The poison?" he asked her anxiously.

"Poison? No, this is exhaustion."

"Good." Tredgett painfully pulled himself erect. "That gives us time to talk. We have some things to settle."

The Temple of the Three Goddesses shone before them, silver in the full moon's light. To Walter it seemed that it stood whole with Enath's fire blazing on the altar, and Anchytel's grove around it, heavy with golden fruit and adorned with leaves like jade and emeralds despite the near winter season. Elun's spring flowed free from its source behind the altar down its ancient course, a silver pathway pulling him toward that golden doorway.

To Walter, now and for many moons, these full moons of completion had lost their terror. No longer was the pull a whirlpool drowning him in black despair or an uprushing fire of red anger. No, it had become the pull of desire, like a lover rushing to his mistress. A capricious mistress, one who must be pleased by how well he had performed her bidding, who might let him fret momentarily in suspense before she opened the door to the paradise beyond.

He felt his men beside him, pulled as he. He knew they felt that pull differently, differently as he had felt it differently over time, but how it felt was too private to share, too personal to ask even Thomas about. Every other time he had let that pull flow through him, pulling the other Huntsmen as strongly as him. This time he tried to block it, stop it within himself, remain rational and in control. They might have failed. He could be calling his men to their destruction. He would have failed them, destroyed them with his weaknesses. Failed Thomas. Failed Reynard. Failed Payne and Justin. Failed Alesander unless Richenza or Tredgett was strong and held him, or if Meriel held Brian. How Meriel had looked at Brian at their marriage feast. If either woman lived to try.

Walter tried to think even as his horse's hooves first splashed in Elun's waters. If one woman was strong enough to hold her man from him, from the Goddesses, then Alesander would not join them, would not burn. If both were held, then Justin, too, would survive even if the Hunt failed. But, if the women lived, the Hunt had not failed.

The temple door was before him now; the fire man-high on the altar. He could hear their horses' hooves on the paving, hear other hooves come up fast behind. He fought to turn from the light, fought the seductive pull into the fire. Usually he could feel the presence of his men, know their closeness to him, but this time the Goddesses' call overwhelmed his senses. Just as he reached the doorway he turned and looked behind. Hamon and Payne joined him, and beyond them? He strained to see as the fire rose to meet him. Two horses galloped toward the temple—riderless horses. There was the chance for freedom.

Walter met the flames with exultation and with hope.